Dead set on revenge, the Presidente launches an attack on Koblan. With the kaavl team split across two continents, and two members battling for their lives, can they find the strength to defeat their enemy? Even worse, Methusal is worried that Mentàll's secret agenda could cost Koblan everything. Will Mentàll's inability to trust others cost him all of his dreams, including the woman he loves?

KAAVL CHRONICLES
(Book Four of Quadrilogy)

KAAVL CONQUEROR

Jennette Green

DIAMOND PRESS

Kaavl Conqueror

A Diamond Press book / published in arrangement with the author

ISBN: 978-1-62964-021-1

Library of Congress Control Number: 2017906526
Library of Congress Subject Headings:
Man-woman relationships—Fiction
Paranormal romance—Fiction
Saga—Fiction

Diamond Press
3400 Pegasus Drive
P.O. Box 80043
Bakersfield CA 93380-0043
www.diamondpresspublishing.com

Published in the United States of America.

Thank you

to you,

my readers.

Thank you for letting me share

a little of my heart

and the characters I love

with you.

Also by Jennette Green

ROMANCE NOVELS

The Commander's Desire
Her Reluctant Bodyguard
Ice Baron
The Pirate's Desire

(Kaavl Chronicles Quadrilogy)
Kaavl Conspiracy
Kaavl Quest
Kaavl Calamity
Kaavl Conqueror

(Christian Apocalyptic, New Adult)
Beyond the Rapture

Castaways
(a novelette)

SHORTER WORKS

Toot of Fruit
(a children's story)

Murder by Nightmare
(a novelette)

Koblan

Quasr
Var
Aestoff
Nelph
Tarst
Ignon Region
Dehre
Rolban
Eerpor
Wyen
Linn
Sasrin

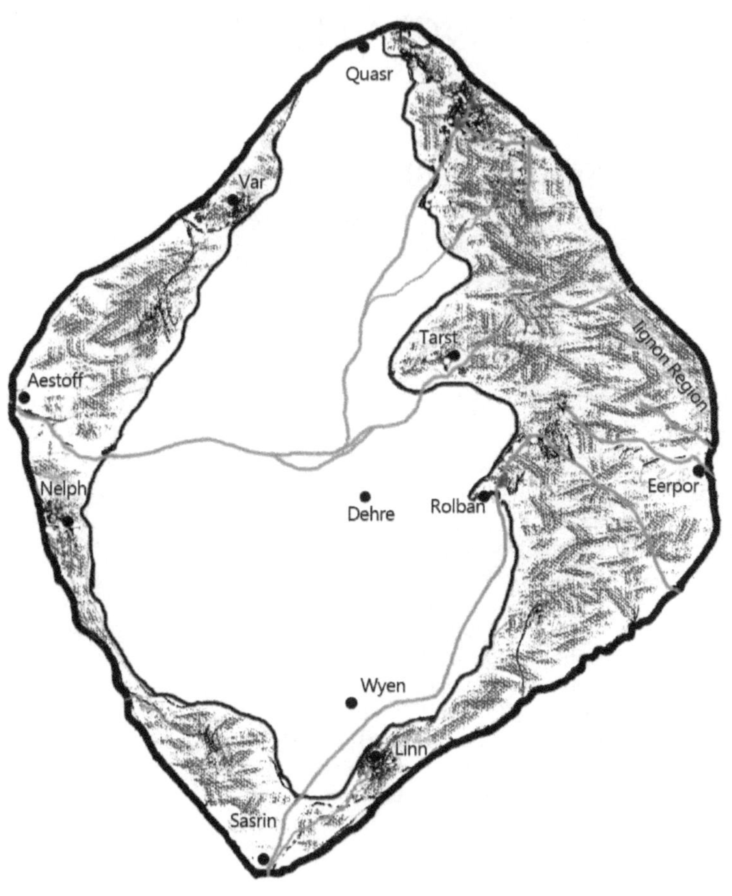

Pronunciation Guide

Kaavl (Kah' vl)

Kaavl levels (from highest to lowest):

Ultimate level (only Mahre ever achieved)
Primary level
Bi-level
Tri-level
Quatr-level (Kwah' tra level)
Quint-level (Kint level)

Places

Aestoff (Ay' stoff)
Carachki (Ka ra' chki) capitol of Zindedi
Dehre (Deh' ree)
Dehrien (Deh' ree un)
Eerpor (Ear poor')
Eerporian (Ear por' ee un)
Koblan (Koe' blun)
Koblani (Koe blane' ee)
Rolban (Role bane')
Rolbani (Role bane' ee)
Quasr (Kay' zer)
Quasrian (Kay zar' ee un)
Tarst (Tarst)
Wyen (Why en')
Zindedi (Zin deh' dee)

Characters

Rolban

Aalicaa (A lee shaw') (Aali (A' lee)) Deccia's sister/cousin, Methusal's cousin, Tri-level
Barak Mehl (Bare' uk Mel) Kitran's brother
Behran Amil (Bee' hrhun/Beh' rhun Uh meel') Tri-level
Ben Amil, Behran's father
Deccia (Day' shuh) Methusal's twin sister
Erl (Earl) Methusal's father
Goric (Gor' ik) Tri-level
Hanuh (Han' nah) Methusal's mother
Mahre (Mah' ree) The Old Kaavl Master
Methusal Maahr (Meth u' zul Mare) Tri-level
Petr (Pet' r) Deccia and Aali's father, Bi-Level
Pogul (Poe' gull)
Poli Amil (Pol' ee Uh meel') Behran's mother
Sims Nalg (Sims Nalg) Supply room supervisor
Timaeus (Tim' ay us)

Dehre

Hendra (Hen' druh) Quatr-level
Mentàll Solboshn (Mn tall' Sole' bah shn) Chief of Dehre, Primary level
Tabor (Tay' bor), Bi-level, Mentàll's second-in-command

Tarst

Aenill (Uh neel') Pan's wife
Dastn (Das' tn), runner for Tarst
Doc, Tarst's doctor
Pan Patn (Pan Pat' tn) Tarst Chief, Primary level
Riln, Bi-level

Quasr

Calbn M'ntoyan (Kal'bn Mn toy'un)
Lylitha (Lil eeth' uh) Calbn's wife
Rartn (Rare' tun) Calbn's son
Trori (Tror' ee) Calbn's daughter

Chief Aarabst (Air' uh bast) of Aestoff
Sozla (Soz' luh) from Eerpor

Zindedi

Ceri (Sair' ee)
Euphira (U fire' uh) shopkeeper in Carachki
General Fitrn (Fie' turn)
Matron Machblin (Mrn. M) Mock' blin), landlady in Carachki
Nygev (Nie' gev) Vitnia's husband
Olita (Oh lee' tuh) friend of Vitnia
Ostl (Oss' tl) the Commander in the Carachki's military base
Presidente of Zindedi
Tisnia (Tiz' nee uh) friend of Vitnia
Vitnia (Vit' nee uh) rents cabins to team on Dakarra
Yalin (Yah leen') Presidente's secretary

PROLOGUE

CARACHKI
CAPITOL OF THE ZINDEDI CONTINENT

IT WAS UNCONSCIONABLE! *Unconscionable!* The Presidente balled up the Koblani peace agreement and hurled it at the whimpering Captain. "How did this happen?" he roared.

The Captain held his splinted wrist to his chest like a mother would hold a fragile infant.

"I do not know, sir. The explosions took place on the base and at the docks. Perhaps the Commanders would know."

"The Commanders know nothing!" The Presidente hefted a stone vase and flung it at the Captain's head.

A quick dodge saved the Captain from being brained. The vase hit the wall, splintering the painted wood.

Seeming to realize that his life was in jeopardy, the Captain leaped to his feet. "I will find out, sir. I will find out everything you want to know, right now!"

"Get out!" His roar of rage filled his head, his eardrums. It shook the Presidente's very soul. He grabbed another vase and flung it at the window. It exploded with a shatter of flying, deadly glass. With a grunt of satisfaction, he threw more baubles, one after another, at any object that pleased him. His breaths came in short pants, and he waited for the pains to start. For death to consume him.

Finally, he collapsed into his chair, winded. A dull pain radiated down his arm. He sat quietly. At last, he realized he would not die. This was not the end, although embarrassment choked him, and utter fury consumed him.

His enemies had succeeded in attacking his military ships and the base. The Zindedi people would think he was a weak, ineffectual fool to have allowed that to happen. It was unconscionable. A humiliation he could never live down. Everyone who failed him must pay the price, and swiftly, before contempt for him swept throughout Zindedi.

"Yalin!"

The door tentatively opened. "Yes, sir?"

"Find out how many ships were destroyed. Tell me the damage on the base. I want a full report, first thing in the morning."

"Yes, sir!"

"And Yalin, as soon as the Captain returns, send him in here immediately."

"Yes, sir." The young man hesitated, throat bobbing with clear apprehension.

"That is all, fool!"

The door closed with a hasty click.

Tomorrow he would order a mass execution. Ostl would die. So would every surviving Commander of the ships that had blown up—after he'd extracted every tidbit of information from them first, of course.

And the attack on Koblan... Fury roared through him, filling his head with violent, red and black images. That attack would have to wait a little while. But he would utterly destroy the Koblani filth. He would ensure that every house was burned, every woman raped and every man dead before he was through.

Zindedi would leave a permanent, scorched blight upon Koblan. He just needed to decide the best way to go about it. One thing was for sure. There would be no peace.

His lips curled back in a bestial snarl. Although perhaps he would *pretend* peace. Those stupid Koblanis would never see death coming.

Chapter One

Day 20/Day 1
At Sea, off Zindedi Coast

The ship's gentle motion was making Methusal feel sick by the time Doc finally exited from Mentàll's room. When she leaped up, the jacket Deccia had put around her shoulders fell to the floor. She barely noticed.

"Is he alive?"

The crewman who'd helped Doc brushed by her with an armload of bloody linens. Methusal turned anguished eyes to the Tarst doctor, who still hadn't answered. "*Doc*. Tell me."

"He's alive. For now."

Relief lasted only for a moment. Fear cramped harder around her heart. "What does that *mean*?"

"The bullet passed through his body. It didn't hit his heart. I think it missed his lungs. That's the good news."

"And the bad?"

"He could be bleeding internally. There's no way to tell at this point. It's not worth the risk to open him up right now. Conditions are less than ideal here. Even in the best of circumstances, I couldn't do much."

"He could still die."

"Yes. If he makes it through tomorrow, that will be a good sign. But even after that, he runs the risk of infection. I disinfected the wound as best I could. But with an internal injury, it's impossible to know if that will be good enough."

Quietly, she said, "Can I see him?"

"He's unconscious." His expression made it clear he thought it would be a miracle if Mentàll ever regained consciousness again.

"I won't disturb him."

"Go on. It can't hurt."

Methusal slipped down the short hall. The floor gently surged beneath her feet. The boat was "running with the wind," as Captain Hilrae had announced with satisfaction a while ago. The wind was behind them, blowing them straight north to Dakarra.

Methusal swallowed back the nausea that was already building in her throat. She put a hand on the wall to steady herself before opening the door to Mentàll's cabin.

A dim torch flickered on the wall, revealing his still form. Even lying there motionless, his powerful body looked deceptively normal, except for the huge bandage wrapped around his left, upper chest region. But his face was as white as death.

"Mentàll," she whispered. "You're a fighter. You can conquer this. Just like you can everything else."

No movement. No response of any kind.

"You *have* to beat this." Her fingers drifted up and gently stroked his soft, white-blond hair, which was always such a contrast to the hard man he could be. "You just *have* to." Tears choked her voice. "You can't leave me, you stubborn man. *I won't let you.*"

She stayed there for a long time, watching his shallow breaths and trying to take comfort from them. He was alive now...and now...and now.

Only the seasick urge to vomit made her leave the cabin. She made it out on deck and vomited over the edge into the white, frothing wake. The freezing wind raised stiff bumps on her arms.

"Do you feel better?"

Deccia and Behran had followed her. Behran wrapped her leather Koblani cloak around her shoulders.

"I guess."

"What happened?" Deccia said. "Behran told us a little. But what happened after they left the palace?"

With short, clipped words, Methusal relayed the facts. She felt raw inside, as if she might fly into a million pieces at any moment. Too many things had happened tonight. She couldn't get a handle on any of them. Emotionlessly, she described what had happened in the Presidente's office.

"He was going to *rape* you?" Fury tightened Behran's voice.

"Oh, Thusa." Deccia hugged her with empathy and grief.

Great, wrenching sobs suddenly gripped her, threatening to tear her soul apart. "But he *didn't*. I'm sorry. I don't know why I'm crying like this." But she couldn't stop.

"You've had a horrible night, that's why," Deccia said. A small movement, and Behran was in the hug, too.

Methusal turned into him, trying to find solace in his strength. In the past, everything had always been all right when she was with Behran. It wasn't now. She wept until she felt utterly drained.

"You need to rest." Deccia's no-nonsense tone reminded her of their mother. "Things will look better in the morning."

She checked on Mentàll before she tumbled into bed. He was still breathing. Hopefully he'd still be alive when she woke up again.

△ △ △ △ △

NEAR DAKARRA

Soldiers patrolled the Dakarran beach when Hendra and Riln arrived near midnight, so they headed further west before stopping to wait for the ship to arrive. They hid among the trees.

Hendra closed her eyes, trying to block out the pain of the horrible scene they'd left behind... Tabor dead. Timaeus shot, and still a helpless prisoner of the General.

It wasn't right. For the millionth time she wanted to run back and do something—anything—to save him. Tears filled her eyes.

Two explosions shook the ground in the middle of the night. Both came from the east. She wondered if the two powder mines had blown up, or if one was from the bomb Tabor had hurled on the base.

Hendra fell into a light, restless sleep, her head cushioned against a tree stump. She dreamed about Timaeus and Doc. Nightmares awoke her over and over again.

The long minutes until dawn seemed to last forever.

Early morning mist cleared away to another blue sky day. She wondered if Doc, Mentàll, and Methusal had succeeded in their mission. Were they on the ship? Worry made her feel sick.

Sozla and Goric still hadn't shown up. She hoped they were all right.

As she chewed on dried meat, waiting for the ship to arrive, Hendra kept several lengths between herself and Riln. Her dislike for the man continued to grow by leaps and bounds. She couldn't stand to even look at him. Although, if she was honest, it wasn't his fault Tabor was dead and Timaeus captured. Maybe she was also angry at herself for not fighting harder to go back and save Timaeus.

She wandered onto the beach and he followed her. Silent moments passed.

"I'm moving west," she finally said. "The ship can't anchor here. It's too close to Dakarra."

Riln said nothing, but his footsteps followed her. They approached a tiny seaside town she hadn't known existed. "Sisln Store" was painted on one building. A few soldiers patrolled the streets.

The ship couldn't anchor near here, either. They needed to go further west and try to flag it down before the Zindedi soldiers could spot it.

Steadily, they hiked west. The soldiers thinned out to a sporadic pair here and there. And Hendra still saw no sign of the ship. But that wasn't surprising, because it had a long way to come. It had to sail north and then east to get here. In walking terms, it would probably take two days.

"Hendra!" Sozla's light, musical voice made her spin, and her heart gave a relieved, glad leap.

"Sozla! You made it. What happened?"

Goric trailed behind the Eerporian girl. A scowl knotted his brows.

Sozla shrugged, her dark eyes snapping. "We set the bombs, but the one for the biggest powder mine did not explode."

"I wonder why."

"I do not know." Sozla glanced from Hendra to Riln, and then back. "Where is Tabor?"

Tears welled in Hendra's eyes. "He's dead."

"What?" Her face blanched with horror.

In halting words, Hendra explained what had happened. As she did so, everyone dropped their packs to the earth. It seemed like a safe enough spot. She hadn't seen any soldiers for a while.

"That is awful!" Sozla said, aghast, when Hendra had finished the horrific telling. "Poor Timaeus. And poor Deccia. We must do something to help him!"

"I'm going further down the beach," Goric muttered. "We need to flag down the ship."

A branch snapped behind them. Hendra whirled, and a gasp choked in her throat.

A Zindedi soldier, black cap pulled low over his eyes, leveled a gun at them.

He smiled. "I think you'll come with me."

To Hendra's disbelief, Sozla burst into laughter.

△ △ △ △ △

Methusal felt awful when she woke up in the morning. She promptly vomited into the bucket tied to her bunk.

She wanted to pull the blanket over her head and pray for oblivion. Three more days to endure until she felt better.

The faint smell of frying eggs wafted to her nose. With a violent gag, she retched again.

Stomach quivering and body trembling, she lay back on the bunk. Her arm hurt. Swallowing, and trying to ignore the pulsing sensation in her head, she lifted it. Dried blood scored the slit in the gown's sleeve. In a rush, it all came back. The skirmish. The pain in her arm, and the soldier with the gun pointed straight at her heart. ...Mentàll shoving her aside and taking the bullet himself.

He lay dying in the room down the hall.

If he wasn't dead already.

A feeling of sick emptiness opened up inside her, and the urge to weep nearly overwhelmed her. Through a sheer act of will, she blinked back the tears. They would help no one. She needed to see how he was doing.

Arms shaking, she pushed herself upright, and then stumbled to her feet. Her head swam and her stomach convulsed. She gritted her teeth, choking back the bile.

Holding onto the doorframe, she peered into the hall. Everything was silent, and she saw no one, but sunshine streamed in through the open hatch. A glorious day. But down here it felt like death.

She staggered down the hall, trying to get a feel for the rhythm of the surging ship. Anxiety grew because of how quiet it was.

Mentàll's door was closed, but she opened it without knocking.

The Tarst doctor looked up. He'd been listening to Mentàll's heart.

"He's alive?" she whispered.

Doc's eyes crinkled at the corners, but his expression remained serious. "He's a fighter. But he's running a high temperature."

Nausea gripped her. "Blood poisoning." She blinked hard, trying to keep back the tears, but one trickled down her cheek anyway.

"How are you holding up? How's the queasiness?"

"I'll live," she choked out.

"A bucket is in the corner. Want to sit with him for a while? I'm going out."

"Yes. Please." Methusal was shaken by how much she did want that.

Doc got a look at her arm for the first time. "You're hurt."

"It's not bad."

"I'll be the judge of that." He swiftly cleaned it. "It doesn't need stiches. But it does need coltac juice every day."

"I'll do it." Doc had enough to worry about."

"Good." He applied coltac juice and a bandage. "I'll be back soon. Get me if there's any change."

When Doc left, Methusal took the stool he'd vacated and got her first good look at Mentàll's face this morning. It didn't look relaxed, like it had last night. A faint frown knit his brows together, and his skin was flushed. Perspiration moistened his brow. The doctor had left a wash rag and bowl of cool water, so Methusal wrung it out and placed it on his brow. His skin already felt hot to the touch.

"Don't give up," she whispered. "You can beat this."

He didn't respond. It scared her, seeing him lying there so motionless, unable to move, or deliver orders. Unable to exasperate and tease her... Unable to kiss her. Tears flooded her eyes, and she lay her head on the uninjured portion of his chest and wept.

The damp bed linen stuck to her cheek, and yet still his quiet breaths went on. So did his slow, steady heartbeat. He couldn't die. He *wouldn't* die. Not if she could do anything to stop it.

Wiping her face, she sat up and reached for the washcloth. She prayed yet again for a miracle.

△ △ △ △ △

The Zindedi soldier shoved up his cap to reveal more of his face. Skyl's familiar grin flashed. "Anyone need a ride home?"

Hendra gasped with relief, and Riln lowered the knife that had suddenly appeared in his hand. "Fool," he growled. "You almost got a knife in your gut."

Skyl jerked his head left. "Follow me."

Everyone grabbed their black packs and followed Skyl west. They crunched in silence through the quiet forest. Sunshine dappled the bright green leaves of the slender trees. To the right, waves crashed on the lonely beach.

"We anchored just past that hill," Skyl said.

"I thought we were supposed to meet you in Dakarra," Sozla said.

"Captain Hil wanted to play it safe."

"Has everyone made it back safely?" Hendra asked anxiously.

"Doc, Behran, Methusal, and Mentàll made it to the ship. But your Chief is in bad shape."

"What happened?"

"He was shot. Doc doesn't think he'll make it."

She gasped. Mentàll. *No.* It couldn't be true! Her cousin was such an indomitable force. She couldn't imagine...

Hendra could not seem to think clearly. She got half-soaked, wading through the breakers to reach the skiff, but she didn't care. She chaffed at the time it took to row through the rolling waves to the ship. All she could think about was Mentàll. And Doc.

Ready hands took the rope and tied it to the ship, while others piled the packs on deck. Swiftly, they helped Hendra and the others out. The moment her foot touched the solid deck, she struggled through the throng of men clogging the narrow walkway and squeezed her way toward the cockpit. She had to see Mentàll.

A familiar red head flashed as a man emerged from the main hatch. She pushed past the last two sailors. "Doc!" Tears flooded her eyes. He pulled her into a solid, comforting hug.

"Hendra." His voice was rough, and he held her tight. "You're safe," he murmured into her hair.

"Mentàll. Is he...?"

"He's alive. But it's bad, Hendra. He has blood sickness and a fever. Methusal is with him now."

"I want to see him."

He nodded. Down below, Mentàll's door was open and Methusal sat on a stool lashed to the bunk. She adjusted a moist cloth on Mentàll's forehead. Her cousin lay perfectly still, and his skin was unnaturally flushed.

Methusal looked over her shoulder. Her face was a sickly white, and purple smudges underscored her dark, anguished eyes. "Hendra."

"How is he?"

"Holding his own. He's still breathing." Methusal put the backs of her fingers to his cheek and sent Doc a worried look. "He's so hot."

"We'll need to start cooling him down."

Hendra said, "I can help." Quickly, she glanced at Methusal. "We can both help."

"Not now," Doc said. "Methusal needs a break, and I need a few minutes alone here before we go out to sea again. Come back in ten minutes."

Hendra touched Mentàll's hand, just to assure herself that he was alive. The sizzling heat of his skin shocked her. He was in very bad shape.

"He's all right for now," Doc said, his smoky gaze finding hers. His steady calmness helped to settle her. "I'll see you soon."

Reluctantly, she left her cousin's cabin, trying to take solace in the fact that he was still alive. And soon, she would be able to sit with him.

Methusal touched her arm. "We need to pray, Hendra." Her voice cracked, and tears glimmered in her eyes. "We need to pray hard."

Hendra, who had recoiled from physical touch for her entire life, drew Methusal into a hug. Something had changed between her cousin and her friend. "He'll be all right," she whispered. "With all three of us helping him, and praying, how could he not?"

Methusal choked back a strangled sound, but said nothing.

"Come on." Hendra gently urged her friend toward the ladder leading to the deck. "We have a few minutes. I'm sure both of our teams have a lot to report."

Δ Δ Δ Δ Δ

Deccia sat crying on deck when Methusal and Hendra arrived. The others stood silently grouped around her. Quickly, Methusal went to her sister and clutched her hand. "What happened?"

Hendra explained what had happened to Timaeus and Tabor. She also reported the damage inflicted upon the Dakarran base, the powder carts, and one powder mine.

Meanwhile, sailors pulled the wet rowboat aboard. At the bow, chain rattled as they pulled up the anchor.

Deccia wept silently. When Methusal put her arms around her, Deccia's shoulders felt stiff, as if she was trying to control the emotions inside her—or as if she was furious beyond words. Methusal wondered about that.

Behran's hard gaze went to Sozla and Goric. "Why didn't the big mine blow up?"

"I do not know."

Goric shrugged. "Maybe the timer failed."

Behran's eyes narrowed.

Deccia sharply shrugged free of Methusal's embrace. "I want off the ship. I'm staying here."

"Deccia—"

"I'm staying until I find Timaeus." She stood. "I want off. Now."

"I'll stay, too," Riln announced.

Hendra shot him a surprised frown.

"No one is going anywhere yet," Behran said. "I believe..."

"*Tell them* to stop pulling up the anchor!" Hysteria edged Deccia's voice. "Tell them now."

Goric slipped away and then returned. The rattling chain stopped. Sailors stared back at their little group, frowning against the glare of the sun.

Captain Hilrae strode forward. "What's the problem? We need to go before the Zindedis spot us."

"You can *wait*," Deccia snapped. "I'm getting off this ship now. Tell your men to lower the rowboat."

Obviously taken aback, Captain Hilrae glanced at Behran, who nodded and said, "Give us a minute to straighten things out."

"Make it quick," he growled, and retreated to the cockpit.

"Like I was saying," Behran said. "We have a problem."

The entire Dakarran kaavl team stared at him with blank expressions. ...Everyone except for Deccia, that was.

"What's wrong?"

"Someone on our team is a spy."

Hendra and Sozla gasped. Riln's mouth dropped open. "What?"

Behran told them about the note the Presidente had received, which had named and described General Greisn's killer.

"No one knew that information except for the people in the General's office in Quasr that day. That includes me, Methusal, Hendra, Riln, Tabor, Timaeus, and Goric. Tabor is dead. Although that doesn't clear him, of course."

All eyes went to Riln and Goric.

Riln's face flushed bright red. "I'm no *traitor!*" he roared.

"I'm guessing the spy will have proof in his backpack. Sozla and Deccia, you're the only ones in the clear. Please look through all of the backpacks on deck."

"What about yours?" Riln blustered.

"Bring it on deck, if you want."

Riln scowled and looked away. Methusal brought her backpack on deck, and Behran's too, for good measure.

Deccia and Sozla took out every item in the backpacks. Behran, Methusal, and Hendra's were quickly cleared. Next came Behran's, Riln's, and Goric's. Also clear. Last, Sozla emptied Tabor's. Nothing. A look of relief crossed Hendra's face, and she sat back on her heels.

"Wait." Sozla frowned. "There is a paper in the inside pocket." She spread it open, and her face drained of color.

"Let me see."

Silently, she handed it to Behran.

Behran read it, and his knuckles whitened. Everyone stared at him with wide, disbelieving eyes.

He read in a hard tone, "The man who killed the General is Riln. In the event names are forged on military papers, he is dark-haired, tall, and muscular."

Methusal gasped. "But Riln didn't kill General Greisn. Why would Tabor lie?"

"We'll never know." Behran refolded the note. "I'd never have believed it."

Methusal didn't believe it either, and the shock on Hendra's face was plain. Tabor had been Mentàll's right-hand man. Could Tabor have duped the discerning Dehrien Chief so completely?

"I guess that's solved," Behran said. "The spy is dead. I guess that's justice."

"Perhaps that explains why one of our bombs didn't explode," Sozla said. "Tabor had them all in his pack before he gave them to us."

More tears streamed from Deccia's eyes. Her white lips were tightly pressed together. "It doesn't matter whose name Tabor wrote down. That description matches Timaeus, too. That's why he was captured." She looked at the sailors still standing motionless on deck. "Why aren't you lowering the *boat?*" she cried out. "I'm getting off. *Now.*"

Two jumped to obey. Deccia headed down below. Methusal followed her to the cabin, where her sister shoved items willy-nilly into her black backpack. Fear made her chest hurt. Mentàll was dying. She couldn't lose her sister, too. "I'll come with you. I won't let you go alone."

"No, Thusa." Deccia's movements slowed down long enough to give her a thin smile. "You need to be with Mentàll. The Presidente will come to Quasr in three weeks. You need to be there. Besides, I won't be alone."

"Do you think Riln will help you? He's a walking bomb."

"I'd do it alone, if I had to. Just remember to send the ship back for me."

All kinds of challenges and problems loomed in Methusal's mind regarding her sister's rash plan. "Where will you go?"

"Probably Carachki. That's where the General was headed."

Methusal thought quickly. "When the ship returns to Zindedi to get you, I'll have a sailor leave a message with Tineia at the Merry Spirits. She's a friend of mine. Just check there every few days after a month has gone by. Then you'll know the ship has arrived to take you home."

Another thought came to mind. "And if you need work or money, she'll help you. It's not the best job in the world, but it pays well. And Tineia is nice. She already knows I have a twin sister. And Mrn. M would help, in a pinch. But you'll need a disguise in Carachki. General Fitrn and the Presidente both know what we look like."

"Thank you, Thusa. But I'll be fine." Deccia's mouth looked grim as she finished tying up her pack.

Methusal fiercely hugged her. "I can't lose you, Decc."

"You won't. I'll come home. I promise." She pulled back. "With Timaeus."

"With Timaeus." Deccia blinked, her eyes shining hard with tears.

"My wedding will be in eight weeks. I want you both to be there." Methusal rubbed away the moisture spilling down her cheeks.

"Oh, Thusa." Deccia's face suddenly crumpled, and she hugged her again, fiercely. "Marry the man you *love*. Life is too short for regrets. Or fear."

She said nothing in reply to that statement. "I'll bet the Captain is getting restless."

"And I'm anxious to find Timaeus."

They both headed outside and joined the little group on deck. In the bobbing rowboat Skyl held the oars, and Riln sat in the bow. Goric, to Methusal's surprise, sat in the stern. He directed a small, self-deprecating smile up at Deccia, who drew in a quick breath. "Goric?"

"I'd like to come. If you'll have me."

"Thank you." A final hug for Methusal, Hendra, and Sozla, and she climbed into the boat.

"Go with The One," Methusal whispered.

Skyl pushed at the ship with an oar and the little boat swished free.

Behran slipped an arm around Methusal's shoulders, and they stood together watching the boat and her sister grow smaller and smaller. Then they were small figures on the beach. ...Then they disappeared into the forest.

"She'll be fine." Behran's arm tightened around her.

She couldn't answer. It felt like her whole world had exploded and all of the vital pieces were flying further and further from her—out of reach of her heart and her control. Now The One was the only one who held them all together.

Δ Δ Δ Δ Δ

The Captain groveled on the floor before the Presidente's desk. "Please," he begged.

The Presidente eyed him with no pity. Blood lust consumed him. Payment must be made for his incompetent military's utter failure yesterday. The bloody retributions would begin closest to home, and then spread out in a dark, bloody wave, consuming every Commander who had failed his post. New Commanders would be assigned. Men in whose hearts terror would strike at the mere mention of the Presidente's name! Fear would whip his military into shape. Laziness would never again infect his ranks. He'd make sure of it!

His clenched fist hit the desk. A brand new vase jumped and rolled. Gently, it rolled to the edge where it quivered, rocking. The Presidente slammed the desk again. It tipped over and shattered on the stone floor.

On his knees, the Captain cowered still more. "Why?" he whimpered. "I have served you faithfully, day after day."

"You *failed,* you miserable rocher!"

"But we killed the Dehrien..."

"He *lives!*" roared the Presidente. "And the girl appeared in my room. She delivered a *peace agreement.* Do you hear me? Those Koblani scum delivered *demands* to my very face!" His tongue twisted into knots, unable to deliver the words fast enough. Spittle flew. "She escaped!" His voice sharpened to a high pitched scream. "You will die for your incompetence. You will *die!*" His breaths came in sharp gasps and pants. A warning pain pierced his chest. His fingers curled hard around his letter opener. He'd do it himself.

A knock sounded at the door.

"*What?*" he bellowed. If it was Yalin, he'd receive a punishment he would never forget.

The door swung open and his son sauntered in. Cold eyes flickered from the Presidente to the Captain, whose face was now on the floor. Sobs wracked his narrow shoulders.

"You are having a party, and you did not invite me?"

A hot ball of pain exploded in the Presidente's chest, and he sat down abruptly. Liquid fire licked through his body.

"Father?" The General looked at him coldly. "Are you all right?"

Each breath was a burning effort. But he could not let his son know. He must distract him, so he could recover from this attack without being analyzed like an insect. Loudly, he wheezed, "Kill the sniveling rocher. Make him an example to the entire palace." The Presidente sat forward on his desk, propped up on his solidly planted elbows.

"Gladly." Fitrn's sword hissed free and he poked it into the Captain's spine. "Stand up."

The Captain refused. Instead, he curled up into a tight ball. That did not prevent the General's lethal slashes, or the Captain's screams as the Presidente's son seized every opportunity to kill the Captain in the most painful, drawn out manner possible.

At one point, the Presidente had to close his eyes. He felt sick. It couldn't be because of all the blood pooling on his floor, or the last, helpless gurgles of the Captain. Even that abruptly silenced.

"Well." Fitrn's sigh sounded regretful. "Yalin!" he shouted.

The secretary entered the room and gaped at the bloody corpse. "Yes, sir?" he whispered.

"Order men to carry the Captain out. He is to be on display in the courtyard for four hours. All servants and soldiers must see him. He is an example to all who fail the Presidente."

"Yes sir!"

"Then you will clean up this mess. Take my sword. Clean that first."

Head bobbing like a mindless fool, Yalin took the blade and fled.

A moment later, two soldiers arrived and removed the Captain's body. Yalin knelt at the General's feet and hurriedly mopped up the blood.

The Presidente and General remained silent while the fool worked. The Presidente would never speak matters of importance to his son while a servant was present. Fitrn knew this, and retreated to a chair to wait, ankle over his knee. He lightly touched his right shoulder and winced. The

Presidente wondered what had happened to him, but refused to expend the effort to ask.

Yalin's thoroughness allowed the Presidente more time to recover from his attack. His breathing was nearly normal when the secretary left. However, his chest still burned. This terrible, lasting pain had never happened before. What did it mean? And yet he still lived. As long as he did, he would seek retribution upon his enemies.

When the door finally clicked shut, the Zindedi leader found the General staring at him. Cruel speculation glittered in his eyes. His son was plotting his assassination.

It disturbed the Presidente, but at the same time pride grew for his son. He felt certain the pup would not attempt to kill him yet. Not until the timing was to his best advantage. In addition, he knew that Fitrn would not attack as long as his desires for cruelty and conquest were still being fully sated. His son was not yet ready to settle down in an office. He wanted to be out in the field, inflicting horror on as many people as possible. The Presidente knew his son well. No better man could follow in his footsteps. The Zindedi leader needed only to keep him occupied until he died in his own time, and on his own terms.

"I have more orders for you."

"I have news for you," the General returned.

The Presidente's brows wrenched together in a heavy scowl. "My orders come first." A gravelly, ominous growl colored the words.

Fitrn did not blink. "Speak then, Father."

The insolent pup. Already flirting with disrespect. Thrust and parry, like a sword fight. Each slice would soon begin to carve closer and closer to the Presidente's heart. But he had no time for games right now. "Ships exploded last night. Every Commander of those vessels is to be executed at once."

General Fitrn sat forward. For the first time in months, surprise flickered across his stony features. "Why?"

Temper surged. "Because they are incompetent! Their ships burned to ash. They are worse than useless!"

Fitrn thought about this. "Yes," he agreed. "Or..." He rose and paced.

The pacing made the Presidente feel nervous. He wished Yalin hadn't returned the sword to Fitrn. "Or what?" he asked, his voice thunderous with disapproval.

The General stopped abruptly, his hands on the Presidential desk, and he deliberately leaned forward. The Presidente glared up at him. Obviously, his son wanted to intimidate him. Perhaps he required a reminder...

Fitrn's smooth words cut into his thoughts. "Which is worse, Father? Death? Or humiliation that one must endure every day for the rest of one's life?"

The Presidente leaned back in his chair in order to create space between himself and his son. He laced his fingers across his soft paunch, striving to appear completely relaxed. "What sort of humiliation?"

The General smiled, but it did not reach his eyes. "The Commanders are prideful. They have worked many years to achieve their position. They crave the respect of others. Take that away from them. Permanently. Make them the slaves of all."

"Demote them? Perhaps below the privates." The Presidente smiled. He liked this idea. Yes. What could be worse? Fresh young recruits would have the power to order the Commanders about; perhaps even humiliate them without fear of reprisal. Living with that denigration each day would feel like death cuts to the pride of the Commanders. "Do it."

"I will order it today." Fitrn's eyes glittered with quickly cloaked triumph.

So. His son wanted to use the Commanders for his own purposes in the future. He would probably promote them again. Once the Presidente was dead, of course. That line of thought tired him. He wanted to rest. But first, he needed to form a plan to keep his son occupied. That meant reminding Fitrn of the upcoming battle against Koblan. Right now, only blood lust appealed more to the General than taking command of Zindedi. It would not remain that way for long, however. Soon, his son would hold a knife to his throat, and the natural ascension of power would turn over to the young, strong, and violently cruel. As it should. But the Presidente was not ready to die yet.

"I have more news," he said. In clipped phrases, he described what had happened in his office last night, including the Koblani girl's insolent demands for peace. "You should have killed her," he snarled. He ignored the fact that he had ordered the General to spare her.

The accusation did not perturb Fitrn. Instead, an unholy light gleamed in his eyes. "I would love to torture and kill that Zindedi whore." He took a deep breath, and his gaze darkened, taking on a glazed, faraway look. Clearly, he was plotting tortures even now.

The Presidente watched with speculative interest. A plan germinated in his head as his son slowly relaxed.

Fitrn nodded. "Death. Very well. We will pretend peace, but prepare for war. I will lead the charge against Koblan."

The Presidente scowled. He did not like it when his son put words into his mouth. However, it was as he wished. And he would keep his life until his son defeated Koblan. "Speak your news," he commanded.

"We captured a Koblani man. We killed another. Unfortunately, the Koblanis blew up all of the powder carts heading into Carachki. They also blew up the small powder mine near Dakarra."

Impotent rage gripped the Presidente. "You allowed this to happen?"

"They are insane. They behaved without reason. Blowing up the carts nearly killed them and my prisoner. At the same time, they seemed frantic to save the prisoner. One died trying to save him."

"Your prisoner must be valuable, then."

"Yes. His papers are clearly falsified. They are missing three important paragraphs."

Grudgingly, the Presidente said, "Your brother's doing?"

"Perhaps." Fitrn dismissed this. "My gut tells me the prisoner is the one who killed your brother—my uncle Greisn."

"Prepare him, then. He will die."

"I would like nothing more." He hesitated. "But he may prove useful as bait."

"How?"

"If he is valuable, they may send more of their top men to save him. Then we can kill them all. In addition, we can use his capture as leverage in our peace negotiations. We will make the Koblanis think we truly want peace. We will haggle over every detail. When they agree to our terms, we can release him."

The Presidente frowned. "What terms?"

"We will demand to learn kaavl. They must send their top five kaavl players to our land for one year. If they comply, the prisoner will be released. Also, the kaavl players will be released at the end of their service."

The Presidente chuckled. "Of course." He did not believe the General would ever release the kaavl players. And yet wasn't kaavl the only weapon Zindedi did not possess? It seemed worth the risk to keep the prisoner alive for that purpose alone.

He nodded. "Let him live. Torture him, though. For my brother's sake, he must suffer deeply. Also, find out who he truly is. I want to find out exactly how important he is to the Koblanis."

General Fitrn clicked his heels together and bowed. "I will order my men to begin immediately." He headed for the door, not bothering to wait for dismissal.

The Presidente's fists tightened in fury. However, he forced his voice to remain calm. "Fitrn." His son looked back. "I have formed a plan to deliver Methusal Maahr and all of Rolban's lush ore straight into your hands."

His son's cruel lips parted in a small, swift smile. "Yes, Father?"

"I will tell you more when it is time to depart for Koblan."

An unholy light shone in his eyes. "I look forward to that conversation."

Satisfied, the Presidente sat back in his chair. His son would make no attempt to take his life yet. All would go according to his new plan. He chuckled, thinking about how easy it had been to manipulate his son. Better yet, soon all of Koblan's treasures would be his, too.

△ △ △ △ △

In the late afternoon, the ship turned SSW, at a tight angle into the strengthening wind and the high, rolling seas. Koblan, however, lay directly south. According to Captain Hil, the necessary tacking to the wind would lengthen the journey home from ten days to fourteen.

The joy of it all.

Methusal felt worse by the minute. Right now she was with Mentàll, but she couldn't sit on the stool because of the violent motion of the ship. She gripped the edge of the built-in bed for balance, feeling too nauseous for words. Pain hammered in her head. It felt like someone was trying to scramble her brain.

Doc had secured Mentàll to the bunk with ropes around his lower chest and legs so he wouldn't roll with the ship. He lay still and quiet, and his skin felt blisteringly hot. Methusal swallowed back a violent surge of bile. She refused to go back to her cabin and collapse into a useless ball of nothingness. She *had* to help him.

Legs braced apart, she dribbled more water on a cloth. The ship lunged, and her hip hit the bunk as she struggled to keep her balance without dropping the water skin. Swiftly, she corked the skin before losing any precious liquid, and then gripped the bunk again with one hand. With the other, she squeezed water drops between Mentàll's dry lips. More cloths lay cooling on his forehead and on his bare chest.

He lay as still as death, although at times his frown deepened and his lips twitched, as if he wanted to say something. She wished he would. His face looked severe. No doubt he was silently suffering in pain, although she knew Doc had given him as much pain medication as was safe.

The ship gave a violent lurch, and a wave cracked into the hull with the force of thunder. The boat shuddered, and for a second she froze with fear, wondering if the boat would break in two.

But she heard only the splash and hiss of waves. The ship plunged on, making her stomach heave.

Hands trembling, she left the wash cloth on Mentàll's chest and gripped the built-in lip that held the bed's mattress in place with both hands. She struggled to conquer her urge to vomit.

Doc lurched in. "How's it going?"

"As well as can be expected," she said through gritted teeth.

Doc shoved the bucket into her hands just in time. He took it when she had finished. "You need to lie down. You didn't get any sleep last night."

With her stomach empty, she felt better. "I can stay longer."

"You need fluids. Or you'll become as dehydrated as he is."

Just the thought of drinking made her feel sick. "Not yet." She picked up the cloth and squeezed more water onto Mentàll's lips.

"Methusal."

"I'm fine."

"Let someone else take a shift."

The thought sounded unbearably appealing. "I can't leave him."

Softly, Doc said, "I'll tell you if anything changes."

"I can't." Her voice broke. Just the thought of leaving him... It terrified her that he might slip away while she was gone. Illogical as the thought was, she felt that if she stayed with him, he couldn't die.

The ship lurched again, and the pain in her head intensified. She pressed a hand to her temple, struggling not to grimace.

Gently, Doc pulled the cloth from her fingers. "Go lie down." His gaze was compassionate. "Hendra or I will tell you if there's any change."

Tears welled in her eyes. "I don't want to go."

"Rest. Come back when you're feeling better."

It would take her body another two days to get used to the motion of the ship. At least. She wouldn't feel better anytime soon. On the other hand, she could lie down for a few minutes. "All right. But I'll be back soon."

Doc turned away and took a packet from a drawer. When he turned back, he held a small glass with water with white powder swirling inside. "Take this. It'll help you keep down the liquid."

"What is it?" She eyed it with suspicion.

"It'll relax your stomach and it will help you sleep for a little while. It'll help you feel better."

"I don't want to sleep." But she did want to feel better. Desperately. Then she could come back and help Mentàll again. "For how long?"

"A few hours."

Her stomach lurched again, and she grabbed the bucket. Her whole body trembled when she was done. She felt awful, and her head felt like it was about to explode. "All right," she whispered. "But just for a few hours." She drank the liquid Doc offered, and then glanced at Mentàll, who lay motionless on the bed. "I'll be back soon," she promised.

In her cabin, she curled up on her bunk. A heavy feeling pushed on her mind, forcing it to relax. The powder was working awfully fast. How much had he given her? With a helpless sigh, she drifted into a deep, dreamless sleep.

CHAPTER TWO

METHUSAL DIDN'T WAKE UP again until pale light streamed in through the porthole. She struggled up onto one elbow and nausea immediately hit her. She lay back down again, swallowing hard.

Hendra poked her head in the door. "You're awake."

"Mentàll! Is he..."

"He's fine. He made it through another night."

"Night? What time is it?"

"It's dawn."

Methusal's jaw dropped. "I slept for fifteen hours?"

Hendra smiled. "You needed it. Are you feeling any better?"

The queasiness had returned in full force. The boat was still bucking and surging with the waves. Up on deck, a hum went through the rigging. "The wind is still blowing hard."

"Yes. But no sign of a storm. That's the good news. Would you like some broth? Coyl has a pot on the stove."

Methusal reached for the bucket and vomited.

"Sorry," Hendra looked chagrinned. "Rest. I'll send Doc to look in on you."

Before she could protest, Hendra disappeared. Methusal thought about sitting up, but just the idea made her feel wretched. She closed her eyes, waiting for Doc to appear.

"How are you feeling?" His quiet voice startled her. He crouched beside her bunk, at eye level. Methusal wondered if she looked as bad as she felt. If so, there would be no fooling the sharp-eyed doctor.

"Not so good," she admitted.

"Want more powder?"

"*No.*"

"Take a sip of water, then." A water skin appeared, and he pressed it to her lips.

"I don't want to be sick."

"Your eyes are sunken and your lips are as dry as Mentàll's. Drink, or I won't allow you out of bed later."

"Later?"

"You're very seasick, Methusal. Ignoring it won't make it any better. Either take care of yourself, or I won't let you get up."

She obediently drank a tiny sip.

Doc recorked the skin and pressed it into her hand. "Drink more in ten minutes. I want that water gone when I come back at lunch time."

Methusal swallowed against the nausea. "I'll try."

"Good." With a smile, he left her.

She couldn't sleep any longer. So she lay there feeling like a dying apte caught in a trap, and alternated between worrying about Mentàll and Deccia, and choking back the urge to vomit.

It was lonely in the cabin, and quiet. For the longest time, she didn't understand why that bothered her so much. Usually she liked time to herself. But this felt.... It felt wrong. Like someone was missing. It took her a while to figure out why.

When she did, she closed her eyes and swallowed against the ache in her throat. She wasn't used to lying alone in bed anymore. She wasn't used to being alone, period. Because for the last three weeks, Mentàll had been with her all day and every night. Every time she lay down to rest, he had been there.

She missed him.

Tears burned in her eyes, and she let them flood over and drip down her cheeks. It seemed silly to hide her feelings. No one was here to see, or to know. No one except for herself.

A hollow place inside of her ached. Yes, she missed Mentàll. It seemed wrong that he wasn't with her right this minute.

He *had* to be all right. He just had to. She was glad that she was alone, so no one could hear her dry, hoarse sobs. Her fragile emotions felt like dry, scattered leaves—as if the smallest breeze could shatter her.

She curled up into a ball and tried to sleep again.

△ △ △ △ △

Deccia paced inside their new, tiny rented rooms in Carachki. The late afternoon sun dimly lit the gray interior. The sagging furniture had seen better days.

Riln and Goric had left hours ago to search out information on Timaeus, and to find food and a disguise for her.

Was Timaeus alive? Being tortured? Her stomach hurt from constant worry, and from a feeling of simmering, impotent rage, too. Tabor had betrayed them. Even though he'd named Riln, Timaeus was captured because of the description he'd given to the Presidente.

Deccia moved to a dirty window and pushed aside the wilted brown drape. It would be dark soon. She hated feeling like a prisoner indoors. She ached to go out and find Timaeus, and do whatever she could to engineer his immediate escape.

The thought of Timaeus in the hands of that evil, deranged General was more than she could bear. She'd seen his dead eyes when he'd come after Ceri. The man was capable of anything. And of course the Presidente would want to extract full revenge on Timaeus for the death of his brother.

She *had* to get out of here! She needed to find Timaeus *now*.

Still no sign of Goric or Riln. The street was empty, except for shabbily dressed children. Dilapidated houses and broken bits of debris lined the dirt road. This squalid neighborhood appeared safe enough during the daytime, but when they'd arrived at dusk last night, men had slunk in the shadows. They were up to no good. This certainty had lodged deep in Deccia's soul.

Anxiety compelled her to pace the room again.

Although she didn't like this neighborhood, finding the rooms in the back of this old, run down house had been a stroke of luck. Riln had struck up a conversation with a traveler on the road and he'd recommended this place. It fit their requirements exactly. The apartment was cheap, and the corpulent owner had asked no questions. In fact, as he'd pocketed five hundred of their remaining seven hundred dascals, he'd done no more than slide his small eyes from Riln to Goric to Deccia with a sordid leer on his lips. She was glad a sliding bolt separated their rooms from the disgusting man's quarters.

Three loud knocks shuddered on the door. A pause, and then two more.

Deccia hurried to open it.

"About time." Riln shouldered his way inside and dropped a cloth sack on the kitchen counter. A glance took in the contents. Eggs, bread, and fruit.

"Any news of Timaeus?" she asked.

"Naw. He's either on the base or at the palace." Riln collapsed on a couch and pulled out a tiny stick to pick his teeth.

Frustration surged so hard that Deccia gripped her fists tightly in order to control it. "I thought you were looking for a disguise for me."

"You want leads on Timaeus, right? That took up all my time."

Another series of knocks sounded at the door. She snatched it open and glared at Goric. His gray eyes narrowed, and his slight body slipped by her to enter the apartment. He carried no bags at all.

"Did you find Timaeus?" she demanded.

"He's probably at the palace."

She glared at them both. "I thought one of you was going to get me a disguise."

Riln's opaque dark eyes flicked away, as if he didn't care. But Goric's set, unrepentant expression bothered her even more. She crossed her arms, trembling with the desire to shout at them both. Slowly and carefully, she said. "Did you two plan this?" Her voice rose. "I need to get *out*. I need to find Timaeus."

"It'll be safer if you stay here," Goric said in an even tone. "At least until the Presidente leaves for Koblan."

She crossed her arms even tighter. In a low voice, she said, "Who are you to decide what is best for me? I'm going to find Timaeus. If that means I find my own disguise, then so be it."

"Fine. Be a fool." Goric retreated to the kitchen and pulled a pan onto the stove.

Quaking with anger, Deccia stared at him, and then at the Tarst man. Riln gave her a hard, dismissive look, and then ignored her. Deccia turned her glare on Goric. Through her teeth, she said, "How dare you call me a fool? We're a team. If anything, *I'm* the leader. You will listen to me!"

On the couch, Riln snorted. "Female having a fit."

Rage consumed her. It was an unfamiliar, overwhelming emotion. In one step, she grabbed the collar of Riln's black jacket and shouted in his ear, "You are an ignorant muscle brain! I want to find my husband, and *you're* going to help me!"

Riln rose and turned on her with a snarl. With one violent jerk, he ripped her hand free and twisted both of her wrists into painful immobility. "Now listen to me, little girl. If you attack..."

"Cut it, Riln," Goric said.

"Who'll stop me? You, pudding boy?"

Riln's sneers and rough treatment made something snap inside of her. She wanted to fight him. She wanted to hurt this wild beast. She wanted to win over all things abominable and hurtful. She twisted her wrists free and attacked him, swinging her fists, and kicking and kneeing him.

When he gave an angry roar and grabbed her arms, she struggled all the harder, panting, taking fierce delight in the burning pain in her arms. She wanted to hurt. She wanted to *bleed* if that meant she could annihilate the monstrous evil that had taken over her life. Over Timaeus' life.

Gasping and panting, she fought with blind fury. Tears streamed down her cheeks. "I hate you," she whispered. "I hate you, I hate you, I *hate you!*"

She wasn't sure how it happened, but a second later she was face down on the floor with Riln's hard knee digging into her back. Her arms were wrenched up behind her.

"Easy, Riln," Goric said.

Above her, Riln's breaths came in harsh pants. "She's strong. Crazy. But strong."

Trussed like an apte, unable to move, Deccia lay still, feeling the hard rug loops digging into her cheek. Fading sunlight shone on the floor, and sanity finally returned. She burst into tears. Embarrassment overwhelmed her. She'd attacked Riln, her own teammate. And *why?* Had she lost her mind?

"Let her go."

Riln's grip didn't ease. "I think she needs to learn a lesson."

"I said, let her go."

Riln's painful knee lifted, and he dropped her arms to the floor. Deccia sat up and curled away from them both. Tears continued to run down her face. Her wrists hurt. Her arms hurt. The bright red marks on her skin indicated that she'd have vicious bruises tomorrow. And why? Because she was a fool! She buried her face in her knees and wept.

The front door slammed. Riln had left the house. Goric returned to the stove. Soon, delicious egg smells drifted to her nose.

Deccia wiped her eyes, feeling stupid and embarrassed. What had come over her? She'd never wanted to hurt anyone before in her life. Was this who she was, deep inside? A monster, wanting to rip apart anyone who made her angry?

She retreated to the relief room and splashed cold water on her face. Afterward, she regarded her swollen eyes in the mirror. She barely recognized the hollow-eyed person staring back at her.

Well, she couldn't hide in here forever.

Reluctantly, she exited from the small room and joined Goric at the counter. He swiftly served eggs onto three plates.

"I'm sorry."

"Riln's the one you should apologize to."

"I know. I will."

Silence ensued as Goric scraped the pan and put it in the sink. He twisted the knob and water exploded into a fitful spray, and then into a steady stream. "Do you feel better?"

"What do you mean? I feel like a fool."

"You're angry about Timaeus. Maybe it helped to take it out on Riln. He deserves it."

Deccia said nothing for a moment. Nothing could justify her hysterical fit. "I don't know what came over me. I was wrong to act like that. But you're right. I am angry. I *hate* this. How could Tabor..." She swallowed back the tight lump in her throat. "How could he *do* that to Timaeus?"

Goric averted his face and grabbed the serving spoon. He stuck it under the running water. "Maybe he didn't mean for Timaeus to get caught. He named Riln, didn't he?"

"Tabor sold everyone out," she retorted. "His description condemned Timaeus just as easily as could have done to Riln. And Riln is innocent. He didn't kill Greisn." She laughed without humor. "How could it be right for a man to die for something he didn't do?"

"Maybe Tabor had no choice. Maybe the Presidente..."

"Tabor was a Zindedi. He had no morals. No scruples. His description sentenced Timaeus to death. If Tabor was still alive..." Deccia swallowed, tears aching hard behind her eyes. She whispered, "I wish I could kill him myself."

Goric eyed her. "Do you want to turn into a Zindedi?"

"Of course not."

"Hatred is the first step. You're not like this, Deccia. Remember who you are."

Tears spilled down her cheeks. "I want Timaeus to be safe," she said brokenly. "I don't want him hurt." She put her hands to her flooding eyes. "I *hate* this."

"I'm sorry," Goric said softly. "I'll do everything I can to help you."

"Then find him. And get me a disguise so I can help look for him."

His movements slowed, and finally he turned off the water. "That might be difficult."

"Why?"

Riln slammed the door open and came in, his face as black as thunder.

"I don't have any more money," Goric admitted.

She gasped. "Why not?" Goric had carried almost a hundred dascals with him today.

"I met an unpleasant fellow. Let's just say I had to give it to him. Or that would have been it."

"Goric!" she stared at him, aghast.

Riln cursed, loudly and colorfully. "I'm stuck with an apte and a lunatic! I don't *believe* this."

"I'll look for a job tomorrow."

Riln swore again. "You're right you will, you puny rocher."

"How much money do you have left, Riln?" Deccia asked. "Fifty."

She didn't ask what he'd spent his money on. The groceries couldn't have cost more than ten dascals. "We'll all need to get jobs."

"You're not getting a job," Riln told her. "You're erratic. You'll jeopardize the mission."

She flushed. "I'm sorry I attacked you. All of the bad things exploded in my head and I took it out on you. I'm sorry."

"Regardless. You're not getting a job."

"I agree," Goric said. "General Fitrn and the Presidente know what Methusal looks like. That means they know what you look like. If you're ever out in public, it has to be for short periods of time."

"Fine. I don't want a job anyway. I want to spend all my time looking for Timaeus."

"You'll need a disguise," Goric persisted. "We don't have money for one."

"Sure we do." She swiftly pulled a knife from a drawer. The blade flashed in the fading sunlight. Both Riln and Goric stared at it with identical, uneasy expressions. She would have laughed if it wasn't so sad that they were wary of her now. She extended the knife, handle first, to Goric. "Cut off my hair."

His mouth gaped, and he stared at the dark tresses tumbling over her shoulders. "Not your hair." The soft words sounded aghast.

"Do it. Zindedi women wear their hair short. I want to look just like them."

Goric didn't move.

"Give me that." Riln snatched the blade out of Goric's hand. "I'll do it."

Instinctively, Deccia's hands flew up and she backed away.

"What are you afraid of? One good whack and it'll be gone."

"I'll do it." Goric held out his hand. With ill grace, Riln shoved it back into his palm.

"Thank you." Deccia retreated to the table and sat down with her back to Goric. His tentative fingers combed through the heavy mass, arranging it into a straight fall. "How short?" His voice sounded a little rough.

"To my chin."

"Are you sure?"

"And cut in some long bangs, too."

Goric set to work, carefully sawing off bits of hair. In soft silence, her long locks dropped to the floor. It felt like death to her. She'd had long hair her entire life. Giving it up felt like losing a part of herself. And yet she'd already lost the biggest part of herself; Timaeus. What did a little hair matter?

Riln wolfed down his eggs while Goric took ages to cut her hair, and then still more time, apparently evening it up. Then he eyed her face. Using the side of the blade, he cut in a few wispy bangs across her forehead and down to her cheeks.

From the kitchen, Riln said, "You missed your calling, pudding boy. You should be a girlie hairdresser."

Deccia ignored him, and Goric appeared to do the same. He critically eyed her face. "Okay. I hope you like it."

Deccia couldn't imagine *liking* it, but she appreciated the effort he had put into trying to make her look presentable. "Thank you, Goric."

He shrugged, and went down on his knees to clean up the mess.

Maybe she'd better take a look in the mirror and get her new self—her new reality—firmly fixed in mind. She headed for the relief room, past Riln, who now forked into someone else's plate of eggs. The Tarst man stared at her as she went by. She cringed. Was it that awful?

In the relief room, she took a deep breath and faced the mirror. A gasp escaped.

The girl in the mirror was a beautiful stranger. Goric had cut her hair so it wisped around her jaw, and pieces of her bangs touched her cheekbones, accenting her bone structure. Her eyes were huge and unblinking and her mouth parted in a soft "O." She stared for another couple of seconds, and then went to the doorway. "Goric. Thank you."

He shrugged again, and disappeared out the door with the trash. Riln stared at her, his dark eyes unblinking. His stare appeared to be involuntary, and it made her feel uncomfortable. She grabbed the remaining plate and sat at the counter with her back to him.

Goric banged the door as he came back inside. "I think we should all have disguises. Tabor might have leaked our descriptions to the Presidente."

"You hide if you want to, apte boy. I'm good as I am."

"Give me three dascals. I know a cheap, easy way to disguise myself."

"So what's our plan for tomorrow?" Deccia asked. It was time for them to work together.

"I'll scout the palace," Riln said.

"I'll get a job," Goric said. "We need money for food."

"I'll go to the Merry Spirits and meet Methusal's friend," she decided.

"Bad idea," Riln said. "She might tip off the military."

"I could get a job there. Sailors talk when they're drunk. Maybe they'll say something about Timaeus."

Both Riln and Goric argued against the idea.

However, Deccia ignored them. She'd made up her mind. Tomorrow she would find out where the Presidente was holding Timaeus, if it was the last thing she did.

△ △ △ △ △

"Methusal." Hendra touched her arm. "Wake up."

She drew in a quick breath and swiftly sat up. The angle and color of the sunlight streaming through the porthole said it was late afternoon.

It took a moment to register Hendra's worried expression. "What's wrong?" Her voice rose. "Is it Mentàll? Has he...?"

"No." But the pucker between the Dehrien girl's brows remained. "He's... Well, he's delirious. He's calling for you."

Ignoring an awful feeling of nausea, Methusal lurched to her feet. "Thank you for coming to get me." She stumbled for Mentàll's cabin.

When she entered, Doc straightened up and draped his heart meter around his neck. His expression was grim. On the bunk Mentàll lay still, but his head jerked back and forth. A low mumble came from his throat. The doctor moved aside, allowing room for Methusal to exchange places with him.

"Try to get him to drink," he said, and left her alone with the Dehrien Chief.

Mentàll's left hand lifted, and then flopped back onto the bed. His chin jerked right, and then left. "Thusa..." he mumbled. Then in a louder, hoarse voice, "Methusal!"

"I'm here." She wrapped her fingers around his hot ones. "I'm right here."

"Thusa." His head continued to move, as if he had not heard her.

"Mentàll." She gripped his hand tighter and pressed her fingers to his blazing cheek. "I'm here," she whispered close to his ear. "Everything is all right."

His restless movements eased. Joy and hope took flight within her. If he could hear her, surely that meant he was getting better?

Then why did Doc and Hendra look so worried? During the war, they'd seen more blood poisoning than she had. Maybe this was one of the stages leading toward death. Despair crushed her hope like sand on a fire.

She touched his hair—something she'd never dare if he was awake—and gently stroked the soft strands; always such a contrast to the hard man he could be. "Fight," she told him. "Fight with everything you have. You can beat this, Mentàll. You can do it. You have to."

He lay very still now, and it scared her. His skin felt like fire. She disentangled her hand from his and prepared cool cloths for his head and chest. As soon as she released his hand, however, the restless movements continued.

"Methus..." he mumbled.

"I'm here. Drink this." Water drops trickled onto his closed lips. She squeezed out a few more drops, but he did not seem to understand that he needed to allow the water inside. Or maybe he didn't feel the liquid. She gently touched his bottom lip, pulling it back a bit so the water rolled inside. "Drink."

His head jerked suddenly sideways. "Methusal!"

"I'm here." She struggled to keep her voice calm.

"Methusal!" His quick movements seemed more agitated than before, and it frightened her. She gripped his hand and spoke near his ear. "I'm here, Mentàll. Everything is all right."

His quick, agitated breaths eased again.

"You've calmed him." Doc appeared at her elbow, his half smile approving. He took in their clasped hands. "Whatever works."

"I need three hands. He won't drink without help."

"We'll do it together." With the doctor's help, they managed to get a few good swallows inside the Dehrien Chief's burning lips.

Doc replaced the cool cloths.

"Is he going to make it?" she whispered. Obviously, Mentàll could hear. She didn't want to discourage him.

"I hope so." He said no more, but his tone was flat. "How's your stomach? Can you stay for a little while longer?"

Methusal didn't want to think about her stomach. The more she did, the sicker she felt. "Please hand me the bucket. I'll be fine."

After he left, she carefully wedged her body between the bunk and the lashed in place stool. Legs braced apart for balance, she looked down at the Kaavl Commander, still holding his sizzling hot hand. A faint frown pinched his brows, but at least he lay quietly now. Too quietly? Methusal wished he would sit up and talk to her—antagonize her—*anything*. Doc obviously didn't hold out much hope that Mentàll would survive the infection raging through his body.

"You can't die," she whispered. "You can't." Her voice broke. She bent and gently kissed his blistering hot cheek. "Fight. Fight with everything you've got. You've *never* let anything beat you before. You can defeat this, too."

CHAPTER THREE

"How is he?"

Hendra looked up. Pale morning sunlight streamed in the window, lighting Mentàll's cabin and the book on her lap. The book she couldn't concentrate on. At least the waves today seemed a little calmer. Doc entered the tiny cabin, carrying a bucket of cold sea water.

"The same. He keeps calling for Methusal." Worry made her feel ill. It felt as if the nightmare of the final night in Dakarra had followed them to the ship. Timaeus. Tabor. Now Mentàll.

Doc took Mentàll's pulse and listened to his breaths. "His lungs are clear. That's good. But he's too hot. I don't know how long someone can survive with a fever this high."

Late yesterday afternoon Doc had removed the remainder of Mentàll's clothes, leaving only a towel for modesty. Four times during the night either Hendra or Methusal had helped Doc cover her cousin with towels dipped in frigid sea water. Mentàll had thrashed when the cold towels touched his fiery skin. It was a good thing the ropes held him down.

Hendra plunged a damp towel into the cold bucket. "Do you think this is helping?"

"It can't hurt," he said grimly.

Mentàll mumbled when the first cloth hit him, and flung out an arm, barely missing Hendra's head.

"Calm down," Doc said in a soothing voice. "Hendra, I'll take that spot."

"Methusal," he muttered.

"Methusal will be here soon."

"Should I go get her?" Hendra asked.

"Not yet. Let her sleep."

Last night Doc had almost needed to drag the haggard, hollow-eyed Rolbani girl to bed. Not long after, he'd ordered Hendra to rest, too.

"How much sleep did you get?"

He didn't answer, and finished draping the last towel over Mentàll's legs. Mentàll mumbled unintelligibly, his fingers twitching.

"Doc." She touched his arm. His normally straight shoulders sagged and lines etched into the sides of his mouth. "You need to rest, too."

"I'll rest later."

"No. Not later." Her grip tightened on his arm. "Methusal and I can watch him today. You need to rest."

He glanced at her hand on his arm. When he looked back up, his eyebrows lifted.

A blush warmed her skin. "Will you rest?" she insisted.

His lips lifted into a grin. "I could be persuaded," he said softly.

Her heart thrummed faster. "How?"

His cool fingers brushed her cheek, and then his palm gently cupped her jaw. "A good morning kiss would help me sleep." He waited. His smoky blue eyes looked deep into her own.

She wanted to kiss him. Her fingers fluttered up and rested, quivering on his shoulder. Why not? If it would encourage him to get the rest he needed...

"Well, if it's for a good cause." With a smile, Hendra leaned forward and tentatively kissed him. Doc went very still, and his breath whispered over her lips. Warmth pooled inside her, and she pressed closer, kissing him more firmly.

"Hendra," he sighed. His fingers slid into her hair and he kissed her with gentle insistency.

Hendra pulled back. Her smile trembled with happiness. For the first time, his kiss had not scared her. It had felt good and right; like breath to her body and joy to her soul.

When he smiled back, the rising sun lit his eyes, turning them a shimmering blue gray. He understood the importance of the moment. "After that kiss, I'll have long, sweet dreams."

"Good. Now go."

His gaze returned to her mouth. "Bossy," he murmured, but he went.

Hendra crossed her arms tightly, hugging herself with joy, and continued to smile.

△ △ △ △ △

"You won't fit into the Merry Spirits," Riln told Deccia when they left the house that morning. Behind them, Goric locked the door. A pair of black rimmed spectacles, inset with plain glass, distorted his features.

"I don't think men in spirit houses have 'types.' Do you, Riln?"

He flushed. "They're rough. Can you handle it?"

"I can handle anything to find Timaeus."

Yesterday's emotional outburst had cleansed away the ick in her soul. Now she felt only a deadly, determined focus. She'd find Timaeus, or die trying. And thanks to Goric, she'd found the perfect addition to her disguise. After she'd seen his glasses, she'd convinced him to buy her a pair. She was glad she had. A glance in the mirror confirmed that she looked nothing like herself or Methusal now. Tineia did not need to know who she was. Deccia would go to the Merry Spirits posing as a Carachki girl looking for a job.

Riln's shoulders lifted in a dismissive shrug. "Your misery."

The man irritated her, but she drew a deep breath to calm herself. She didn't want to respond in emotional, reactionary ways, like she had yesterday. She wanted to be herself. Mildly, she said, "Thank you for the warning."

He shot her a suspicious look, and hiked abruptly north.

Goric followed Riln. He had been withdrawn ever since he'd come back from buying spectacles this morning. Any questions put to him were answered with curt, monosyllabic answers. Deccia wondered what was wrong.

Quickly, she walked for the wharf, which was two blocks south and eight east. She wondered if Riln and Goric had argued early this morning. She had no idea, since they'd given her the lone bedroom while they slept on the floor in the living room.

Deccia forgot about Goric when tall masts came into view and the briny sea breeze blew stronger. She stopped dead in her tracks when she got her first look at the bay and the docks. The smell of smoke and burnt gun powder permeated the air.

A long pier led to what must have been a network of docks—except now the docks consisted of broken slats of blackened wood, and charred posts jutted up through the gently rolling waves. Large chunks of blackened ship debris bumped between the posts. Smaller pieces bobbed on the waves and battered the rock wall which enclosed the bay. Mentàll's bombs had utterly destroyed the docked military ships.

In the bay, a dozen ships rode the waves, Zindedi flags fluttering in the breeze. Small figures moved on the decks.

On shore, tens of men scurried, dragging charred wreckage into a huge pile in a large stone courtyard. Men in long boats fished debris from the water. They had a lot of work ahead of them. But considering all of this activity, it was very quiet. Unnaturally so. Unease stirred in her spirit.

Deccia spotted a small, neat building labeled "Merry Spirits." Its roof was black, the building brown, and the door blue. The blank-faced structure had no windows, but that didn't explain why she sensed it was empty. She didn't dare walk straight up to the door, or she'd draw the attention of the soldiers. Instead, she crept a block north, and then cut down a side street and slipped to the back of the Merry Spirits.

She peered around the corner at the men at the quay. Her sense of unease deepened as she took in the scene.

She was much closer to them now. Loud thwacks and grunts, punctuated by small cries, filled the air. Stocky older men were stripped naked to the waist. Blood dripped down their backs. A whip hissed, and another cry choked out. The whip wielder was a young man. Likely a Private.

A new figure, dressed in crisp black, and with his beret perched at a precise, jaunty angle, strode up to the two men. His back was to Deccia, but something about him was familiar.

"Twenty lashes for Mekl." His own whip licked out, catching the skinny, dark-haired man square across the back. Mekl made no sound. The black clad man's jaw clenched and the whip hissed again. A bark of pain erupted from the other man. A grin twitched, and the cruel officer's sharp features turned in Deccia's direction.

She gasped, and jerked out of sight. *General Fitrn.*

"Hiding's a good idea," rasped a voice behind her. "Don't wanna get on the bad side of anyone in that family."

Deccia whirled. A woman with long, curly dark hair and a tired smile lounged against the wall, holding a smoke stick. She must have just exited from the back door of the Merry Spirits. A match flared at her fingertips and she lit the stick.

Her brown eyes looked kind, but Deccia's instinctual empathy probed into the other woman's spirit. She was older than she looked. Maybe fifty. And a cynical edge sharpened her soul. But she was forthright. She'd say what she meant.

Deccia relaxed a little. Not that she'd trust a Zindedi completely, of course, but this one seemed all right. "Do they have a good side?"

The woman's barked out a laugh. "That's debatable. I'm Tineia, by the way." Smoke streamed from her nose. "Who are you?"

Of course she couldn't give her real name. Methusal might have told Tineia, and Deccia didn't know how far to trust this woman. "Hanuh." It was her mother's name, and one she could easily remember.

"Hanuh," she rasped, and inhaled another lungful of smoke. "It suits you. What are you doing here, Hanuh?"

"I need to find a job to support my family. I was hoping I might find one here."

"We're closed. For the time being."

"Why?"

Tineia nodded toward the General. "Until that one leaves. After the explosions, the Presidente ordered punishment for all of the troops. Especially for the former Commanders. This morning the order came down—no spirit houses can practice business until he lifts the ban."

"I hadn't realized."

"Come back when the ban lifts. Do you have experience?"

Deccia thought it might be best to tell the truth. If she did get a job here, Tineia would find out soon enough. "Not much. But I'm a fast learner."

She laughed harshly. "You just need to be fast."

Tineia seemed to have a finger on the pulse of the city. Maybe she'd heard something about Timaeus. Carefully, Deccia said, "Have they caught the ones who set the explosions yet?"

"No. And that's why that one's so crazy to beat the troops into submission."

"Who could have done it?" She tried to recall bits of Zindedi history. "The eastern Zindedis?"

Tineia shrugged. "I don't care. As long as I can earn dascals and take care of my daughter, that's all that matters to me."

Deccia decided to press harder. "I heard they'd taken a prisoner."

"Really?" Tineia's dark brows arched. She inhaled more smoke.

Disappointed that Tineia clearly knew nothing about Timaeus, she said, "Maybe it's just a rumor."

A scream drew their attention to the quay. Deccia peeked around the corner while Tineia sauntered closer to take a look. Two privates held one of the half-naked men upside down by his feet, dangling him over the water.

Deccia closed her eyes and jerked back, swallowing back nausea. She had just felt, as sharp as a blade, the man's humiliation and absolute terror.

General Fitrn's cool, cutting voice said, "Tie him up and throw him in."

"No!" screamed the man.

Deccia's hand flew to her mouth, and she choked back bile. Tears surged. "I have to go," she whispered.

Tineia regarded her with pity. "Come back in a couple weeks. I hear the General's going to Koblan with the Presidente. Things will calm down then."

With a nod, Deccia dashed for home. Although "home" might be a dilapidated, dreary shack, and as depressing as death, it was safe. And she wouldn't hear anymore screams.

△ △ △ △ △

The morning slowly passed and Deccia remained, still trembling, in their rented rooms. The screams and inhuman treatment she had witnessed refused to leave her. Finally, she grabbed a rag, a bucket, and soap and attacked the grimy kitchen counter. The floors were next.

Cleaning the filthy shack helped to clear her mind, too. She cleaned until the tiny apartment shone, and her stomach reminded her to eat. After she ate bread and cheese, she felt even better, and thought about the empty afternoon that stretched before her.

Before she could decide what to do next, the door banged open. Both Riln and Goric headed for the food.

Elbows out, keeping Goric away from the food, Riln compiled a massive sandwich at the counter. Finally, after taking his sweet time, he ambled to the couch and collapsed onto it. He ate the sandwich in gigantic bites, scattering crumbs everywhere. Quietly, Goric made his own lunch.

Riln burped. "Found your boy, Deccia."

She gasped, not quite sure she'd heard right. "You did? Are you sure?"

"Yeah, I'm sure. I heard guards talking at a restaurant. By the way, the last of my money is gone."

"Is he alive? Where is he? Tell me everything!"

Riln noisily chewed and swallowed another bite while Deccia waited impatiently. "He's in the palace dungeon. Still alive. I guess the Presidente wants to use him to get better peace terms from Koblan."

Relief overwhelmed her. Timaeus was alive! And if the Presidente wanted to use him as a pawn, that meant he'd keep him alive—at least until the peace deal was finished.

Unfortunately, despair quickly followed that line of reasoning. What was she thinking? The Presidente could not be trusted. He could kill Timaeus whenever he wanted, and Koblan would never know.

"We have to rescue him. *Now*."

"It's too dangerous," Goric said.

"I don't care! I'll do whatever it takes. Or die trying."

Riln rolled his eyes. "An apte and a lunatic," he muttered.

Deccia clenched her fists. "What's your plan, Riln? You seem to think you know everything."

"I say wait. Mentàll—if he survives—will probably order Timaeus to be exchanged in return for peace. All we have to do is wait for the ship to come back. Then we'll go home."

"So you think we should do *nothing*?"

"No." An evil grin curled his lips. "I'll do a little reconnaissance. And give the Zindedis a few unpleasant surprises. And when the ship comes back..." He chuckled.

"What?" Deccia stared at him with suspicion.

Riln smiled. "Let's just say if the Presidente doesn't sign the peace agreement, he has some surprises ahead."

Goric's gaze sharpened.

Deccia said, "Did Mentàll give you new orders?"

"Not new. And I'm sworn to secrecy. Sorry." He didn't look sorry. He looked smug.

Frustrated, she surged to her feet. Riln could have his little secrets. Only one thing mattered to her.

"I won't leave Timaeus in prison! They could be torturing him. And he's injured! Besides, the Presidente could order him killed any minute. We can't trust him."

Goric said, "We'll try to rescue him, Deccia. We'll work on ways to get into the palace. Maybe one of us can get a job there. But it'll take time."

"*Time?*" Tears filled her eyes. She grabbed her glasses and headed for the door. "I'm not waiting one more minute. I'm getting a job right now."

Goric's surprisingly strong fingers closed around her arm, stopping her. "No, you're not."

Deccia stared at him, and then at his offending hand. Anger surged. "Let go!"

At once, he released her. "They might recognize you. It's too dangerous. Riln and I will try first."

"I don't *care* if it's dangerous. I want to rescue Timaeus."

"Do it smart," Riln advised from the couch. "Leave it to the men. Well—a man and pudding boy." He laughed loudly.

"I won't sit here and do nothing!"

"Cook the meals. Clean the house. Isn't that what a good woman does?" Riln snorted.

Deccia crammed her fake glasses on her nose and burst out the door. She slammed it and sped away from the house and the two men who seemed more interested in creating stumbling blocks than plans to rescue Timaeus.

Somehow, she'd get a menial, inconspicuous job in the palace.

Timaeus, I'm coming.

△ △ △ △ △

Aali felt lonelier than ever. Almost a week had passed since playing Hide and Find with the children, and the unpleasant scene in Calbn's office. Lylitha was apathetic, and slept most of the time, and even though Aali loved the kids, she wanted to talk to another adult.

Right now the children were with the cook, and Aali sat outside alone, in the shade, contemplating her cracking cast. The garden glowed with beautiful flowers, but she barely noticed. She felt depressed. Five more weeks to endure until she could go home. It seemed like an eternity.

"Hey, Aali." A shadow fell across her lap.

She looked up. "Dastn!" Her heart leaped, and she reached for her crutches.

"Don't get up." He pulled off his heavy pack and sat beside her on the bench. "How's your leg?"

"It doesn't hurt anymore."

His brown eyes sharpened, and he intently scanned her features. "What's wrong?"

She heaved a quick breath. His kind question lanced open the misery that had been festering inside of her for weeks. "I miss home. The M'ntoyans are nice. Mostly. But kind of... Weird."

His brows drew together in concern, and that made her feel better. "Weird how?"

"Well, the kids are normal. Lylitha is nice, but she's tired all the time. Calbn isn't nice. He doesn't trust me. In fact, I think he hates me."

"Did you spy on him?"

Aali flushed. Unfortunately, Dastn knew her too well. "Well, a little. And GG—their great grandmother—is the strangest of all. Ever since I talked to her a week ago, she's been giving me the evil eye."

Dastn gave a snort of laughter. "Evil eye? Why?"

"I don't know! I wonder if she's...losing it."

"Senile, you mean?"

Aali shook her head. "I'm not sure. Sometimes she seems sharp, and other times she's hard to figure out."

Dastn pulled a parchment from his pack. "Here's a letter from your father. Maybe that will make you feel better."

Aali took the precious letter, but did not open it. Instead, she tucked it in her pocket. Time with Dastn was precious, too. She'd missed his smile, and even his teasing.

Dastn said, "I've met GG. She's a tough old lady. Don't let her scare you. You're as spunky as she is."

"Is that a compliment?" Aali wanted to know. "She's rude!"

"And since when do you take disrespect from anyone?"

"But she's old. I have to treat her with respect."

"Yes. But call her on the rudeness. She speaks her mind. Speak yours."

She smiled. "Thanks. I feel better."

He stood. "You had me worried. All pale and lifeless looking."

She playfully poked his arm. "Stop it."

"Sure." Dastn dropped his chin to his chest and drooped his broad shoulders. "I'm poor, pitiful Aali. My leg's broken and people are mean to me. Life stinks!"

She levered herself up on her crutches. "You *are* a whip beast!" She gently kicked him with her good foot.

He grinned. "There's my feisty girl."

She rolled her eyes, but smiled. "I haven't been that bad."

"It's good to see you smile again."

Tears suddenly blurred her eyes. "Oh, Dastn." She wobbled forward a step.

He moved to meet her, and his arms went around her. The crutches felt awkward under her arms, but she gripped him tight, her face pressed into his chest. Tears flowed then, and she gulped and sniffled.

Apparently feeling impatient with the impeding crutches, Dastn knocked them onto the stone walkway. They fell with a clatter. His arms tightened around her, holding her close. "Shh. It's all right."

"I'm sorry," she hiccupped.

"It's all right." She felt his cheek against her hair. His breath warmed and soothed her in a way no words could. She felt safe and complete in his arms; as if she was finally at home in this new place.

At last, her tears trickled to a halt. She wiped her eyes with the backs of her hands.

"Sorry," she said again.

"Why?"

"Because I *am* feeling sorry for myself."

"I think you're lonely. You miss home."

"Yes. I do."

"But you're strong, and you're going to be fine."

"I know. Thank you." She gave him a watery smile.

"Come take a walk with me," he said. "Show me the sights."

"I haven't been out much," she confessed.

"Why not?"

"I spend most of my time taking care of Trori and Rartn. They're great kids," she added hurriedly.

"What is Lylitha doing?"

"She's tired a lot. And she has dizzy spells. She's going to have the baby any day now."

"You have a soft heart, but you're not their servant. You're their guest."

"But I feel like I should help out."

"Help, okay. But don't give them free child care all day long." He held the gate open for them. They exited from the courtyard and walked into the street.

"GG said that, too. Well, more like, 'Don't let Lylitha run you ragged.'"

"She's right."

"I didn't tell them I'm leaving the house." Aali stopped, feeling a pang of conscience. "Someone needs to watch Rartn and Trori."

"I'll tell them. Wait here."

He soon returned. "They're eating dinner. They're fine."

"What will we eat? Oh, I guess we can get something later from the cellar," she decided.

"No."

"What do you mean, no?"

"Follow me. I have a treat for you."

"You do?" She grinned, and swung a little faster on her crutches. "I love surprises. Give me a hint."

"No."

Dastn led her to the waterfront, where several ships were docked. Shops lined the quay. Many showcased bright, beautiful blankets, beaded clothing, and woven grass bags and hats. She'd never seen a marketplace like this before. During the war everything had been burned and closed down. And Rolban was a communal village; everyone worked to provide the necessities. Very few frivolous items were produced.

"It's beautiful," she said, her eyes wide with wonder.

"We'll eat dinner here." He stopped on a flat strip of land located between the shops and the beach. Tables and chairs were set up there, and nearby was a little shop with its door open. Delicious smells drifted out. "Sit down, and I'll get us some food."

He disappeared into the cottage and reappeared a little later with plates of steaming seafood and plump grain kernels, which were covered in a delicate sauce. Tagma tarts were for dessert. A man brought out cool cups of water.

"This is fabulous!" Aali breathed. "Thank you, Dastn!"

His lips edged up. "Eat up."

She enjoyed every morsel. And she loved sitting outside as the sun sank toward the dark blue rim of the ocean, too. The cool sea breeze slid fluttering fingers through her hair. It felt as if it swept away the dark, closed in feeling she'd been feeling in the mansion lately. It made her feel alive and refreshed. She drank in the sound of flying beasts cawing to each other, and the shouts and clanks of fishermen docking their boats as they prepared to bring in the day's catch. It all felt fresh and exciting. And she had Dastn to thank for it.

She finished the last of her tart. "This was the greatest! Thank you."

His intent brown eyes held hers, smiling a little. "You're easy to please."

That's right, she agreed silently. Give her the great outdoors, delicious food, and Dastn, and she was happy. No. More than happy. Filled with joy.

His gaze ran over her face, taking in her happiness, and something flickered, deep within. He stood abruptly.

"It's getting late. We should head back." His warm hand closed around hers, helping her up.

Aali chattered happily all the way back to the Chief's compound. There, the familiar flowers looked brighter than they had before.

Trori and Rartn rushed outside to greet them. "Goodnight, Aali!" They hugged her tight, and she kissed their heads and sent them back to Lylitha, who stood in the doorway.

Twilight was falling fast now, enfolding the courtyard in shadows.

"I'm leaving early tomorrow," Dastn said.

"Already?" she felt dismayed. "But you just got here."

"You'll miss me." That wicked brow tilted up a bit.

She would miss him. More than she wanted him to know. "I haven't had a chance to read my letter yet."

"Do you have one to give Petr?"

"Yes. In my room. I'll get it."

Dastn followed her into torch-lit hallways. He waited in her doorway while she fetched the letter.

"Here." She pressed it into his hand. "How early are you leaving?"

"Dawn."

"I'll see you in a few weeks, then." She tried to sound flippant, as if she didn't care too much, but didn't think she pulled it off.

"Don't let GG push you around."

"I won't. Thanks, Dastn." On impulse, she went on tip toe and kissed his scratchy cheek. He stiffened, but his hand curled around her arm, steadying her.

"'Bye," he said roughly. After a long look, he turned on his heel and left.

Heart thumping pleasantly, Aali watched him go. If only he didn't have to leave so soon. She'd miss him. ...Who was she fooling? She missed him already.

But this time, she wouldn't sit around feeling sorry for herself. No way. Tomorrow she'd talk to GG.

△ △ △ △ △

A noise teased Methusal from sleep. She opened one eye. The gray cast of the sunlight slanting through the porthole said she'd slept until late afternoon again. The motion of the boat felt gentler. She didn't feel very queasy, either. Finally!

A disturbance sounded in the hall.

"I'm trying, Doc, but he broke free..."

"Get Methusal!"

Methusal was down the hall before Hendra made it to the cabin. In the Dehrien Chief's cabin, Doc pressed a firm hand against Mentàll's chest, who was struggling to sit up.

"Relax, Chief," he murmured. The rope that had secured the Dehrien onto the bunk now trailed on the floor. The Tarst doctor coaxed him to lie back down on the bed.

"Methusal!" Mentàll croaked. A frown tensed his flushed face.

Doc spotted her. "He's a little agit..."

"*Methusal.*" With a gasp, the Dehrien Chief sat straight up again. "*Methusal!*" It was a shout.

She rushed in. "I'm here." Gently, she gently urged him to lie back. He refused.

"Methusal!" he said again, harshly.

She took his hand. "Shh. I'm here. Everything is all right."

He looked directly at her, and for a second it seemed as if clarity sharpened those glazed eyes. "Methusal?"

"Yes. Lie back. You're too big for me to fight." He settled back down, but his hand painfully gripped hers.

He gradually relaxed, and apparently fell back asleep. His hand still held hers tightly, though.

Doc sent her a faint smile. "You're just what the doctor ordered."

"He's not in his right mind," she said anxiously. "What does that mean?"

"It's common with fevers. People often work through their personal demons."

"So I'm his personal demon?"

He smiled. "I think he's worried about you."

She glanced back at Mentàll. A frown still tugged at his brows. "Maybe he's reliving what happened in the Presidente's palace."

"Maybe. Earlier he threatened to choke someone with a whip. He seemed sure the man wanted to hurt you."

Her face warmed. "Well. Yes. That did happen." She looked down at their interlinked hands and with a tiny, involuntary movement, stroked his thumb. She knew Doc was watching, but couldn't meet his gaze.

He said, "I'm glad you're here for him. But I have to tell you, Behran's been worried about you."

Behran. Guilt almost made her drop the Dehrien Chief's hand. "When I'm done here, I'll go see him."

"Could I send him in now? He wanted to see you when you got up."

"Sure." Finally, she looked up. Now she felt more compelled than ever to let go of Mentàll's hand, but did not.

Doc sent her a discerning look. "I'll be right back."

Behran. She briefly closed her eyes. While she'd been feeling sick and worrying constantly about Mentàll, she'd barely spared a thought for Behran at all. She'd been living in survival mode. She hoped he would understand.

Since Mentàll seemed to be asleep, she gently disengaged her hand and set to work wringing out a new, cool cloth for his forehead.

"Thusa."

She turned. Behran stood in the doorway, his hands in his pockets. With a smile, she crossed the gently rolling deck and hugged him. "I'm sorry, Behran. I didn't mean to ignore you. I've been so sick and worried that I haven't been able to think straight."

"It's okay." He rubbed her back before he released her. "Are you feeling better now?"

"Yes. I haven't thrown up in three hours."

He grinned. "Good." He glanced at the bed. "And how is Mentàll?"

Worry clogged her throat and closed like a fist around her heart. "I don't know." Her voice caught. Quickly, she cleared her throat. "Doc says the next two days are critical. If he survives, his chances are good."

Behran said nothing for a moment. "He's tough."

"Yes." Methusal looked up and found his deep blue eyes watching her.

She turned away. "Would you mind helping? We could use some fresh sea water."

"Sure." He fetched fresh water and spent the rest of the afternoon with her, helping to lay cool cloths on Mentàll's fevered body. His presence was undemanding, and she relaxed as quiet conversation ebbed and flowed between them.

Dinner smells drifted in from the galley, and her stomach rumbled. She laughed. "This is the first time I've felt hungry in three days."

"Go get some food. I'll stay with him."

"Are you sure?" She felt reluctant to leave. "I could get something and bring it back, and then you could go eat with the others."

"Is that what you want?" he asked quietly.

"I'd like to eat with you, of course. Maybe Doc..."

"I'm here," the Tarst doctor said. "Both of you go."

Behran grinned. "Thanks."

Methusal smiled, but sent a backward glance at Mentàll as she exited.

Chapter Four

Day 4

THE NEXT MORNING MENTÀLL SEEMED even hotter. His skin blazed like the sun. Deep lines furrowed the doctor's brows when he lifted the heart meter from the Dehrien Chief's chest.

"Well?" Methusal's throat felt so tight with worry that she could barely swallow.

"His heart is thundering so hard it sounds as like it could explode." He slowly folded away the medical device. "I don't want to scare you, but this could be it."

"No!" she gasped, and grabbed Mentàll's hand. It felt limp and unresponsive. "*No!*" she repeated forcefully. As if denying it could change the facts.

With shaking fingers, she pulled the hot rag off of his forehead. "We need more cold water. We need it *now*." She couldn't look at Doc, but heard him leave.

"No," she told the Dehrien Chief. "Don't do this to me. You ornery man, don't you dare *die* like this!" Her shoulders convulsed. With a strangled sob she pressed her cheek to his blazing hot chest. His heart galloped like explosive thunder under her ear. It terrified her. "Oh help, The One, please," she whispered. "*Please.*"

"Water, Methusal." Doc reappeared with a sloshing bucket. Hendra was right behind him.

"We need to get liquids into him."

"We need to pray," Hendra said quietly.

"Yes." Tears welled in Methusal's eyes. She lay her palms on his scorching hot chest.

Hendra and Doc took up positions on either side of her, each touching a part of Mentàll's body. Hendra prayed softly. "The One, please calm Mentàll's fever. Please kill the infection in him. Please see him through this, and heal him."

Doc cleared his throat. "Give me wisdom. Tell me if there's anything else I can do."

"Don't let him die. *Please* don't let him die," Methusal whispered.

"Amen," Hendra said.

"All right," Doc said briskly. "Let's work on cooling him down again. Methusal, you'll drip water into his mouth."

The hours slowly passed. Behran brought fresh, cold sea water and dumped the warm. Doc, Hendra, and Behran took half hour rest periods. Methusal refused.

In the late afternoon, Mentàll twitched. For a second, she felt a spark of hope, but when she touched him, he felt just as hot as ever.

"No," he mumbled, and his chin jerked right.

"Shh," she whispered.

He growled, and his shoulders twitched. Doc checked the ropes, his expression calm, but set.

Mentàll suddenly surged upward, straining against the ropes. "*No. Mama. Don't die!*"

They both tried to urge him to lie back, but his muscles were rigid, and he did not seem to sense their presence at all. "No," he said hoarsely. Then he whimpered, and it sounded like the wail of a little boy. "*Nooo!*"

He flopped backward, his teeth gritted. "You *scienth*," he snarled. "I hate you. I'll find you..." His chin jerked from side to side. "Kill you, you scienth. Kill you..." The words faded into unintelligible mumbles for a little while. And then, "Your fault. Kill you." His face contorted, as if he was trying to cry, but no tears fell from those sunken eyes. He whispered, "*Why?* Mama, why?"

Methusal's heart broke, listening to him. She wanted to shield him from those listening to him. She knew that the pain came from his deepest heart, and that he wanted to keep those things hidden. He would never want anyone to know his vulnerability, or his fear.

He would hate that his weakness and vulnerability were being exposed like this. He would utterly hate it.

He finally quieted, and with a trembling hand, Methusal squeezed more water between his lips.

When reaching to get more, her shaking hand hit the lip of the bucket, and only Doc's quick reflexes kept it from falling to the floor. He pulled the cloth from her fingers. "You need to rest. This could go on all night."

"I'll be fine," she said shortly.

Behran arrived with another bucket of water and deposited it on the wet cabin floor.

"Have you eaten today?" Doc persisted.

"I had toast for breakfast."

"It's four o'clock. Take a break. Get some food."

"I don't *want*..." Then she noticed Behran watching her, his expression inscrutable. "I'll take a short break." Without another word, she headed out the door. Behran followed her.

"Thusa. Stop for a minute."

Reluctantly, she faced him. She knew what he wanted to say, but couldn't handle it right now. She felt ready to fly into a million pieces.

With compassion, his gaze held hers. "What's going on?"

How could she make him understand? *She* didn't even understand. "I can't bear for him to die, Behran."

"You care about him."

"I don't want him to die."

Behran watched her, his blue eyes dark. "How deep does it go?"

"You don't understand. That should be me in there." Her throat ached. "He took the bullet for *me*."

"I understand." He nodded once, took a deep breath and glanced at Mentàll through the doorway. Then he brushed by, heading for the main cabin.

"Behran, wait!"

"What?" His voice sounded weary and resigned.

"It's not..." She couldn't find the right words.

"Every minute you're awake, you're with him. What does that say to you?"

"I need to help him."

"I get that. But ask yourself why you're still wearing his marriage necklace."

Her fingers flew to her throat. "I...I forgot I had it on." Behran stared at her, eyes dark with disbelief. With shaking fingers, she reached for the clasp, but found she couldn't make herself unlatch it. Quivering with sick confusion, she stared at him. "Please. I just..." How could she explain that she didn't know if up was down right now? That she was terribly confused, and sick with worry?

Pain flashed in his eyes, and she hated it. "Behran..."

"Maybe you need to take a step back and look at everything objectively."

With quick relief, she latched onto that explanation. "Yes. You're right. I've been too close to him for too long, and then he was shot... Behran, don't..."

"Give up on you?" he said softly. "Never that, Thusa. Never. All I ask is that you be honest with yourself, and with me, too." This time he did leave.

CHAPTER FIVE

AALI DECIDED IT WAS TIME to stop walking on eggs around GG. That old woman was stronger than she let on.

She knocked on her door.

"Who is it?" The old lady sounded querulous. So what else was new? Aali was done being scared of her.

"It's Aali. I'd like to speak to you."

"What for?"

"Because I'm bored. And because you're one of the most interesting people I know."

A smothered snort came from the room. And then something clattered. It sounded like a tea cup had dropped onto a tea plate.

"Come in, then. Be quick about it. I'm too old to wait forever."

She opened the door and found GG mopping the front of her dress with a clean cloth. The old lady scowled. "See what you did. Shut the door. You're letting in a draft."

She obeyed and sat in the chair near GG, just like she had last time.

"Presumptuous girl."

"Why are you mad at me?"

"Figure that out for yourself," she snapped.

"Let's talk about something else, then."

"What?"

"You pick."

"Hmmph." The old lady fell silent for a moment, but a small smile worked at her mouth. Maybe she wasn't as displeased with Aali as it had seemed. Or maybe she was ready to move on and create new dramas. It was hard to tell with GG.

"Deccia," GG said. "It's a shame about her."

Clearly, GG knew about Deccia's imprisonment during the Quasr War. And likely the General's violations of her, too. Still, it surprised her. Few people knew how he had abused her. "How do you know about that?"

"I was kept a prisoner. But my mind still works. So do my ears. What happened to her, after?"

"Deccia's okay. She married Timaeus, and they're on the spy trip to Zindedi. Did you know about that?" She gently baited the old woman.

GG narrowed her eyes. "I know everything. What do you take me for? An old fool?"

Aali deliberately changed the subject, determined to glean new information from the cantankerous old woman. "I heard that Calbn and Mentàll are planning a treaty. What do you know about that?"

She snorted. "If you don't know, I won't tell you. But I will say it is for the good of all."

Good of all? But who was included in that "all"? Was her definition as narrow as Mentàll's? Meaning only for the good of Mentàll and the M'ntoyans. She frowned.

GG cackled with glee. "You want to know more. Well, go find out. Surely you're a resourceful girl. Don't you know kaavl, like your cousin, Methusal?"

"Of course."

GG smiled, and sipped her tea. She said nothing more. Clearly, the visit was over. But at least she was speaking to Aali again. Unfortunately, she still hadn't learned why GG had flipped out last time. Next time she'd finagle more answers from the crafty old woman.

△ △ △ △ △

Methusal felt ready to keel over from exhaustion. It had been a long night. Mentàll's outburst yesterday afternoon had been the last time he'd spoken. He'd lain as still as death all night long, and still the fever raged out of control. Doc shook his head more than once. "I'm not sure how he's surviving this."

"It's a miracle," Hendra said softly.

Right now, Methusal was alone in the cabin with the Dehrien Chief while Doc and Hendra ate breakfast. She lay her head on his bunk. Exhaustion pulled at her spirit, and she could barely keep her eyes open. But she'd stay and continue to fight for him, as long as there was breath in both of their bodies.

The cold, damp cloths would keep him cool for another few minutes. Maybe it wouldn't hurt if she closed her eyes for just a moment...

△ △ △ △ △

Deccia stood in line with the other women outside the palace gates. Dew clung to the grass inside the metal fence, and cold bit through her jacket. Ahead of her, ten women awaited their opportunity to interview for the positions of washer woman or maid in the palace. Deccia would be happy to gain either position.

Ahead of her, a short, middle-aged woman with gray-streaked black hair, and her thick figure wrapped in a long, tan coat, stamped her feet against the cold. "Be the death of me," she muttered.

The line moved forward. At last. For Deccia, the last two days had crawled by. The palace only interviewed for women's jobs one day each week, and she'd been advised to get there early. All the same, ten women were in front of her. What if she never got a chance to interview for the job?

She tried not to think about that possibility, or the other frustrations she'd encountered over the last two days. She'd investigated the maze through which Behran and Doc had transported Mentàll the night of the ball. But the center of the maze was closed now, and guarded by three soldiers. She shouldn't have been surprised.

The good news was that yesterday Riln had managed to get a job as a groundskeeper at the palace. Of course, ever since then his ego had swollen all out of proportion. Especially since Goric had tried and failed to win the same position.

Deccia was getting to the point where she didn't want to go home anymore. Riln's constant small digs at Goric and herself were trying her patience.

The short woman was next. A soldier held up his arm, forcing Deccia to stop a length short of the interviewing table. Two women sat behind it. Crisp Zindedi black and red uniforms hugged their figures. The first one had chin length dark hair. Her tan skin was pock-marked and frown lines creased deep into her forehead. The other woman was thin, with curly white hair.

The woman ahead of Deccia waved her hands, clearly trying to convince the palace supervisors why she needed to win the position. The dark-haired one pointed to a bench where two other interviewees sat. With a quick nod, the woman hurried over and settled her handbag in her lap.

"Next," the first supervisor said in a hoarse voice.

Deccia smiled and hurried forward. "Good morning."

The dark-haired woman eyed her critically, her gaze moving from Deccia's hair to her spectacles. "Why do you want the job?"

She got the strangest feeling that the woman had already made up her mind about hiring her. At the same time, she sensed a dark, thick kind of curiosity in the Zindedi—the kind of curiosity often present in minds that worked slowly and were closed to new ideas.

"I need to support my family. I have lots of experience washing clothes and cleaning."

"Hmph. What do you think, Ilna?"

Ilna looked quickly at Deccia, and then away. In a low voice, she said, "Whatever you think is best."

Deccia refocused her smile upon the first woman. "I'd be happy…"

"No. Go." The dark-haired woman dismissed her and looked left. "Next."

Deccia's jaw dropped. "But why?"

The woman sent her an unfriendly look. "You won't fit in. I've seen your type before."

"But…" Her gaze slid to Ilna, who looked down, avoiding her gaze.

"Next!"

She moved away, unable to believe what had just happened. They had barely spoken to her. She was younger and stronger than the three women awaiting second interviews on the bench. Didn't they want strong, durable employees?

Apparently not.

Dazed, she found another bench and sat down. Now what would she do? She'd put all of her hope into getting that job, and now she had no backup plan to help her get closer to Timaeus.

△ △ △ △ △

"Should we wake her?"

Methusal fought the soft, comforting tendrils of sleep. A hard surface dug into her hip. It reminded her of the stone floor in Mrn. M's house.

Zindedi.

Mentàll! With a gasp, she sat up and realized she was lying on the deck floor in Mentàll's room. Doc and Hendra looked down at her.

Hendra smiled. "Good afternoon."

"Afternoon!" She stumbled to her feet. "You let me sleep all *afternoon*? Mentàll!" Filled with fear, she spun to look at him. "Is he..." His skin looked like bleached parchment, and he lay unnaturally still. "*No!*" Her knees buckled. Doc caught her and drew her against his strong, wiry frame. *"No.* Why didn't you wake me? *Why?"* Sobs seized her. A vast, bottomless pit of despair engulfed her. "No." She couldn't bear it. She couldn't *bear* it.

"Methusal." Hendra touched her arm. "Methusal!"

She couldn't listen. She couldn't think.

"Methusal," Doc said. "He's alive. The fever broke."

"What?"

"He's going to make it. He has a tremendous will to live. And he's the strongest fighter I've ever seen. Not that that surprises me."

"He's *alive?"* Methusal pulled free of Doc's supporting arms and stared at Mentàll. "But he looks so white. What's wrong with him?"

"Nothing. Finally, he's sleeping peacefully."

Methusal burst into tears again. Arms crossed tightly, she stood very still and wept. Now she saw the gentle rise and fall of his chest and the relaxed lines of his angular, gaunt face. He was alive. He would live. Without thinking, she touched his rumpled hair, but after that barest caress, she pulled back.

"Thank The One," she whispered. She drew deep breaths, trying to calm down. She shouldn't be so emotional. She shouldn't be falling apart. What would people think?

"I'm glad he's okay," she said at last, wiping her face. She stumbled backwards. "Does everyone know?"

"Yes," Doc said.

"Good."

"We were about to leave," Hendra said, with a speaking look at Doc. "Would you like to sit with him for a minute, before the others come in?"

She drew another shaky breath. "Yes. Maybe for a minute. Thank you."

The two withdrew, and Methusal carefully wiped away the last of her tears. She felt raw and clean inside. Reborn. Everything would be all right now.

She sat on the stool beside him and watched him sleep peacefully. He had made it.

"I'm glad you're alive," she whispered. "You'll probably start making my life complicated all over again, but I don't care. It's worth it. *You're* worth it." Unable to help herself, she pressed her lips to his cool temple. "You're a maddening man. But my life would never be the same without you in it."

He didn't stir. Gently, she slid her fingers down his stubbly cheek. His beard had grown long enough that it felt soft, rather than scratchy, against her skin. "Please don't scare me like that again."

Footsteps sounded in the hall, and she withdrew her hand. She turned to greet Behran and the others.

Behran touched her shoulder. "He made it."

Methusal smiled. "He made it."

△ △ △ △ △

Deccia wandered through the city all day, looking for soldiers she could shadow, and always hoping to hear a tidbit of information about Timaeus. It earned her a few suspicious glances and one indecent proposal.

When the sun sank toward the western mountains, she headed home. The day had been a complete waste of time, and she felt depressed.

Goric and Riln were both home. Fresh food lay on the counter. Riln sat on the couch drinking a bottle of spirits and crunching savory discs. Goric stood at the stove, folding an omelet over vegetables.

She pulled off her glasses and dropped them on the table. They pinched her nose, and she was glad to take them off.

No one said anything to her. It hurt.

Deccia turned on the faucet and water sprayed into her cup.

"Hungry?" Goric asked, sliding the omelet onto a plate.

Her stomach rumbled loudly, and a small smile lifted one corner of Goric's mouth. "I guess so. I haven't eaten all day."

"Why not?"

"Because we're out of money, remember? And I didn't think of it." She'd felt too sick at heart to eat. If she couldn't help Timaeus, did anything else matter?

He shoved the plate toward her.

Her mouth watered, despite everything she'd just told herself. "Isn't this yours?"

"I can make another."

"Thank you."

Riln rose from the couch. "Well. The lunatic and the loser. The whole happy family is home."

Deccia wasn't in the mood for his digs. "Step off." She placed her plate on the table and dug in.

"Step off? Is that any way to talk to the bread winner of this house? Oh, and the *only* source of information on Timaeus."

"I got a part-time job as a stock boy today," Goric said.

Riln snorted as he straddled a chair. "Stock *boy*. Just right for you, loser."

"Stop with the *names!*" Deccia's frustration exploded. "Shut your mouth. If you don't have something good to say, be quiet."

"Oh!" Riln grimaced, and made a show of clutching his chest. "I'm cut to the heart." The mockery morphed into a black glare. He rose, swigging back spirits. "Guess you don't want to hear the latest about your hubby."

Deccia eyed him with suspicion. "Did you learn something?"

"Yeah. But if you don't have time for me..."

"Cut it, Riln," Goric muttered.

Riln rolled his eyes. "You have a valiant champion, lunatic."

Deccia stabbed her fork into another bite of delicious eggs. Calmly, she said, "What did you learn, Riln?"

He settled back at the table. "Maybe you'd better finish your food first."

"Why?" Deccia put down her fork. "What happened?" Her voice rose. "Is Timaeus alive?"

"Yeah, he's alive. For now. Sources told me he's being tortured. Presidente's orders. General is carrying it out."

A high, keening sound escaped from Deccia's throat, but she swallowed hard, choking it off.

To the side, Goric made a sudden, restive movement. "Still? Or when he first got here?"

Riln shrugged. "All I know is he's missing a body part."

"*No!*" Deccia cried out in anguish, "*No!*"

Goric abruptly got up and left the room.

She couldn't seem to stop her wailing whimpers. They escalated into hysterical screeches, but she didn't know how to stop them. She didn't know how to think. "*No!*" she cried again and again. She screamed, "Say it's *not true*, Riln!"

Riln looked very uncomfortable. "Hey. Calm down. It's just the top of his finger."

"Just the top of his finger?" Deccia gasped. She leaped up and fled for her bedroom. A slam and she was alone. She collapsed onto the bed, overcome with hysterical grief. Timaeus was being tortured, and she could do nothing to stop it. *Nothing.*

Time passed and she didn't notice. Her mind was consumed with rage and grief. She imagined clawing Fitrn's eyes out. She imagined attacking the Presidente with a knife. But nothing helped.

Nothing blocked out the awful horror consuming her soul.

Late in the black night she fell asleep. Her nightmares returned. Only this time, they were so much worse.

She was in a dark prison cell. A scuffle came from the hall.

"Move it."

She ran to the small, barred window in the door and peered out. Two soldiers dragged Timaeus down the hall. His head was down and back bared. General Fitrn followed. His whip hissed repeatedly into Timaeus' flesh. Blood poured from the stripes in her husband's skin.

"Timaeus!" she cried out. "Timaeus!"

He looked up. His nose was broken and blood streamed down his face. Even so, love shone in his weary eyes. "Deccia," he mumbled.

"Timaeus, I love you! I love you!" The men dragged him further down the hall. The evil General sniggered. "Now the fun will begin."

"No," she screamed out. "No! Take me, instead. Take me!"

Her prison door swung open. Were they freeing her? When she tried to step through, the stocky, dead General Greisn blocked her exit. His amber eyes looked lit from the fires of hell.

"You will be mine forever," he hissed.

But she wasn't afraid of him anymore. "Take me, instead of him. Let him go."

He chuckled. "I will finish what I began."

"Let him go!"

He laughed. "I have more interesting things on my mind." He shoved her hard, backward into the cell.

Deccia realized that her hands were free. This was different. She could hit him. She could stop him.

Screams echoed down the hall. Timaeus' screams.

"No!" She attacked Greisn with fury. "I'll kill you. I'll kill you!" She struggled against his binding arms and screamed and bit him and clawed. The constricting arms fell away. She was winning! "I'll kill you," she panted. "I will kill you!" Her fist hit his jaw with a satisfying thud. Pain bit into her knuckles. Good.

"I hate you!" she screamed, and hit him again.

A choked sound erupted. Maybe she'd hit his throat. Or his nose? "I hate you," she snarled. "I'll kill you for what you're doing to Timaeus."

"Do it." An unidentifiable sound of pain hissed. "Do it," he whispered. "I deserve it."

He was taunting her!

She attacked him with blind fury, hitting and punching him as hard as she could.

"Deccia." Was that Timaeus? She hesitated. "Deccia." Suddenly, she was punching empty air.

"Deccia. Wake up."

She blinked. Light poured in from the living room illuminating Goric, who stood beside her bed. Blood streamed from his nose and dripped from his split lip.

What was happening? She breathed in short gasps, trying to understand. And then the dream flooded back. And Greisn, whom she had punched.

She looked at her blood smeared knuckles, and then at Goric's face. "I hit you," she said stupidly. "I hit you. I'm so *sorry*."

"It doesn't matter." He shoved his hands in his pockets. A wince flickered.

Deccia felt aghast. "Why are you... Why did you let me hit you?"

"You were having a nightmare. I wanted to wake you up."

She felt horrified by her behavior. Was this what she had become? A violent beast, hitting people? Hurting them? Tears filled her eyes. "I'm so sorry!"

"I'll live." Abruptly, he said, "Goodnight." The door closed with a quiet click.

Deccia fell back on her bed, feeling utterly horrified and sick to her stomach. She pressed her hands to her eyes. "Oh The One, what is happening to me?" Her heart ached for Timaeus, but the rage that still consumed her—the craving for vengeance—was it wrong?

The Prophet's words slipped into her mind. "'Vengeance is mine. I will repay,' says the Lord."

She burst into tears. "The One, *please* help Timaeus."

Out in the living room, she heard Riln mutter, "What'd you do? Make an advance on her?" He barked out a laugh. "At least wait 'til her husband's cold in his gr..."

"Cut it!" Water blasted in the sink.

Silence. Another rumble came from Riln. His tone sounded derisive. Goric said something curt.

Riln laughed, and then all was silent.

Deccia curled up in a ball and pressed her wet face into her pillow. She'd really hurt Goric. Clearly, in order to wake her up, he'd stayed close long enough for her to inflict physical damage upon him. Why had he endured it? For how long had she hit him? Deccia tried to separate the dream from reality, but couldn't.

The simple fact was, he'd suffered because he had wanted to wake her from the nightmare. It was a long time before she fell asleep again.

Chapter Six

Day 6

METHUSAL SLEPT WELL, and awoke with a feeling of peace. Mentàll was alive. Finally, life could return to normal.

Last night, she'd been so emotionally exhausted that she'd gone to bed early. Now that her mind was clearer, she lay still and allowed the memories of the last few weeks to replay through her mind. It was time to make sense of everything that had happened with Mentàll.

At last, she admitted to herself how close she'd grown to him in Carachki. She remembered their missions together, and how he had maddened her, and how his kisses stole her breath. She remembered lying in his arms the night before the ball, and his gentle, soul stirring kiss the next evening. And the look in his eyes when he'd held her hand.

If he hadn't thrown himself in front of the bullet, she would be dead right now. Watching him suffer and battle to live these last few days had been the most agonizing experience of her life

And she remembered falling apart when she'd thought he was dead. Her fingers touched her marriage necklace. Her fake marriage necklace. The one she should have taken off days ago, but had not.

She closed her eyes. It was time to face some hard truths. Deep feelings stirred in her for the Dehrien Chief. It was foolish to deny it.

His death would have destroyed her.

Her fingers involuntarily stroked the flowers and smooth chain of the necklace. She should take it off. She wasn't really married to him.

And Behran. She cared for him very much. There was no doubt about that.

But the Dehrien Chief evoked feelings in her that she'd never felt before for any man. Deep, complex feelings that she was afraid to name.

How could she love a man that she did not fully know? Who was he? The man she had come to know in Carachki? Or was he the power hungry man she'd known for the last three years?

He'd accomplished his goals in Zindedi. But what were his goals for Koblan now? And what had been his goals for her, all along?

Could she trust him? This was the question that mattered more than the state of her foolish heart.

Things had happened so fast, and so intensely in Carachki that it might be foolish to trust her feelings. As she'd told Behran, she did need to take time to step back and try to see things clearly. If at all possible, she needed to hold Mentàll at arm's length until she could sort out the truth, and the complex, confused mess of her heart. She had to find out who he was before she could ever make any decision about him or Behran.

Reluctantly, she unclasped the marriage necklace and placed it in her pocket. She would give it back to him later.

She joined Behran and the others in the main cabin for breakfast. After a delicious meal of Coyl's fluffy eggs, everyone left the table except for Behran, Methusal, and Sozla, who quietly ate a piece of fruit. The conversation turned to Mentàll's miraculous recovery. Soon afterward Sozla scooted down the bench, heading for the aisle. "Behran, perhaps you will play whaal with us on deck a little later this morning?"

Behran glanced at Methusal.

"You are welcome, too, Methusal." Sozla's dark eyes looked horrified, clearly afraid that she'd hurt Methusal's feelings.

"No, that's fine, Sozla. I need to see Mentàll for a minute this morning, and then I need to do a few other things. But Behran, you go ahead."

He looked from Sozla to Methusal. "Are you sure?"

"Of course."

Sozla's smile brightened. "Good. I will see you on deck soon, Behran." She disappeared outside.

Methusal smiled at Behran. "Now. Tell me everything that happened in Dakarra."

△ △ △ △ △

Mentàll was awake for the first time in days. Hendra smiled at her cousin as she entered his cabin. To her immense relief, he smiled back. After all of the worry, it seemed too good to be true that he would actually recover. He was fully dressed now, but lay quietly on his bunk.

She gently touched his shoulder. "You have no idea how relieved I am that you're all right."

"Give you a scare?" His voice was raspy.

"And not just me. Would you like some water?"

"No." He closed his eyes, clearly tired. "Doc made me drink a whole glass."

"Good. Methusal will be happy to hear it."

"Methusal?" His eyes opened again, and the ice blue looked sharp and clear. "She...was here?"

"She's been here every minute, day and night. Even when she was so sick she could barely stand. She refused to leave you."

"Really." A faint smile curved his mouth, and he fell silent, contemplating that thought with obvious pleasure.

"You're a lucky man. By rights, you should be dead. Doc is amazed you pulled through."

"I have much to live for."

"But now you'll rest. Doc says you can't get out of bed for two days."

He smiled faintly. "I'm too weak to argue."

"Good. Would you like something to eat? Toast?"

"Coyl's pudding sounds...good."

Hendra smiled. "I'll talk to him. I'm sure he'd be happy to whip up a batch for you."

Before she could go far, he grated, "Hendra."

She turned back.

"Thank you. For everything you did for me. Doc told me."

"Of course. I would do anything for you." She loved him, just she knew he cared for her, although he'd never said so.

But he'd proven it by his actions, over and over again, through the years.

"Thank you." His eyes closed.

She turned to leave.

"Hendra. Send in Methusal. I want to speak to her."

"I'll tell her." With a smile and a light step, she left her cousin. He would be all right. *Thank you, The One.*

△ △ △ △ △

The Presidente felt better today than he had in ages. Satisfaction filled him with a feeling of peace and great pleasure as he thought over his recent achievements.

The Commanders who had failed him were suffering humiliation at the hands of their former subordinates every single day. His prisoner was suffering greatly, as well. In addition, tomorrow he would set sail for Koban.

At first, the idea of sailing to that backward continent had felt like a slap to his dignity. But now he saw it as it was; the perfect opportunity to exact his revenge.

Soon his detested enemies would choke on their supposed victory over him. This very morning he had ordered his most clever scientists to cook up the perfect retribution for Methusal Maahr. Not only would he kill that detestable trollop, but he would also twist the entire peace negotiations into knots. He hoped Mentàll Solboshn was still alive, too, because he burned to see that arrogant man brought to his knees.

Then he would top it all off with a death blow to Koblan's heart, which would secure him the most important victory of all.

For such sweet morsels of revenge, he was looking forward to his voyage.

△ △ △ △ △

Nerves beat like feathered wings in Methusal's stomach when she entered Mentàll's cabin. "Hendra said you wanted to speak to me?"

Ice blue eyes cut to hers and held them. "Methusal." His voice sounded hoarse and raspy.

With a slight smile, she came closer, even though her heart fluttered like a caged flying beast. It was good to see him awake, and his smile slid joy, like sunshine, into her soul. "I'm glad to see you're awake."

"And in full possession of my faculties? Doc told me about my delirious rants."

"Yes." She stopped a small distance from his bunk.

"Thank you for everything you did for me."

"You're welcome." With a soft smile, she scanned his features, taking comfort from the warmer tone of his skin this morning. "You're feeling all right?"

His teeth flashed in a small smile. "Thanks to you. Hendra said you refused to leave me."

Feeling a bit flustered, she looked down. "I was worried about you. After all, you took the bullet meant for me. Thank you."

"I would do nothing else."

She looked back and saw only blue intensity. She glanced away again. "Is there anything I can do for you? More water…"

His hand caught her ridiculously fluttering one. "Sit down and talk to me."

Matters were not going according to plan. Hadn't she just decided to put distance between them so she could view their relationship more objectively? As usual, he was flipping her world upside down in the space of a moment.

She perched on the edge of the stool, but her gaze skittered from his to the porthole.

She felt very aware of his strong, warm hand holding hers. Her plan to create distance between them was definitely derailing rather quickly. She needed to get back on track.

"Why won't you look at me?" Her gaze swung back, and his narrowed with unnerving perception. "Tell me the truth, Methusal."

He wanted the truth? "You're well now." She tugged her hand free. "So it's over." The words were surprisingly hard to say. Perhaps because they weren't fully true.

"It will never be over between us."

Agitated, she stood up and moved away.

"I do not remember much, but I do remember two things."

Her gaze returned to his face. "What?"

"I remember your tears on my cheeks. And I remember you begging me not to die." He watched her quietly. Waiting for her to deny it? She did not.

"I was worried about you."

"Why? I have been a thorn under your skin for three years. If I died, you could marry Behran with no second thoughts."

Angry tears sprang to her eyes. "How could I want you to die?"

"You do not hate me, still?"

"No! Of course I don't hate you."

"Tell me, then. Why wouldn't you leave my side? Why did you become hysterical when you thought I was dead?"

Why did he have to push and push, and *push*? "Because it was too horrible. I couldn't bear it."

"You want me in your life." That certain statement was soft.

Yes. Yes, she did, and the truth scared her. "As a friend," she said, clinging to her original plan. "I think we became friends while we were in Zindedi. I hope that can continue."

He closed his eyes, and then she realized how exhausted he must still feel. He always projected such a forceful, confident persona that he'd fooled her into thinking he was himself again. He was not.

"We will...finish this conversation another time, Methusal. It is not over."

It *was* over—at least, their intense, close relationship in Carachki had ended. But sorting through what was real between them and what was not was a task for another day. Until then, it had become abundantly clear that she must try harder to put emotional space between them. "You need to rest. I can come back later."

"No." His eyes opened again. "Tell me what happened...with the Presidente. You delivered the papers?"

"Yes." Relieved by the neutral change of topic, Methusal settled back on the stool and told him everything. She skimmed by the Presidente's attempted rape, but evidently not fast enough, because his hands fisted white, and color seared high in his cheekbones. "I will kill the scienth," he mumbled.

"The explosion distracted him. I escaped before he could do anything. I think he'll come to Koblan."

"Good." The red in his cheekbones faded, and he closed his eyes again.

"You're tired," she said gently. "I'll leave you to rest. Do you need anything? More water?"

Voice barely audible, he said, "Why are you so nice to me when I am weak, and prickly when I'm strong?"

"Because when you're sick, you only have the energy to be yourself. You don't have the strength to cause trouble."

"You still do not trust me."

"I know you're a complex man. You're not entirely who you appear to be."

He was quiet for a moment. "Will you never forgive me for the past?"

"I have forgiven you. I've told you that. But the past is a warning to me, too. I know how clever you are. How your obvious plans can have deeper, more complex motivations. I don't know what your true objective is for Koblan. Or for me. That makes it hard for me to completely trust you."

"You're afraid. But of what?"

"I'm afraid if I trust you, you'll end up destroying me and everyone I love."

He smiled faintly. "I am not that powerful."

"I know you have a big plan for Koblan. But you won't tell me what it is. Right?"

He didn't deny it.

"See? That makes me feel suspicious. I don't know if it will benefit only you, or the rest of us, too."

"Is that why you stay so close to me?"

Her eyes narrowed. "I'll will be here when you show your true hand."

"What do you want it to be?"

She did not reply.

He said, "You are protecting yourself. Everyone else has given me a second chance. Everyone except for you."

And yet her heart *had* given him a fresh chance. She couldn't tell him that yet. Her possible gullibility frightened her. "I know you better than they do."

He grasped her wrist, and the strength in his hand belied the exhaustion on his face. "Tell the truth, Methusal. What do you think about me?"

She blinked in quiet agitation. "I know you can convince anyone to believe anything. Mrn. M believed everything you said to me. She's a trusting lady. She just didn't know..."

His fingers relaxed their hold, and his thumb caressed her palm. "Know what?"

"She didn't know..." She swallowed and said in a low voice, "That you may not really know how to love anyone. Even yourself."

He stared at her for a long time. "You may be right."

"I need to go."

"Come back tomorrow."

She lifted a brow, but offered a small smile, too. "Still giving orders? I'll look in on you. Maybe." She felt his gaze follow her into the passageway.

Nothing had been settled. Worse, she felt more confused than ever. And she still hadn't returned his marriage necklace.

Chapter Seven

Methusal spent most of the seventh day at sea out on deck with Behran and the others playing whaal, or staring at the sun dazzled, rolling blue ocean. Although it felt nice to relax in the sun, part of her lived below deck, with Mentàll. She wondered how he was doing. She'd been avoiding him, and she felt a little guilty about that.

In the afternoon, Hendra arrived with a bowl of grain discs for everyone to share. "Methusal, Mentàll is asking for you."

"Shall we deal you out this hand?" Sozla asked.

"Yes. I'll be back soon."

She stopped by her cabin to retrieve something before arriving at Mentàll's door. Although it was cracked open, she knocked.

"Come in." His voice was a gravel rasp.

The Dehrien Chief sat propped up with pillows into a half sitting position today.

"You're looking better." The lines of exhaustion had eased from his features, although his angular face still looked gaunt.

"Tomorrow I will get out of this bed."

It must be terribly hard for him to be cooped up in this tiny sick room. "I heard that you'd like to see me. And I came to return this." She let his marriage necklace stream from her palm into his. An unexpected sense of loss pinched her when the last link slipped through her fingers.

His fingers curled around the necklace. "Does Behran believe your pledges of love yet?"

She turned for the door.

"You are running because you fear your feelings for me."

With a frown, she turned back. "How quickly you recover. Yesterday you were too weak to attack me."

He held out a hand. "If you do not fear me, then come here."

"No."

Softly, he said, "You are afraid."

More to prove him wrong than anything else, she closed the distance between them. "I'm here. See? But I told you, it's over, Mentàll. Whatever did or didn't happen in Zindedi doesn't matter."

"Behran is safe. That is why you want to choose him." An edge bit through his words. His warm, strong hand wrapped around hers, locking her into place beside him. She made no move to extricate herself, because that would only fuel his belief that she wanted to run away from her feelings for him. And he'd be right.

He said, "I did not ask you here to talk about Behran. Tell me what happened when you hid the bombs on base. Did anything unusual happen?"

Methusal thought back, and realized that she'd never told him about Sergeant Kirkwn, and how he'd indirectly helped her plant the bombs.

As she related the story, he nodded slowly, and Methusal realized that the longer he held her hand, the more relaxed she felt. Her anxiety dissolved as they quietly talked about eastern Zindedi.

She said, "Do you think they could be an ally, if we need one?"

"Possibly. I am forming a backup plan in case the peace agreement doesn't work."

An idea struck her. "We destroyed one powder mine and most of the Presidente's ships. Do you think eastern Zindedi might make a power grab? What if they decide to go to war against the Presidente again?"

"I have thought about that, too." His thumb absently caressed the back of her hand. "This Kirkwn. Do you think we can trust him?"

It felt like they were back in Zindedi again, in Mrn. M's house. This closeness and quiet conversation seemed entirely natural. The last of her tension eased away. "If we can offer what he wants, I'm pretty certain he'd ally with us."

"Good. I hope it will not come to that."

"I feel the same. I'm not sure how far I would trust him, to be honest. The peace agreement has to work. We've worked so hard for it."

"Nothing is ever certain. Even the best laid plans go awry."

"Not yours," she said with a faint smile.

"I did not plan to be shot. I cannot control everything." His pale gaze met hers. Unexpected vulnerability flashed in it.

Her heart thumped. "Don't look at me like that."

"Like what?"

"Like you're human. Like your heart isn't made of ice."

"I am human, Methusal. I almost died. It reminded me that nothing lasts forever. While we have life, we must grab what we want with both hands." His other hand closed around her free one. "I did not want to die, because I had not told you what I feel for you."

She shook her head. "You don't..."

"You do not think I can love. But I do care about you, Methusal, as much as I am able. Forget Behran," he said roughly. "Take a chance with me."

"Mentàll." He'd actually cracked open the door of his heart. She knew how hard that speech had been for him, and his admission triggered a break in the careful protection she'd built around her own heart.

Soft emotion swiftly filled her up. "Mentàll," she whispered again. An agony of conflict gripped her. She wanted to protect herself, but at the same time, she wanted...

With a gentle tug, he pulled her down and kissed her. Emotion swamped her, stealing her breath and her thoughts away. Tenderness. All the feelings for him that had blossomed in Zindedi, combined with the hopeless despair she'd felt when he'd been so sick, all overwhelmed her. She couldn't fight them. She didn't want to. Helplessly, she returned his kiss, wanting more and more, and ever more. And he gave it. Tenderness, desire, and need licked deep into her heart. It felt as if his kiss might steal her soul...

Gasping a little, she jerked back.

He held onto her wrist. "Do not run from me. From us."

"I...I have to go."

"Your kisses to Behran will be a lie," he told her in a low, harsh voice.

With a gasp, she pulled free and fled.

△ △ △ △ △

Methusal sat curled up on her bunk, knees tucked tightly under her chin. What was she going to do? Much as she wanted to be smart and careful, her feelings for Mentàll defied logic.

She was sick of the conflict tearing apart her soul. She did care about Behran. But if she was to remain engaged to him, he deserved her whole heart. She wanted to give it to him, but Mentàll kept cutting in and upsetting everything. He would not be ignored. More importantly, she could not ignore her own feelings for him.

"Oh, The One, what should I do?"

She couldn't be falling in love with Mentàll! Didn't she have a choice in the matter? Behran was her logical choice. She knew him, and she trusted him.

Her explosive feelings for Mentàll were rash and completely illogical.

Methusal faced the deepest truth. She was afraid of what falling in love with the Dehrien Chief would mean for the rest of her life. She cared about Behran. She would be happy with him. What more—sanely—could she want? Because giving her heart to Mentàll would be insane. Wouldn't it?

The Dehrien Chief was a complex, difficult man, and yet when she was with him... Methusal closed her eyes tightly. How could she know what was real?

Behran was a wonderful man, and she felt guilty, not to mention sad and scared, to think about breaking their engagement. But if her heart belonged to Mentàll, then she needed to figure that out, and soon. Behran deserved to know the truth.

Chapter Eight

THE NEXT AFTERNOON A FLURRY of activity in the cockpit drew Methusal's attention.

"Sit down here. Do you want something? Maybe a pillow?"

"No. Thank you." Mentàll's voice sounded strained and harsh.

Footsteps *thunked* back down the ladder, into the belly of the ship.

Unable to help herself, she headed toward the cockpit, where the Dehrien Chief sat with his eyes closed, his face white, and breathing labored.

"Are you all right?"

His eyes flew open. He drew a deep breath, perhaps to try to calm his rapid breathing. "I am fine."

"You don't sound fine." Concerned, she sat beside him. "Don't have a heart attack. Then all our hard work would be for nothing."

A faint smile glimmered on his lips.

She felt relieved when his color slowly returned to normal.

"Is this how I must capture your attention, Methusal? By remaining an invalid?"

"You know I can't resist an injured wild beast."

His sudden grin disarmed her.

For the first time in weeks, the Dehrien Chief wore his usual bleached leather clothing. The scent of sun warmed leather pleasantly mingled with the scent of his skin. It was a potent combination, and unfortunately heightened her awareness of him.

When she drew a quick, agitated breath, his blue eyes sharpened. He leaned close. "Thank you for watching over me." His breath gently touched her lips.

Before she caught herself, Methusal slightly arched toward him. "You're..."

Those light eyes gleamed at her.

Appalled, she jerked back.

He smiled. "A kiss would make me feel better."

"I am not going to *kiss* you." She glanced quickly toward the bow of the boat, but no one was watching them.

His wicked grin remained. "I will accept your kisses in private. Come to my cabin, and you can help me recover more fully."

Methusal blushed red hot. "I am not going to your *cabin!*" She jumped up, but he caught her hand. A rusty chuckle escaped.

"I am sorry, Methusal. Earning such a heartfelt response is a difficult temptation to resist."

Warily, she sat back down. "You're teasing me."

"I would not proposition you on this ship. Especially when I do not have the energy to climb down the stairs."

She refrained from rolling her eyes.

He said, "I am glad you came to speak to me. Tell me why Deccia left the ship."

Relaxing again, she related the entire tale, and ended with telling him that Riln and Goric had accompanied Deccia to Carachki. Mentàll nodded, not appearing to be surprised. Perhaps Doc or Hendra had already told him, but he'd also wanted her perspective on the situation.

His expression looked remote now, and his eyes hard. It must be difficult for him to hear again that his right hand man had been a Zindedi traitor all along.

He said, "Doc said Sozla found the note Tabor wrote. Do you know where it is? I want to look at it."

"It's probably in his pack. I'll go get it." It took only minutes to find it and bring the folded paper back to Mentàll.

He studied the parchment for a long moment, and then crushed it in his fist. "Tabor is not the spy."

"But he wrote..."

"That is not Tabor's handwriting. Deccia has gone to Carachki with the real traitor."

She gasped. "What? That can't be true!" It *couldn't* be. The implications were too terrible to consider. "If Tabor didn't write that note, then how did it get in his pack?"

"The true spy planted it there in order to turn suspicion away from himself. He probably put it in Tabor's pack after he died."

"You think Riln or Goric is the spy?" Methusal felt even more horrified. "That means Deccia is in terrible danger!"

"Yes." Mentàll closed his eyes, face pale again. "Her only hope is if the traitor chooses to remain undiscovered."

"But why would he? Why would he allow Deccia to rescue Timaeus?" Her voice rose. "He's probably turned her over to the military. To the Presidente! They could all be in prison right *now*."

"Yes."

"We need to go back. We have to save them!"

"No." His voice was little more than a thin whisper, and his face looked like translucent chalk.

"Mentàll!" His torso tilted sideways, and she caught him before he could hit his head on a metal sail crank. "Doc!" she shouted.

The Tarst doctor swiftly arrived and helped her lay the Dehrien Chief down on the deck. He whipped out his heart meter and listened to his chest. "A little fast. He'll be fine."

Even as he spoke, Mentàll opened his eyes. For a second, his expression was completely blank, but then he frowned. "Help me up."

Doc helped him sit up. "Take it easy, Chief. I'll get more blood builder. That should help."

Worried, Methusal watched as color slowly returned to Mentàll's cheeks. "You need to lie down and rest," she fussed. "Why are you out here, and demanding to see Tabor's note? You're in no shape to do anything."

"I am fine. I do not like to feel useless."

"Give yourself a break. For goodness' sake!"

He did not reply, but instead continued their previous conversation as if there had been no interruption. "After the Presidente signs the peace agreement, and we are certain he will abide by his word, we will send a ship back for Deccia and Timaeus."

"It may be too late."

"Do not underestimate your sister, Methusal. If she is anything like you, she will find a way to obtain her goal."

"But with a traitor..." She tried to imagine either Riln or Goric as the Zindedi spy, but failed. Riln hated the Zindedis—or so it seemed. Goric was sulky, and appeared to lack a spine. Either would make a poor spy. "Who do you think it is?"

"I do not know." Mentàll closed his eyes again. The warm rays of the late afternoon sun touched his face, and the lines of tension relaxed.

Methusal touched his arm. "Rest."

Without opening his eyes, he said, "You will come back and see me later?"

"I'll see you later," she agreed.

He smiled. "Soon I will feel better, Methusal. Soon the game will end with you in my arms."

She snorted, and left him with his over-sized ego. At least he wouldn't lack for company.

△ △ △ △ △

Deccia had wandered about for several days in a fog, consumed with grief and worry about Timaeus.

This morning it had taken all of her willpower to drag herself from bed. Now, sitting hunched over on the bed, head in her hands, she contemplated her day. Should she wander around Carachki again? Or curl back up on the cot and never get up again?

Contemplating that thought scared her enough to lurch for the door. She couldn't give up on Timaeus. She would not give up.

In the living room, Goric said to Riln, "See if he's still being tortured. It's killing her."

"I'll do what I can, rocher." Both men's eyes turned to Deccia.

She shuffled to the counter and set water on to boil. A loaf of sliced bread caught her eye. She should eat.

With hearty bluster, Riln said, "Watcha doin' today, sad girl?"

Deccia bit into a plain hunk of bread, unable to find the motivation to spread jam on it. "Wander. Scout. I don't know."

Riln raised his eyebrows, but said nothing.

Deccia didn't care what he thought. She turned to the whistling pot and poured hot water into a mug for tea.

"The ban lifts tomorrow," Riln told no one in particular. "I can't wait. I can't take another night in this funeral house."

"It lifts tomorrow?" A spark of interest lifted her spirits.

"Yeah. The Presidente left yesterday, and Fitrn leaves tomorrow."

Hope finally budded in her heart. She grabbed the jam pot and slathered a spoonful on her bread. The sweet tartness shocked her system. But it tasted delicious. It also made her feel alive again.

"Good," she said. "Tomorrow I'll get a job at the Merry Spirits."

Riln's expression turned openly skeptical. However, he said nothing.

Goric looked up from the table. His split lip had almost healed. She was grateful that the damage she'd done to him had begun to fade. "A spirit house is not the place for you," he told her.

Irritation surged, and that emotion felt good, too, after the apathy that had sucked the spirit from her over the last few days. "I'll do anything to help Timaeus. I don't care how awful it is. If I can get information, or find a way inside the palace, I'll do it."

Goric looked back at his plate and said nothing more.

"I'm outta here." Riln lumbered to his feet. "Rocher boy, it's your turn to bring home food. Put dascals in the community pot, too."

"Forget it," Goric muttered. "Spend your own money on spirits."

"What do *you* spend your money on, loser?" Riln retorted. "You never have two dascals to rub together."

"It's none of your business." His face looked cold.

Deccia interrupted the familiar argument. "Tomorrow I'll have a job. We'll have plenty of money then."

With a snort, Riln headed for the door. "The apte will let a *girl* carry him." The door slammed.

"Don't let him bother you," she advised.

In one swift, violent movement, Goric stood. "I don't let wild beasts manipulate me. Later."

Deccia's thoughts returned to the Merry Spirits. Tomorrow she'd go early. Surely Tineia would give her the job. Hope bloomed, and she plotted out every detail of her job pitch. She had to get this job.

Chapter Nine

DAY 9

AALI CONTINUED TO WONDER what GG's secret might be. Although it was clear GG wouldn't tell her about Calbn's treaty, the older woman's mysterious secret was another matter.

She decided to pay the old lady a surprise visit. Hopefully she wouldn't need to dodge crockery this time.

"Come in," the querulous voice said. Aali fumbled with adjusting her crutch and reached for the door handle. "Come *in*, I said."

She maneuvered both crutches and herself through the door. "It takes me a minute," she informed the old lady.

Was that a smile? It quickly disappeared. "What do you want?"

"You have bad manners. My father would switch me if I talked like you."

"Well, look forward to old age. You can say whatever you like."

Aali saw no need to beat around the bush. "Why did you have a fit when I mentioned Sims' name?" She cast a wary eye at the tea cup at GG's elbow.

GG's mouth opened and shut. Aali could almost see the wheels turning as the old woman decided which reaction to portray. She stayed in the doorway, ready to make a quick escape.

GG narrowed her eyes and pressed her lips into a thin line. "You are an impertinent, sassy girl."

She smiled. "People say that."

"Dastn, I'm sure. You probably drive him crazy." The old lady sipped tea.

Aali refused to take the bait. "Why did you have a fit?"

"Can't you guess?" She waved a hand. "Must I spell it out for you?"

"Please do."

She raised her eyebrows. "We had an affair, long ago. I thought he was dead. It shocked me to learn he's alive. That's all."

Aali doubted that was all. "Is he the wanderer you talked about? The father of your first son?"

GG's hand trembled as she poured more tea. "You're a smart girl to stay near the door. I can't throw anything that far."

"*Is* he?" A theory was beginning to form in her head, but she didn't want to articulate it. Not yet.

GG set down the pot and stared into her tea. "My father never approved of Sims. His family worked on the docks. They were poor. But he had a verve I liked." She slurped tea. "I liked it very much.

"When my father found out I was pregnant, he chased Sims out of town. I was young, weak, and foolish. I didn't fight for him. I married the man my father chose for me. And that is that." She calmly sipped more tea.

"You obeyed your father? I find that hard to believe."

"You think you wouldn't do the same. But this was long ago. I was pregnant, and my family shamed. I took the easy way, which turned out to be the hard way. I learned from it. Don't take the long way, like I did, young lady. Go for what you want."

Aali thought about Dastn. She wanted him. More than as a friend, but he thought she was too young for him. And her father would likely think the same. Her father was just as unbending as GG's.

"I will."

GG nodded. "I believe you."

"Do you want to see Sims again?" Aali dared to ask.

GG dropped the tea cup with a clatter onto the table. "You are a *most* impertinent girl."

"Would you see him, if you could?"

"No. Well, maybe. But it's too far. Rolban, didn't you say?" GG's pseudo-forgetfulness didn't fool her.

"Methusal will get married soon. I could invite you to the ceremony."

"Who is she marrying? That Mentàll? Is that his name?" Interest sparked in the old eyes.

"*No*." Aali felt shocked by the very idea. "She's marrying Behran Amil. They've been dating for three years."

"Mmmhuh!" She snorted. "Too long, if you ask me. Why haven't they married yet?"

"I don't know."

"She doesn't know her own mind, that's why."

Aali returned to GG's earlier statement. "Why in the world would you think she'd marry Mentàll Solboshn? She hates him!"

"Oh, an old lady hears things. Can't say more."

Then the truth dawned on her. "Well, they *are* pretending to be married on their trip to Zindedi. But it's only a cover. It's not real."

"The ship will dock here in Quasr when they return." GG changed the subject.

"It will? I thought they'd sail back to Aestoff."

GG shook her head. "When it arrives, bring Methusal to me. I want to meet her."

"Okay." She wondered what the cagey old lady was plotting now. Sometimes she wondered if GG was in her right mind. And other times she seemed completely sane and sharp.

"Leave. I'm done with you. Tell Lylitha I need more tea."

As if GG had summoned her here in the first place! Aali rolled her eyes, but obeyed. The ideas circling in her mind started to fall into place. She took a quick breath.

Could it be true? If so, then everything GG had just said would make perfect sense. ...Even if some of it might be wishful thinking on the old woman's part.

∆ ∆ ∆ ∆ ∆

"What are you thinking?" Doc eased down beside Hendra on the cabin top.

She shivered in the stiff breeze, but he made no attempt to put his arm around her. In fact, ever since their kiss below deck a few days ago, he'd made no attempt to touch her at all. Hendra shivered again. Zindedi's cold winds still followed them, but the sun-warmed deck, soaking into her breeches, felt good.

"I'm worried."

"About what?"

"Deccia and Timaeus. And I'm worried about Mentàll."

"Why? He'll make a full recovery."

"I know. And I'm glad. I'm just worried about Quasr. Do you think the Presidente will come?"

He remained silent for a moment. "I only saw the Presidente for a few minutes. But it was obvious he's not a man who likes to take orders from anyone."

Hendra believed that. "And I'm sure he's furious at Mentàll for blowing up his ships and powder. If he does come to Quasr, I'm afraid... I'm afraid he'll pretend peace, but order Mentàll's assassination."

"Have you told Mentàll your concerns?"

"Not yet. I'll wait until he feels better."

Doc chuckled softly. "Your cousin doesn't need to be baby coddled."

"He's not invincible," she said with a catch in her voice. She'd always halfway believed he was. When she'd been a teenager, Mentàll had always seemed bigger than any circumstance—like he could demolish any force that came against him. But the bullet had almost taken his life. And he was vulnerable in other ways, too. She saw the way he looked at Methusal. The Rolbani girl had the power to hurt him—not that she would. Not on purpose, anyway.

Ever since being shot, Hendra had sensed cracks in the armor around her cousin's heart. She wanted to protect him, but she wanted the best for him, too. She wanted him to be happy.

"He's a grown man," Doc said. "He can handle his own affairs."

She sighed. "I know. Maybe when he's stronger I'll feel less... protective."

"You love him. That's natural."

"I hope the Presidente doesn't come."

"How will we have peace if he doesn't?"

"I don't think we can trust peace with him, anyway. If he comes, he'll find a way to retaliate against Mentàll."

"You could be right. But I think he probably will come."

"Yes." Of course he would. The Presidente would want revenge. "I'll warn Mentàll later, in case he hasn't thought of it already." The wind sliced through her tunic, and she shivered.

Doc frowned. "Where's your jacket?"

"Down below, in the nice warm cabin." She smiled. "At least the sun is out. We're lucky we haven't had any storms."

"Maybe those are waiting until we get home."

"Aren't you full of sunshine."

Doc smiled, and curled his warm hand around hers. Happiness thrummed through her. During the last few days, she'd begun to wonder if he had decided to take a step back from their relationship. The idea worried her. Was he still interested in her, or was he having second thoughts? And if he was having second thoughts, wouldn't that be for the best?

"Doc," she said quietly.

"Hmm?"

"Well... Never mind."

She wouldn't upset the fragile balance between them again. After all, this new, slower pace was perfect, wasn't it? It didn't scare her, but it didn't challenge her, either.

Maybe he wanted to build a firm foundation before they moved forward again. Maybe. Cautious hope filled her. If that was true, it meant that he valued her. He wanted to take the time to get to know her better as a person. It made her trust him even more.

His hand around hers felt nice. Small shimmers of happiness streamed into her at the point of their contact. She closed her eyes as the warm sun toasted her skin, melting her fears away...at least for a little while.

△ △ △ △ △

Deccia smiled hopefully at Tineia. She had just explained how much she wanted the job, and how hard she was prepared to work. "So, may I have the waitress job?"

"I'm sorry." Deccia sensed no regret in Tineia's voice, however. "I just hired someone."

"Oh." Disappointment crushed into her like a mountain. This had been her last hope. Yet again, she was denied a job where she most needed one. It was so unfair. Almost as if fate was plotting against her.

"I'm sorry." Tineia's warm voice sounded kind. "Hanuh... Does your husband know you're here?"

Surprised by the question, Deccia touched her marriage necklace. "Not exactly."

"Do you think he'd like it?" she said gently. "Most men don't like their wives to be molested."

Deccia gasped and flushed. She'd had no idea.

Softly, Tineia said, "Your husband loves you very much. Go put his mind at ease."

How could Tineia know how much Timaeus loved her? And Deccia couldn't put his mind at ease. *He was in prison.* With tears in her eyes, she thanked Tineia and left.

Depression weighed upon her spirit again. Out of habit, she trudged to the palace and circled it. It was quiet now that the Presidente and General were gone. That should have brought her peace, but Timaeus was still inside. What were they doing to him?

She sat down on a cold, shadowed park bench. Despair choked her, and she prayed to The One for help. She didn't know what else to do. How could she help Timaeus now?

Sunshine warmed her feet, and then slid down the bench, thawing her legs, and then her face. It was a beautiful day, with bright blue skies, and the crisp air smelled fresh and clean. Shop windows across the street from the palace reflected the bright red banners festooning the palace gates. A woman came out of one of the shops and turned the "closed" sign to "open." Bright, jewel colored dresses filled the display window. And in the bottom corner a sign said, "Help wanted."

Help wanted? Fresh hope surged through her. If she could get a job in that dress shop, then she could watch the palace gate all day long. She could see who came and went. She could see if a prisoner was transported out.

Where did they take prisoners? To the military base for execution? Or maybe to a cemetery.

She tried to close her mind to those dark thoughts. If she couldn't get a job *in* the palace, then maybe right outside the gates was the best she could do.

Deccia entered the dress shop's cool interior. A woman with spectacles hanging from a silver cord around her neck stood behind the counter, totaling receipts. She wore her graying hair in a short, attractive style, and her pale blue dress and long white sweater looked fashionable.

Deccia self-consciously tugged down the bottom edge of her plain white blouse. Her black slacks didn't look too fancy, either, but the mirror this morning had assured her that she looked presentable.

"Good morning," the woman said pleasantly.

"Good morning. I see you're looking to hire someone." With a smile, Deccia approached the counter.

The woman's sharp gaze assessed her. "Do you have experience?"

"My mother is a seamstress. She designs her own clothes, and I've learned a little from her. I'm a hard worker, and I learn fast."

The woman eyed her until Deccia began to feel uncomfortable. Finally, she said, "Do I know you? You look familiar."

"My sister was in town recently. Maybe you met her."

The woman nodded, but still looked uncertain. She hadn't made the connection. Deccia hoped she never would. "I'll give you a try," she said at last. "When can you start?"

"Today."

The woman smiled, and extended her hand. "I'm Euphira."

"Hanuh."

"Nice to meet you, Hanuh. How about I show you around the shop?"

The day passed quickly. Euphira gave Deccia a few dascals at the end of the day and gently suggested that she take full advantage of the fifty percent discount in the store. "Start with two blouses," she advised. "We'll work from there."

Deccia felt surprisingly good as she headed home. She'd accomplished something today, and she'd been able to watch the palace all day long. Maybe she'd learn something that would help rescue Timaeus. Maybe.

At home, Goric leaned against the counter, reading the paper. It was dim inside and reminded her of the gloom that had enshrouded her spirits over the last few days. At least Riln wasn't there. He made the place seem even darker.

"Hi," she said. "I got a job."

"At the Merry Spirits?"

"No." That disappointment hit her again, full force. Truly, the Merry Spirits would have been the ideal job. She could have spoken to soldiers with direct access to the palace. Instead, now she had to watch the palace through a glass window. A catch of depression gripped her again. Would the new job be helpful, after all? It had felt good to do something constructive today, but would the job really help them rescue Timaeus?

Goric eyed her. "Good." He returned his attention to the paper.

Unwanted frustration simmered again. "Thank you for the interest," she mumbled. She tested the pot to see if it was hot. It was cold. Impatiently, she switched the flame on high.

Goric murmured, "Where did you get the job?"

"In a dress shop. It's across the street from the palace."

"Good." A tiny smile eased the tight, perpetually unhappy line of his mouth. "It suits you. You'll be safe."

She rolled her eyes. "Safe. Right. I probably won't learn a single thing."

"Women from the palace probably shop for clothes. Maybe they'll say something."

"Maybe. But unlikely." She changed the subject. "What did you do today?"

"Work."

Curiosity registered for the first time. Goric never said much about his job. "Where do you work?"

"Down near the docks."

An unexplainable suspicion suddenly dawned on her, and she frowned. When he said no more, she said, "Aren't you a fountain of information."

He barely glanced up. "What else do you want to know?"

"Have you ever been to the Merry Spirits?"

Slowly, he said, "I've passed by once or twice."

"Oh." Sick disbelief crept into her spirit as her empathic hunch inexplicably deepened. "And did you happen to pass by yesterday, or maybe early this morning?"

He put down the paper and directed his full attention to her. "What are you trying to ask me?"

"Tineia didn't give me the job. That isn't suspicious. But she said something else that was."

"What?" His expression looked wary.

"She said, 'Your husband loves you very much. Go put his mind at ease.' Why would she say that? It's funny, because it sounded like she'd actually *met* my husband. But we both know that is impossible."

Goric's eyes slid away. "So?"

Her suspicions solidified in one hard, angry heartbeat. She gasped, "*You* did it. You sabotaged the best job lead I had!"

Discomfort twisted his features. "Listen, Deccia..."

"No! *You* listen. How dare you?" Her voice rose an octave. She felt shocked, betrayed, and furious. "I could have learned all kinds of information from those men. Why would you *do* this to me? To Timaeus?"

"Sailors know nothing about the palace. Commanders do."

"Well then, I'd focus on the commanders!"

Goric flushed, and suddenly his murky gaze sharpened into glittering ore. "Do you want information? Do you want inside the palace?" He faced her now, and she was vaguely surprised that he matched her height. He always seemed so short and slight, and insubstantial.

"Of course I want those things!" she shouted back.

"Then you'd better be prepared to sleep with them," he told her. "That's the way it works down at the docks. If you want a backdoor entrance into the palace, you've got to sell your body to do it. That starts with tickling their fancy in a brothel. Is that what you want? Will you prostitute yourself for information?"

Deccia slapped the table in fury. "How dare you? I would never..." Tears sprang to her eyes. "I would *never!*"

"Are you so naïve, Deccia?" he hissed.

"I could spy for information! I wouldn't have to sleep with them. You have a sick, dirty mind!"

"Yeah?" His gaze raked down her body, and then back up. "When they get a look at you in that short uniform Tineia wears..." His face flushed dark. "They wouldn't leave you alone. They'd touch you and grope you..."

"Stop it!" Deccia wanted to cover up her ears.

"I won't. You will hear the truth. And the truth is, after what Greisn did to you..." He drew a quick breath. "Working in the Merry Spirits would destroy you."

"How do know what would destroy me?" she cried out. "Being without Timaeus is destroying me! Him being tortured is destroying me! I have to do something...*anything* to stop it."

"The sailors at the Merry Spirits would torture *you.* Would Timaeus want that?"

"I'd do anything for him," she wept. "Tomorrow I'm talking to Tineia..."

"No. You're not." The gray, fade-into-the-background man Goric pretended to be had vanished.

"I am! You can't stop me." She burst into angry tears.

"Well, well." The door banged shut. "The lovers are having a quarrel."

"Cut it," Goric snarled.

"I have good news for the lunatic."

Deccia quickly turned. "Timaeus. Is he all right?" She waited in fearful anticipation.

"The guards say he hasn't been tortured in a week. Sounds like he'll be all right until the Presidente comes back."

"Thank The One!" Then fearful suspicion dawned. "You're telling the truth, aren't you?"

Riln raised his hands. "I swear. Don't freak out. Don't attack me."

"Oh, thank goodness! Thank you, Riln!" Deccia rushed forward and threw her arms around him.

"Well." She heard the grin in his voice as his burly arms closed around her. "Looks like all the lovin's for me, apte boy. Maybe if your shorts weren't twisted so tight she'd save a little for you."

Deccia jerked back. The disgusting slug! But she felt too relieved to scold him. And then she remembered something else, too. This morning, Goric had asked Riln to get the information about Timaeus.

"Thank you, Goric," she told him.

"Yeah." He shoved his hands into his pockets and hunched his shoulders, visibly withdrawing into himself again. The mask had returned. He'd done a good job of fooling her...but no longer. He muttered, "I'm trying to look out for you. Believe it or not."

Although she did not feel comfortable with the idea of hugging him, she could do something else. "I'm sorry for yelling at you."

"Yeah." His lips twitched. "I probably deserved it."

"I mean it. I'm grateful to you both. What do you want for dinner tonight? I'll cook anything."

Goric's face lit up, and she laughed. "Yes, I'll make pudding."

Relief made her spirits soar. She was too happy to pay any attention to the mild squabbling now between the two men. Timaeus was all right. And he would stay okay for a few more weeks. They just had to rescue him before the Presidente returned.

CHAPTER TEN

AFTER LUNCH, only Doc, Mentàll and Methusal remained at the table with Hendra. Across the table, she noticed that a wide gap of space lay between the Rolbani girl and Mentàll, and wondered why.

"Hendra and I were talking about the Presidente," Doc said, and glanced at her. "Have you told Mentàll about your theory?"

She'd been reluctant to worry her recovering cousin. But Doc was right. It was time to warn him. The more time he had to formulate counter moves to the Presidente's schemes, the better.

"What theory?"

"I think you should be careful. I don't think you should trust him."

Her cousin waited for more.

Hendra explained, "At first, I didn't think he'd come all the way to Koblan to sign the peace agreement. In his eyes, it would be the same as humbling himself and admitting defeat to you. I couldn't imagine him doing that. After all, he must hate you. He must want revenge."

"True."

"And then I realized that's exactly why he *would* come." She involuntarily shivered. Unfortunately, years of trying to predict and counter Jascr's attacks had taught her too much about how cruel, arrogant minds worked. Humility wasn't an option. In fact, any imagined defeat or humiliation had enraged Jascr still further, stoking the fires of his hatred, and lowering his mind to darker, more evil paths, just to reclaim his power over her. On one occasion, when she was fifteen, she'd managed to evade him for weeks on end. It had resulted in one of the most terrifying, humiliating episodes of abuse she'd ever received from her step-brother.

Struggling to keep her voice steady, she said, "He'll come, pretending peace, but in his heart he'll burn to hurt you. To defeat you. I think he'll come for one purpose only. To kill you."

Methusal looked quickly at Mentàll. Fear darkened her gaze.

Mentàll's arm moved toward the Rolbani girl, as if he'd reached for her hand under the table. "I will order men from Dehre to protect both Methusal and myself."

The Rolbani girl's posture relaxed a little. By contrast, tension tightened the powerful muscles in Mentàll's upper body. His hand returned to his side, and his lips curled back in a snarl. "The Presidente will lick my boots before I allow him any kind of victory over me."

Doc said, "Calbn could order his men to watch the Presidente's entourage, too."

"Better yet," Methusal said, "only allow the Presidente and two or three of his closest advisers to come ashore."

"He may not agree to those restrictions," Mentàll said. "But between Calbn's men and mine, we will match every Zindedi who comes ashore. Guards will protect the private wings of the mansion. All Zindedi movements will be restricted in both Quasr and the mansion."

"Sounds like a solid plan." The Tarst doctor's concerned glance rested upon Hendra. He seemed to sense how upset she was. She felt cold inside. The old fear and the memory of the evil things Jascr had done to her made her feel sick.

"Yes," Methusal agreed, and scooted toward the aisle.

"Methusal. When the Presidente is in Quasr, you will go nowhere without a guard," Mentàll said harshly.

Her eyes narrowed. "Of course. I'm not foolish. A guard sounds like a good idea."

A frown flashed. Mentàll watched Methusal disappear up the ladder.

Doc chuckled. "A word of advice. Women don't like to be ordered."

Mentàll frowned again. Hendra touched his hand. Softly, she said, "You care about her. And I know you don't want her to get hurt. But Doc is right."

Mentàll gave a curt nod. "I will remember." He left them at the table.

Doc turned his attention to her. "What's wrong?"

"Nothing, really. It's just the past. I was remembering all of the horrible games Jascr used to play with me." Emotion suddenly choked her voice, and he reached for her, pulling her close to his side. She buried her face in his shoulder. "I hate this." She drew a shaky breath. "Why can't I forget it? He's dead."

"The terrible things you lived through may have helped us, just now."

"What do you mean?"

"How else could we understand how the Presidente might think?" His voice roughened. "Because of Jascr, you know how twisted minds work. Your insight will help protect innocent lives."

She hadn't thought about that before. "So good might come from it."

"It may help save your cousin's life."

Yes. That would be worth it. All those years of torture would be worth it, if it ended up saving Mentàll's life. With a smile, she kissed Doc's bristly cheek. "Thank you."

Chapter Eleven

Captain Hil estimated that they'd reach Koblan in another five or six days. For Methusal, it could not come soon enough.

Tonight she stood with Behran on deck, riding the dark, rolling waves, and enjoying the peaceful night. She'd spent more time with him lately. It had been fun and relaxing, but at the same time, she'd avoided physical contact with him. He didn't comment on it. Maybe he sensed that she was struggling to sort out her feelings for him and Mentàll. That particular endeavor wasn't going so well.

As much as she tried to avoid Mentàll in order to gain needed emotional space from him, she was still painfully aware of his presence. Worse, the warm recollection of when he'd taken her hand at lunch the other day, to comfort her, still lingered. Even though he'd turned harsh and dictatorial afterward, she'd *felt* his care and concern for her. It licked under her defenses, eating away at the distance she was trying to create between them.

Mentàll still retired early every night. By the end of each evening, his face was pale and he was clearly exhausted. But his health was definitely improving.

Yesterday, for instance, he'd made it up on deck without turning as pale as a ghost. This morning he'd startled her when she'd opened her cabin door and discovered him striding down the short hall with an echo of his former vigor. His left arm movements, however, remained stiff, but Doc reported that the wound had closed and was healing nicely.

She was glad for all of those things. But it deeply disturbed her that he could still easily capture all of her attention with one look. Even worse, her heart raced whenever he lingered nearby. Avoiding him did not appear to be helping her perspective at all.

Ryon loomed above the rippling black water. A cool breeze filled the sails.

The two of them had remained silent, watching the waves, for a long time now. The undemanding quiet was nice. Behran always made her feel calm and safe.

"Tell me something, Thusa," he said at last.

"Sure." For the first time, she noticed how serious he looked. The breeze ruffled the lock of hair drooping over his forehead.

"Why don't you want to spend time with me in the evenings?"

For a second, she stared at him, surprised. "We spend most of the day together!"

"Yes. And I enjoy that. But we're never alone. If I want to spend time with you in the evening, I have to ask."

It was true. Most nights she went to bed after the usual games of whaal ended. Even when Behran, Doc, Hendra, and Sozla lingered, talking and laughing, she usually made her excuses and left. The truth was, she wanted to be alone. She didn't feel like giggling and laughing. She felt... It was hard to find the right word. "Depressed" couldn't be it. Maybe "unsettled" was a better one.

"I'm sorry. I guess I've been tired. And I've been worrying about Deccia, too."

He frowned. "I'm sorry. Of course you're worried about her. I guess I was afraid it might be something else."

"Like what?"

He shrugged. "After dinner..." Voice firmer, he said, "After Mentàll leaves, you seem to check out. It's as if you've gone somewhere else."

Appalled, she wondered if that might be true. This evening flashed to mind. Mentàll had sat across from her at dinner. He'd spoken to the others more than he had to her, but every time his gaze rested on her, energy thrummed through her blood. When he'd retired for the night, that edgy excitement had deserted her, too. Seen from this detached perspective, the implications were alarming. How could

Mentàll's absence affect her just as much as his presence? Her fists tightened in frustration.

"Thusa?"

She blinked. His eyes looked dark in the moonlight.

"I'm sorry, Behran." Behran deserved better. She was trying to put space between herself and Mentàll. Unfortunately, it wasn't helping.

She settled for part of the truth. "I'm overwhelmed. I'm trying to make sense of everything that happened in Zindedi, and I've been thinking about what will happen when the Presidente comes. This mission feels like it will never end."

"When the Presidente comes, you'll have to pretend to be Mentàll's wife again. How will you handle that?" Behran's dark eyes asked an even deeper question.

"I don't know. I haven't thought about that." But he was right. Since her fictitious union with Mentàll irrationally seemed to scare the Presidente, they'd need to continue the charade. It would help them keep the upper hand in the negotiations.

But the thought of several more intimate days with Mentàll scared her. What would happen? Would she finally make an irrevocable mistake? One that would tie her life to his forever? Just remembering the intimacy they had shared in Carachki caused guilt and shame to burn her cheeks. Behran still didn't know about that. She couldn't tell him.

"I don't know," she said again. "But it'll only be for a few days, and then it will end."

"You're telling me you have no feelings for Mentàll at all."

"I do care about him, Behran. But you know I care about you, too."

He stared at her. Hurt registered in his eyes, and she couldn't bear it. She slipped her arms around him and held him tight. "Behran, I'm sorry."

He held her tightly against him. But it didn't fill the emptiness inside of her. She felt lonely, standing in his arms. Her heart struggled to find his—to find the closeness that had budded all those years ago on Rolban's plateau, just after Mentàll had been defeated. A little of that old feeling trickled in. She cared about him a lot. He was her friend. And she didn't ever want to lose him.

Finally, Behran released her. His expression was almost severe in its bleakness. "You're upset. But I still need to know the truth. What do you feel for him? And what do you feel for me?"

She opened her mouth, but before she could speak, he said, "Tomorrow night. We'll finish this conversation then. Be prepared to tell me one thing: Do you still want to marry me?"

He turned on his heel and left her.

△ △ △ △ △

Dark night enshrouded Hendra and Doc, and a cold, stiff breeze tried to slide inside her warm leather jacket. She held onto the rail, feet braced apart as the ship rode the choppy ocean. Water hissed by the hull. With a lurch and a wave slap, the ship reared high and then plunged forward, conquering the eager, adolescent waves.

Doc murmured, "Methusal's at the bow. Did you see her?"

She hadn't, and peered over his shoulder. "She's all by herself."

It didn't surprise her. Both Methusal and Mentàll had seemed troubled lately. Her cousin watched Methusal like a prowling wild beast waiting for nightfall to stalk his prey. Methusal took care never to be alone with him. Behran didn't seem happy, either. When he thought no one was looking, he eyed Methusal with a dark, troubled look.

"She needs to make a decision," Doc said.

"I think she's still planning to marry Behran."

"Is that why she's so unhappy?" he said dryly.

"Maybe." Lately, feeling protective of her cousin, Hendra had been observing Methusal's body language around him. It spoke volumes. Even though Methusal frequently angled her body away from him, she jumped whenever he accidentally touched her, and every time he spoke to someone, she slid a quick glance at him before looking way. She was very aware of him. That meant that she was battling deeper than casual feelings for her cousin. Good.

"I think she's afraid," she said softly. An emotion she could certainly understand. Trusting men was an uphill battle for her, too, and Mentàll had hurt the Rolbani girl more than once in the past. "Actually, it's a miracle he has a chance with her at all."

"Yes. She's a tough girl. But Mentàll will need to play it slow and easy if he wants to win her. I think he realizes that."

Hendra blurted, "Is that what *you're* doing?"

Doc looked at her quickly, in obvious surprise. "What?"

Hendra blushed. "I mean... Well, ever since we kissed a few days ago, you've seemed kind of distant." There. She'd said what was troubling her. Her heart pounded, afraid that he might tell her he was having second thoughts about their relationship.

He laughed. "Distant is not how I feel. I felt like I was pushing you too fast. All I could think about—all I *do* think about is touching you and kissing you and holding you in my arms."

Tremendous relief filled her. "I was afraid you'd had enough of me."

"*Never* that, Hendra." His voice thickened. "Never that. But I do want to make sure you know I care about *you*. Not just your outer beauty." He laughed, and it sounded a little choked. "You're *gorgeous*, Hendra, and you're sweet, and.... Did you know that? I just wonder... Sometimes I wonder if I'm good enough for you."

"Doc!" Aghast, she wrapped her arms tightly around him. "*You* are the most wonderful man in the world. You're so patient with me, and you're sweet, and honorable...and you're everything I've ever dreamed of finding in a man."

"I am?" His teeth flashed in a small grin.

"Yes. And while I think we should go slow—I *need* to go slow—I think one little kiss, every now and then, wouldn't hurt, would it?"

"No," he murmured. "I don't suppose it would." And he proved it. His hands remained light on her arms, so she did not feel enclosed or trapped. Instead, she felt the glorious freedom and joy of kissing the man she loved.

She loved him. Wonder took root in her soul. She loved him with her whole heart. She'd never believed she'd fall in love.

With a light rub of her arms, he let her go—with obvious reluctance, if his rueful smile was any indication. "You're shivering. We should go below."

Heart full to bursting, she nodded. Doc took her hand and they walked together to the stern of the boat. But before she climbed down the ladder, she caught a glimpse of Methusal sitting alone at the bow.

The Rolbani girl was unhappy, and it didn't seem right. Hendra wanted everyone to feel the same happiness that she was feeling right now. But Methusal appeared to be avoiding her problems, rather than solving them. They were festering.

Hendra knew better than most the consequences of trying to repress problems. At one point or another, the root of the difficulty would erupt in a messy, hurtful way. It was time for someone to make a move. And she knew exactly who that person should be.

△ △ △ △ △

Methusal shivered as the stiff ocean breeze slid under her clothes. She wished she'd worn an extra tunic tonight, but right now she couldn't muster up the will to go below and fetch it. She couldn't face Behran again. Not yet. She felt torn, confused, and desperately unhappy.

Hendra and Doc lingered on the opposite side of the boat, enjoying time alone together. She was glad for them. Hendra's fragile vulnerability seemed to be softening into trust in Doc. And to think just a few weeks ago she'd thought Hendra was in love with Behran!

Feeling colder than ever, she retreated to a sheltered spot on the cabin top where the rowboat, lashed on deck, provided protection from the wind. The breeze was a little softer there.

Hendra and Doc were quiet now. A quick listen revealed that they had gone below. She was alone on deck, except for Skyl, who was in the cockpit. Good.

Her cheeks felt wet, and she closed her eyes and brushed away the tears. Even before her conversation with Behran that evening, emptiness and depression had been eating away at her, growing steadily worse over the last few days.

It didn't make sense. Everything had been going exactly how she'd wanted. She'd spent most of her time with Behran. She'd put space between herself and Mentàll. In fact, she'd tried to ignore him as much as humanly possible. And ever since that afternoon in the cockpit, he'd only initiated cordial conversations with her.

Wasn't that what she wanted?

A cold breeze swirled up under the edge of her tunic, sending icy fingers up her back. She shuddered, and crossed her arms tightly. She didn't want to go below with the others, who were happily playing whaal in the warm cabin. She didn't want to pretend to be happy anymore.

A whisper of movement teased her ears.

Mentàll. Her heart jerked in surprise when he sat down beside her. His warm, muscled thigh eased up against hers.

After the initial shock, her tension slowly eased away. All of a sudden she wanted to give up. She was so tired of fighting her feelings. She was so tired of feeling desperately unhappy, and unable to admit it, even to herself. With a sigh, she closed her eyes. When he put his arm around her shaking shoulders, she leaned into his warm body and lay her head on his shoulder.

"Where is your jacket?" his low, harsh voice said.

"In Zindedi." With a shiver, she pressed closer to him. "Does this hurt?"

"No."

She felt safe. She felt content, and for the moment, refused to think at all. Instead, she absorbed his presence, drinking it in like a parched person.

He said softly, "You are not fighting to escape from me."

"Not at the moment."

"I may have that pleasure later?"

"Please," she whispered. "Just hold me."

His arm tightened, and his breath warmed her hair when he kissed her. "What is wrong, Methusal?"

"Everything."

"Has Behran hurt you?" The harsh note returned.

"No."

"Then who has?"

"Me."

He fell silent. Her feelings for this man had grown too deep. He'd rooted down into her heart, and now filled it up, forcibly pushing Behran into one of the small side chambers. She wanted to give in. She wanted to stop fighting, because she wanted to be in his arms. She *liked* being in his arms. Could it be? Was this where she was supposed to be?

The moonlight sculpted his features into angular planes. He watched her, perhaps waiting for an explanation for her mood. With a small, choked sound, she gave in to the longing that ached through her soul. Her hands curled around his shoulders, and she reached up and kissed him.

It wasn't enough. Her fingers slid over his smooth, tense shoulder muscles and buried themselves into the soft, thick hair at his nape. With a small sound, she pressed closer to him and kissed him with hungry desperation.

With a soft growl, he came alive. The intensity of his kiss consumed her. Before realizing what was happening, she was on his lap, and his hand ensnarled in her hair, and his arm felt like an ore band, low around her waist. His injured arm.

"Are you all right?" she whispered. "Am I hurting you?" Every part of her that touched him felt like it was on fire.

His hot breath curled in her ear, and she shivered. "No. I feel better now than I have in months."

Mindlessly, she pressed closer to him, returning his kisses.

He was the one who pulled back, his breaths harsh. His chuckle sounded a little unsteady. "We had better stop, Methusal, before I take you on this deck."

She buried her face in his neck, feeling their hearts pound in tandem. Tightly, she clung to him, unwilling to let him go. She pressed her eyes shut, fighting the tears.

Mentàll's heart rate returned to a slow, steady thump. When she continued to hold him, he loosened her arms from around his neck so he could look into her eyes. "What is wrong, Methusal?"

Wordlessly, she shook her head.

"Tell me the truth." The Kaavl Commander came through in that order.

"I don't want to want you."

"But you do," he said with fierce satisfaction.

She wiped away the tears and climbed off of his lap to sit beside him.

He watched her, but said nothing. When she finally met his gaze, she saw he was still waiting for an answer. He would not beg for it, but he expected her to be honest.

"Yes," she said, and closed her eyes. Because that meant the death of her relationship with Behran. Even while she still believed marrying Behran would be the safest and smartest decision for her, he deserved her whole heart. If she couldn't give it to him, he deserved to know the truth. And she would tell him, tomorrow.

Not that she believed any future could exist for her and Mentàll. She knew who he was. If she chose to enter a relationship with him, it would be with her eyes wide open. Much as her illogical heart wanted him, any relationship with him would most likely end in pain and disaster.

The thought scared her.

"I...I probably shouldn't have kissed you." She rose, but he blocked her path.

"It was not a mistake. Let me prove it to you."

How could he prove that he would never hurt her? Or never break her heart? He was still a ruthless man. She knew him. He was still the same man, underneath it all. Wasn't he?

He desired her. That much was obvious. But how deep did his emotions go? Did he love her? Or was he incapable of love, like he'd admitted before? And what if she was only a conquest he wanted to add to his list of achievements? Would he quickly bore of her, once he'd made her his own? Would he move onto his next challenge and leave her behind, heartbroken and forgotten?

Was she a fool? Behran would never hurt her.

His eyes narrowed. "What are you thinking about, Methusal?"

"Behran."

"How much longer will you string him along?"

"I'm not." She stopped. That wasn't true. She had been. And it made her feel terrible. "I do love him, you know."

"As a friend." An edge cut through his voice.

"I trust him. He'd never hurt me."

"You will break his heart, Methusal. Better a clean break now, than a messy one later."

He was right. She stared at him for a long moment. "I'm afraid."

He frowned. "Do not fear me, Methusal. I have sworn I will never hurt you again."

"I don't believe you will. Not on purpose, anyway."

"I will not," he stated harshly.

With a sigh, she went into his warm arms, and they closed securely around her. She could not believe that she had just chosen Mentàll over Behran. But finally, a sliver of peace soothed her heart. She felt as if she had finally come home.

Chapter Twelve

THAT NIGHT EVERY DREAM started with Mentàll and ended with Behran staring at her with hurt and devastated reproach. Then he walked away. When Methusal called to him, he refused to turn back.

She awoke with a gasp.

As she watched dust particles float in the gray dawn light, she knew it would be that way when she told Behran the truth. He would not take her back, not for any reason. Of course, he would not reject her as a friend, but their future together would never happen.

It scared her, the idea of throwing away their future for a man who admitted he didn't know how to love. A man accustomed to being alone; a man who needed no one but himself. He didn't need her. But he wanted her.

And she wanted him—in fact, more of him than he could ever probably give her.

Tonight she would tell Behran the truth.

△ △ △ △ △

Later that morning, Methusal lay on deck. The ocean surged gently beneath the ship, and the sails hummed, driving the *Sea Mistress* ever southward, toward Koblan. The sun warmed her eyelids, and she felt tired and lazy.

Behran and the others were playing a game of truth or dare nearby. She'd declined. She'd felt uncomfortable, knowing what she needed to say to him later. Although she'd seen the reserve in his dark eyes this morning, he still treated her with the same easy warmth as always. That made her feel even more awful for what she was about to do.

She'd taken a nap in the sun, instead.

The nap had come and gone, but she felt too comfortable to move now. She was in her own little world, and the others were happily playing their game. Everyone was playing, except for Doc and Mentàll. Captain Hil had invited them to his cabin a half an hour ago to celebrate Mentàll's recovery with a toast of spirits.

Methusal's stomach rumbled, but it was too early for lunch. Maybe she'd sneak down and pilfer a snack from Coyl's food lockers.

She shaded her closed eyes with her hand, and slowly opened them. Pink and orange spots danced before them. The world seemed unnaturally bright.

"I'm in." Doc appeared on deck. Hendra slid sideways to make room for him.

Captain Hil's party must be over. It seemed the perfect time to go get a snack. She sat up. "I'm going to get something to eat. Anyone want anything?"

"A pitcher of water and glasses," Behran suggested.

"Okay."

Methusal climbed down below. After the bright sunlight, it seemed darker than usual inside. The main cabin was empty, but voices came from Captain Hil's quarters. The door was half open. Methusal knelt down and pulled open Coyl's food lockers. Grain discs. Yes. Those looked good. But maybe dried meat would be better. That would give her energy until lunchtime.

She straightened, nibbling on the salty, savory strip. Now to find a pitcher. Where did Coyl keep those...?

Voices tickled her ears. "A beauty," Captain Hil said with a knowing snicker. "You planned well to be paired with her. A lucky man. Did you get what you wanted?"

"I will get what I want."

"Oh? You're a patient man. More than I would be."

She glanced at the partially opened door. She carried with vision and saw Mentàll and the Captain sitting at a round table. Mentàll's glass of spirits was half gone. The Captain's was empty.

Mentàll said, "I have waited a long time to achieve my goal. I will make no hasty mistakes."

"Have to admire a man with a plan. Chief Aarabst admires you, as well."

Mentàll's eyes glittered, and his half smile didn't look like a smile at all. His cold expression reminded her of the man she had feared so long ago. The man determined to take over Rolban, and to win the Quasr War. The man bound and determined to make her pay for humiliating him, no matter the cost.

Captain Hil chuckled. "You have courage, my friend, going up against those chiefs. Especially Rolban's. How do you think it will turn out?"

Mentàll's lips curled back, resembling a wild beast's snarl. "I will let no one take what is rightfully mine. With this successful mission, I have earned it."

The Captain nodded his grizzled head and sloshed more liquid into his glass. He raised it. "To the future of Koblan."

"To my victory." The Dehrien Chief drank deeply.

With a gasp, Methusal stepped backward.

Mentàll meant to take over Koblan. It was the only thing that made sense. The plan they were discussing must have something to do with the secret agreement he'd discussed in Aestoff with Chief Aarabst. Clearly, Rolban knew nothing about it.

In addition, Captain Hil had just said Mentàll had planned well to be paired with her on the mission. So somewhere, in his devilish plots, he'd planned all along to use her to achieve his biggest goals, as well.

How did he plan to use her?

She'd begun to trust him. But he hadn't changed at all. How could she have been such a fool? She felt sick.

Her worst fears had just been proven true.

A chair scraped backwards.

He was about to come *out!* Whirling, she ran for her cabin.

It had all been a game, from the very beginning. He'd planned to get close to her. Every calculated move he'd made had been performed only to advance his power hungry schemes.

With a sob, she shut the door. She'd *known it.* All of those weeks in his close company she'd struggled to cling to that certainty. But he'd gotten to her. He'd burrowed under her skin until now...now...

She collapsed on the floor and wept, hands on her face, teeth clenched in agony. She had let him in. He'd slid into her heart like a knife. "Oh The One," she moaned. "Help me. *Help me.*"

That his betrayal could devastate her so utterly, that she was face on the floor, weeping—what did that say?

The searing pain terrified her.

She tried to stop her tears, to get a grip on herself, but could not. Her foolish heart had begun to trust him. Right now, it felt as if cruel blades cut that organ into painful, bloody bits.

She felt raw inside, as if torn to pieces. She couldn't go back outside. She'd plead a headache. Later, she'd try to piece her life together again. Right now, all she could do was curl up in a ball and grieve.

△ △ △ △ △

That night, Methusal retreated to the bow of the boat to be alone. She had successfully fooled everyone into thinking she was fine. And she'd avoided Mentàll like a sickness all day long.

The others were down below, laughing. She'd come outside to be alone, and to cry again, which would be the first time since her meltdown this morning.

A storm of furious tears overtook her, and she was glad for the solitude, and that no one would hear her breaking down over a man who was the lowest sort of a wild beast.

"Thusa." Footsteps broke into her soft, hiccupping sobs. Behran. She'd forgotten they had planned to talk tonight.

She wiped the tears away with her sleeve, and averted her face to look out at the sparkling waves. Ryon's luminous green glow lit the sea and the high, wispy clouds.

"What's wrong?" His tone was unexpectedly gentle, and when his arm went around her, she turned into him, clutching his tunic in her fists. She drew a deep, watery breath, trying to calm herself.

"What happened?"

"I hate him." Her teeth clenched so tight her jaw hurt. "I *hate* him."

His arms closed around her stiff body, and he held her tight. Her rock. As always, her shelter from the storm.

"Oh, Behran, I'm sorry."

"For what?"

Methusal pulled back. Wiping her cheeks, she turned to look at the rolling sea.

"What did he do?" he asked quietly.

"I finally found out the truth." She told him everything she'd overheard, and ended with, "He's secretly plotting to take over Koblan."

Behran remained silent for a long time. Finally, he said, "It's not a secret if Captain Hil knows his plan. And Chief Aarabst, too."

Behran did not appear to be nearly as perturbed as she'd expected. "*I* didn't know about it," she retorted. "And neither did you."

"Think back. Remember how he traveled all over Koblan in the months before our trip to Zindedi? Wouldn't it make sense that he's been setting up a new Alliance of some kind?"

"If that's true, then Rolban doesn't know about it. Papa hasn't been consulted. Tell me—why would Mentàll exclude Rolban?"

"Are you sure Rolban has been left out? Does your father tell you everything?"

Methusal said nothing.

"Maybe you're jumping to conclusions."

"I *heard* him, Behran! I saw the expression on his face. It was all cold and hard, like when he tried to take over Rolban three years ago."

"Do you think he wants to take over Rolban again?"

"I don't know what he's planning! But I'll bet he's plotting something much bigger than that."

"What?" Behran said simply. "And how? What can he do?"

"He can make an Alliance and trick everyone into signing it. I'll bet he wants to grab power over all of Koblan, like...like the Presidente!"

"Thusa. That's impossible. Koblan's chiefs are smart. They know what he's done before. They're not going to sign a document that gives Mentàll supreme power over all of Koblan!"

"I don't like it, Behran. I tell you, he's up to no good."

"Instead of talking to me, maybe you should talk to him. Ask the hard questions. Make him answer you."

"He won't answer me."

"He will. If you apply the right pressure."

"What do you mean?"

"If he thinks he's going to lose you, I think you'd be surprised by what he'd do. And he won't lie, will he?"

"No." Because he hated liars. But he may not tell the complete truth, either, if it benefited him to keep silent about the deeper part of his plots. On the other hand, what if Behran was right? What if she had jumped to conclusions?

She looked down at the dark, glittering waves. White froth chased the peaks into the gullies. "I'll talk to him. But I won't expect much."

"When you've figured it all out with him, tell me, Thusa. I need to know if it's over. I need to know where I stand."

"Behran..."

"I can see that you're confused about him, but I can't walk this line anymore. Like I said last night, I need to know what you feel for me. And what you feel for him. Don't you think I deserve to know the truth?"

"Yes. You do."

"Get the facts, and then tell me your answer." His gaze looked hard and a little bleak, and he abruptly left before she could speak.

△ △ △ △ △

Methusal knocked on Mentàll's door. Instead of being bid to enter, the door opened and he smiled down at her. "Methusal. This is a pleasant surprise."

"I need to speak to you. Will you come out on deck?" She didn't want everyone to hear the argument that was sure to come.

That discerning gaze read her expression, and his smile faded. "Of course. You know I am always happy to spend time with you."

Methusal ignored this. Not waiting for him to get his jacket, she rapidly climbed the ladder and gained the quiet spot near the bow of the boat. It was chilly again, but she'd had the foresight to throw on an extra tunic.

"What do you want to speak about?" He was right behind her.

Methusal swallowed a soft gasp and quickly faced him. When she stared at him, she saw two men—the man she'd come to know in Zindedi, and the ruthless man who had tried to take over Rolban, and who had also done his best to get under her skin during the Quasr War.

"You haven't changed. You'll never change, will you?"

Wariness cracked his perpetually confident façade. "Explain what you mean."

"*You* are the one who needs to explain. I heard you talking to Captain Hil this morning.

A beat of silence elapsed. "What did you hear?"

"You want to take over Koblan. And you have a plan in place to do it."

"No..."

"Yes!" Her voice rose. "Tell me the *truth.*"

"The truth, Methusal? Think about the Quasr War. With countless ships at his command, the Presidente could not take over Koblan. With what army would I try to do the same?"

"Tell me your plan."

"Now is not the time to discuss..."

"*Tell* me!"

A muscle worked in his jaw, and he looked away for a moment. "Nothing is completed. You must trust me."

"Trust you? *Why?*"

He flinched a bit. Harshly, he said, "Even after our time together in Zindedi, you still do not trust me?"

"When I hear you boasting of a plan to take over Koblan... Gee. Maybe that makes me suspicious. Maybe that brings to mind your plots to overthrow Rolban!"

"Methusal!"

Through gritted teeth, she said, "Tell me the truth. All of it."

A frown hardened his expression. He did not like being put on the spot. Would he humble himself and answer her? Or was Behran wrong? Did his pride and endless quest for power mean more to him than she did?

A breath hissed through his teeth. "I plan to unite Koblan. We need a system in place to deal with threats from Zindedi."

"System?"

"Government."

This was a new concept. "What do you mean?"

"Each community will have a vote. If two-thirds of the chiefs agree on a course of action, everyone will work together to achieve that goal for Koblan."

Methusal thought it over. "That's a good idea," she admitted. "But where do you fit in?"

"I am a chief. I will have one vote."

"And?" She knew him too well. Not for one second did she believe that was all.

"Time will tell, Methusal."

"Tell me everything."

"The facts are not fixed yet."

"You want to be Presidente of Koblan, don't you?"

Something hard and fierce glittered in his eyes. He did.

She felt sick. "You want to be just like him. The Presidente."

"I want to be no one but myself."

"You're power hungry. Just like he is."

"Methus..."

"You always have been! Why did I think for one minute that you'd changed?"

She turned away, but his grip on her wrist pulled her back. Warm breath stirred the hair at her temple. "You do know who I am."

"Then tell me your whole plan. Tell me how you plan to become the Presidente Supreme of Koblan."

"Trust me."

She gasped at the pure, arrogant nerve of him. "I *don't*. I will *never* trust you. And think about this—you ask me to trust you, but you don't trust me. Otherwise, you'd tell me everything right now!"

His gaze flickered.

"Is it hard for you to trust *me*, in particular, or people in general? Or is your plan is so terrible that you know I won't like it?"

"My plan will hurt no one. Trust me."

"*Trust*. That is the real issue here, isn't it?"

How could she trust a man who kept secrets from her? And he still had not told her everything. He'd as much as admitted it. It made her feel sick.

Softly, he said, "If you had listened longer to the conversation, you would have heard more. The Captain and I mostly discussed you. Not Koblan."

"That's right." She gave a sharp, bitter laugh. "Do you mean how you plan to use me to achieve your goal? How *do* I fit in? I am so curious."

"Sarcasm does not suit you."

"And you possess so many charming, stellar qualities."

"Why were you spying on me?"

"I wasn't *spying*," she snapped. "I just happened to overhear. And then you got that cold look—like when you're planning to be a whip. Like when you tried to take over Rolban." Her voice rose. "Like when you threatened to *kill me!*"

"Methusal!" It was a guttural rasp.

Tears stood in her eyes. "Don't deny it. I know who you are. I *know...*"

He kissed her. Its hot fierceness shook her to her toes. After a shocked second she struggled, but his strong hand on her back drew her closer. The savage heat threatened to consume her.

To her chagrin, her struggles quieted, and her head swam. She could think of nothing but him and his kisses, which commanded her complete surrender. Her trembling hands went to his chest, meaning to push him away, but instead crept up, across his hard muscles, to grip his shoulders. An insane part of her longed to melt into him. What was *wrong* with her?

When he deepened the kiss, a violent tremble gripped her and a soft moan escaped. She didn't want to free herself.

His lips strayed across her cheek, and then his hot breath seared her ear. "You are mine," he murmured.

"No," she denied, even as she quaked in his arms. "*No.*"

Sanity finally presented itself. With a gasp, she wrenched free. "It's over. This lie is *finished*. Don't touch me again. *Ever.*"

She fled down the deck.

What was wrong with her? She must have lost her mind, to have responded to him like that! She took a deep breath, trying to calm her expression before she went down below.

Behran lifted an eyebrow when he saw her, but it lowered when he scanned her face. His attention returned to the cards on the table before him.

Was her face flushed? Was it obvious that Mentàll had kissed her?

Desperate to pretend that all was normal, Methusal plopped down on the bench to watch the game.

Behind her, the Dehrien's steps *thunked* down the stairs. Behran glanced from him to Methusal. She frowned. Mentàll strode by without pausing. A loud snap indicated that he'd closed his cabin door.

Behran's brow lifted again.

"We need to talk," she told him quietly. It was time to put an end to every lie in her life.

Slowly, he nodded, "Let me finish this game."

She climbed outside again. It was over with Mentàll. Forever. He hadn't told her the full truth, and he probably never would. She couldn't trust him. Not ever.

△ △ △ △ △

Behran joined her on deck a few minutes later. She felt cold to her marrow. This was the last conversation she'd have out on this freezing deck, that was for sure.

"Is it over with him?"

"Yes." Although it hurt to say it, she had to tell him the full truth. "And it's over between us, too, Behran. I'm sorry."

He was silent for a minute. "I saw that coming."

"I'm sorry. I didn't want this to happen. You have to know that my head chooses you, but my heart won't listen to reason."

His shoulders moved restlessly, but he said nothing.

Feeling even worse, she said, "You deserve my whole heart, Behran. I do care about you, very much, but you deserve someone who loves you with her whole heart. I'm *so sorry*." Tears blurred her vision.

"The heart wants what the heart wants."

"I'm sorry," she said again.

"You're sure you won't be with him?"

"*Never*."

A long silence elapsed. "Then be with me."

"Behran! What are you saying? I can't. I *won't*. It wouldn't be fair to you."

"You said you still care about me."

"Of course I do. But..."

"Is there *any* chance for you and Mentàll?"

Despair threatened to overwhelm her. "No. I can't trust him." Her voice caught. "Honestly, right now I wish I could get off this ship. Because I know he'll try to convince me to trust him again. And I'm so weak with him that I'm afraid he'll succeed."

"Would it help you to have an excuse to push him away?"

"Yes. But what do you mean?"

Softly, he said, "Let's keep our engagement going for now. I know how you feel. I won't expect anything from you. But if you want to keep a barrier up between you and Mentàll, our engagement is the only thing that will do it."

An incredulous laugh escaped. "You'd stay engaged to me just to protect me from him?"

"*Yes*," he said fiercely. "I love you, Thusa. If this is how I can protect you, then this is what I want to do."

"But it would be a lie. I have feelings for him, Behran. I care about you, too, but..."

Bleakly, he finished, "It's not the same."

"No," she whispered. "I don't want to hurt you. And I won't take advantage of you like this, either."

"*Yes*," he said. "Let me protect you from him. Let's keep up the engagement until we get home. And then...then we can end it, if that's what you want."

Methusal didn't feel right about this. "It's not honest. I don't want to lie to you, or to others about our relationship."

"Tell me the truth. If Mentàll was out of the picture, would you still consider marrying me?"

"Yes, but..."

"Then it's not a lie. It's a reconsideration period. I know where you stand. You won't be leading me on. I want to do this. I don't want him to hurt you again. And if this is the only way I can do it, then so be it."

Tears filled her eyes. "Behran."

"At the very least, we're still friends, Thusa. Friends look out for one another. And if you want to keep Mentàll at arm's length, I want to help you do that."

She could not believe how unselfish this man was; the man who had been her first love.

"Behran." She wrapped her arms tightly around him and wept. For friendship. For the loss of their old relationship. But perhaps it was the start of something new. A deeper, stronger friendship. She pulled back and wiped her eyes. "All right, thank you. I know it's wrong, and I shouldn't. But I accept your offer."

Chapter Thirteen

Lylitha delivered twin boys in the middle of the night. Aali learned about it when she went to breakfast that morning.

An excited Trori chattered nonstop. "I can't wait to see them! Papa'll take us right after breakfast."

Sure enough, shortly after breakfast Calbn collected his children. "Take a half hour off," he told Aali curtly.

"Thank you," she said, in an equally cool tone.

A half an hour, hmm?

A quick plan formed while she brought her breakfast dishes to the kitchen. So far, she'd discovered nothing about Mentàll and Calbn's secret plans. Now was her opportunity. She would sneak into Calbn's office while he was busy with his new babies.

Her heart hammered, remembering the last time she'd been in his office. He'd almost burst an apoplectic blood vessel. If he caught her again, his threat to throw her out of his house might be the least of her worries.

While she knew that searching his office wasn't the most prudent thing to do, she'd promised Methusal answers. By her timetable, the kaavl team could return any day. She had to discover at least one fact about Calbn's nefarious plots before it was too late.

Firmly gathering up her courage, she slipped down the hall. A few lengths from the Chief's office, she pretended to adjust her crutches while several people passed by. When the hall was empty, she slipped into kaavl. The office was quiet. No one was inside.

She swung quickly toward Calbn's office.

"Where are you going in such a hurry?"

She gasped with joy and turned. "Dastn! When did you get here?"

"Late last night."

She frowned. "But wasn't that dangerous? To travel at night?"

"Pan had an important message for Calbn. And I have to return Calbn's reply today."

"When do you leave?"

"Now."

"*Now?*" She'd barely had a chance to see him!

Maybe she could convince him to stay for a few more minutes. "I need a lookout. Will you help me? This is my only chance to search for the documents."

"You want me to spy for you?"

"Please! I need you."

His grin edged up. "How *much* do you need me?"

Her heart fluttered. "Don't expect payment, because you won't get it, you mercenary!"

He folded his arms across his broad chest. "Then what's my incentive?"

Aali felt indignant. "To save Koblan from an evil plot!"

"Do you really believe there's an evil plot?"

"I need to find out the truth."

"Aali..."

"We have to protect Koblan. I won't steal anything, I promise. I'll just read documents. Come on, Dastn. Please?"

"One minute."

She grinned. "I knew I could count on you!"

He muttered something that sounded suspiciously like, "...lost my mind."

She swung into the office and headed straight for the desk. But the shiny desktop was empty, so she pulled open the top drawer. Nothing but small parchments. She opened the other drawers, one after another.

Nothing! Now what?

Frustrated, her gaze zipped around the room. Where would Calbn hide important documents?

"Aali." Dastn's warning whisper came through the door.

"I can't find them!" she hissed. "I need another minute."

"Hi, Chief M'ntoyan," Dastn said, his voice louder than normal. "I was about to deliver your message to Pan. Do you have anything else to add?"

Calbn! Horrified, she scanned the room. Where could she hide with a cast and crutches?

△ △ △ △ △

Koblan! Home at last. Methusal stood at the railing with the others, feasting her eyes upon the familiar Quasr Mountains, which loomed up from the continent before them.

A warm breeze caressed her skin. Cold Zindedi was long gone. Half of the team had come home. Her heart still longed to be with her twin. Even now, she worried and prayed for her.

Behran stood beside her.

Avoiding Mentàll over the last few days had been easy. Seeing him caused physical pain, like an open, bleeding wound, in her heart.

She told herself that she was relieved their volatile relationship had ended.

Over the past few days she'd spent most of her time with Behran and the others, even though she'd really wanted to hide in her cabin and lick her wounds. She was grateful for Behran's steady, supportive presence. Their continued "engagement," combined with her fight with Mentàll, had finally managed to create a division between herself and the Dehrien Chief. She told herself she was glad.

Mentàll, for his part, had spoken little to her. But when her gaze occasionally caught his, frustration registered in his. Often, his lips were a hard line.

"Behran." Sozla appeared at Behran's other elbow. "Which mountains are those? The Iignon, no?"

Behran grinned down at the petite Eerporian girl. "You see the two white mountains? Those are Quasr's twin peaks."

Sozla pressed her hands together. "So, we are almost home!"

"Will you stay in Quasr for a while?" Methusal asked Sozla.

"Oh, yes. Mentàll said he will ask all of the Chiefs to come to Quasr to meet the Presidente. My father will come. I will wait to meet him."

"You're still welcome to come to Rolban afterward, if you'd like."

"Yes." Sozla cast a quick glance up at Behran. "I...I think I would like that. For a few days, or perhaps a week."

"Good." Behran grinned again. "I'll show you how our water systems work."

Sozla beamed. "I would like that, thank you." Her hands fluttered. "Well. I will leave you two alone."

"Why?" Behran said. "Stay with us. Thusa and I were just taking bets on how long it will take before we see Quasr's buildings. What's your guess?"

"Mmm." She pursed her lips. "Ten minutes, perhaps. Or fifteen."

Methusal listened to Behran and Sozla chat as she watched the dark strip of land grow closer. Her guess was a half an hour.

The soft breeze caressed her face, bringing with it the faint scent of flowers. Her mind drifted ahead, and it felt as if she was flying over the water.

Her mind relaxed further into kaavl, and Koblan zoomed two times closer, and then three and four times larger. This was a first for her in kaavl, and it was amazing. She saw Quasrians wandering on the beach. Couples held hands. Others shopped in the open, colorful stalls. One stall displayed huge bunches of orange and yellow flowers. They were not nasrias or ortangias.

A fierce pang of homesickness struck her. Not for Rolban, but for Zindedi. For Mrn. M's house.

She remembered when she and Mentàll had admired one of Mrn. M's flower arrangements on the dining table. Afterward, Mentàll had casually taken her hand and urged her to come out and walk the quiet streets with him. For a mission, of course, but in Mrn. M's house their closeness had felt so natural. And real. As if they truly were married, and intimately in tune with one another.

Methusal drew a quick breath and gripped the deck railing harder. Emptiness ached inside of her. *Stop it,* she told herself. *It's over. Stop thinking about him.*

With a forced smile, she turned to Behran and Sozla, "Change my guess to five minutes. Ready or not, we're almost home."

△ △ △ △ △

"No," Calbn told Dastn. Aali heard the frown in his voice. "I gave you my full message an hour ago."

The door knob turned at the same moment she noticed a closed door on the other side of the room. She hurried over and slipped inside. It was a closet.

Quietly, she closed the door to a crack and peeked out. Calbn still hadn't come in. Dastn was still talking to him in the hall.

Good old Dastn! What would she do without him?

She took the opportunity to look around, and realized she was wrong. It wasn't a closet. It was a small room with a window. Shelves lined two walls, and a chair was positioned beneath the window, next to a table and a lamp.

Stacked parchments covered half of the shelves. None of them were rolled up, however, like the official ones she'd seen before.

A large wooden trunk near the chair caught her eye. It was big enough to store secret documents. She abandoned her station at the door and hurried over as fast as her crutches would allow. She sat on the chair and tested the lock on the chest. Open.

Heart beating faster, she flipped open the lid. Jackpot! Several rolled up parchments lay inside. Quickly, she pulled out one and began to read. It was the document Rolban had signed, agreeing to a tentative treaty with the invader land.

Not what she was looking for. She quickly scanned another parchment. She smiled. This was it. There was Mentàll's signature. And Calbn's. And the signatures of many others chiefs. Her eyes widened. There were signatures from every community on Koblan, except for Rolban!

Quickly, she read, "We agree to become a unified continent, and to elect one Presidente..." She gasped.

In the other room, a drawer snapped shut.

Too late, she realized that she'd left the door cracked open. She swiftly placed the parchment back where it belonged, and looked around for a way to escape.

The window. If she slid it up...

She tugged up at the bottom edge. For a second it didn't move, and then suddenly, with an awful screech, it shot up. She swallowed a gasp.

Panicked, she threw her crutches into the bushes and then hoisted herself onto the window ledge. No. That wouldn't work! How would she get her cast out, except by falling backwards? Not a good idea.

She stood on the chair and poked her cast out the window, and then grabbed the window edges and teetered there, trying to work her other leg through. Panic rushed through her when she heard footsteps approach.

She pushed off the ledge and thankfully fell on her good leg.

With haste, she grabbed her crutches and hobbled as fast as she could away from the window. She realized she was in the side garden, and hurried to the front of the building. She didn't want to look suspicious, but she didn't want to get caught, either.

Heart pounding, she swung around the corner and barreled into Dastn. "*Ooomph!*"

He felt like an immovable wall, and he grabbed her so she wouldn't fall.

She gasped. "*Dastn.* You scared me to death!"

He gripped her arm and propelled her forward. "Come on."

"Stop." He was pulling her too fast. "I'll fall."

Dastn growled under his breath, but released her. She followed him to a bench. "Sit down," he ordered.

"I'll sit," Aali agreed with a frown, "but only because I want to." Her leg ached. Hopefully she hadn't re-injured it.

Dastn sat beside her. "I shouldn't have helped you spy. What if he'd caught you? What would he have done to you? And me?"

"He doesn't know you're involved," she scoffed.

"Right. I blocked the door to his office and gave him a lame story, too."

"It all worked out."

"Did it? Aali." His fingers caught her chin, so she was forced to look at him. His brown eyes looked angry and concerned. "Promise you won't do something so stupid again."

She couldn't decide if she liked that he was touching her or not. His face was very close. If she leaned forward, just the littlest bit, she could kiss him. But he didn't look very approachable right now. Not with that frown.

She pulled free. "I won't." Airily, she added, "I won't need to."

His frown didn't lessen. "What did you learn?"

"Mentàll and Calbn are setting up a massive Alliance all over Koblan. Everyone's signed it except for Rolban." Her eyes narrowed. "Did you know about it? Pan signed for Tarst."

"No. But I do know Mentàll has traveled all over Rolban. And I know he talked to Pan a few times. But I didn't know anything about an Alliance."

"You. A runner? I thought you knew everything that happens on this continent."

His eyes flashed. "Do you think I read the messages I carry?"

"No. But you hear things. How *couldn't* you know about this? Why didn't you tell me?"

"That is unfair," he said through his teeth.

"Did you know the Alliance will create the new position of Presidente for Koblan?"

"Aali!" Fists clenched, he stood abruptly. "This conversation is over." He reached for his pack beside the bench. He strode away, tossing it onto his back as he went.

"Dastn." What had she done? She stumbled to her feet. "Dastn! *Wait.* Please! I'm sorry." She hobbled after him, but he was too fast for her.

She whispered, "I'm sorry, Dastn."

Chapter Fourteen

Aali watched Dastn, his shoulders stiff with anger, turn the corner. And then he was gone, heading south, for Tarst.

A great shout sounded from outside the courtyard gate.

She hurried to see what was going on. Dastn retraced his steps, too.

"A ship!" A man shouted, running toward them. "Tell the Chief!" He sprinted by Aali to continue spreading the news.

"What ship?" she called, but he didn't answer. Dastn strode north now, toward the harbor.

Was it an invader ship? Or—joy flooded her—was it the ship carrying Deccia and Methusal home? Had they finally returned?

"Aalicaa!" Calbn appeared in the gateway. "Watch the children."

With something so exciting happening, that was the last thing she wanted to do. But she rounded them up as quickly as possible and hustled them into the courtyard. At least there she could see what was going on.

Trori tugged at her hand. "Is it a good ship, Aali? Or a bad one?" The little girl still clearly remembered the terror of hiding from the Zindedis during the Quasr War. Aali placed a comforting hand on her shoulder. "A good one, of course. See how excited everyone is?"

Time passed slowly as they waited to learn more. She made up games for the children to play, so they wouldn't be bored.

Finally, two people turned into the gate of the compound. Hendra and Doc!

Aali struggled to her feet and swung fast to meet her friends. "Hendra!" she cried out.

"Aali!" Hendra hurried over and gave her a careful hug. She looked down at the cast. "Dastn told us what happened. Are you all right?"

"I'm fine. It's wonderful to see you both. Where's Deccia and Timaeus and Methusal? Did everyone make it home safely?"

Hendra's smiled faded. "Deccia and Timaeus are still in Zindedi. Timaeus was captured, and Deccia is trying to rescue him. Goric and Riln stayed behind to help her."

Aali's high spirits crumpled. "Oh *no*."

"The Presidente should arrive in Quasr in one week. When he leaves, we'll send the ship back to get them."

It felt as if a horrible rock had lodged in the pit of her stomach. Her sister was still in danger in Zindedi, and Timaeus was captured. "What about the others? Methusal. Is she here?"

"Yes. Behran, too. Mentàll was shot. He's all right now," she hurried to explain, "but he's walking slowly."

"Shot?" It was hard for her to imagine the giant Dehrien incapacitated.

"It just missed his heart. He's lucky to be alive."

Aali felt more shocked by the minute. "Do we have peace with the invaders?"

"We'll find out soon. Methusal invited their Presidente to come here for peace talks. We hope he'll sign the agreement then."

"That would be good."

"We hope so."

"I'm glad to see you both. I just wish Deccia and Timaeus were here, too."

"I'm glad *you're* all right," Hendra returned. "We were worried when Dastn told us what happened."

She swallowed a lump in her throat. "Did he say anything good about me?"

Hendra glanced at Doc. Dastn and Doc were cousins. It seemed as if she wanted him to answer that question.

Dryly, he replied, "He said you were uncontrollable. And he didn't look happy just now. What have you done to him?"

"Nothing!" Tears ached in her throat, but she determinedly swallowed them back. "We had a fight. It was my fault."

"Apologize. And treat him right," he advised. "He's a good guy."

"Don't you think I know that?"

"You have feelings for him, don't you?" he guessed with surprising gentleness.

She sniffed. "You've been halfway around the world. How would you know?"

"Aali." With compassion, Hendra touched her shoulder. "We care about you. And we can see you're upset."

"You're starting to grow up," Doc said. "Your feelings are natural."

"I'm not *starting* to grow up! I *am* grown up. I'm sick of people treating me like a child!"

"Is that why you fought with him? Because you're tired of him thinking of you like a child?"

Could it be true? "Maybe."

Doc's next words were infuriatingly reasonable. "You're sixteen, and he's four years older."

She rolled her eyes. "Please. Is that all you guys think about? Age?"

Doc smiled. "No."

Hendra frowned at him.

"I'm not a baby," she insisted. "He has to stop treating me like one. My feelings are just as real as...as Deccia and Timaeus' are!"

"Tell him how you feel, then," Doc advised.

"Why? So he can laugh at me?"

"He won't laugh at you."

"No. He'll give me the same dumb speech you just gave me."

"Maybe not."

"Oh, please. You know he will. He's too..."

"Decent? Honorable? A friend to you, even though you drive him crazy?"

"How do you know?"

"Dastn and I are cousins. We talk. I have a pretty good idea of what's going on."

She looked down. "Exactly, then. All that."

"Aren't those qualities the reason why you like him so much?"

She didn't answer. "What about Dastn? If he tells you everything, then what does he feel about me?"

"Ask him."

"He's mad at me."

"Apologize."

"I will. When he comes back."

They both smiled at her. Impulsively, she hugged them both. "I *am* glad to see you. And I can't wait to see Methusal. I have some shocking, important news for her."

△ △ △ △ △

"I'm Trori." The little girl beside Aali spoke up, evidently tired of being ignored. "And that's Rartn. My brother."

Hendra went down on her knees, so she'd be on an equal level with them. "I'm pleased to meet you." She smiled. "I'm Hendra."

Trori smiled back and looked at Doc. "Who are you?"

"I'm Doc." He bent and shook her hand with solemn formality.

"Do you heal people?" Trori asked with interest.

"I try."

"Can you heal mistemper? Papa says GG has it. It's why she's as mean as a whip."

Aali snorted.

"Who is GG?"

"My great-grandmother." With round, entreating eyes, Trori said, "Can you fix her? I love her. But sometimes she scares me. I want her to get all better."

A twitch of amusement pulled at Doc's mouth, and he glanced at Hendra. "I can't promise anything. But I'll talk to her, if she'll allow it."

Movement flickered at the front gate, and Methusal and Behran entered, followed more slowly by Calbn, Captain Hil, and Mentàll.

Mentàll's face looked pale, but he appeared to have made the long walk from the ship with little ill effect. Hendra noticed his long glance at Methusal and Behran. A muscle twitched in his jaw.

Hendra had been worried about him lately. He'd been cold and distant ever since his fight with Methusal a few days earlier. But his cold mask was just that—a mask. Years of reading her cousin allowed her to see the small clues that proved he was upset and deeply unhappy. Hendra had no idea what had happened, but it was clear the two had had a terrible fight. Equally clear, they were both still hurting. And, based upon a comment she'd overheard Methusal tell Behran, the Rolbani girl did not trust Mentàll anymore.

Hendra wished she could help. But whatever pit Mentàll had dug for himself, he'd have to dig himself back out. She was under no illusions that he was innocent in the matter. But she did hate to see him so unhappy.

A small hand grabbed hers. "Will you eat lunch with me?" Trori asked.

Hendra smiled back. "I'd love to. Thank you."

"Good!" The little girl tugged her toward the mansion. Over her shoulder, she told Doc, "You can come, too."

Amusement deepened a dimple into his cheek. "I would be honored."

Hendra offered Doc her free hand, and when he took it, he murmured in her ear, "You have a gift with children."

"So do you." She grinned. "You're a charmer."

"How many orphaned children do you care for, back in Dehre?"

"Eleven." Wistfulness caught at her heart. She missed them. It had been a long time. She hoped they were all doing well.

"You would make a wonderful mother."

Hendra flushed. She'd never allowed herself to think about having children. Considering her paralyzing fear of men, it had seemed inconceivable. But with Doc...it almost seemed possible.

She flushed again, but her hands felt suddenly cold and clammy. *Was* it possible? Or was she fooling them both into hoping for something that could never be?

Doc's grip tightened. "What's wrong?"

"I just..." She offered a wobbly smile. "I just hope I make it that far."

His smoky gaze ensnared hers. With quiet confidence, he said, "You will."

Trori's tug on her hand provided a welcome distraction. "There's GG. Come on. You can meet her now."

△ △ △ △ △

"Thusa!" Aali grabbed Methusal's arm before she could slip into the room that she would share with Hendra. "Come over here."

Methusal wondered what her cousin was up to now.

Moving with exaggerated stealth, Aali urged Methusal into a small room off of the main hall. It was lined from floor to ceiling with shelves containing parchments and books. A wooden table and chairs took up most of the remaining floor space. Late afternoon sunlight streamed in. It smelled faintly of dust and sun toasted wood.

Her cousin peeked out the door, quickly checked both ways down the hall, and shut the door.

"What's this about?"

"The super spy mission you gave me." Her eyebrows arched meaningfully. "I completed it, and I have all the answers you want."

Methusal didn't have the heart to tell her that Mentàll had already confessed his plan. Well...*part* of his plan. Maybe her cousin knew more. Curiosity grew, laced with a feeling of dread. "That's great. How did you do it?"

She rolled her eyes. "You don't want to know. But here's the facts: Mentàll made an Alliance with almost all of the chiefs of Koblan. I think Calbn is helping him, but I don't have proof." She shuddered. "Calbn's *not* nice. He has a nasty temper."

Interesting.

Methusal said, "Mentàll told me he wants to set up a government. He thinks all the communities should work together to face Zindedi threats."

Aali's face fell. "Then you *know*, already?"

"He didn't tell me every detail. I think he's hiding something. What else did you find out?"

"Not much. I read the Alliance. It looked like all the chiefs signed it. All except for Uncle Erl."

"You're sure?" The sick feeling in her chest felt like a lump of ore. She had been right, then. He was hiding something from Rolban.

"Yes. I double-checked, because it seemed so strange. So why would Mentàll form an alliance with everyone except for Rolban?" She gasped. "It's a plot, isn't it? He wants everyone to come together and attack Rolban!"

"I'm not..."

"Ore means power," Aali said sagely. "If Mentàll and Calbn can control all the ore on Koblan, that means they'd control the most important substance in the world."

The idea seemed both far-fetched and terrifying. "Did the Alliance state their purpose in banding together?"

"No. Only something about the good of Koblan. What is it, Thusa?"

"Nothing." But this didn't bode well. Not at all. Why had Mentàll excluded Rolban from the negotiations? What was he hiding? Suddenly desperate to be alone and think, she said, "Thank you. You've done a wonderful job. Now I've...I have to figure out what to do with this information."

"You're welcome. Oh, and Thusa? I'm investigating something else, too. I think you'll find it *very* interesting. But I have more research to do. I'll tell you about it later." A mysterious smile tugged at her lips.

If Methusal wasn't feeling so agitated, she might have been amused by her cousin's flair for the dramatic. "I can't wait to hear," she murmured.

Hopefully it didn't have anything more to do with Mentàll or his possibly selfish, greedy plots.

∆ ∆ ∆ ∆ ∆

Brooding over Aali's facts made Methusal tremble with anger. What was Mentàll hiding? Clearly, he hadn't told her everything on the boat, and no wonder. She walked faster. Well, he would tell her now.

She spotted Hendra in the dining room talking to a short, squat woman. Quietly, and with an apologetic look for the interruption, she asked, "Excuse me, but have you seen Mentàll?"

"He's talking with Calbn, Dastn, and a few runners in Calbn's office. Why? What's wrong?"

"Nothing—I hope. We'll see," Methusal murmured. As she waited for the Dehrien Chief to appear, she paced the dining room, and from time to time peeked down the hall at Calbn's closed office door.

The more time that passed, the more upset she felt. Was Mentàll planning to lead a united attack against Rolban? Did he still want to seize power over her community, like he had tried to do three years ago? Did he want to steal their ore, so he could gain power over the entire continent? Had he told the other Chiefs that they all needed to unite together and gain control of Rolban's ore, because it was the one vital thing they needed to be able to defend themselves against Zindedi?

Her heart thundered in sick, agitated anger. Surely none of those things were true!

Hendra cast several worried looks her way, but she soon disappeared to take care of her own affairs.

At long last, Calbn's door opened. Mentàll's harsh voice said, "Remember. Tell the chiefs they need to be here within the week."

More voices murmured, and Methusal paced faster, itching for him to come out so she could ask him a few sharp, heated questions. *No.* She drew a deep, calming breath. She would speak to him rationally.

She managed to smooth a pleasant expression on her face. When Dastn and the others passed by, they responded with quick smiles, unaware that she felt like a boiling volcano inside.

Last of all, Mentàll finally exited with Calbn. Methusal ground her teeth behind her smile. The Dehrien's cool blue gaze rested upon her. It seemed about to slide away, but then sharpened with perception.

Her false smile twitched wider. "Mentàll. May I have a word with you, please?"

Calbn sent her a dark, dismissive look, but Mentàll murmured a few words to him, and the Quasrian Chief disappeared down the hall.

Mentàll turned his full attention upon her. It was disconcerting, once again, to realize how big he was. And what a formidable foe he could be.

In low voice, he said, "*Now* you want to speak to me?" The subtle inflection on the first word was unmistakable. His expression looked remote, as if he disliked speaking with her, period. It hurt, but she tried to ignore it. After what she had just learned, it was for the best.

"Why can't you ever tell me the whole truth, Mentàll?"

"What do you mean?" Wariness tightened his features.

"You excluded Rolban from your new Alliance. You've talked to every chief on Koblan except for Rolban's. Why is that?"

To her surprise, his shoulders relaxed. "For one reason only. Rolban does not trust me. I had planned to invite your father to Quasr after the successful Zindedi mission. I have already given Timaeus the invitation. When Erl gets here, I'll discuss the Alliance with him."

"So you don't want to take over Rolban?" His glacial glare made her falter. "...Or steal our ore?"

"*No.*"

Relief made her feel dizzy. "Then why didn't you tell my father about the Alliance? Was it because you didn't want him to derail your plan before it even started?"

"Yes."

Even more taken aback by his stark admission, she said, "You didn't trust my father to give you a fair chance. But clearly you don't trust me, either. Why didn't you tell me your whole plan on the ship?"

"I do trust you, Methusal." His voice was harsh. "But it is hard to tell all of my hopes and plans to a woman who is determined to think the worst about me."

"I am not."

"You are. You run from me like an apte from its shadow." Anger hardened the words. "You *look* for reasons to distrust me."

"You're right. I am afraid. Part of me wants to trust you...more...more than *anything*." To her consternation, her voice wavered. "But then all of these questions keep coming up. Why didn't you tell me the whole truth at the beginning of the trip? Why did the Alliance have to be a secret from me? I *knew* all along that you were hiding something. It made me feel suspicious. And when it turns out my suspicions were right, it makes it even harder to trust you now. Because you still haven't told me everything, have you?"

Regret flickered, and uncertainty, too. His warm hand closed around hers. "Come. I will tell you everything."

She allowed him to lead her into a small room off the main hall. He shut the door, so they were alone for the first time in days.

She pulled her hand free. "I have hard questions for you, Mentàll. Please tell me the whole truth. About *everything*."

He crossed his arms. His features looked carved in stone, but determined, as if his mind was made up. "Ask me anything, Methusal, and I will answer you."

"You've waited to tell my father about the Alliance. He'll learn about it here, with all of the other chiefs present. Did you plan it this way so the chiefs would pressure him into signing the agreement?"

"No. I hoped that all of Erl's questions could be answered at once, in an open discussion. Then he could make an informed decision."

"With some gentle coercion thrown in for good measure?"

"I need Erl. I need Rolban, and I need you. To face the Presidente's demands, we must all stand together."

"You mean you need Rolban's ore under the control of your Alliance. Then you will control what the Presidente so desperately wants."

"Methusal." Weariness pulled at the lines of his mouth.

"Tell me the truth, Mentàll. *All* of it. I mean it. What is your ultimate plan after my father signs your Alliance, and after the Presidente signs the peace agreement?"

He drew a deep breath. Only the emotions flickering across his face gave clue to his internal struggle. It must go against every one of his self-protective instincts to bare his deepest plans and desires to her. And to trust her with them. How many people had he truly trusted in his life? Not many. ...If any at all.

He said, "Koblan will need a Presidente. This Presidente will lead the continent and speak to the leaders of other countries, like Zindedi." Harshly, he finished, "I want to be that person."

So, he finally admitted his deep lust for power. She nodded. "I guessed that back on the ship." Heaviness settled in her heart. "Now, will you tell me the deepest truth? How do you intend to steal that power over us all?"

The pale blue eyes flashed freezing ice. "I do not steal, Methusal. I will put in my bid to be elected Presidente of Koblan. Any or all of the other chiefs can contest me in that bid. The man with the most votes will win."

"An election?"

"We will make laws to determine how long a man may remain Presidente. Then a new election will be held."

She eyed him for the first time with doubt...and hope. It sounded like a good plan. And strategically sound for the governance of Koblan, too. "How much power would a Presidente wield over the rest of us?"

"That is yet to be determined. But I have drawn up a plan."

"Of course you have," she murmured. "How much power do you desire?"

His eyes flashed. "As much as necessary to act swiftly against threats. And the power to suggest new laws and to direct campaigns to strengthen Koblan's inner structure."

"Sounds pretty broad," she said softly. "We'd need a trustworthy man in a role that large."

"I am that man."

She eyed him. Mentàll was a strong, confident man, and a brilliant strategist. He possessed many qualities that would make an excellent Presidente. All except for one. "Tell me. If you win, how hard would it be for you to relinquish power at the end of your term?"

"I will put in another bid to be Presidente."

Not the answer she was looking for. "Would you be able to give up power?"

"I must follow the laws, just as all future Presidentes will. Both Koblan and you will have to trust me, one step at a time."

"Trust," she agreed softly. "That is always the core issue, isn't it?"

"Trust is your choice. I have told you more than I have told anyone else."

"Is that everything, then? You're not holding anything else back?"

"What do you want to know, Methusal? The Alliance and the role of Presidente will evolve as I speak with the other chiefs."

"I know." Was she being unreasonable, expecting him to spell out the entire future for her? Trust was her choice, but could she take that leap of faith? Could she forget the past, and all that he had done to Rolban, and to her? At heart, was he no longer the insatiably power hungry man she had met in that jail cell years ago? The man who had held a knife to her throat because she'd threatened his plan to take over Rolban? Had he truly changed?

She wanted to believe him. She wanted to trust him.

And she *did* know him much better now. He'd protected and saved her life many times. She did believe that he would never hurt her. He said that he cared for her. Maybe that was enough.

She hated the cold distance that had grown between them. She hated being distant from him, period.

While she still wasn't ready to blindly step forward into a relationship with him, surely, at the very least she could give him the respect and trust due a friend. He had certainly earned that much. "Thank you for trusting me with the truth."

Relief eased the tension from his features. Triumph flickered. "Then all is well between us."

"We are friends, Mentàll. I can't promise more." For now, she needed to tread carefully where he was concerned. The core issue of trust still needed to be laid to rest. Perhaps in the coming days, as the talks about the Alliance advanced, that would happen. For now, though, she would think with her head, and not with her heart.

Frustration glimmered again. "You are afraid," he said harshly.

"Friendship is all I can offer. Accept it or not."

"I will accept it," he said with a soft edge to his voice. "For now. But I will pursue much more."

"Accept what I can give you."

Uncertainty flickered for the first time. "Do not do this."

"Do what?"

"You insist on putting a wall between us. I will strip it to the foundation, if I must."

She turned away.

"Methusal!" Anguish roughened his voice.

A glance back saw the raw emotion etched into his features, and it hit her hard. "Don't look at me like that."

"I have a heart, Methusal," he said in an uneven voice. "Stop dismissing me as if I mean nothing to you."

She closed her eyes, unable to look at him. "I'm sorry."

When he was vulnerable like this, and she could see his heart, she utterly couldn't resist him. It reminded her of the pain he'd revealed to her when he had told her about being abused as a child. It also reminded her of the closeness they'd shared in Zindedi, and the heartbreak she'd felt when he had almost died on the ship. She cared too much for him. "Please. Don't make this any harder than it is."

"Your engagement to Behran is a lie."

Methusal's lashes fluttered. He didn't know how true that was, and she felt guilty about furthering the deception. But she still needed to tread carefully.

A few more days of distance and carefully moving forward in her relationship with Mentàll seemed like the prudent course of action.

"Thank you for telling me everything. I should go."

"*Methusal!*" He stepped toward her.

"Don't." She swiftly backed up, desperately afraid of succumbing to her own weak will regarding him. He stopped, and his expression said he did not like her fearful response. "Just accept it."

"I cannot," he said harshly.

"Please," she whispered. "Just..." Catching her bottom lip between her teeth, she wrenched the door open and fled.

△ △ △ △ △

Hendra looked up in surprise when Methusal burst into their room. The Rolbani girl looked distressed, and when she saw Hendra, she wheeled back around.

"Wait," Hendra said softly. "What did Mentàll do?"

Of course this had everything to do with her cousin.

Her friend hesitated, and then slumped onto her cot, head in her hands. For a few moments the only sounds were her soft, agitated breaths.

Hendra waited, feeling compassion. For being such fiercely independent individuals, she suspected both Methusal and Mentàll were fiercely lonely people, as well. Both were afraid to trust others with their emotions. She understood that only too well.

"I'm so confused." Methusal finally whispered. "I don't know what to *do* anymore."

"What did he do now?"

"He kept the Alliance a secret from Rolban. From me. I asked him on the *ship*..." Her voice caught. "I wanted so much to trust him, but he wouldn't tell me everything. I *knew* he hadn't. And when Aali told me, I confronted him. I demanded that he tell me everything."

"Did he?"

"Yes. I think so. But why wasn't he honest from the beginning? I *knew* he was hiding something. I knew it. He says he's told me everything now. But how do I know if that is true? How do I know if he's *still* hiding something from me?"

"He doesn't want to hurt you. Surely you know that."

"I know. I believe that. It's just..." The Rolbani girl searched for the right words. "I want to trust him, more than anything. But I'm afraid to."

"Why?"

"I'm afraid he's not the man I came to know in Carachki. I'm afraid I'm wrong about him. I'm afraid he'll break my *heart!*" Tears filled her eyes.

"Do you love him?"

She closed her eyes, but didn't answer.

Softly, Hendra said, "What about Behran? How does he fit into this? You're engaged to him."

"It's not..." With a quick agitated movement, Methusal abruptly stood. "Behran knows what's going on. I'm not misleading him." She paced the room.

Hendra didn't push for more information. "It sounds like you're confused. Maybe you need to take time away from both men."

"Really?"

"Yes. Definitely. If you like, I could tell Mentàll to step off for three or four days, and you can tell Behran the same."

Methusal visibly relaxed. "That does sound like a good idea."

She smiled. "All of us girls should get together and shop. Or go out for dinner tomorrow night."

"Do you really think that will help?"

"Yes. I think we all need to clear our heads."

"I thought you and Doc were doing okay."

"We are. But a little time away won't hurt."

"All right." Hope lifted Methusal's voice, and she sat down again. "Let's do it."

"After that stressful trip, it's just what we need." Although she hadn't admitted it, Hendra needed time to wrap her head around the idea of actually having a future with Doc.

Methusal lay back on the cot and rested her arm over her eyes. "I feel much better already." The relief in her voice was clear. "I just want to be *me,* and no one else for a while. Not Behran's...fiancée, not Mentàll's..." She shook her head. "No. I'm starting now. I won't think about either one of them."

"Good. I'll leave you alone for a bit. And I'll deliver the message to Mentàll."

"Thank you. I feel so much better. You have no idea."

Hendra left the room. She understood the need to escape, and to think. This retreat would help her, too.

She spotted her tall cousin at the end of the hall. "Mentàll!"

He waited for her to catch up. His discerning gaze scanned her face. "You are all right, little cousin?"

"Yes. I'm delivering a message for Methusal. It would be best to stay clear of her for a few days."

His brows wrenched together.

Hendra added softly, "She'll tell Behran to do the same. I think she's confused, Mentàll. About both of you."

His frown eased. "Good."

"But be careful. I think she's on the edge. Pressure might push her in a direction you don't like."

"I understand Methusal very well. I will give her space."

"Good luck." She wanted very much for Mentàll to be happy. She hoped one of them, at least, would enjoy a love that would last a lifetime.

∆ ∆ ∆ ∆ ∆

Dastn hadn't left yet after all, Aali quickly discovered. The news the kaavl team had carried from the invader land would need to be spread throughout Koblan as fast as possible. Dastn would be a part of the messenger team that accomplished it. When he did leave, he probably wouldn't be back for at least a week—maybe longer.

Right now, he was conferencing with Calbn and Mentàll, writing messages as fast as he could, and then coordinating with the other runners. He'd probably leave first thing tomorrow morning.

But she wouldn't let him leave until she'd apologized and made things right between them.

The children were in bed now, and Aali hobbled out to the courtyard. It was the only quiet place on the compound. The household was a hubbub of activity and excited plans.

She lay her crutches against the bench and looked up at the dark sky. Ryon wasn't up yet, so the stars looked like bright pinpoints in the dark sky. The flowers smelled heavenly, and filled the quiet space with a sweet, heavy fragrance.

It was late, and she was starting to feel sleepy. She didn't really expect that Dastn would come out here. But he'd leave first thing in the morning. She knew that. Maybe she'd wait out here all night, and catch him before he could leave the compound.

Aali giggled at the thought. Her cast would turn to mush in the dew.

More time passed. She really should go inside. Otherwise, she'd never wake up early enough tomorrow to catch him before he left. She took a final deep breath, drinking in the heavenly scent, and the quiet peace of the courtyard. Then she grabbed her crutches and maneuvered onto her feet.

"Going so soon?" Dastn's voice came from behind her, and she awkwardly spun.

"Dastn. How long have you been there?"

"A minute. Maybe two." He came out of the shadows.

"Why didn't you say anything?"

He didn't answer, just looked down at her, his dark eyes unreadable in the soft torchlights.

She reached for his hand. When he didn't pull away, she took it as a good sign. "I'm sorry," she said softly. "I said some horrible things to you. But I knew none of them were true."

"Then why did you say them?" He looked down at their loosely linked hands. His warm, strong fingers closed around hers.

Aali heaved a breath. Joy and delicious tingles rushed through her. "Hendra helped me realize that I'm tired of you treating me like a little girl. I'm not. I feel the same things as any other woman."

"You're not eighteen."

"I know. But I'm not twelve, either. Don't treat me like I am."

"Aali, I won't take advantage of a sixteen-year-old girl."

"As if you would take advantage of anyone," she scoffed.

"We can be friends. Nothing more." Unsmilingly, his gaze held hers.

"All right. Friends." It wasn't fine, but what else could she do? "Will you forgive me?"

"I can't help but forgive you. I can't help a lot of things where you're concerned."

"What do you mean?"

"I mean," his thumb brushed her knuckles, and then he released her hand. "I can't seem to escape being drawn into whatever web you're spinning."

She smiled. "Am I spinning a web around you? That sounds so wicked."

"Not wicked. But inescapable."

"I like you, Dastn. A lot," she said, with her heart in her throat. "You're a great guy. I want you to know that."

"Thanks. So we're friends?"

"Yes." *For now,* Aali finished silently. Because her feelings for this man just continued to grow, and she couldn't seem to escape them, either.

"I'd better go in. I have an early start tomorrow."

"I'm glad you came out. I was going to get up early tomorrow and track you down," she confessed. "I didn't want you to leave still mad at me."

One corner of his mouth curled up in that special smile, just for her. "Sounds like something you would do."

"And be safe," she told him.

"I'll be back in a week. Mentàll is sending me and a few other runners out to request that all the chiefs of Koblan get here as soon as possible."

She nodded.

"Come on. I'll walk you inside."

She swung on her crutches beside him, and stopped outside her room. She looked up at him, feeling shy all of a sudden. "'Bye, Dastn."

His gaze ran over her face. It looked dark and gentle. "'Bye, Aali." He grinned a little. "Stay out of trouble."

It was hard to smile and glare at him at the same time.

With a wave, he disappeared down the hall. Aali sighed, her heart beating fast. She felt warm inside. That Dastn. He always knew just how to get under her skin. Now, if only she could find a way to break down that wall he'd placed between them.

Chapter Fifteen

"GG WANTS TO SEE YOU. She's cantankerous," Aali warned.

From the little Aali had told Methusal, the unpredictable old lady sounded like someone she should meet.

Her cousin showed her into a little sitting room cluttered with books, papers, and furniture. A slightly hunched old lady with ore gray hair sat at a little table, stirring tea. She turned as they entered, and Methusal's breath caught in her throat. Her eyes were such a pale blue that they looked almost colorless.

"I'm Methusal," she smiled. "Pleased to meet you."

"Call me GG. Everyone does." Her eyes narrowed. "Leave us, Aali."

Aali sent Methusal a speaking glance and shut the door behind her.

"So. You're Methusal. Aali has spoken of you." The old lady's almost colorless eyes continued to watch her intently, as if trying to bore a hole straight into her soul. "Are you as good at kaavl as I hear?"

"Probably." It was an honest statement.

The old lady cackled. "Good. I like you. Now, tell the truth, young woman. Will you make the right decision?"

"About what?"

"Don't be a fool." GG slurped tea. "You haven't set a date yet, have you?"

She finally followed the elderly woman's thoughts. Her engagement to Behran. Well, her *false* engagement to Behran. She hated continuing the deception, and struggled to find an answer that wasn't an outright lie. "Awhile back we set the wedding to take place in six weeks."

"Mmmhuh." GG sniffed, and snapped, "Do you know your own mind?"

"I'm not sure what you mean." Uneasily, she wondered why it felt as if the old lady could see straight into her heart. And why would she want to do so?

"Coward. Face your destiny."

"What?"

"Take advice from an old woman. I made the mistake you're about to make. There's no going back. No going back."

"I know my mind." But she didn't. Not really. How could this old woman know that she was struggling to make sense of her feelings for Mentàll?

"Don't be a fool, girl."

A knock came at the door. "GG?" It was Calbn's voice.

Methusal stood. "I should go. It was nice to meet you."

"You can't run away from the truth. It always catches you. Pray it won't be too late."

Chapter Sixteen

Day 19

It had felt wonderful to ignore all of her problems—namely Mentàll—over the last several days. Methusal had enjoyed shopping, chatting, and playing whaal and several new card games with her friends. She'd grown to know Sozla better, and liked her sharp wit. Aali and the Eerporian girl had often wandered off together, looking at hats or other trinkets.

Behran had thought it was a good idea for her to take time away from the Dehrien Chief. She felt guilty for continuing to take advantage of him, and for continuing the deception of their engagement. She hoped she wasn't making things worse for him by doing so.

And whatever Hendra had said to her cousin worked. Mentàll kept his distance. However, whenever they passed in the hall he murmured, "Methusal" in a low voice. She responded with a polite murmur, and he thankfully kept walking. However, that low, harsh voice of his vibrated like the finest instrument down her nerve endings. She almost wished he wouldn't speak to her at all, because it made her think about him for a long time afterward.

As she relaxed and laughed with her friends, ate a few meals out, played card and board games at the mansion, and spent time alone, something inside of her slowly began to heal. Until then, she hadn't fully realized how much the time in Carachki had cut deep wounds into her soul; namely, being tortured by General Fitrn, and the Presidente's attempted attack in his office. Not to mention the terror of

Mentàll being shot and hovering for days on the brink of death.

So much had happened. No wonder she felt so raw and vulnerable inside. She needed this time to heal and take care of herself.

As the days passed, she missed her sister more than ever, and prayed for her several times a day. She missed Deccia's wisdom and practical advice. She could use that right now.

But her mother would be coming soon. Thank goodness. Methusal longed to see Hanuh. Perhaps her empathic mother could help her figure out what to do about Mentàll.

CHAPTER SEVENTEEN

HENDRA SIPPED her cooling breakfast tea and reflected that the last few days had been rather peaceful and pleasant. She wondered how many more safe, idyllic days remained. Already, Calbn had ordered guards to be stationed all over the compound, on every street corner in Quasr, and of course many men watched the bay, on alert for the possible soon arrival of the Presidente's ship. A few carried guns. The others bristled with knives and bows and arrows.

She took another sip of the minty tea. She had enjoyed spending time with Methusal, Sozla, and Aali over the last few days. Yesterday Methusal had invited Hendra and Sozla to visit Rolban after the Quasr talks ended. She'd invited them to stay for as long as they liked; even as long as a month. Hendra remembered that was when Methusal's wedding to Behran would take place, although Methusal hadn't mentioned that fact.

The idea of visiting Rolban tempted her. Even though she wanted to go home and see the Dehrien orphans again, nothing else awaited her in Dehre. And, knowing Mentàll, he'd be gone traveling the continent, trying to secure the votes of the other chiefs so he could become Presidente. She didn't want to be alone in Dehre.

Then again, Mentàll was still recovering from his injury. He probably wouldn't be ready to travel the continent for another week or two after the talks. Maybe she'd stay with him in Quasr, and then go to Rolban and stay until the wedding. Two weeks didn't seem quite as long to be a guest as four did.

"Hendra." Above her, Doc's voice made her jump. He sat down on the bench beside her. She hadn't seen much of him over the last few days, although they usually shared at least one meal together. "Would you like to help me out this morning?"

Her brows flew together with worry. "The twins still aren't doing well?"

"No. Their skin is still yellow."

"Quasr's doctor won't try your new treatment?"

"No," he said grimly. "But Lylitha will. She turned the care of the twins over to me this morning."

"Quasr's doctor can't be happy."

"He's not." Doc said this through tight lips.

Hendra wondered if Quasr's middle-aged doctor had caused a scene. "I'd be happy to help. What can I do?"

"We'll walk with them in the sunshine. One of my instructors in Wyen believed that fluids and sunlight can help heal yellow-skinned babies."

Sounded harmless enough. "Of course. I'd be happy to help."

Hendra deposited her dirty mug in the kitchen and then followed Doc to the nursery, where a worried looking Lylitha waited. Dark shadows underscored her eyes, and her long black hair was plaited into a straggly braid. Both tiny babies slept in their baskets, little arms crooked up around their heads. Their skin had a sickly, yellowish pallor.

Doc gently lifted one dark-haired infant. Hendra had seen those hands work with quick, skilled precision to save a man's leg during the Quasr War. They were capable, gentle hands. "You're a fighter, *palteect*," he murmured. "You'll beat this."

He lay the infant on a towel padded table, and with quick skill, peeled off the baby's outer garments. He left on the cloth diaper. The child screwed up his face and let out a pitiful mewl of outrage. Hendra followed his example with the other infant.

Lylitha looked on with a worried expression. "They won't get too cold? They won't get sick outside?"

Calmly, Doc soothed, "It's warm in the garden. Hendra and I will hold them the entire time."

"If you're sure." Lylitha bit her lip.

"We'll be gone for an hour. Take the time to rest. It's important that you take care of yourself." When Lylitha frowned and opened her mouth, Doc firmly but gently said, "A fresh, happy mama will do the twins good."

Lylitha's shoulders drooped, but she nodded.

Hendra cradled the miniature boy close in her arms. Gradually his tiny, spitting cries of anger subsided. Out in the garden, Doc found a bench in the sun, and Hendra sat beside him. Warmth toasted her skin, and soon the infant in her arms drifted off to sleep. Doc's, however, continued to belt wails from his tiny lungs.

Doc rose and put the child against his shoulder. With gentle pats on the infant's back, he strolled the garden, murmuring soothing words to the baby's fuzzy black head. The bleats quieted, but when Doc tried to sit down again, the child let out another lusty howl. Doc chuckled, and kept walking. Finally, the child's head sagged on his shoulder, his mouth slack.

"You're good with him," Hendra whispered when he sat down again.

He smiled. "Babies just need a lot of love and a little patience. Most things sort themselves out with time."

He'd make a great father.

Doc glanced at her. In his eyes, she saw the same gentle, steadfast patience he'd shown the child. *He'd be a wonderful husband, too.* He'd love and accept her, just as she was.

Warm flutters beat inside of her. Could she marry him? ...If he asked her, of course.

When he looked at her like this, she wanted to believe that a future was possible for them. She wanted to believe it so much it hurt. She wanted to throw open her heart to a future that—in this sparkling sunshine—seemed only full of wonderful possibilities.

But for now, she would enjoy these peaceful moments. For soon this idyllic bliss would end. The future and all of its problems waited outside the garden walls.

Soon the Presidente would come.

Chapter Eighteen

Day 21

THE LONG DAYS in the Zindedi capitol passed slowly for Deccia. She watched the palace every day at work. Few people came and went into the Presidente's compound. It was quiet with the Presidente gone.

Riln had heard no more about Timaeus, either. Deccia prayed for him constantly, and her mind twisted in endless circles, trying to figure out how to rescue him from prison. Unfortunately, the palace was a fortress. The guards did not allow Riln access inside the building. His job on the grounds was basically useless, except for gleaning occasional tidbits of information.

The Koblani team needed to get inside that palace. Today, at long last, a new idea had begun to germinate in her mind. She'd broach it to the others after dinner tonight.

To pass the time in the evenings, she'd taken to playing whaal with the men. The game of strategy kept her mind fully engaged, so she couldn't worry about Timaeus—at least that was true for a little while.

"That's *it!*" In disgust, Riln threw down his cards and levered himself to his feet. "That game makes my head hurt." He rarely lasted longer than two rounds. Gulping the dregs from his bottle, he shuffled to the counter. "Hey, apte!" His voice rose to a belligerent bellow. "You been drinking my stash?"

"You're the only one who drinks." Goric dealt neat piles for Deccia and himself.

Riln cursed and yanked on his jacket.

"You coming back?" Goric asked.

"What's it to you, apte?"

"Take your key."

Riln mumbled something filthy and headed for the door. "I'll be gone a couple hours, loser. Plenty of time for you to make it with the lunatic." He laughed. "Wait. You'd need equipment for that." Chuckling loudly to himself, he slammed the door behind him.

Goric's face turned a dull red.

"Ignore him," Deccia advised.

"I always do."

They each played two preliminary cards, and then discarded one. Goric's color retreated, returning his skin to its normal pale color. His murky eyes sharpened to intense gray as he concentrated into the game. Deccia enjoyed matching wits with him. She also noticed that he immersed himself so completely into whaal that his true self always crept free at one point or another. She wondered if he realized it.

Deccia smiled at her cards. "You're going down, Goric. Might as well start planning breakfast right now."

A tiny smile glimmered. He plucked a card from his hand. "You haven't seen all my cards yet."

"I don't need to. Let's see. I think I'd like fried cakes..."

"How about a pit o'three?" A card slapped down and he shoved it toward her.

Deccia's jaw dropped. "That's not fair. We just started the game!"

"I like to win. Pay up."

With reluctance, she scooted her three highest ranking cards over to him. "Slug," she mumbled. "But you haven't beaten me yet."

He gave her highest ranking card a smacking kiss. "But I will. It's only a matter of time."

"You're smug and annoying."

He grinned. "Did I tell you how much I like baked tubers with egg sauce?"

"I am *not* getting up in the middle of the night to cook breakfast for you." Goric usually left for work before dawn, which meant he ate breakfast at an unconscionably early time.

"You don't have to. Tomorrow's my free day, remember? I can sleep in."

She growled, and frowned harder in concentration. Goric won the game, to her annoyance. However, she challenged him to a rematch, and felt satisfied when he accepted.

He said, "If you win, you're freed from breakfast duty. But if *I* win... Let me think about what I want. In addition to breakfast, of course."

"I have a new bet." It was time to broach her new idea. However, suggesting it to Goric presented a bit of a problem. She didn't want to imply that his job wasn't helping the rescue mission. He did bring in a little money. But maybe her plan would solve two problems at once.

"What?" His posture was still relaxed, his expression trusting.

She hated to break that. "The Presidente will arrive in Koblan soon. He'll probably be back here within three weeks."

Goric visibly retreated behind his mask again. "So?" His face looked a little hard.

"I'm frustrated because we haven't come up with a plan to rescue Timaeus yet."

Slowly, he dealt the cards. "What do you want to do?"

"Riln can't get into the palace. The only way to get Timaeus out would be to put one of us on the inside. I think one or both of us should apply again for jobs in the palace."

Goric said nothing for a long time. "I guess that'll be me," he said finally, and picked up his cards.

"Maybe both of us should apply. If we both got jobs..."

"No." He flipped down two cards.

Deccia paid little attention to the cards she lay down. "Why not?"

"Methusal was at the ball. Most of the servants probably saw her. Your glasses help, but no. It's too dangerous."

"Timaeus is my husband. I'll do any..."

"Anything. Right." His tone was difficult to decipher. "You'll do anything to rescue him. I understand that. But a suicide mission doesn't strike me as very bright."

"Then what do you suggest?"

"I'll apply under one condition."

"What?"

"You stay clear of the palace."

She frowned. "You're a hardheaded man."

A smile glimmered. "Finally. You see the real me."

"I'll agree with your deal for now. But if you don't get a job, all bets are off."

"Okay. Are you going to take one of my cards? Or will you give me the advantage?"

"I won't give you anything." She snatched up his heavily embossed card.

Another smile gleamed, and then vanished. He remained withdrawn, however, and lost in his thoughts for the remainder of the game. Deccia won.

"Another game?" she asked.

"I'm tired." He scooted back his chair.

"Can I ask you something?"

"What?"

"Why do you do that? Withdraw, I mean, and hide inside yourself."

"We all need walls. Some of us need thicker ones than others."

"Why?"

"Maybe I have more to hide." He headed for the cabinet.

"What do you mean?"

Back to her, he said, "Let it go."

"If you never let anyone in, you're going to be awfully lonely."

Goric stilled for a moment, and then shoved the drawer shut. "Maybe I've accepted that."

How could he so matter-of-factly accept such a bleak fate?

"That's a shame," she told him. "Even though you can be stubborn and hardheaded, you're a pretty nice guy underneath it all. Choosing to close yourself off is a waste, if you want my opinion."

"We are who we are." His gray eyes met hers, murky now. "Some things will never change." The bleak statement sounded faintly ominous.

An unexpected shiver slid down her spine. "Good night."

"'Night."

Curled up in her room, Deccia wondered why Goric chose to close himself off from everyone. But when she fell asleep, she dreamed about Timaeus. She ran from door to prison door, pounding on them, and calling out his name. There were so many cells. He was locked inside one of them. If only she could find him, she could set him free.

Chapter Nineteen

ALL OF THE KOBLANI CHIEFS had finally arrived, except for Erl and Wyen's chief.

Methusal hoped her parents would arrive today. The Presidente could come any day now. His possible arrival made her feel uneasy.

Mentàll showed no signs of worry.

The flurry of preparations Calbn's servants had made for the arrival of the chiefs and their families settled down into a quiet routine. Now a huge group crowded the dining hall every night. All of the chiefs treated Mentàll with deferential respect. A few appeared to admire him.

Sozla's father and mother had arrived this morning, and the stocky, balding Chief of Eerpor had shaken Mentàll's hand warmly, and then directed the Dehrien Chief to a quiet corner to talk.

Sozla had immediately grabbed her mother's hand and urged her over to meet Methusal and Behran.

"Hello." Sozla's mother extended a slim hand to Methusal. "I am Ralnta."

"Nice to meet you. I'm Methusal."

Ralnta was a lovely, dark-haired woman who only looked a decade older than Sozla. Both mother and daughter were petite, with lively dark eyes. Methusal liked Ralnta immediately, and Behran appeared to, also.

Ralnta shook Behran's hand firmly, and her smiling dark eyes seemed to take his measure in one quick, intent glance. A smile said she liked what she saw. She turned to her daughter, "You have made many good friends on this trip, Sozla. You are indeed blessed."

"We are the lucky ones," Behran said. "Without Sozla, I would never have figured out the detonators for the bombs."

Sozla blushed. "It was a team effort."

Ralnta sent Behran an approving smile. "Of course. Koblan is fortunate to have had two such gifted engineers on the mission. If it is all right, I will take my daughter away. We have not had a chance to speak in weeks. But perhaps we can meet later, and have lunch?"

"We would like that." Behran watched Sozla go, and then turned to Methusal. "She's told me about her father. He's a hard man. I'm glad she has a mother like Ralnta."

Methusal nodded. "I hope my mother gets here today. I can't wait to talk to her."

Behran's deep blue gaze settled on her face. "How are you doing, Thusa?"

"The same." In other words, still conflicted.

She'd resumed spending time with Behran, particularly at the evening meal. He treated her with easy friendship, which quieted her fears about their pretend engagement. He did not appear to expect anything more from her, for which she was grateful. Despite what a wonderful man Behran was, the time away from both men had only confirmed her decision that he was not the man for her. Whether or not Mentàll was the man she hoped and needed him to be remained to be seen.

During the last few days, Mentàll had still made no effort to directly approach her; perhaps because he'd been so busy helping Calbn ready Quasr for the arrival of Koblan's chiefs and the Presidente. And, as the chiefs arrived, he had spent a great deal of time speaking with each of them.

For the most part, his only comment to her had remained a quiet "Methusal" in passing.

The day before yesterday, however, he had stopped midstride and his long fingers had gently touched her shoulder. In a low voice, he said, "You are well? Do you have all you require?" His manner mirrored that of a husband who had been distracted too long by work, but wanted his wife to know he cared for her. In that moment, the intimacy they'd shared in Zindedi rose like a consuming wave and threatened to swallowed her up. She'd murmured, "I'm fine. Thank you," and hurried away.

Clearly, her feelings had not changed at all. But her uncertainty concerning their relationship remained. Should she take that step of faith and fully trust him now? Was she foolishly clinging to her fears just to protect her heart?

She didn't know what to do, and desperately needed some good advice. That was part of the reason why she longed to see her mother. She needed to talk to someone about Mentàll, but that person could not be Behran.

"I'll be fine," she told him now with a small smile. "Thank you for asking."

With a serious look, he said, "What are friends for? You know you can tell me anything, Thusa. Any time. I'm here for you."

Her smile wobbled. "Thank you. I don't deserve you."

"Yes, you do," he said firmly, and pulled her into his arms. With a sigh, she hugged him back. If only he was the right man for her, everything would be so simple.

△ △ △ △ △

At the end of a pleasant lunch with Behran, Sozla, Ralnta, and Aali, Methusal's stomach felt uncomfortably full. "I think I need a walk. Those cheese tarts were too delicious."

Sozla laughed. "Yes. The chef has saved all his best recipes until now. I wonder what he will serve when the Presidente comes."

Behran groaned. He'd eaten five tagma tarts. "I'll take that walk with you."

"No need." That harsh voice spoke directly behind Methusal. She drew a startled breath. Mentàll's light touch felt disturbingly possessive. "Methusal and I have matters to discuss."

A faint frown flickered across Behran's features, and then vanished. "Be my guest."

"Your permission is appreciated." Mockery laced Mentàll's low tone.

Behran nodded to Methusal. "I'll see you later."

She gave him an answering smile and turned to Mentàll. For a moment, his sheer size unexpectedly surprised her. After a week of seeing him from a distance, his close proximity felt like a bit of a shock.

His discerning gaze ran over her features, and he smiled. "Come."

She followed him into Calbn's flower garden. It was warm out here, and smelled sweet. Buzzing insects flew from one green, lushly flowered plant to another. The air felt close and still, and slightly humid. The stone walls were as high as her head.

"Would you like to sit?" With chivalry, Mentàll indicated a bench.

"No, thank you."

"The Presidente will arrive soon." How like him, to state as a fact what others would only hope to assume. "Are you ready to resume your role as my wife?"

"Will that truly be necessary?" Perhaps she could save herself from several days of confusing intimacy with Mentàll. "Think about it," she urged. "If he comes, that means one of two things. Either you've won, or he's plotting to kill you. Either way, our fake marriage won't make any difference. The outcome is decided."

He smiled, and it wasn't a nice one. "I will put the fear of The One into him. He fears our unity. And I will give him more reason to fear if he tries to kill either one of us."

"Mentàll..."

"It would be foolish to discard any advantage over him, no matter how small. We will win peace with Zindedi by force or by their voluntary submission. Are you prepared to stand by my side and help me? Or will you continue to run from me? Choose now."

She scowled. "I'm not running from you."

"No? Isn't that why you wanted to keep distance between us all week?"

She didn't answer.

"It is time for you to face the future, Methusal. You are not a child. Give me your answer."

With annoyance, she retorted, "I'll help. Are you happy? Better yet, are you finished?"

"Good." His shoulders seemed to relax.

"If you're done..." She made to go around him.

His strong hand gripped her arm. "No, I am not finished, Methusal."

"Stop touching me."

His hand dropped. "Give Behran a message. When the Presidente comes, he is to stay away from you."

"To support the lie of our marriage?"

"Yes. It is only fair. Behran has enjoyed your company for the last few days. Now it is my turn."

"*Now* are you finished?"

"No. When the Presidente comes, we will live in the same quarters."

Methusal's jaw dropped, although she should not have been surprised. It made sense that they would live together in order to support their fictitious cover. However, the thought of living with him again, in such close quarters, frankly panicked her. "Not like in Carachki. I won't stay in the same room with you."

"We will share a suite of rooms. You will have the bedroom to yourself."

"Well, then. Good."

Mentàll smiled faintly. "Yes. It will be good."

She frowned. "Stop it."

Softly, he said, "You are running again, Methusal. Have you ever asked yourself why?"

"Because you're a ravenous wild beast? I don't want to be eaten up like...like one of your sweet tarts!"

Mentàll threw back his head and laughed. It startled her, and she stared in surprise. With a wolmite grin, he said, "Yes, you are right, Methusal. You are exactly like my favorite sweet tarts—only you are better. You are sweet and tart and beautiful and fiery. I can never get my fill of you. Looking at you makes me hunger, and kissing you makes me thirst."

"Mentàll," her face flamed hot and she stepped backward.

"I speak only the truth." His voice sounded gentle now. "I want these next few days with you. I want to prove exactly how much you mean to me."

She briefly closed her eyes. He'd make their time together incredibly difficult. It would be unbearably hard to resist him, because he planned to pull out all the stops to make her his, once and for all. That determined glint in his eyes said so.

"Don't," she whispered. "Just..."

"Give up? Never. And I will personally make sure Behran receives that message."

"I'm not *yours!*"

"Behran may be your fiancé, but he is not your husband."

"*You* are not my husband, either."

He only smiled. "You feel more married to me than you've ever felt engaged to Behran."

He was right. Frustrated by her response to him, and fed up with his arrogance, she snapped, "Are you finished? Because I'm going to take a walk with Behran."

His confident smile slipped. "Soon the game will end. Show him mercy, and tell him goodbye now."

Methusal ground her teeth. She left him alone in the garden.

△ △ △ △ △

Aali's squeals drew Methusal into the main hall after she'd reentered the mansion.

"Mama! Papa!" Methusal cried, and ran forward. Erl caught her in his arms and twirled her around, her feet barely off the floor.

Her mother was next. She hugged Methusal tightly. "We've missed you so much!"

"I've missed you, too, Mama." It felt like such a relief to be in her mother's arms. Finally, she no longer felt so alone.

Hanuh pulled back. "There now." She gently wiped a finger across Methusal's cheek. "I'm supposed to be the one crying. Not you."

"I'm so happy to see you. I'm glad you're both here." She turned to her father. "Did you know Mentàll wants to talk to you about an Alliance?"

"Yes. He explained everything in the letter he sent with Dastn."

She searched her father's eyes. "And you're not upset he kept it a secret from you?"

"I was at first. Then I realized he did it because he felt insecure. I can understand that."

Methusal couldn't imagine Mentàll being thought of as "insecure." Her confusion must have shown, because Erl chuckled. "He thought I could kill his plan. That's a compliment. But the Alliance is a good idea, and I would have told him so from the beginning."

"So you'll sign it."

"And I'll throw in my bid to become Presidente."

Methusal choked on a laugh. "So he told you that, too."

"He wants to hold the elections in Rolban. It's his way to make amends for keeping me in the dark. I'll take every concession he'll give."

Awareness prickled down her back. She turned.

"Mentàll." Erl shook the Dehrien Chief's hand. "I received your letters. I've made my decision."

"Would you like to speak privately?"

Methusal thought she detected a hint of uncertainty in his voice.

"Yes. And then I would like to speak to the other chiefs. Are they all here?"

"Wyen's should arrive later today."

"Good. We have much to discuss."

"I can show you to your room," Aali piped up.

"After you've settled in, meet me in Calbn's office," Mentàll invited.

"I'll be there shortly," Erl agreed.

After the luggage was dropped off in a spacious room dominated by a wide bed covered with a white, frilled comforter, Erl departed, and so did Aali.

Hanuh took Methusal's hand and pulled her down beside her on the bed. "Now. Tell me why you're so upset."

"You just got here. You don't need..."

"I'm your mother. Tell me." Softly, she said, "You look sad, Methusal. What can I do to help?"

She shook her head. "I'm such a mess. You have no idea."

"Start from the beginning."

So she did. She outlined the trip to Zindedi, the time she'd spent in Carachki as Mentàll's wife, the ball, and how Mentàll had been shot. The trip home and the subsequent problems took a few more sentences.

"How did you feel when he was shot?" Hanuh watched her with intent compassion.

"Awful. Like I was living in a nightmare. I was so scared. I couldn't leave him. Not until I knew he would make it."

"And then the arguments started again."

"Yes. I care about him so much, Mama, but he's such a complex, difficult man. All we ever do is fight and hurt each other, over and over again."

"Is that all you do?"

She flushed. "For our cover...in Zindedi...he kissed me." She didn't mention the other things they had done.

Hanuh made no comment. "What about Behran? He's waited patiently all this time. What do you feel for him?"

"I care about him." Methusal abruptly stood and began to pace.

Hanuh said, "Stepping back from both relationships has been a good idea."

"I have to tell you the truth. Behran and I...we're not engaged anymore."

Her mother frowned. "You're not? But I thought..."

"We're pretending to be engaged."

Hanuh's brows climbed her forehead. "Explain that, please."

Methusal did, to the best of her ability, and finished with, "I feel like I'm taking advantage of him. I am, aren't I? It's been the wrong thing to do?"

"Behran calls it what? A 'reconsideration' period? And this was his idea?"

"Yes."

"Has it helped?"

"Some, but I'm still so confused. I don't know what to do."

"Listen to your heart," Hanuh said simply.

"That's what Deccia said, but..."

"Let yourself *feel*. Stop judging your thoughts and feelings. And stop worrying about Behran. While I don't think pretending an engagement is the best idea, that's your choice, and his, too. Behran knows what he's doing. It's certainly unselfish of him, and it sounds as if he's trying to be the best friend he can be for you."

"I know. I'm so lucky. I don't deserve him, Mama. And I don't want this fake engagement to hurt him even more."

"He wants to protect you. I think *that* is making him feel happy. Behran is a big boy. But your real problem, it seems, is in trying to figure out your true feelings for Mentàll."

"Yes. And you haven't heard the best part. Mentàll and I have to pretend to be married again when the Presidente comes." She explained the ridiculous reason why. "I'll have my own room," she hastened to explain. "It'll be perfectly respectable."

Hanuh gave her a peculiar look. "Did you have your own room in Zindedi?"

She flushed. "No. But nothing happened. Well, not exactly..."

"I won't ask you to explain that. Here's my advice, if you want it."

"I do."

"Experience your time with Mentàll when the Presidente is here. Allow yourself to feel the truth in your heart."

"But if I do that, he'll dig in even deeper. I'm afraid I'll never get him out then."

"Don't be afraid of your feelings."

"But I *am* afraid of my feelings! I'm afraid I'll do something stupid, like fall in love with a man who still might be a wild beast, after all."

Hanuh gripped her hand. "I know you're afraid. And I agree that you need to be cautious. But you also need to discover the truth, don't you?"

"Yes. But how? What do you sense about him?"

Hanuh's eyes clouded, and she retreated into an empathic trance. After a long moment, she blinked. "He's changed. To a small degree. But he's a closed man, so it's hard for me to see deeper, into his heart."

"I know."

"If you love him, make the effort to find out who he really is. Stop pushing him away, and then maybe he'll let you deeper inside that heart of his."

Methusal smiled, and unexpectedly so did her mother. Hanuh said, "He's already let you in the cracks. But you know that, don't you?"

"I want to believe it, but I'm scared."

Hanuh patted her hand. "You'll figure it out. I have full confidence in you. Will you follow my advice?"

"I will."

△ △ △ △ △

Hendra sensed tension in the dining hall that night. The last of Koblan's chiefs had arrived, but the Presidente's ship still hadn't been spotted. She'd heard a few chiefs mutter under their breaths, wondering if the Zindedi leader would come at all.

He must, for the sake of peace, and for Mentàll's sake, as well,

Her cousin had worked hard for months forming the Alliance, and putting together and leading the mission to Zindedi. Not to mention formulating the peace plan. All of his hard work and the proof that he was fit to lead Koblan rested in part upon the Presidente's arrival and the events that followed. She wanted Mentàll to win the position of Koblan's first Presidente. He had earned it.

That afternoon the Koblani Alliance had been ratified, and the candidates for Presidente decided. Erl and the Chief of Wyen would contest Mentàll for the position. But for now, during the Zindedi Presidente's visit, the men had elected Mentàll as the interim Presidente, with full rights to negotiate with Zindedi on their behalf. Of course, all terms would be agreed upon by all of the chiefs before the final peace agreement was ratified.

It was obvious to Hendra that the chiefs respected Mentàll. If the Zindedi Presidente came, it would dramatically increase his chances of becoming Presidente. So much depended upon the cruel Zindedi leader. It was frightening.

If that wasn't enough, Mentàll's guards from Dehre had arrived this afternoon. He'd assigned one to her. She wasn't sure how she felt about a man stalking her every move. Especially since Hlmut was her youngest brother's best friend. She shivered. He was a big man with a thick neck.

Doc's fingers closed around hers under the table. He offered a small smile. "Want to walk on the beach?"

Happiness bubbled up, chasing away the worry. "I'd love to."

It was dark outside. With their fingers interlaced, they meandered down the main street.

"The twins are looking better," she said.

During the past several days she'd helped Doc sun the infants in the mornings and afternoons. She'd enjoyed every wonderful moment spent with him and the babies.

In bits and pieces, Doc had told her his dreams and plans for the future. He'd like to begin training young men and women in Tarst to become nurses and doctors. He believed Koblan needed more skilled physicians, and Hendra couldn't agree more. She wished she could be a part of Doc's plan. She'd love to learn more about healing people.

"I think the twins have turned the corner," he agreed now. "We'll know for sure in the next day or two."

They walked down the beach steps and onto the fine sand. She pulled off her shoes and left them beside the stairs. Doc did the same, and rolled up his pant legs.

She giggled. "Do you plan to wade in the water?"

He grinned. "Yes."

"You're crazy! That water has to be freezing."

"It's not. Come see," he coaxed.

She walked with him to the water's edge. Cold water swirled around her toes, and she squealed. "It's *cold*."

"Give it a minute. It'll warm up."

Hendra only remained beside him because she enjoyed being close to him, and his hand around hers felt warm and secure. To her surprise, the icy water did seem to warm up— a little, anyway—the longer her feet were immersed.

"You're right. I think. Or maybe my toes are turning blue."

He chuckled. "You can still feel them, can't you?"

"Yes. But I wouldn't want to go for a swim, that's for sure."

"Baby steps," he murmured, and urged her to walk on. He strolled the closest to the ocean, so water swirled around his ankles, but only tiny rivulets ran over Hendra's toes.

Baby steps. Holding Doc's hand now, walking with him like this, and even kissing him no longer frightened her. While these accomplishments made her feel happy, and gave her a sense of hope, none of them required deep emotional intimacy. True intimacy would mean stripping away the guards from her heart. Could she do it? Could she let him in? Could she be the woman he needed her to be? The woman she wanted to be.

These questions had rested heavily upon her heart for days. And over that period of time she'd thought of only one way to test the waters, so to speak. One way to figure out, once and for all, if she could overcome her fears.

Mentàll would utterly disapprove, but what he didn't know wouldn't hurt him.

Doc, however, was the one she'd need to convince.

"What are you thinking?" he asked.

Should she tell him her idea now? Nerves made her feel sick. Water swirled around her toes and ebbed away. She glanced out to sea, hoping for inspiration—or courage—to strike.

Twin yellow lights pierced the blackness.

"Look. What's that?"

Ryon's pale light didn't help much. The moon was at its half, and shimmered off of the dark, rippling water.

"A ship."

"One of ours?"

"It's too late to be a fishing boat."

"Maybe it's the Presidente."

"It probably is."

"We need to warn the others!"

Doc gave a short chuckle. "This isn't how I planned this evening to end."

"What do you mean?"

"We'll talk about it later, when we have more time." Still holding her hand, Doc set a quick pace for the steps, where they slipped on their shoes, and then hurried for the mansion.

She wondered what he had wanted to say. At the same time, she was relieved that she hadn't been able to tell him about her plan yet. Soon, though, she'd need to grit her teeth and take the plunge.

△ △ △ △ △

Methusal looked up when Hendra and Doc burst into the dining hall. Hendra ran over and whispered in Mentàll's ear. The Dehrien Chief stood. "The Presidente's ship has been spotted."

A murmur swelled. Excitement and dread filled her.

"I will go to the docks," Mentàll said. "A few chiefs may join me. We will welcome the Presidente's men, and invite them to visit the mansion tomorrow morning."

Every chief scrambled to his feet. It appeared that everyone wanted to be included in the initial delegation.

"For security purposes, only half of us should go." Mentàll glanced at Quasr's chief. "Calbn, we'll need twenty armed men to accompany us to the docks."

"Of course." Calbn swiftly exited.

Erl had risen too, but Hanuh wordlessly clutched his arm. With a smile, he patted it. "I'll be back soon."

Mentàll strode in Methusal's direction. Even so, she was surprised when he stopped beside her. With a hand on her shoulder, he murmured in her ear, "Transfer your belongings to my rooms tonight. The bedroom will be yours."

"But..."

"And take this." A warm, silky weight pooled into her palm. Their marriage necklace. A host of old feelings swamped her. The intimacy and familiarity of their closeness in Zindedi gripped her heart like a glove. "Wear it tomorrow morning when we meet the Presidente together."

Before she could speak, he was gone, striding to confer with the other chiefs.

Beside her, Behran said, "Now it begins."

"Will you help me move my things?"

Thanks to her earlier conversation with Mentàll, she had already packed for the move. Now it only took a minute to throw in a few extra necessities. Silently carrying her bag, Behran accompanied her to Mentàll's quarters.

She had never been inside the Dehrien Chief's rooms, and was glad Behran was with her for moral support. Much as Hanuh had encouraged her to honestly experience her emotions, the thought of being alone again with Mentàll made her heart pound with a bit of panic.

The main room of the suite contained a desk, chairs, and bookcases, all stained dark brown. On the right side of the room was a long couch. To the left, a wooden door led to a relief chamber, and straight ahead another door opened into a bedroom.

Methusal headed for this and dropped her bag inside. A large bed, framed in large-beamed, dark wood, and covered with a soft amber and ochre quilt dominated the room. A curtained window promised plenty of sunshine during the day.

It smelled of Mentàll. Of leather and male and power. And it felt like a man's room. Although his belongings were neatly stacked on the shelves, his presence felt so strong she felt she might drown in it.

A protective frown creased Behran's forehead. "He'd better stay out of here."

"He will." Not that it would make living with him any easier. "He'll sleep on the couch."

"You're not moving here tonight, are you?"

"No!" she blurted. "No. The charade begins tomorrow morning, when the Presidente comes."

"Good. Let's go." To her surprise, he took her hand and urged her at a fast clip from the room.

"Slow down," she protested. "What's wrong?"

"Sorry." He released her. "I need fresh air. Let's go outside."

When they reached the flower garden, she touched his arm. "What's wrong?"

He released a sharp breath. "Do you realize what you're getting into?"

"Unfortunately, I do."

His gaze looked bleak. "I guess...I guess I'm finally realizing it's over. Between us, I mean."

"Behran." Her heart hurt. "I'm sorry..."

"No. You have nothing to be sorry about. I just don't want him to hurt you."

"I don't want him to hurt me, either."

He stared at her in silence for a moment, his chest heaving slightly. "I'm here. If you need anything, I'm here."

With tears in her eyes, she hugged him tightly. "Behran. You are such a good man. I love you. I always will. You know that, right?"

He sighed, and kissed her temple. "I know you do." His voice roughened. "And I love you too, Thusa."

After a long moment, he put her from him. "I have something to say. I've kept quiet about for a long time, because I respect your feelings. But I need to warn you."

"About what?"

"Mentàll. He knows this is his last chance to steal your heart. He won't play by the rules."

"I know. But..."

"He knows he already owns a piece of your heart. And he'll sink in his teeth and rip it out if you let him."

"Behran, I don't..."

"Don't trust him, Thusa. I'm telling you to be careful, because I care about you. He's still that same man who threatened to kill you three years ago. He stole the *Second Book of Kaavl* right out of your hands eight months ago. I don't trust him. Not one fingerbreadth."

"You don't think he's changed? Even a little?"

"For your sake, I hope he has. But think about this logically. Why does he want you? Is it because he loves you? If so, great. But to be honest, I'm really concerned another reason might be motivating him." When she didn't answer, he said, "You do you realize he's been chasing you ever since the Quasr War ended, right? Why else would he send you those kaavl pages every month?"

"I'm not sure. "It felt odd to have her own suspicions articulated by someone else.

"He planned the mission to Zindedi just right, so he could get close to you. Ask yourself why."

"I have. I can't figure it out. Except..." she hesitated to say it. "I think he desires me."

Behran gave a short, mirthless laugh. "That's obvious. But lust isn't love. He thinks he owns you. When he came up to you today..." He broke off and looked away for a second. "I wanted to punch him."

"Behran," she whispered.

"All I'm saying is be on your guard. I'm afraid you're going to get hurt."

"I'll remember everything you've said."

"Good." He hugged her again for one hard, long moment. "Take care of yourself. That's all I ask."

He walked her back to the room she shared with Hendra, and she bid him goodnight. Her heart felt heavier and more troubled than ever before.

Behran had just resurrected every doubt she'd ever had about Mentàll. Hearing all of her worries spoken out loud, and really contemplating that they might be true—that Mentàll had been pursuing her for some selfish, cold purpose of his own for months—scared her.

Was Behran right?

Had Mentàll told her everything? Or was he keeping one, final secret from her?

Surely not.

Oh The One, help me. Please help me to see the truth.

CHAPTER TWENTY

Day 23

Sun shone in the window when Methusal woke up. Hendra was already gone, and breakfast smells seeped under the door. She didn't particularly want to get up.

The Presidente would arrive at the mansion this morning. Last night he had agreed to stay on his ship until the new day had started.

Methusal put her head in her hands. She did not want to see that horrible man again. The last time she'd seen him, he'd been about to violate her. She shuddered, remembering that moment, and how his soldiers had held her pinned on the floor while the Presidente...

The door opened and Hendra poked her head inside. "Thusa? Mentàll is asking for you."

"Is the Presidente here?"

"Not yet."

"I'll be out soon."

Hendra hesitated. "Are you all right?"

"I will be."

"Act like you don't remember," the other girl said softly. "Hold your head high."

Methusal hadn't been sure if Hendra knew what had happened the night of the ball. "Thank you. I'll do that."

With a smile, she closed the door.

It had been the boost of encouragement she'd needed.

Methusal dressed and gathered up the last of her belongings.

Last of all, she hesitated at the small dresser where the glittering gold and silver marriage necklace waited for her. Sunlight sparkled off of the green stones, and glowed like fire in the pale blue ones. It was time. She clasped the smooth, silken weight around her neck and left the room.

First, she stopped by Mentàll's room. A knock drew no response. Good. She slipped inside and glanced left and right. Empty. Sunlight streamed into the large bedroom, making the room feel bright and welcoming. Quickly, she dropped off her last bag and left Mentàll's compartment. When she closed the door behind her, she relaxed.

"Methusal." Mentàll's harsh voice made her jump. The Dehrien Chief approached, flanked by two large, burly men. "Just the person I was looking for." He introduced the men as Jsan and Tumel. The first had blond hair, and the other, dark. "Jsan will be your guard. Any time you leave our rooms, he will accompany you. Go nowhere without him."

"All right."

He turned his attention to Tumel. "Methusal may enter my private quarters at any time. However, she is the only one who may do so."

Tumel nodded, and stationed himself outside the door.

"Where's your guard?" she inquired, as they headed down the hall.

"He will assume his duties when the Presidente arrives." His tone was curt.

She glanced at him. "You're nervous, aren't you?"

"No. I am torn between wanting to kill the scienth or make peace with him."

She looked at him in surprise. "Because he ordered you shot?"

"No, Methusal." His pale gaze seared like blue fire. "Because he almost lay his filthy hands on you. I have not forgotten."

Unexpected warmth crept into her heart. She offered him a small smile. "For peace we can do anything. Right?"

"For peace I would charm a whip into the trap of my choosing."

She grinned, and he unexpectedly did, too.

Δ Δ Δ Δ Δ

Nerves crawled through the pit of Methusal's stomach. She stood next to Mentàll, just inside the mansion's open massive wooden doors. Calbn, the guards, and the Presidente and his men had just cleared the compound gates. She stiffened her spine and schooled her features into a cool, expressionless look.

Mentàll's wide hand touched her back, and then slipped lightly around her waist. Although it was unspoken, he offered his assurance that he would stand between her and the Presidente. The Dehrien Chief would not allow the Zindedi leader to touch her. It comforted her, and she relaxed a little.

The stocky, thick-limbed Zindedi leader stalked into the mansion. His black and silver hair looked crisp against his head, and the black and red uniform had no wrinkles. Dozens of medals, no doubt awarded to himself, twinkled on his chest beneath his drooping jowls. His face looked flushed, perhaps from the exertion of walking all the way from the docks. Methusal wondered if he traveled anywhere in Zindedi without a carriage.

Two Zindedi soldiers flanked him, and seven trailed behind. Their eyes darted to and fro, and their fingers hovered over the knives in their belts. No guns were visible, however. Perhaps leaving them on the ship was one of the conditions Mentàll had laid down last night when he'd met with the Zindedis.

In the shadowed interior of the mansion, the Presidente's eyes looked almost black, and they landed swiftly upon Methusal. They glittered, and his thick lips pulled slightly away from his teeth, clearly remembering how she'd been pinned helplessly on the floor of his mansion, and what he'd wanted to do to her. A shudder went down her spine, and then Mentàll stepped forward, blocking the Presidente's view of her.

"Presidente. It is an honor. Thank you for coming to our land." The men shook hands, and Mentàll stepped back again.

"The pleasure is all mine." The Zindedi's smile looked false, and his eyes glittered at Methusal again. He seemed to sense her revulsion. Perhaps it fed the evil fires in his soul. She stared back impassively.

The Presidente stepped forward, hand outstretched. "And your wife, the lovely Methusal. I am enchanted to see you again."

He meant to take her hand and perhaps kiss it with his slimy lips.

She gritted her teeth, determined to endure it, for peace's sake. But before he could touch her, the Dehrien Chief's arm came between them.

"No one may touch my wife, except for me." His smile looked pleasant on the surface, but Methusal recognized the cold snarl curling the ends.

The Presidente's gaze flickered to Mentàll, revealing faint surprise that was quickly cloaked. His false smile edged higher. "Of course."

Mentàll said, "We have lunch prepared. If you would like to join us?"

With a quick hand jerk, the Presidente indicated the young soldier beside him, who held a small box. "Artn is my food taster. He understands which foods best complement my palate." So. The games had truly begun. "As an expression of good will, I have brought a gift. Artn," the Presidente prompted.

Artn stepped forward and presented the box to Methusal. It was the size of her hand and three finger widths high.

"Open it," the Presidente encouraged with a smile that Methusal could not quite decipher.

She glanced at Mentàll, who nodded. His smile looked just as false as the Presidente's.

She lifted the lid, and saw a glistening brown cake, covered in a soft brown frosting inside. It smelled sweet and delicious, and faintly of ortangias blossoms.

"The most expensive cake money can buy," Artn said. "Made fresh is morning."

"A rare delicacy," the Presidente interjected. "Even young Artn here has never tasted it before."

"Perhaps he would like a piece," Mentàll suggested, directing a feral smile at the young man.

Artn blanched, but only for a split second.

"Come," Mentàll said. "Let's enjoy lunch together."

Methusal accompanied Mentàll to the table, where he held out a chair for her. It was placed to the left of his chair, at the head of the table. In an undertone, he told her, "Dispose of the cake."

"My thoughts exactly," she whispered back.

The Presidente took his position at the other end.

Calbn sat on Mentàll's right, as did the other seven Chiefs of Koblan. The Presidente's advisors took up positions to Methusal's left, all the way down the table. Adversaries stared at one another. Silence ensued, and Calbn raised his arm to signal the servants.

Beverages were served first, and Artn sipped from the Presidente's cup. With a nod, he handed it to the Zindedi leader. The Presidente raised his silver goblet. "A toast to the peace process. May it be profitable for both countries."

More toasts ensued, with each Koblani chief and each Zindedi advisor taking the opportunity to introduce themselves and proclaim their interest in peace, as well.

The first meat course was served.

After sampling several slow, carefully chewed bites, the Presidente said, "A fine meat. It compares favorably to one of our common animals in Zindedi. Ours is a fine land, ripe with the choicest delicacies, is it not, Presidente Solboshn?" With swift, deadly slices, he forked up another bite of meat. "Tell me what you enjoyed most about our bountiful land."

"The climate is cool. A welcome change from Koblan at this time of the year."

"Ah, yes." The Presidente smiled, still chewing. At intervals his lips parted, showing some of his masticated food. It was disgusting. Either he didn't know good manners, Methusal reflected, or it was a slap at Koblan, because he didn't think them worthy of basic civility. "How many of your people are enjoying our cool climes right now, Presidente Solboshn?"

Methusal glanced quickly at Mentàll. He looked unperturbed. "The minimum required to ensure a permanent peace."

The Presidente chuckled. "I am happy to provide shelter for our new friends. In fact, I am pleased to report providing protection to a man in my palace right now."

Timaeus was a captive in his dungeon. Methusal's fingers fisted.

Mentàll said coolly, "My countryman's release will be required for peace."

With a self-satisfied smile, the Presidente patted his mouth with a cloth. "I will happily release him. Once you agree to all of my terms, of course."

An uncomfortable silence followed. Erl frowned heavily, and the eyes of every Koblani at the table turned to Mentàll.

Although his face remained expressionless, lightning fast thoughts flickered behind that cool blue gaze. The Presidente clearly had come to make demands. Any peace would come at a steep price.

He said, "After lunch, we will begin discussions."

With a wide smile, the Presidente raised his goblet. "To satisfactory terms. May the shrewdest and strongest prevail."

△ △ △ △ △

"He's a beast!" Aali said indignantly. Her eyes shone with tears.

Methusal, Aali, and Hanuh had gathered in Hanuh's chambers while Erl, Mentàll, the chiefs, the Presidente, his advisors, as well as a legion of guards now filled Calbn's office. The discussions were underway.

Methusal wanted to eavesdrop, but had refrained with difficulty. "He's a horrible man." A few minutes earlier she had deposited the cake in a cooking fire in the kitchen. She felt certain it was poisoned, and didn't want to take any chance that an animal might get a hold of it and eat it in the trash heap.

"Do you think Timaeus is still alive? And what about Deccia?" Aali's high voice trembled.

Hanuh put an arm around her niece's shoulders. "They'll be fine. We must believe that."

"But how can we *know*? That wild beast could lie and lie and lie!"

"We have to trust your Uncle Erl, Mentàll, and all the others. And we need to pray that The One will give them wisdom," Hanuh said.

"Why did he *come* if he doesn't want peace?"

"He's angry," Methusal said. "He wants to make us suffer for the harm we did to his military. But he's afraid of us, too, which is why he's here. He'll agree to peace. Mentàll will see to it."

"It takes a wild beast to corner a wild beast, you mean?" Aali said.

"Yes."

Hanuh said, "You have full confidence in Mentàll, don't you, Methusal?" Wisdom and a hint of humor warmed her gaze.

"I trust he'll do the very best for Koblan. If he had his way, he'd make the Presidente crawl back to his ship licking the dust from the earth."

Hanuh raised an eyebrow. "Sounds like you know him well. Or maybe that's the way you feel, too?"

"I do. The Presidente is a murderer, and he's sick in the head. I think he's insane. He deserves to die. The only trouble is if he does, his son will take over Zindedi. He's even more twisted and cruel than the Presidente."

"If they're truly insane, how can we trust any promise of peace from them?"

"We can't. I think Mentàll plans to work out a peace agreement that's acceptable to both sides. But I also think he'll be subtly threatening the Presidente at the same time. If the Presidente breaks the peace, Mentàll will order more destruction upon Zindedi."

Aali piped up, "I think the only way to have peace is to kill the Presidente. And his son."

"That's murder."

"They need to be stopped! Just think about what they're doing to poor Timaeus!"

Softly, Hanuh said, "Vengeance is The One's. He will repay. But if the Presidente breaks the peace, that will mean war. The Presidente will suffer Koblan's retribution. Do you think Mentàll has men in place in Zindedi to assassinate the Presidente and his son, Methusal?"

She had never considered that possibility. It sent a chill down her spine. "Riln and Goric are still in Zindedi. I could see Riln cheerfully carrying out that assignment." Provided he wasn't a Zindedi spy. Provided they weren't *all* in prison right now, including Deccia.

"It's a dangerous game Mentàll is playing."

"Unfortunately, that's his favorite type of game."

△ △ △ △ △

The talks went late into the afternoon, and then the men broke up. Dinner was delayed because the Presidente inexplicably remained in his room for a long period of time.

Methusal waited with the others until the Zindedi leader finally arrived. Red mottled his face, and sharp huffs wheezed from his chest. With a heavy plop, he sat in his chair and said little, except for a few abrupt words to his officers.

Methusal turned to Mentàll and said in a low voice, "How are the talks going?"

"He refuses to speak about peace. He is demanding that shipments of ore be sent from Rolban to pay for the damage we caused in Zindedi."

"What about Timaeus? Has he said more about him?"

"He does not know his true identity, and we will not tell him. However, he is threatening to torture him still more if we do not agree to his terms."

"*More?*" Methusal felt sick to her stomach. She clenched her fork tighter. "What has he done to him? Oh, poor Timaeus. And Deccia!"

The Dehrien's hand closed over hers. "I will make him pay if he kills Timaeus. Be sure of it."

"That's not good enough. Aali's right—the only way to get rid of that monstrous man is to kill him!"

To her surprise, his lips twitched. "I thought you were above murder and vengeance. What about the Prophet's directives to forgive your enemies?"

"I can't forgive someone who plans to torture someone I love! Besides, the Prophet meant that I should forgive you."

"Yes." His thumb gently rubbed her fingers. "You and I have peace now, Methusal. Once I thought that was impossible, too. It gives me hope for peace with Zindedi."

"But how can we possibly trust him?"

"We cannot. We will pretend peace, just as he is pretending peace. But a man like the Presidente understands only two things: fear and destruction. By the end of these negotiations he will fear me. Then he can choose. He can follow through on our agreement, or I will order one final, crippling blow against Zindedi."

"What do you mean?"

"Mentàll Solboshn!" the Presidente boomed. His color had returned to normal. "Truly, your wife is delectable. I understand why she has captured all of your attention. However, if you can tear yourself away, I would like to resume negotiations after dinner."

"I would be pleased to do the same."

"I will not speak to *them* any longer," the Presidente motioned to the Koblani chiefs and his own advisers. "I will speak to you alone. With our guards, of course."

"Of course." A faint smile touched Mentàll's lips. He raised his goblet. "To fruitful discussions."

Cruel and evil were the only adjectives that could describe the Presidente's smile. He raised his glass in salute and drank deeply.

Methusal glanced sideways at Mentàll. "Be careful," she murmured. "I don't trust him."

"He wants to intimidate me." A pleased, feral smile curled his lips. "I look forward to our negotiations."

At the moment, she wasn't sure who looked more dangerous or pleased with the upcoming confrontation. With a shiver, she ate the last of her dessert.

"Be sure to go nowhere without Jsan," he said through thinned lips. "The Presidente knows he can hurt me best through you."

"I'll be careful."

She guessed Mentàll would probably not come to their rooms until late tonight. Which meant she'd have his entire suite to herself. That should have made her feel relieved, but instead, the thought of being alone in those large, unfamiliar rooms made her feel uneasy. "This may seem silly, but the back window..."

"Guards are patrolling it. Do not fear. You will be safe."

She believed him. Mentàll would make sure of it. But after the questionable cake the Presidente had given her, she wondered what tricks he meant to employ next. Although it was probably unnecessary, she worried about Mentàll. And she wondered who would be victorious in the battle of their wills tonight.

Chapter Twenty-One

Day 24

METHUSAL HADN'T SLEPT WELL, and when she exited from the bedroom for breakfast, Mentàll was gone. Had he ever come to their rooms last night?

Yawning, she put her plate of food on a table. Dawn peeped through the trees outside, turning the leaves a slivery white color. The sky was a deep, milky blue. Few people were stirring this early. A few servants ate near the end of the hall, and Wyen's chief, a swarthy man with a lot of black hair, sat at another table across from a red-haired woman.

Methusal stared at the woman. She looked familiar. And red hair was uncommon in Koblan.

The woman fed Wyen's chief a piece of toast, and a dimple creased his stubbled cheek. He grabbed her hand and kissed it.

Methusal looked away. Obviously the woman had serviced Wyen's single chief last night.

She wondered where Mentàll might be. As she ate, she slipped into kaavl and listened to the conversations around her. The chief and the woman flirted outrageously. The servants worried about cleaning up after the dozens of guests. Her hearing drifted down the hall to Calbn's office, and there she picked up Mentàll's low murmur.

"The talks last night achieved nothing." A raspy sound indicated that he'd rubbed his jaw.

"He threatened you."

"And he threatened Methusal. He dared to demand that we send a high level kaavl player to Zindedi."

"That will never happen."

"And he wants three ships full of ore sent to Zindedi. If we comply with those terms, he will agree to leave Koblan in peace."

Calbn snorted. "What did you tell him?"

"I asked him how many Zindedi ships he would like me to sink."

Calbn chuckled. "And?"

"He demanded that I recall every Koblani from Zindedi soil. I told him we had become accustomed to Zindedi's cool climates. Perhaps we would like to claim it as our own. Finally, his face turned purple and he pulled at his neck cloth. It appeared that he was having trouble breathing. I suggested he lie down, because I did not want to take advantage of a weakened man. His servants pulled him from the room. That was at midnight. I have not seen him since."

Calbn's hard laugh sounded triumphant. "A toast to you, Mentàll. Your tongue cuts like a knife. The battle will continue today, no doubt. A man as prideful as the Presidente will not humble himself willingly. You must offer an enticing morsel. That way he can grasp it and it won't appear that he's lost his dignity."

"I will negotiate a contract that will allow Zindedi to buy half a ship load of ore. In exchange, he will give us two hundred guns. I will point out that a free trade agreement will be profitable to both lands."

"He will accept that?"

"Eventually. Either it will be a pretense, or it will be the truth. Our next moves will depend upon his actions."

"If we cannot trust him, why make a peace agreement at all?"

"Peace is our best goal. I will encourage him to accept it. I will make it clear to him that it is the best, most profitable solution for Zindedi. I do not want war."

"He fears kaavl. If he has two sane thoughts to rub together, he will fear you, too. We will be victorious."

A hesitation elapsed. "I hope so." The caution in Mentàll's tone surprised her.

"What's wrong?" After a moment of silence, Calbn guessed, "Is it his threats against Methusal?"

Mentàll said nothing.

Voice disapproving, Calbn said, "She is a mere woman. They are good to warm a cold night, but that is all. If the

Presidente believes she means more than that to you, he will bring you to your knees."

"My relationship with Methusal is no concern of his or yours. He will not succeed in using her against me."

"Really?" Calbn's tone sounded sharp. "Remember, Mentàll. She is only a means to an end. Just as these talks with the Presidente are a means to an end. Keep your priorities in order. Only then will we gain victory over Zindedi."

"Do not speak to me about priorities, Calbn." Mentàll's voice sounded like ice. "I choose my priorities. And I repeat—my relationship with Methusal is none of your concern."

"Fine." A chair squeaked, as if Calbn had relaxed back. "Do what you think is best. But our chiefs would like to meet with the Presidente today."

"Yes. I have set up a meeting for later this morning."

"Good."

The men's conversation turned to other matters, and Methusal slowly finished her breakfast.

It appeared that Mentàll had made no headway with the Zindedi leader last night. But she thought about the new information she'd learned about the Presidente's health.

Mentàll had said he'd turned purple and had had trouble breathing during the meeting. And before dinner last night, she'd also observed the Presidente's mottled face and labored breathing.

Was the he ill? Was something wrong with his heart? Maybe his death was not far off.

It seemed wrong to feel happy about that prospect. And yet a quiet death for the Presidente—perhaps slipping peacefully into the eternal hereafter—did not seem right. Considering all of the deaths and tortures he had ordered, he deserved to suffer mightily.

But for now, he remained alive, and a thorn in Koblan's side. Until his death, they would have to deal with him and his unreasonable demands for peace.

"Good morning, Thusa." Hanuh sat down across from her.

"'Morning, Mama." She spotted her father filling his plate at the buffet counter.

"I had an idea for today," Hanuh said. "Since the men are busy with the talks, maybe you, Aali, Hendra, Sozla, and her mother and I could all go shopping. I've never seen Quasr. Does that sound like fun?"

"Yes." It sounded terrific, in fact. Sitting here in this mansion and feeling the tension thickening between the Zindedis and Koblanis made her feel on edge. She grinned. "Maybe our bodyguards will enjoy it, too."

Hanuh laughed. "I've already spoken to Aali, and she said she'd speak to the others. We'll meet here in an hour."

Carrying their breakfast trays, Hendra, Doc, Behran, and Sozla arrived just then. Behran sent Methusal a brief smile, and spent the meal talking to Sozla. The Eerporian girl giggled often, and Behran appeared relaxed. A grin occasionally tugged at his lips.

Methusal was glad that he seemed so happy. It made her feel better about the whole situation with Mentàll.

She told her mother, "I'll be back soon. I need to clean up before we go."

"Take your time. We're in no rush."

△ △ △ △ △

Aali frowned. Who *was* that man? The familiar figure lurked in the morning shadows near the main doors.

The short, stocky figure looked vaguely menacing. Unease thrilled down her spine.

Moving with smooth nonchalance, she moved closer, and then the man shifted into the sunlight.

Kilum! A runner from Tarst. She hadn't seen him since the war with Dehre. His hair had receded a bit, and a scar slashed across his temple. It looked wicked.

She hadn't seen her favorite Tarst runner in over a week. Not that she'd been yearning to see him, or counting the days, of course.

It seemed very strange that Kilum would be here instead of Dastn. She approached the Tarst man. "Kilum?"

His black gaze slid to her. It looked dead—even evil, if she wanted to be fanciful. Whip beast eyes.

Ignoring her unease, she inquired, "Where's Dastn?" A horrible thought dawned on her. "Is he hurt?"

Kilum scowled. "How would I know? Maybe."

He didn't look at all disturbed by the possibility.

The man gave her the creeps, so she left him without saying anything else. But now fear now crowded into her heart. Dastn! Was he missing? Hurt? Where was he?

If Pan had sent for Kilum, then Dastn must be hurt!

She had to find Pan right away. He would know.

She swung quickly on her crutches for Calbn's office. People scattered as she barreled toward them. She rounded a corner, and her crutch caught on the leg of a table. With a cry, she pitched forward.

Strong hands caught her. "Careful. Do you want to break your other leg?"

"Dastn!" The minute she regained her balance, she flung her arms around him. "I thought you were hurt!"

He laughed, and it was a wonderful sound. So was the healthy, strong feel of his chest against hers. Instantly, she felt better.

"Why did you think I was hurt?"

"Because of Kilum," she said, pulling free.

"Kilum?"

"He's a Tarst runner." At his sudden frown, she added, "Isn't he?"

"No. Where is he now?"

They both scanned the great hall.

"I don't see him," Aali said. "Why are you frowning?"

"Kilum disappeared after Mentàll's war against Rolban. Thusa mentioned seeing him later, during the Quasr War. At that time, he was with the Wyen. No one has seen him since."

"Well, he's gone now. I'm just glad you're okay." She hugged him again tightly.

"I can see that." She heard amusement in his tone.

With a frown, she stepped back. "Is it a crime that I care about you?"

He smiled. "No. I'm touched."

He was laughing at her! Well, maybe not. But he did find her amusing. She saw it in his eyes. "You ungrateful slug. When do you leave again?"

Dastn laughed out loud. He slung an arm around her shoulders. "Come on, Aali. Tell me what new trouble you're plotting."

She shrugged his arm off. He was not taking her seriously at all. And she'd thought, especially after the way they'd left each other last time, that they were finally growing closer.

"You might want to step off," she advised. "Just in case I accidentally poke you with my crutches."

Dastn only smiled. "Did you tell Methusal about the Alliance?"

Forgetting her pique, she grinned. "Yes, and she was shocked. She and Mentàll had a big fight about it."

"Things seem smooth between them now."

"Maybe," she said doubtfully. "The Alliance has been ratified. And the chiefs like the the idea of electing our own Presidente, too. For defensive purposes."

"It is necessary," he said grimly. "We won't survive without it."

"Who do you think should be elected? Wyen's chief, Uncle Erl, or Mentàll?"

"Not Wyen's chief. I can't read that guy. Erl is fair and level-headed. But Mentàll led the mission to Zindedi. His peace plan got the Presidente here."

"Methusal did, you mean. She presented the plan to the Presidente."

"Yes. But Mentàll planned the trip, and he thought up the defensive national alliance. He has courage, and he's a visionary. Zindedi's Presidente hates him, but he respects him at the same time."

"I guess that's important," she agreed. "We want the invaders to be scared of our Presidente. That way they won't cross him."

"Yes. What do you think? Who do you think should be our Presidente?"

Her heart swelled, happy that he wanted to know her opinion. "Well," she said, "Methusal hates Mentàll. But I think I agree with you. I think he'd be the best Presidente. At least for now. Won't they re-elect in three years?"

"That's the plan. You'll be old enough to vote next time."

Aali rolled her eyes. "Rub it in, why don't you?"

His mouth curled up at one corner. "You're getting there."

"Not fast enough for me," she muttered.

Dastn stopped in front of Calbn's office. "Don't be in a big hurry. Adulthood and responsibility will come all too fast."

She raised an eyebrow. "Like I don't have responsibilities now? I take care of Trori and Rartn full-time. I've been *spying,*" she whispered this, "to protect Rolban. Among other things," she finished mysteriously.

He did not answer, but sent her a measuring look.

"So you see, Dastn, I do adult work. I *feel* grown up. But you still treat me like a child."

He still didn't respond.

Frustrated, she stomped her foot. Her good foot. "Why won't you say anything, you stubborn man?"

He smiled a little and glanced down at her tapping foot. "I rest my case."

Aali gritted her teeth and glared. Really! He was impossible. She swung off down the hall without bothering to say goodbye.

△ △ △ △ △

Methusal returned to Mentàll's suite to brush her teeth. She was glad her mother had suggested shopping. Even though she'd spent plenty of time over the last week wandering through Quasr's shops, it was a sunny day, and she'd be glad to leave the mansion and soak in a little healing sunshine. It frustrated her that the Presidente was here, causing all sorts of problems, and she couldn't be a part of the solution.

She exited from the relief room and stopped short with a gasp. Her hand flew to her racing heart. Mentàll stood beside the desk, his broad back to her, stripped to his breeches.

He turned. A slow smile curved his lips. "My missing wife."

"I am not your wife," she stated with agitated irritation. "Have you had enough sleep? Put your shirt on."

He did so, still eying her like a delighted whip with a new apte. "You were worried about me," he finally murmured.

"Did you come in last night? Did you ever rest?" Methusal immediately wished she could bite back the concerned words.

"Yes. The couch was quite comfortable."

A rap came at the door. Glad for the interruption, she watched her fake husband open it.

What had happened to her tongue? It seemed to have developed an unfortunate mind of its own.

Mentàll opened the door wide enough for Methusal to spot the red-haired woman on the other side. She blinked. It was the woman who'd been with Wyen's chief at breakfast this morning. She still looked so familiar.

But why?

And then it hit her. Three years ago in Dehre she'd seen this woman fawning all over Mentàll. Hendra had said the redhead was just one of his many women.

"Mentàll." The woman ran a finger down his chest. "I have missed you."

"Wyen's chief entertained you last night."

"Yes, but he is not you." Her full red lips pouted.

As Methusal watched this interplay, a sickened lump lodged in her throat. The woman was flagrantly flirting with the Dehrien Chief. Worse, he didn't seem to find it offensive, judging by his smile. Methusal sharpened her hearing to dishonorably eavesdrop again, but only caught Mentàll's seemingly regretful, "You must go," and then he shut the door on the hussy.

Why had that woman *come* here? Methusal turned away, feeling sick to her stomach. The woman was clearly familiar with the location of Mentàll's room.

Had he spent time with her this last week?

She felt shocked by the idea of Mentàll being intimate with that woman. It made her feel queasy and hollow inside, as if her stomach had been ripped from her body. Turning her back on him, she picked up a writing stick from the desk, trying to gather her chaotic thoughts.

She swallowed. Had he been seeing other women all along? Not in the invader land, of course. But earlier— perhaps after the Quasr War had ended? And again now, after they'd returned home? How many women had he seen? Just the one?

Methusal didn't know why she felt so shocked by the idea. He was a man. Hendra had told her three years ago how heartlessly he went through women. "Never the same one, and never for long," Hendra had said. Why had that phrase stuck in her head?

Of course he'd had women. Men had women.

Then why did her soul feel like it had begun to bleed?

The writing stick dug sharply into her palm, on the verge of puncturing her skin. Methusal let it drop from her fingers, feeling dizzy and disoriented. She clutched Dehre edge of the desk for balance, and became aware that Mentàll was facing her on the other side. Bewildered, she stared back at him.

She needed to be alone. Abruptly, she bolted, but he caught her arm and moved into her line of vision. "What is it, Methusal?"

She glanced up, still unable to speak, and then drew a quick breath. His light eyes actually looked pleased. Was he *laughing* at her?

That loosened her tongue.

"Haven't you warned off your women, Mentàll? Don't they understand that they might break our cover? But maybe it's worth the risk to you!" She jerked free.

He smiled. "You could not be jealous?"

"Never!" she said fiercely. "But I'm surprised you'd risk the mission just to satisfy your base lusts!"

He said nothing for a moment, and then, "Lust does not motivate me, Methusal. Would you like to know what brings me pleasure?"

She didn't like the gleam in his eyes. "Step off, you *whip*!" Furiously, she steamed into her room. Unfortunately, the Dehrien Chief filled the doorway before she could slam the door. With sudden suspicion, she accused, "Did she *follow* you here?"

"No. Marla lives in Quasr."

"How convenient for you. Well. Go find your good time girl. Only be discreet about it. Once one lie collapses, the whole house crumbles."

"Which house do you mean, Methusal?" he said softly.

"The peace agreement, of course. And the house of dry grass you've built of our fake marriage." She glared. "It's about to burn."

"I agree it is starting to smolder."

"Go," she ordered. "Quit wasting my time."

The Dehrien Chief did not comply. Instead, he advanced further into the room.

She held her own, refusing to back up. To her consternation, he erased the distance between them. His large, warm hands encircled her upper arms. "I did not think you cared, Methusal."

"I don't."

"Then why do you look so disappointed in me? Like I have not lived up to your high expectations?"

"I have no high expectations of you," she retorted, giving her arms an experimental tug. He did not release her, surprise, surprise. She hissed, "You're a whip."

The pale gaze gentled, and his smile disappeared. "I have had no women, Methusal."

Her heart gave a fast bump. "Right. She just came to visit, out of the blue. One of your old Dehrien women, no less."

He smiled again. "That was three years ago. You barely knew me then. Should I be flattered that you remember every detail of my life?"

"I don't. I only remembered her because of her unusual red hair."

"I see. But the fact remains—that happened three years ago."

"You haven't been with her since?"

"No."

"But of course you have been with others."

"None since the Quasr War started." Mentàll held her gaze, his eyes intent, watching her response to that surprising statement. And he never lied, so it must be true.

"But... That's been ten months! I mean, I know during the war you had little opportunity, but since then..." She couldn't believe what he had just told her. What was he trying to say?

He said nothing, but his level gaze told her the truth.

"Why?" Her heart beat faster.

"I think you know."

"No. I don't."

"I want only one woman."

"Who?" she asked faintly.

"You, Methusal."

She couldn't wrap her mind around that statement. "Why? I thought you hated me during the Quasr War."

"I did, at first. But things changed."

"How? Why?"

"Every time you cared for my injuries with a gentle touch, you challenged my hatred for you. And then you did something that changed everything."

"What?" She still couldn't believe what she was hearing.

"Even though you despised me, you went beyond your duty and massaged my shoulders to ease my pain. I found I liked your touch. I wanted more of it, and it disturbed me. I wanted to hate you, but I did not any longer. That disturbed me even more. After that, I did not know what to think about you."

Each of his words felt like a shock to her heart. His feelings for her had changed *during* the Quasr War? Her pulse pounded in her ears.

In a low voice, he continued. "Don't you know, Methusal? Even a wild beast can be gentled with the right touch."

She stared at him, speechless. He'd changed his mind about her because she'd tried to be kind to him? Because she'd tried to follow The One's instructions? All of this was because of what *she* had done?

Mentàll said, "I began to question my perceptions of you, although I did not admit that to myself for a long time. It took longer to realize that I had misjudged you. You were not the selfish, arrogant girl I thought you were."

She found her tongue. "I thought those words described you."

"I make no excuses. But the fact remains—I have had no women since before the Quasr War began."

Everything he'd just said challenged everything she'd ever believed about him, and also challenged her interpretation of every event that had happened during the last ten months. It was difficult to absorb. Without thinking, she blurted, "Do you have children...with those women?" She flushed.

"None."

She glanced away, trying to ignore her fierce feeling of relief. She couldn't take it all in.

His eyes glinted. "So you see. You have no need to be jealous."

"I'm not," she replied automatically.

His palms stroked her upper arms, and she shivered.

"Stop lying to yourself." His warm breath caressed her temple. "We both know the truth. Think about what I have told you." He released her, and unexpectedly headed for the door. "I must go. But I will see you later, at dinner."

The door closed with a quiet *click* behind him.

She felt bereft. And why? Because she hadn't wanted him to leave yet? Because she'd wanted him to kiss her? Yes. Yes, she had.

She rubbed her suddenly goose pimply arms. Good had come from following The One's instructions to love her enemy. Mentàll had changed his mind about her. He'd begun to like her...perhaps even trust her a little. Peace had begun with her enemy, and she hadn't even known.

She thought back over the last part of the war. She'd been convinced that the Dehrien Chief had still wanted to take revenge on her, and hurt her. In fact, she'd still believed it in Zindedi, too.

But had revenge motivated him when he'd kissed her so passionately at base camp? Was it revenge when he'd sent her the copied pages of the *Second Book of Kaavl*? And was it revenge when he'd used every verbal tool in his arsenal to convince her to play the part of his wife during the peace mission?

No.

She leaned against the wall to support her suddenly quivering legs. Mentàll claimed that he had completely changed his mind about her *ten months ago*. He had pursued her all of this time because he wanted *her*. Period.

Could it be true? Could it all be so very simple?

△ △ △ △ △

His spy should arrive soon. The Presidente smiled, and decided the Koblani chiefs could wait a while longer for the peace talks to begin this morning. The fools. In the meantime, he would plot Koblan's destruction right under that prideful, detestable Dehrien's nose.

The Dehrien deserved to pay for his sneers last night, and for witnessing the Presidente's heart weakness. And clearly he had warned Methusal to dispose of his "gift." Thanks to Solboshn, the clever work of his scientists had been a complete waste of time. Methusal was still alive. And no one in the mansion had even complained of a stomachache.

The Zindedi leader clenched his fists hard in impotent, visceral fury. He would destroy that Dehrien.

Like that. His fist drove into a nearby vase. It hit the floor with the force of a gunshot.

And this. His violent arm swept across a shelf filled cheap glass baubles and worthless trinkets. They shattered into thousands of satisfying fragments on the stone floor.

Soon he would bring that arrogant Mentàll Solboshn to his *knees!* He would crawl to the Presidente, begging for mercy.

He chuckled with relish. The Dehrien would receive no mercy. His torture would last forever.

But first, the Presidente would continue to play his game of whip and apte with Mentàll and his ice maiden whore, Methusal. He still did not believe for one minute that they were married. But the fact they pretended to be so, just to trick him... Well, it pleased him that he could manipulate them so easily. And better yet, he had another, even better plan in store for Methusal. The Dehrien would not save her this time.

With further contempt, the Presidente's gaze flickered over his shabby accommodations. The irritation of his surroundings felt like a needle poking under his skin. And yet what else could he expect? The Koblanis were mere tribesmen. They stupidly thought he would feel honored by a tiny room with threadbare linens and earthenware pots with the glaze worn off.

His eyes skimmed the fresh cut flowers and the shining, polished floors. If he didn't feel such contempt for the Koblanis, he'd feel insulted. Quasr's Chief should have given up his own lush chambers to the Presidente if he'd truly wanted to negotiate profitable terms from a rich, powerful country like Zindedi. Of course, he was a fool. As all Koblanis were fools.

He would grind them beneath his heel.

The Presidente couldn't wait until this charade was over, and he could return to his opulent palace. But for one more day, he would twist the Koblanis into knots, pretending to consider their ludicrous terms. Exacting these small tortures provided him with much pleasure.

Of course, he'd sign...eventually. Like rochers, they'd be easily fooled, and just as easily squashed. Their misplaced trust would give him the advantage of time—time to attack their weakest community when their Chief and all of their kaavl players were missing.

A knock at the door interrupted his self-indulgent chuckle.

"Enter!" he thundered. He missed Yalin, but the fool got seasick, and he'd had to leave him at home.

Kilum's swarthy face and compact, muscled body silently entered the compartment. Shortly, he said, "You have orders for me?"

The President "*tsked.*" "You have been on your own too long, Kilum. You forget how to pay respect to your leader."

Something black flashed in the dark eyes, but it was quickly masked. Kilum went down on one knee and bent his balding, wind snarled hair to the floor. "I am honored you need my services. What can I do for you?"

"Better. No. I did not tell you to rise." With satisfaction, the Presidente watched Kilum sink back to his knees. The muscles in the spy's shoulders tightened as hard as ore.

The Presidente smiled. "Be prepared, my servant. When the negotiations are over, you will follow Methusal. Here are your instructions."

With relish, he outlined his plans twice. Then he made Kilum repeat them—still kneeling, of course. "Do you understand?"

Head still bowed to the floor, Kilum said, "Yes, sir."

"Good. Rise." When Kilum obeyed, the Presidente eyed him with a small smile. "Do not fail your mission. Your success is vital to Zindedi's national security. Do you understand?"

"Yes, sir."

"Failure will bring you unpleasant consequences."

A long pause elapsed. Belatedly, Kilum said, "Yes, sir."

"That is all. You may leave."

"Yes, sir." Kilum left quickly. The door slammed behind him. Fear chased his footsteps, the Presidente deduced with satisfaction. He smiled, dreaming of his plans for the future...for his enemies' defeat, and for the many pleasures to come.

△ △ △ △ △

Hendra pulled on her hat, grabbed a small purse filled with money that Mentàll had given her, and hurried out of her room. The others were about to leave for another day of shopping in Quasr. She wanted to go too, and find a new scarf.

"Hendra." Doc strode from the direction of the nursery.

Her heart leaped with joy, as it did every time she saw him. Over the last few days, Doc had magically appeared by her side for every breakfast and dinner. In addition, several times a day she'd helped him walk the twins in the garden's sunshine. She hadn't seen him yet this morning, and hurried toward him, suddenly feeling worried.

"The twins. Are they all right?"

He grinned. "The yellow is gone. They're completely healthy."

"Oh, Doc!" She flung her arms around him and held him tight. His arms felt strong and secure around her. Flushing a little, she stepped back. "I'm so happy," she said softly. "And it's all thanks to you. You've done a wonderful job."

"I couldn't have done it without your help."

She smiled. "Any pair of arms would have done."

"Not for me." His gaze flickered to her purse. "Where are you going?"

"Shopping with the girls."

"Oh." His shoulders shifted, as if trying to rebalance whatever he'd been about to say.

"What?"

"I was about to ask if you'd like to go to town with me. I need to get supplies for my medical kit. But..."

"I'd love to!" She blushed again. "I mean, as long as you don't mind helping me shop for a scarf, too."

He smiled. "I would feel honored."

They joined the others at the mansion doors—one of which was propped open to let in the warm morning sunlight. Hendra explained their plans, and with knowing smiles, the others agreed that was a fine idea.

Methusal appeared to be lost in her own thoughts. She trailed behind as they left the mansion. Her expression flickered between joy and uncertainty. Hendra and Doc fell into step beside her.

"Is everything all right?" Hendra said in a low voice.

Methusal glanced at her, clearly startled. "Yes. I'm fine. It's nothing. Just Mentàll. He's confusing me." With a rueful lift of her lips, she added, "But what else is new?"

Hendra smiled. "I think he's pretty wonderful. But I'm biased, I guess." She sensed that the Rolbani girl was teetering on the brink of a momentous decision regarding Mentàll. Selfishly, Hendra wanted to push her squarely into his camp. She wanted her cousin to be happy, and she thought Methusal could make him so. Even more, she believed he would make Methusal happy, too. In fact, she suspected the Rolbani girl might already be halfway in love with him.

Methusal smiled too, and a bit of hope battled the anxiety in her eyes. "You completely trust him?"

"Yes. If he gives you his word, you can count on it until his dying breath."

"I know."

Softly, Hendra pushed a little harder. "Will you give him a chance?"

"I want to."

"Do it," she encouraged. "You both deserve to be happy. He's had no one to love him his entire life—you know that. He's been broken, but I think the pieces can still be put back together with care. By the right person."

"You think I could be that person?"

"I *know* you are that person."

More hope flickered. And anxiety. "Thank you, Hendra."

Doc's hand closed around Hendra's. "My supplies are down this street. Are you ready?"

She said goodbye to Methusal and walked with Doc down the cool, tree-lined avenue. They ducked in one shop and he found a length of cloth for bandages, as well as pins. The shop smelled of spices and soap.

After paying for his purchases, he gathered up the package and they left. On the street, he said, "Help me look for a garden store. I need coltac and tacky leaves."

"What about blood builder? Look, there's a powder specialist across the street."

Doc bought an assortment of healing herbs and powders. He lingered afterward, reading the description on a bin which contained needle sharp leaves. "Golgnt," he mused. "I've heard of it, but never used it."

"What is it used for?"

"Healing the heart. Sometimes clots form, and they make it hard for the blood to pass through. Golgnt clears all of the garbage out, so the heart can get healthy blood again. Old tales warn it's poison. But one of my old instructors in Wyen tried it on an old man on his death bed. It cured him."

"Will you buy some?"

"I'm not sure of it." He sniffed a pinch between his fingers, and let the leaves flutter back into the bin. "Anything to cure the heart can be risky. My patients may not want to take that risk, and I'm not sure if I want to, either."

She touched his arm. "Don't we sometimes need to face our fears in order to get better? Sometimes the only way to get well is to risk it all." She referred to her bold, crazy plan, which was still simmering in the recesses of her mind. It might be the only way to clear her heart and mind from the garbage of her past. But now wasn't the time to speak to Doc about it. Not yet.

He unexpectedly smiled, and held the door open for her as they left the shop. "Have you appointed yourself Mentàll's heart doctor?"

She blinked.

He chuckled. "You were subtle. But it was clear to me that you'd like to match up your cousin and Methusal."

"She'd be good for him. I think they'd be good for each other."

"You may be right. But sometimes it's easier to cure other people's problems, instead of our own."

Softly, she said, "I'm trying."

"I know you are." He dropped his parcels on a shaded bench beneath a tree, and turned her to face him. His palms on her arms felt warm and gentle. He took a deep breath. "I think we've come a long way, Hendra."

"Yes." Her heart suddenly beat fiercely with agitation, because she guessed what might be on his mind.

"When this is over—when the Presidente leaves—would you have dinner with me? At the Poctlo." It was a seafood restaurant near the pier. Hendra and the girls had had lunch there once, and it was very expensive.

"I would love to."

"Good." With a smile, he kissed her. His warm caress lingered, until her heart raced and her skin felt flushed. When he pulled back, his gaze traced her features. A faint smile curved his lips. "That pink blush makes you look even more beautiful."

"Thank you." She smiled, and took one of the packages on the bench and he took the other, and then claimed her free hand, as well.

"Wear sandals," he suggested. "I'd like to walk on the beach with you afterward. Okay?" He looked at her, and his serious gaze looked tender.

"Okay," she whispered.

He meant to ask her to marry him. She was fairly certain of that fact. And she knew how she wanted to answer. But she could not make that promise—not until Doc agreed to one stipulation.

Her heart beat harder, in sickening thuds. He would not be happy when he learned what that caveat would be.

Oh for courage to do what must be done—to make sure their marriage would not fail before it even began.

△ △ △ △ △

The Presidente raised his goblet. "To peace."

Mentàll watched him with a hard look in his eyes. After a long delay, which was not quite rude, but not cordial, either, he raised his own cup to his lips and drank. Methusal wondered what had happened during the talks today.

She had enjoyed lunch and shopping in town, but when she'd returned to the mansion in the late afternoon, the tension between the opposing leaders was as thick as a Tarst fog.

Her father had told her the Presidente had made outrageous demands all day. Her mother and father now sat to her left at dinner this evening.

The Presidente licked his lips. "Regrettably, tomorrow is the last day I may remain in your fine country. Duties require me to return home."

Methusal glanced at Mentàll. Clearly, no peace had been brokered yet.

Beside her, Hanuh murmured, "Tell Mentàll that the Presidente desires to play us all for fools. He enjoys making the men dance at the end of his strings, like helpless puppets. He relishes Mentàll's fury, and he desires your hatred, Methusal, most of all."

Her empathic mother's eyes looked dark and troubled.

Methusal leaned close to Mentàll and repeated her mother's warning.

He covered her hand and gently squeezed it. In a low voice, he said, "Thank your mother for me."

Methusal did, but Hanuh's visible tension did not ease.

At the far end of the table, the Zindedi leader chuckled. "The trouble, gentlemen, is that our talks have become clogged with the vain posturing of little men desiring power. It sticks most unpleasantly in my throat. What we require is the grace of a woman's presence. I feel certain that this sweetest of oil could speed along our negotiations most satisfactorily."

Hanuh gripped her hand, hard.

"What do you want, Presidente?" Mentàll asked through thinned lips.

"Why, your wife's presence, of course. I..."

"No."

The Presidente continued, "I require her presence at the peace talks tomorrow. Only she may soothe the damage your words and actions have inflicted upon both myself and Zindedi. Perhaps if she could serve me... Yes. That would please me greatly. I would be willing to consider once again some of your lesser demands if she serves me."

"Don't *do* it," Hanuh whispered vehemently.

"When aptes fly," Mentàll said. Although his features were expressionless, aggression tightened his body.

The Presidente burst into laughter. "Oh. No. I do not want her to serve me like *that*. Privately. No. I meant she could serve me drinks and refreshments. A small enough request."

"My wife serves no one."

The Presidente leaned back, lacing his thick fingers over his portly belly. His features hardened. "Why did you ask me here then, if you do not want peace?"

"Perhaps it is time to remember why *you* are here," Mentàll said icily. "Why did you leave the safe comfort of your palace to beg peace from me?"

His face mottled. "You dirt eating..."

"You fear destruction. If I give my kaavl soldiers one order, it will mean the end of your military. Do not threaten *me*," he hissed.

"Mentàll." Erl cleared his throat.

The Zindedi Presidente glared. "Listen to your lessers, Solboshn." He levered himself up from his chair. Artn rushed to help. "Be certain of one fact. I will sign no peace unless Methusal attends the talks tomorrow. And she *must* serve me, as is fitting a woman."

The Presidente and his advisors' heavy boots clumped from the room.

Tension tightened the cords in Mentàll's neck, but he made no effort to call the Presidente back.

The chiefs silently looked at Mentàll. Wyen's chief sent Methusal a baleful look.

It all rested upon her. The Presidente would be willing to sign the peace agreement, but first he wanted to unleash some of his anger and feelings of humiliation upon Methusal. Hurting her was the only way a man that prideful would agree to be humbled.

She touched the hard muscles of Mentàll's forearm. "I could..."

"You will not." Mentàll did not look at her. "You absolutely *will not.*"

"But..."

"Do not speak of it again." He abruptly rose and left. Calbn and Erl followed.

Methusal turned to her mother. "If it means peace, I could..."

"No," her mother said sharply. "Mentàll is right. That sick Presidente will not humiliate you for his own pleasure."

"But..."

"No, Methusal. He is like a small child. If you give in, his respect for Mentàll will evaporate. And he will demand still more."

Her mother was right. Had the mission and these talks been for nothing? Were war and destruction the only currencies the Presidente feared and valued?

Her mother patted her hand and released it. "Your Dehrien Chief just rose higher in my estimation."

"He's territorial. While I'm under his protection, he'll let no man hurt me."

"I think it's more than that. Don't you?"

Methusal looked down. "Maybe."

"I'm going to turn in. Think about what I said. And I'll be praying for a solution with that ridiculous Presidente."

"I told you he was insane."

"He is not insane. But he is thoroughly corrupt, and completely and selfishly evil. He cares about no one and nothing except for his own pleasure. And he only derives pleasure from hurting other people."

"I know."

"Be careful. Because he wants to hurt you, very badly. Mentàll, too. In fact, I don't think he'll rest until he's accomplished that goal." Hanuh kissed the top of her head. "Goodnight."

Accompanied by Jsan's solid presence, Methusal soon retired, too. Before she went to bed, she prayed for wisdom for Mentàll as he dealt with the Presidente. She also prayed that she could help out in some way. And she tried to close her mind to her mother's frightening warnings.

Soon the Presidente would leave. Peace or no peace, he would be gone forever. He would never hurt Mentàll, or herself. Never, she told herself.

She dreamed of Zindedi.

Mentàll sat on their bed, lacing up his boots, and she knelt nearby, stuffing food into her pack for their hike. "Will we have time for a picnic?"

"Yes. If you would like one." He finished knotting the laces.

She grinned at him. "Mrn. M only packed eight tarts. Is that enough for you? Because if you need more..."

He laughed, and the sound was so natural that she stared.

"You should do that more often," she murmured, feeling disconcerted. "You look almost human."

"Come to me."

Willingly, she did so. It was so easy to scoot closer. He drew her into the "V" of his legs. Her hands went to his chest, but instead of pushing him away, they slipped around his torso, and she felt his hard muscles beneath his tunic.

His wide palms cupped her face, and the ice blue eyes seemed to look deep into her soul. "How much more human can I be?"

She closed her eyes and leaned into him, aching for more of his touch...

Methusal awoke with a start. Ryon's moonlight streamed into the room, spilling pale green moonbeams across the wide bed.

Her heart beat heavily. She lay still, remembering the dream, and she pressed her hands to her eyes. A deep yearning prickled through her blood. She wanted to cling to the dream, to slip back into his embrace.

No. She pushed up on one elbow. *No.* She needed to clear her head. A trip to the relief room might do the trick.

She tiptoed to the door and peered out. The outer room was pitch dark, but when she opened the door wider, moonlight spilled inside. Mentàll was asleep on the couch. His quiet, even breaths touched her ears.

He must be tired. She wondered how little sleep he'd had last night.

Methusal tiptoed to the relief room. It only took a minute, and when she slipped back out, her involuntary footsteps took her to Mentàll. He slept facing the wall. The couch was long enough for him, but too narrow. It reminded her of the night he had slept on the couch in Zindedi. He'd never told her why.

She remembered the deep red couch marks on his cheek, and how she'd touched them. She also remembered the flash of vulnerability in his eyes, and she'd sensed his deep need for love to soothe away the hurts of his past.

It was hard sometimes to believe that vulnerability could live in this big man. When he was awake, he seemed so large and indomitable. As if nothing could shake him. And yet...

Methusal moved closer. She yearned to touch his hair. Giving in to an insane, foolish impulse, she did so. It felt soft, as she'd known it would. Always such a contrast to the hard man he could be.

His fingers unexpectedly curled around her wrist. She gasped.

"Methusal," he murmured.

"Let me go."

Instead, his fingers slipped down to enfold her hand. His thumb stroked her sensitive inner palm. "*Saltisienna.*" The word stole across her senses like a tender caress. What did it mean?

He turned onto his back and pulled her closer, so that now her hands touched his chest. To her chagrin, she made no attempt to break free.

His heart beat slow and heavy beneath her palms. He tugged her still closer and raised his head to capture her lips in a soft, beguiling kiss. "Lie with me, Methusal."

"No!" She gasped. "*No,*" she said again, more to convince herself than him. Trembling, she pulled back and he released her.

A moment elapsed.

In a quiet voice, he said, "Why are you here?"

"I don't *know!*" Her voice twisted in anguish. "Goodnight." She fled to her room, fighting the urge to do exactly as he wanted and stay with him. She leaned against the closed door, shaking.

What was wrong with her? Why did she have the insane urge to go back and take him up on his offer?

She pressed her hands to her flaming cheeks. The man was a menace to her peace of mind. He'd thoroughly worked his way under her skin, and she feared she'd never be able to get him back out again.

She felt so confused. What, exactly, did she feel for him? What did he feel for *her*?

Although he'd clearly changed his mind about her, and equally clearly desired her, she'd heard no words of love from him yet. And she was honest enough to admit that she was scared to death to completely open up her heart to him. To love him.

She crawled onto the wide bed and curled up on her side. She knew Mentàll would not join her in this bed. Not ever. And yet she wanted him there with a passion that frightened her.

Chapter Twenty-Two

Day 25

WHEN METHUSAL FINALLY EXITED from her bedroom the next morning, Mentàll was gone. Not that she was surprised. Like a coward, she'd puttered around in her room until he'd finally left. She joined Hendra for breakfast.

"Where is everyone?"

"At the beach."

"So early?"

"Apparently last night was the highest tide of the year. They want to check for shells. Doc and I might head down in a little while."

"Have the talks begun again?"

"No. I haven't seen the Presidente yet this morning."

Methusal nodded, and quietly ate her breakfast. A question burned in her mind. Finally, she said, "What does 'saltisienna' mean?"

A knowing smile lit her brown eyes. "It means 'fire of my heart.'"

"Oh." She blushed furiously.

Hendra's smiled widened, but she but tactfully changed the subject. "Here comes Mentàll. I'll leave you two alone."

"Thanks," she mumbled.

Hendra greeted her cousin with a big grin, and speedily left them.

Mentàll faced her across the table. "Good morning."

"Morning." Methusal glanced at him, and then back down at her scrambled eggs.

"Did you sleep well?"

Warmth flushed her cheeks. "Fair." Which meant very poorly. "And you?"

Those pale eyes seared into hers. "Would you like the truth?"

She stiffened her spine, and offered saucily, "Of course. Husbands and wives have no secrets, right?"

He smiled. "I dreamed of you all night."

"Then you must be tired of me by now," she replied. "Why aren't you meeting with the chiefs?"

His smile lingered. "We are waiting for the Presidente to appear. I have a proposition for you."

"What?" she said warily.

"Join the meeting. You will not serve the Presidente, of course. But he wants you there. I think your presence could benefit the peace process."

"How?"

"He continually interrupts the meetings to whisper to his advisors. They appear to be preparing a long document. Your kaavl skills could help us discover what he is doing."

"He dictates this document *during* the meeting? That's rude."

"It is a game. But the game will end today. What do you say, Methusal?"

"I'd be happy to help. I'm sick of sitting around, doing nothing."

He smiled. "That's my girl."

"For one more day," she murmured.

His eyes narrowed, apparently not comprehending.

"I'll be your girl for one more day."

"And one more night," he agreed. She frowned, but he tilted up her chin and to her shock, leaned across and kissed her. "The Presidente is here." With a smile, he kissed her more thoroughly, making her blood heat and her heart race. "Let the games begin."

△ △ △ △ △

Methusal shifted on the uncomfortable wooden chair, which was positioned to Mentàll's right. She had a direct view of the Presidente and his posturing advisors. The meeting had yet to begin, and yet already Artn knelt by the Presidente's side, listening intently to his superior's directives. The Presidente's thick lips were pulled back in a self-indulgent smile, and his eyes flickered smug, condescending glances at the Koblani chiefs.

Dishonorably eavesdropping was a pleasure...and a bore.

She murmured to Mentàll, "He's dictating his packing list. He wants everything pressed. No wrinkles, or Artn will be severely flogged."

Disgust curled the Dehrien Chief's lips. He gripped the white decision stone and rapped it three times on the long table.

"The meeting will begin. Last night, Pan was good enough to write up the list of demands from each side. He will read them now."

The Tarst Chief cleared his throat.

"Zindedi demands include: First, one high level kaavl player must travel to Zindedi to teach their troops kaavl; second, three shiploads of ore must be sent to Zindedi to pay for the destruction of several powder mines, and one boatload of ore every month must be sent thereafter, to be paid for by Zindedi goods and materials. Third, all Koblanis who visit Zindedi must be registered into the country; and finally, while the Zindedis do agree to free trade, Koblani merchant ships will be taxed before goods are offloaded."

Methusal rolled her eyes. Was the Zindedi President serious about peace at all?

Pan cleared his throat again. "Koblani demands include: First, Zindedi will cease and desist invading our land; second, any and all Koblani prisoners will be released immediately; third, Zindedi ships will remain six hundred lengths offshore, until invited to dock by Koblani ships; fourth, in exchange for a half boatload of ore, Zindedi will give Koblan two hundred guns; and fifth, free trade is acceptable, but taxes will be taken after merchandise has been sold, but before the barterers return to their ships."

Artn scuttled from the room, and the Presidente settled back with a satisfied smile. His fingers laced over his thick middle. "We appear to be at an impasse, gentlemen...and lady." His false, ingratiating smile made Methusal grit her teeth.

The negotiations began again, but the Presidente patently refused to budge on any issue. Servants finally served lunch, and the interminable meeting wore on. The Presidente did not look frustrated at all. Instead, a self-satisfied smirk continued to pull at his lips.

After lunch, Artn reappeared—this time with a scroll in his hand. While Wyen's chief and a Zindedi official argued about the number of firearms Zindedi should deliver to pay for the hundreds of lost Koblani lives during the Quasr War, the Presidente whispered into Artn's attentive ear. Methusal focused again into kaavl to listen to the Presidente.

"You fool, I said ten cases of racmun spirits, not two. ...Yes, a fourth of their cargo is an acceptable tax."

With a frown, Methusal glanced at the long document in the Presidente's hand. Performing a quick visual carry to the top of his head and then looking down, she zeroed in on the writing on the other side.

We, Zindedi, do solemnly agree to uphold peace under the following conditions:

1.   All Koblani citizens and ships must register within one hour of arriving in Zindedi waters.

2.   Free trade is acceptable, but one fourth of a Koblani ship's cargo must be paid first to Zindedi tax officials before any merchandise is unloaded onto Zindedi soil.

3.   Two cases of racmun spirits will be sent home with the Presidente as an expression of good will.

4. A humble apology from Presidente Solboshn, along with three boat loads of ore must be paid for the destruction of several Zindedi powder mines and countless Zindedi war ships.

Under these conditions, Zindedi will cease and desist attacking Koblan. However, any further Zindedi deaths by Koblani hands will break all agreements and be grounds for war. All Koblani ships in Zindedi territory will be seized and all Koblani citizens put to death.

So. The Presidente was making up his own peace agreement on the side. A few of the demands seemed surprisingly reasonable. On the other hand, others differed from the ones Zindedi officials were arguing about so vehemently right now. The *scienth*. No other word could describe a man who created turmoil just for the pleasure of twisting others into knots.

She touched Mentàll's arm. At once, she had his full attention. "May I speak to you privately?"

"Of course." In one fluid movement, he helped Methusal scoot back her chair. He told the others, "We will return shortly."

In the hall, Methusal looked both ways, and wasn't pleased to see two Zindedis lurking at the far end of the hall. "The flower garden."

Outside in the warm, humid heat, she explained what she had seen.

Anger tightened his features, but he remained calm. "I have a plan. Write down what you saw on a fresh parchment. Then follow my lead."

Back inside, Mentàll relaxed back in his chair, long legs stretched out under the table. He appeared to be listening idly to the arguments flying back and forth between the Zindedi advisors and the Koblani chiefs.

Meanwhile, Methusal procured a parchment and swiftly wrote out what she'd read on the Zindedi paper. When she'd finished, she rolled the parchment back up and handed it to Mentàll. His wide palm silently asked for the writing instrument. His fingers brushed hers as he took it.

With swift, bold, black strokes, he marked cryptic notes beside each of the Presidente's demands. At the bottom, he scribbled Koblan's demands. Then he rolled the scroll back up again.

At the far end of the table, the Presidente's eyes had narrowed, watching this interchange. Artn returned and murmured in his ear, but he ignored the young man. When Artn hesitantly tried to speak again, the Presidente snapped, "Sit!" and pointed to the floor beside him.

Cringing, Artn quickly obeyed.

Methusal looked away. Revulsion curled through her. A grown man forced to sit like a child at the Presidente's feet was horribly demeaning. It embarrassed her to see it.

The Presidente smashed his white rock on the table. Abrupt silence fell, and all eyes turned to him. His chest puffed out. "Honorable Presidente Solboshn. I see that you and your wife have been indulging in negotiations of your own. Are they private, or will you share them with me?"

Mentàll offered a thin smile. "We have no secrets." He handed the parchment to Chief Aarabst, on his left.

"No!" the Presidente thundered. "Methusal must bring it to me."

Chief Aarabst glanced at Mentàll.

"No," the Dehrien stated.

"Mentàll. I'm happy to do it." The idea repulsed her, but she would do it, for peace.

His frowning gaze held hers for a long moment. "Very well."

Methusal took the parchment and strode to the Presidente's end of the table. However, every step that brought her closer to the Presidente thickened the feeling of revulsion within her. She stopped just short of Artn, on the floor. When the Zindedi leader took the parchment, she turned with relief to make her escape.

"Stay, Methusal. I will wish to make my response to Mentàll's demands."

A glance took in Mentàll's frown, but he remained relaxed, sprawled in his chair, so Methusal stayed where she was. The Presidente's thick fingers unrolled the parchment. Surprise stiffened his corpulent body. She battled a smile from her lips.

"So." The Presidente's voice sounded congenial, but warning prickles crept down Methusal's skin. "You have stooped to espionage. You have succeeded in procuring secrets from young Artn." Light purple mottled the skin above his collar.

Artn glanced quickly at the Presidente, and stark terror stared from his dark eyes.

"No." Methusal instinctively defended the helpless Zindedi soldier. "I stole the secrets from you, Presidente, while you read the document. I heard you whisper to Artn that you wanted ten cases of racmun spirits, instead of two."

The Zindedi leader said nothing. Indecision flickered. He did not know how to respond to this new development. Finally, he shoved the scroll away and stared at Methusal with hard, calculating interest. "How? Tell me all, and I will strike the last condition from the agreement."

"Methusal," grated the Dehrien Chief.

She sent him a reassuring look, and returned her attention to the Zindedi leader. "I have very sensitive hearing. And I can see everything in this room—even hidden objects."

"How?" The Presidente sat forward, looking fascinated. "Are papers—clothes—invisible to you?"

Methusal chuckled merrily. "You don't want to know, Presidente. But realize one thing; I can see everything I want to see."

"Ah." His gaze ran down her body, and a leer curled the ends of his mouth. "I wish I could do the same."

Mentàll half rose from his chair. She sent him a quelling look.

"Tell me," the Zindedi leader said, "does kaavl allow you to perform such feats?"

"Of course. It is why you can never defeat us, no matter how hard you try. To your soldiers, we are invisible. We can see and hear every conversation from a great distance. Stone walls are no barrier to us."

Methusal rested her hip against the table near the Presidente, easily holding his rapt attention. "So do not provoke us," she said softly. "We are not creatures of war. But if we must, we can strike with swift, deadly precision. We have proven it, both here and in Zindedi. You have no defense against us. And yet," her laugh tinkled like a bell, "we are willing to let you walk in peace. This is your last chance, however, Presidente. If you choose war, we will be forced to annihilate your military." She smiled. "And last of all, we will come for you."

The Presidente's eyes bulged for a moment. Then he sat back in his chair. Expression as hard as a stone, he laced his hands across his paunch. "Prove it."

Methusal smiled. "Leave this room. Go anywhere you wish and speak to your advisors. Then come back, and I will tell you what you said. And where you went."

He frowned. "That is impossible."

Koblan's chiefs, including her father, stared at her with disbelieving expressions. Mentàll, however, crossed his ankle over his knee and eyed her with amusement, laced with resignation.

"All right." The Zindedi leader pushed his fists onto the table and levered himself to his feet. "Artn. Nmol. Come with me."

The three left, and the last man shut Calbn's office door behind them.

"Methusal," Erl said with a frown. "How can you..."

"Shh, please, Papa. I need to concentrate."

Methusal carried with vision to the dark strip under Calbn's door, and then carried, looking down the hall. With ease, she followed the Presidente's slow, lumbering footsteps.

He led his advisors outdoors, into the courtyard, and then just outside the compound's gates. The sound of pedestrians on the street and carts rumbling down the road battled for her attention, but with ruthless precision, she cut them out and focused only on the Presidente's conversation.

"I will say several numbers. If the Rolbani slut can repeat them back to me, we will know she is telling the truth. Listen carefully. Eight, nine, zero, eleven, one-hundred ninety-nine and eighty-seven." Artn wrote them down on a parchment, and showed it to the Presidente. "Good. Put it in your pocket."

The procession headed back inside. Methusal hastily wrote down the numbers too, and watched the Zindedis' every moment until Calbn's office door opened again.

The Presidente resumed his position at the head of the table. He gave Methusal a faint smirk. "Well?"

"You went outside the compound gates. You said six numbers. I wrote them down. They will match the numbers on a parchment in Artn's left pocket."

The Presidente's eyes narrowed.

Mentàll said, "We will exchange numbers. Methusal, give your parchment to the Presidente. Artn, give yours to me."

The exchange silently took place.

Mentàll said, "I will read the numbers Artn wrote." He did so. Incredulity crossed the Presidente's features. "Now you, Presidente."

Of course, the numbers matched.

Erl stared at Methusal, his mouth slightly agape, as did everyone else in the room.

She smiled. "Now do you believe in kaavl, Presidente?"

A lacy, blotched purple rose from his collar. "You are gifted, no doubt. However, I do not believe that your powers could destroy my military."

"Kaavl is multi-faceted, Presidente. This is only the tip of the stone."

A darker, ugly flush colored his skin now. "We will take a break. Negotiations will resume at dinner."

"Take our peace conditions with you," Mentàll said. "I look forward to fruitful discussions this evening."

The Presidente stalked from the room, shaking off Artn's tentative arm of help.

The Koblan chiefs gazed at Methusal with varying expressions of awe.

"You didn't really do that, right?" said Wyen's chief. "It was a trick. Did you have a spy at the gate?"

"It was no trick," Mentàll said harshly. His gaze held Methusal's, and fierce blue fire—pride, she realized with a jolt of warm satisfaction—burned in his eyes. "She is greatly gifted, just like her ancestor, Mahre."

Erl said, "Methusal. I am speechless. You have never made me prouder."

"Can kaavl players really do all those things she said?" Wyen's chief asked Mentàll.

Quietly, he said, "We can do everything we need to do." He stood and extended a hand to Methusal. "Come. I want to speak to you."

She allowed him to take her hand and accompanied him outdoors, to a bit of shade in the flower garden. Insects buzzed, and the sweet scent of flowers hung heavily in the warm, humid air.

He held both of her hands now, and drew her to face him. "I am very proud of you, Methusal." Faint amusement twitched his lips. "No doubt your kaavl tales will spread far and wide throughout Zindedi."

She smiled. "And they will fear us even more."

"I did not know you could spin half-truths into such convincing tales," he murmured. "An unknown talent."

"You approve?" Her breaths quickened when he drew her still nearer to him.

"I approve of any truth, half or not, that will give us the advantage over our enemies."

"Good. I wouldn't want you to think I'm a liar."

One hand cupped her jaw. He gently stroked her cheekbone, and her breath caught. "It is not a lie when we can do everything you said, and more...with the right kaavl players."

"If they were sufficiently gifted," she murmured.

"Yes. Gifted like you."

"And you."

His fingers stroked her hair. "We make a fine pair, Methusal."

She felt like she might drown in his clear blue gaze. "Maybe," she allowed faintly.

"Tonight, I want..."

"Mentàll!" Calbn called. "Good news. The Presidente has already cut one of his demands and agreed to one of ours."

"I am coming." With regret, his gaze traced Methusal's features. "I will see you later."

She nodded, but her mind felt sluggish and dreamy, as if entranced by a heady, hypnotic spell.

As she watched Mentàll stride away, her heart beat with slow, heavy thrums. This one man—could he possibly be her destiny?

△ △ △ △ △

Methusal pulled a long, mauve colored dress from the closet. It was sleeveless, and tied over one shoulder, leaving the other bare. She'd found it while shopping a few days ago. It seemed appropriate for the last night of peace talks.

The Presidente had agreed to all of their terms, and he'd cut out his demand for three boatloads of ore. Koblan had agreed to all of his other demands, except for his stipulation that one fourth of a boatload's cargo must be paid as tax before unloading and selling merchandise in Zindedi. Perhaps that last detail would be hashed out over dinner.

Tomorrow the vile Presidente would go home. Could all of their problems possibly end so soon?

Methusal brushed her hair and examined herself in the small mirror. Her skin looked clear, and her green eyes luminous. She looked presentable. Maybe even pretty. Would Mentàll think so?

She took a deep breath. Time to face the gauntlet with the Presidente one last time.

As she twisted the doorknob, a small sound came from the outer room. The door swung open to reveal that Mentàll was standing before the mirror, which hung above the couch, naked to the waist. Shaving lather obscured the lower half of his face.

"Sorry!" she gasped, and reached for the doorknob again.

"Do not be." A smile flickered through the foam. "You are always welcome to be here with me."

She eyed him again, and then edged inside.

He watched her in the mirror, and drew the blade down his cheek. "You look beautiful, Methusal."

Her cheeks warmed. "Thank you." She watched the hypnotic ripple of his muscles as he rinsed the blade in a cup of water. With a quick, smooth line, he drew it down his face again.

"Why are you shaving in here, instead of the relief room?"

"It has no mirror."

She wandered around the room, trying to ignore him, but finding it increasingly difficult to do so. The scent of his soap was leathery and spicy, and smelled like heaven. Her gaze returned to his back. The last rays of sunlight shimmered off of the hundreds of thin silver scars lacing his skin. A testimony to his uncle's cruelty. His shoulder muscles tightened, completing the last strokes down his face.

On the left side of his back, the round bullet wound was still puckered and pink. The scar from the Quasr War stretched down his right side. It was a fingerbreadth wide and five handbreadths long. She'd cared for that wound for weeks, tending it and massaging the knotted muscles in his shoulders to ease the pain. It had healed well.

Not sure how she suddenly had arrived there, Methusal reached out and traced it. "This scar is horrible." He had many scars—but most, she realized now, were on the inside.

His muscles stiffened beneath her touch and she froze, appalled by her thoughtless action. His hand hit the shaving cup, nearly knocking it over.

He grated, "Your touch maddens me." A plea and a warning.

She snatched her hand back. "I'm sorry."

He faced her. "Are you?" Two rough swipes of the towel erased the last of the soap, leaving only the harsh planes of his face. Some unknown emotion—it couldn't be pain?—dilated his pale eyes.

Wordlessly, she stared back at him. "I wasn't thinking," she said, to explain her action. "I remembered when you got that scar, that's all. I was remembering..."

"Our past."

"Yes. But our present—has it changed so much?" Had it? It was a plea from her heart for understanding.

Peace lived between them now, and he desired her, but did he care for her?

What did she feel for him?

She was afraid to face that truth. But Methusal could not deny that invisible threads bound her to him now. She couldn't break free from his gaze.

"You tell me," he said.

She regarded him for a moment. "Aren't you the same man?"

The one who had tried to take over Rolban.

He knew what she meant. He turned away and put the cup and towel on a side table. Harshly, he said, "I am still that same man."

Methusal wanted to reach out and draw him back. She had wanted him to deny it. But he hadn't. She didn't understand him. Not at all.

Mentàll pulled his tunic over his powerful, sleek muscles. "It is time to go."

"Wait."

He hesitated.

Helplessly, she said, "You have changed. Haven't you?"

He took a step toward her, and his hands curled around her upper arms. "I am no longer filled with hatred. I have changed in that regard. I was wrong to hurt you, and Rolban. But at heart, I am still the same man I have always been. I will not lie."

Methusal said nothing, but her heart filled with a bit of hope. Although he denied it, he *had* changed. As he said, he was no longer driven by hatred, and he had admitted to his wrong deeds. In Rolban, he'd even apologized for them before the trip to Carachki. She hadn't believed him then, but she did now.

"So you have changed," she said softly.

"I am no saint, Methusal."

She felt as if he was warning her, but she wasn't certain why.

He could not abide to live a lie. Perhaps that was why.

"I know you're not." She offered him a smile.

"You know who I am," he said harshly. "Do not tell yourself fairy tales, Methusal."

Without speaking, she looked at him, and wondered what he was trying to tell her.

He pressed, "Can you accept me as I am?"

At last, she understood. Inexpressible emotion filled her, and tears prickled in her eyes.

Before she could speak, he whispered again, roughly, "Can you accept me as I am?" He bent his head suddenly and kissed her, a burning whisper across her lips. Her hands went to his chest, and she made a small sound when he pulled away.

"Would you like another?" he murmured.

"Yes," she whispered, and swayed into him. This kiss was tender, and even a bit tentative. Familiar stirrings of fire licked through her and she melted into him, sliding her arms around his neck, and her fingers into his hair. His chest felt hard and warm and very strong against her.

He nibbled kisses down her jaw. "Will you?" His teeth grazed her earlobe. "Will you accept me as I am?" he whispered.

Overwhelming tenderness welled up in her, so strong she could barely contain it. And then she knew. Perhaps she'd known all along.

She loved him.

With a shudder, she gripped his shoulders more tightly. His muscles felt like smooth ore beneath her fingers.

He whispered again, "Will you accept me?"

"Yes," she whispered. Lord help her, she could not deny him anything, not even her own heart. "I do. I can...I want to, more than anything."

"Then choose me over Behran. I promise that you will not regret it. Not for one day." His hot kisses traced the column of her throat, and she arched her neck back, breathing faster.

"I...I can't think when you kiss me like this."

His lips left her throat, and she drew a deep, shuddering breath.

He watched her, his pale eyes burning as hot and clear as blue fire. "I want your entire heart and mind, as well as your body, Methusal. Answer me when you are ready."

She still clung to him. When she realized it, she let go and stepped back.

Harshly, he said, "Something special lives between us."

"I know. And...and I'll give you my answer. Tomorrow."

Disappointment flickered. But he said, "Fair enough," and offered his arm. "The Presidente is close to capitulating. Should I try to charm him?"

"Maybe *I* should try to charm him."

"Perhaps," he murmured. "But if he comes within one step of you, I will kill him."

Methusal smiled. "There's the wild beast I know."

He chuckled. Securing his hand around hers, they entered the bustling hall, joined as one to face their final battle.

△ △ △ △ △

Everyone wore their best tonight in the dining hall. Mentàll solicitously pulled out Methusal's chair. As he helped her slide it back in, he murmured in her ear, "Now the show will begin."

She squashed a smile. Smoothing the napkin onto her lap, she glanced down the table at the Presidente. His color was high, and his skin looked faintly mottled again. At the moment, he gulped deep swallows from a glass of spirits. The ever-hovering Artn quickly refilled it.

Once again she wondered how serious his health condition might be. Even if he signed the peace agreement and meant to abide by it, what would happen if he died? Would General Fitrn uphold the peace, too?

Mentàll lifted his glass. Sparkling amber liquid shimmered. "Presidente. To peace, and to the beginning of friendship between our lands."

The Presidente did not drink. "Did you agree to my last request, Solboshn?" His voice sounded harsh and ugly. Methusal wondered if he had begun to regret his concessions to Koblan.

"Let us celebrate the points we have agreed upon. Our final negotiations can conclude after dinner."

The Presidente frowned, but said no more. He attacked his first course with violent jabs of his fork.

Methusal murmured to her mother, "What's wrong with him?"

Hanuh glanced at the Presidente. "He is angry about his health, and he hates appearing weak to us. He wishes he could order his soldiers to kill us right now."

Mentàll had been listening. "Is he pretending peace?"

"I can't tell. He fears you, Mentàll, and you, too, Methusal. He doesn't want peace—I sense that very clearly. But that's not to say he won't follow through with it."

"Do you sense anything else?"

Hanuh again glanced down the table. "Malevolence blackens his soul. It's difficult to read deeper into him. But one thing is certain. He would like to hurt us, and if he can find any possible way to do so, he will."

Methusal said, "So, we still don't know if we can trust him."

"We cannot," Mentàll said. "However, we will proceed with peace as though we can."

"Why?"

"Peace is better than war. We must pursue even the slimmest chance for peace. But we will not be fools. We will watch him. If he breaks his word, we will strike before he can." The cold, uncompromising threat in his voice made her shiver.

She blurted, "I know how to agree to his last demand."

Mentàll regarded her. Harsh lines etched the sides of his mouth. He wanted this peace. She felt it viscerally. And if it failed, it would deeply disappoint him.

"Agree to pay them a twenty-five percent tax on the cargo—but only on the portion that is actually sold in Zindedi. Payable in cash. Offer the same terms if they'd like to sell cargo here."

Hanuh put in, "He will see it as another concession."

Another idea popped to mind, and Methusal addressed the Quasr chief, sitting across from her, "Calbn, do you have a singing and dancing group in Quasr? Could you ask them to come in quickly?"

He frowned. "Why?"

"They could put on a performance tonight in honor of the Presidente. Make it look like it's been planned all along. Maybe some of the girls could pretend to fawn over him." She grimaced as she said it. "Just as part of the act. He'd feel honored and important. Maybe his pride won't feel so squashed. Maybe then he'd be willing to graciously agree to our last request."

"I think that's a good idea," Hanuh murmured. "He enjoys having his ego stroked."

"Well, Calbn?" Mentàll said.

"My wife may know of a group. I will speak to her now." Calbn left the table and headed toward their private quarters. Lylitha hadn't joined them for dinner this past week. Methusal assumed it was because she was caring for her infant sons. Either that, or she and her husband did not have a good relationship.

Calbn returned just as a maid scuttled out of the mansion's main doors. "They will be here within the half hour."

The Presidente slammed his fist on the table. "To the fair Methusal. Your beauty turns every eye in the room." Mocking malevolence glittered in his dark eyes.

Mentàll's fingers tightened around his fork.

Methusal, however, decided to play along. She lifted her own cup. "To the distinguished Presidente." For a second, she floundered. What other positive thing could she say about the bestial Zindedi dictator? "You... You rule a beautiful and bountiful land. I look forward to trading ore for your fine fabrics and pottery."

A disbelieving frown puckered the Zindedi's brows, but he raised his glass still higher. "To wise and fitting words from a beautiful woman." He drank deeply, and Methusal did the same.

She coughed in surprise, because the liquid burned like fire down her throat. She hadn't expected racmun spirits to be in her cup. It was the first night it had been served to everyone.

Her mother smiled with amusement, but Mentàll did not.

The spirits in her cup went quickly to her head, perhaps because she'd eaten little, or maybe because she wasn't used to the alcohol. In any event, she soon felt giddy.

The Presidente raised his cup again and stared at Methusal. "To the many fine Koblani delicacies I look forward to sampling."

The Dehrien Chief stiffened.

Methusal giggled, and raised her glass. "To nasrias and ortangias. Perhaps Calbn could plant them in his garden. Their fragrance could surely sweeten the sourest temperament."

Calbn scowled, and his dark eyes hardened to contemptuous black. The Presidente, however, bellowed with laughter. "To sweetening the sourest Koblani." His faintly appreciative gaze turned to Methusal. "And to even sweeter lips. They must pleasure Ment..."

"Enough!" Mentàll thundered. Red scored his cheekbones.

A cruel, satisfied smile curled the Presidente's lips. He drank deeply.

Methusal looked at Mentàll, confused. "What's wrong?" She patted his arm playfully. "They're only harmless toasts. Look how happy the Presidente is. He's smiling."

"Enough, Methusal," he said harshly. He pried the cup from her fingers, and the liquid sloshed onto the table cloth.

She glared, but it was hard to hold the expression, because she felt the irrepressible urge to act silly. "You're no fun," she pouted.

The singers and dancers arrived, followed by musicians who pounded on drums and played upbeat tunes on reed instruments. It was all very loud and merry, and when the girls sashayed to the Presidente and caressed his thick, wiry hair and exclaimed over his medals, the Zindedi leader relaxed. For the first time, he smiled with genuine enjoyment.

Methusal was thirsty, and piqued that Mentàll had stolen her cup. So she drank deeply from his. When she put it down, he removed it from her reach. Irritated, she grabbed for her own cup, but his large hand trapped hers on the table. "Enough." Over his shoulder, he said, "Water, please."

A servant immediately delivered a full glass of water, but Methusal glared at Mentàll. Soon, however, a deeper, rosy glow warmed her senses. She smiled. He frowned. "You're a contrary man," she told him.

"And you, *ce'cemone*," he said in a low voice, "cannot handle racmun spirits."

She giggled, entranced by the soft, lyrical Dehrien word. "What does "'say say mone' mean?"

"Tonight I will tell you. After the spirits wear off."

She gazed at him, smiling, chin in her hand.

A faint smile twitched one corner of his mouth, softening his stern expression. "Do not look at me like that, Methusal."

"Why not? You like it."

"If you were in your right mind, I would enjoy it even more."

The tempo of the music increased, and the dancing women tied bells to their wrists. The dazed, happy fog in Methusal's head slowly dissipated, and a dull ache followed.

It was so loud. When would the dancers leave? She drank more water, hoping it would flush away the effects of the racmun spirits.

Artn appeared at Mentàll's shoulder. "The Presidente will sign the agreement. Prepare two copies, and he will sign them tomorrow morning."

Both Mentàll and Calbn blinked in surprise. Mentàll recovered first. He glanced at the other end of the table. The Presidente was gone. "Very good. Thank him for me."

Artn bowed his head and trotted down the hall toward the Presidente's room.

Calbn stood. "A toast! The Presidente will sign the peace agreement."

Zindedi officials and Koblani chiefs cheered, their joy no doubt amplified by the racmun spirits and dancing women. More toasts circled the table.

Methusal was surprised that the Presidente hadn't insisted upon his last condition. She also wondered why he'd left so abruptly. Perhaps his heart was troubling him again, and he didn't want to appear weak.

Calbn said in a low tone to Mentàll, "Let's go over the draft. I'll have a servant make two copies tonight."

Mentàll nodded, but before he stood, his gaze snared Methusal's. Faint amusement lurked there. "I see you possess your full mind again. Please wait up for me. I would like to speak to you tonight."

"I will. As long as you're not too late."

"I will not be late," he promised in a low voice, and left with Calbn.

It was still noisy. Her mother touched her arm. "Your father and I are turning in. We'll see you in the morning."

"'Night, Mama."

Her mother smiled, and squeezed her hand. "Goodnight, Thusa." Her serious, knowing gaze held a mixture of joy, tempered with concern. "Be happy," she said. "That's all your father and I want for you."

She watched them go. Her mother seemed to sense that something portentous might happen tonight. And Mentàll had made it clear that he wanted to speak to her.

But about what? It couldn't be... Her pulse accelerated. No. Certainly not. However, suddenly she needed to find some solitude.

She left the room and escaped into the quiet garden next to Calbn's office. A light shone inside. Mentàll and Calbn pored over documents on the desk.

She sat on a bench in the shadows. In the quiet, the ache in her head subsided. Invisible insects chirped and hummed in the soft, dark shadows of the garden. It smelled sweet and heavenly. Perfect.

Could a life with Mentàll be perfect? Would it provide the deep joy that she had always wanted in a relationship?

In the past, that very question would have made her laugh. But now she prodded the idea from every side. With her whole heart, she wanted it to be true.

She didn't want to leave Quasr and go home soon. In fact, the thought of leaving him and never seeing him again terrified her—it felt as if she'd be making the most horrifying mistake of her entire life.

Methusal closed her eyes. What was she thinking? It *would* be a mistake.

She loved him.

As terrifying as it might be, she must finally take her courage in hand and tell him how she felt. Then she'd move forward and try to make their relationship work.

Yes, she was scared. But since she loved him, she must put everything she had into their relationship—even if he broke her heart in the end.

Otherwise, she would regret it forever.

Peace finally filled her heart.

Tonight she'd tell him that her engagement to Behran had ended several weeks ago. And she'd ask him to forgive her for the lie. Then all of the deceptions between them would be finished, and they could move forward.

"Methusal?" Calbn's voice tickled her ears. For a second, she thought he was in the garden and had spoken to her.

Then she realized that she'd relaxed so much that kaavl had taken over. Calbn was speaking to Mentàll.

"Why her?" Calbn asked. "You've pursued her all this time, and for what? You still haven't won her." Ice clinked in a glass. "Drop her. You could have any other woman on the planet."

"None can offer me what Methusal does."

"And what's that? ...Ah, yes. A close alliance with Rolban's Chief." Calbn's nasty chuckle sounded approving. "Smart. It's the richest community in Koblan. Before long, much power will be seated there."

"True."

"Is that the only reason?" A silence elapsed. "What more does she offer, then?" Calbn laughed sharply. "Wait. That's an easy guess."

A hard, sick lump lodged in Methusal's throat. She peered through the bushes, so she could carry with vision into the room.

"It's because she's Mahre's descendent, isn't it? She'll give you lots of kaavl sons. Not a bad exchange for your freedom."

"It will not hurt matters." A small smile pulled at Mentàll's lips.

She gasped.

Calbn's laugh sounded clearly approving. "You're as sly as a whip. Was that your plan from the beginning?"

"It would be a lie to say I have not considered it at length."

Calbn laughed again. "But she refused your first offer of marriage. Judging by the smile she gave you tonight, however, this time she'll accept you with open arms."

"I will seal her commitment to me tonight." The Dehrien Chief raised a spirit glass. "To Methusal."

Calbn raised his glass. "To a firm alliance with the most valuable commodity in Koblan. And to the extraordinary sons you are sure to beget. Power and kaavl married together—certain immortality for your line, Mentàll. Clever. You have my deepest admiration."

Mentàll's lips curled back into the barest snarl. "Not bad for the son of a bastard." He tossed back the rest of the amber liquid in one gulp.

Methusal gasped again, and pressed her hand to her heart. Jagged, raw pain tore through her.

This was why he wanted her. On the ship, after hearing his conversation with Captain Hill, she'd wondered how he wanted to use her to gain his goals. Now, finally, she understood. By marrying her, he could obtain access to Rolban's riches. Not only that, but he would gain the power he'd always wanted, and kaavl immortality, too.

No wonder he had pursued her with single-minded determination since the Quasr War. In fact, ever since he'd discovered he could stomach her presence, and in fact lusted after her. What more could he want in a woman? Yes, his feelings had changed. And now she understood why!

She choked back a sob. He didn't love her.

But he'd never said he did. He'd only said he wanted her. *But he'd said he cared for her.*

Did he? Or did he only care about power and his future legacy?

Hot tears slipped down her cheeks. She didn't know what to believe anymore. Her heart felt ripped out, as if she'd been gutted and left to bleed.

"Oh *The One*," she whimpered. "Please no. *No.*" She crumpled forward, fists on her knees, unable to control her frightening, visceral sobs. "No. *No. Please.*"

"Methusal." Behran's deep voice was a surprise, but only for a moment.

She turned into him. While he held her, she sobbed out her agony.

△ △ △ △ △

When Methusal's blinding tears finally stopped, Behran walked her back to Mentàll's suite.

He'd asked few questions, which was good, because she was barely able to speak. But when Tumel opened the door so Methusal could slip inside, Behran touched her arm. His gaze was dark with compassion. "It's over?"

She nodded jerkily.

"I'm sorry." With a soft goodnight, he left her.

Inside, she washed her face in the relief room, and shied away from the quick glance in the mirror over the couch. Her eyes were red and puffy, and her face an unsightly, blotched mess. In the bedroom she quickly pulled on her soft pajamas and slipped between the cool sheets of the gigantic bed.

More tears streamed down her cheeks. Mentàll had shown his true hand tonight. At last.

Now she knew everything.

She'd repeatedly wondered why he'd pursued her ever since the Quasr War had ended. He'd claimed it was because he desired her. Maybe he did. But now she finally knew what he really wanted.

Why was she so surprised? Power was all he'd ever wanted. She knew that, but had blindly forgotten about it. At his core, he was a power hungry man. He always had been, and he always would be. It was the driving force of his life. His consuming passion. He had said this afternoon that he hadn't changed. He had told the truth. He hadn't changed at all.

And kaavl children would be the topping on the proverbial tart. With her, he could gain everything he'd ever desired.

She'd foolishly hoped he might love her. But she'd been wrong. Mentàll was not the man for her. The logical part of her brain had warned her, over and over again, and yet she had not listened.

She wept silently. In the three long years they'd known one another, the one thing they still did best was hurt one another. It had to stop. Once this last charade with the Presidente ended tomorrow, she would go home and never see Mentàll again.

It was over. Forever.

In the dark quiet of the room, she finally fell into a light sleep.

Δ Δ Δ Δ Δ

A rap at the door teased her awake. Her eyelids slid open. Another firm, decisive knock.

Mentàll.

Through her thick, muddled thoughts she remembered that he'd wanted to talk to her. He'd asked her to wait up for him.

Tough tagma berries.

They could talk in the morning.

She didn't answer.

The door opened. "Methusal?"

"Get *out*," she whispered.

He hesitated. "What is wrong?"

When she didn't answer, the edge of the bed sagged down. She curled up, away from him. "Get *away* from me," she hissed.

He rose. But now a match flared the lamp to life. The sharp smell of smoke drifted to her nose. He stared down at her. Methusal knew she looked like a wreck, but didn't care.

"Who hurt you?" Anger harshened his voice.

"Go *away*." She closed her eyes. "Please!"

A waft of a breeze told her that he'd knelt beside her. "Tell me, Methusal," he said softly. His hand reached out, perhaps to stroke her hair, but she reared back. "Don't *touch me!*" she snarled, and rolled quickly to the far side of the bed. There, her feet found the cold floor. She stood there, shaking, arms crossed. The whole bed stretched between them.

He rose. Caution stilled his features. "What happened?"

"*You* tell me," she bit back.

"You are speaking in circles."

"Calbn seems to understand everything perfectly. Why don't you go talk to him again?"

He cast a perplexed look toward the door. "What did Calbn do to you?"

"*Calbn* didn't do anything to me. It's *you*. It's always *you* who hurts me, over and over again. Why don't I ever learn?" she cried out. "Why did I start to trust you? I *hate* you! I hate you with my whole heart!"

He stood very still. "You heard my conversation with Calbn."

"Give the man a prize!" she said sarcastically. "I know everything now, Mentàll. I know how you want to use me. I'm just a stepping stone on your path to greatness."

"No."

"Looks like you'll need to tell your friend Calbn that you failed again. I'm not as stupid as you want to believe."

"Methusal."

"Be quiet!" she snapped. "I won't listen to more of your 'half' truths."

After a second, he said, "I would be foolish if I did not consider how an alliance with you would affect my future."

"Alliance!" she cried in disbelief. "Yes, finally. Tell me the truth."

"Our relationship is about more than an alliance. You know that."

"Do I? Because you're so open and honest about *everything*? Oh yes, I can trust you completely. From the first moment you held a knife to my throat so you could gain power over Rolban, until you ripped the *Second Book of Kaavl* out of my hands. You said you haven't changed. And I believe it now. It's always been about power with you. It will *always* be about power. Don't insult me by telling me it's about anything else between us!"

A flush scored his cheekbones. "Something bigger lives between us, Methusal. Do not deny it. I have told you that I care for you. I have proven it over and over again. I have protected you. I have saved your life too many times to count!"

"Thank you, then. *Thank you!* But it's over. Whatever might have been there, it's dead. I want you out of my life, now and forever."

He gritted, "You are lying to yourself."

"Get out! I hate you."

"This is not over," he stated. "We will discuss it tomorrow, when you've calmed down."

Fury flared. "I *am* calm, you arrogant, cold-blooded wild beast! Get out!" When he didn't move, feeling enraged beyond all reason, she grabbed a book off the bed table and threw it at him. "*Get OUT!*"

Swifter than thought, he rounded the bed and closed the distance between them. Tears streaming, she snatched up another book, but he twisted it from her grasp. He held her wrists immobile in his fists.

"Do not attack me." Threat shivered in that low tone. When she struggled, his grip tightened.

"Why not?" she spat. "Treating a beast like a beast is the only thing you understand." She had to get away from him. His nearness both infuriated and confused her.

He hissed, "Do you think I am a wild beast? Then a wild beast I will be." Thickly, he murmured, "I will do whatever it takes to make you mine."

"I hate you. I *hate* you!" She struggled harder.

His warm lips found the pulse point below her ear and lingered. She gasped aloud. And then he forced her backwards, onto the bed.

"What are you *doing?*"

He ignored her. Holding her wrists pinioned to the bed on either side of her head, he kissed down her throat to the hollow between her breasts. She gasped again and involuntarily arched against him.

His kisses traced a delicate path beneath her breasts.

"Mentàll. Oh, don't. Please." Her breaths came in sharp gasps, and she was overcome by confusion and a frightening, aching passion. His heavy breaths hovered, hot on her skin. He remained stationary there.

"Mentàll." She wasn't sure if it was a plea for him to stop or continue.

After a long moment, he rose up and buried his lips in her hair. Only now did she feel how fast the breaths shuddered through his body.

He kissed below her jaw, where her pulse pounded, and then her lips. Harshly, he whispered, "I am sorry, Methusal." Then he levered himself to his feet.

Instinctively, she quickly sat up, too.

He said, "We will finish this discussion tomorrow." And then he was gone, closing the door with quiet force behind him.

Methusal crossed her arms tightly. With a soft sob, she crawled back into bed, curled up into a ball, and wept herself to sleep.

Chapter Twenty-Three

The next morning, Methusal lay awake in the predawn light, carefully touching last night's memories. The hurt, pain, and confusion of what she had learned felt like an oppressive weight on her heart. In comparison, the bright morning sunshine felt like it mocked her.

Was Calbn right? Did Mentàll only want her for power, and for kaavl progeny?

Her feelings for the Dehrien tormented her. She wanted to run away and escape from them. But wasn't that the coward's way to protect herself? How could she ever discover the truth if she didn't face him calmly, and demand answers?

Her mother's advice, given several days ago, returned to mind. "If you love him, make the effort to find out who he really is. Stop pushing him away, and maybe he'll let you deeper inside that heart of his."

Did he truly have a heart? Or did he just want to use her for his own purposes, like Calbn believed? Most damning of all, Mentàll had not denied Calbn's claims.

The Dehrien Chief definitely desired her. That was abundantly clear. Even worse, his behavior last night had not shocked her, as it should have done. Instead, she had wanted him. She'd wanted to give herself to him utterly.

She loved him. This truth again scorched her heart, as hot and clear as the morning sunshine. She loved him. She could not stop.

Appalled, she choked on a sob and pressed her hand to her mouth. She loved him. But did he want *her*, or only the benefits he could gain by joining with her?

She had to ask. It was time to have a final, honest conversation with him.

Methusal crawled out of bed, dressed, and brushed her hair.

In the other room, a writing stick scratched on parchment. He was waiting for her. Stiffening her spine, and feeling unbearably vulnerable, she opened the door.

Mentàll immediately rose to his feet. This morning he wore the dark blue shirt that he'd worn the first day in the invader land. It emphasized the breadth of his shoulders and brought out the blue of his eyes. His blond hair was damp. He was devastatingly handsome.

He moved from behind the desk. "Good morning, Methusal."

"Good morning," she said quietly.

His pale gaze looked cautious. It was the first time she'd ever seen him when he did not appear completely confident. He said, "I deeply apologize for my behavior last night. Will you please forgive me?"

"Yes." His aggressive seduction had disturbed her far less than her response to it had. "I'm sorry for throwing the book. I shouldn't have done that."

His shoulders relaxed. "Then we may have peace." It was too quiet to be a statement, but it wasn't quite a question, either.

She took a deep breath, clinging to her courage. "I want to trust you. But I can't. I'm afraid."

He sat on the edge of his desk, which put him on eye level with her. "Because of what you overheard last night."

"Because of everything, Mentàll. The secrets you kept from me about the Alliance. And Koblan's Presidente position. Not to mention our whole sorry past. We hurt each other really well. I want it to stop."

"I do not want to hurt you. It is the last thing I want to do."

"I believe you."

Hope flared in his eyes. "Then half the battle is won."

"No. It's not. Give me an honest answer. Why do you really want me?"

Surprise flickered, and then resolution. "Because you are an extraordinary woman. No other woman sharpens me like you do. No other woman matches me like you do. You are the only woman for me."

"Tell me the truth. Is it because my father is Chief of Rolban? Because Mahre is my ancestor?"

"They are a part of who you are. I cannot separate those things from you."

"You're not answering the question."

"What is your question?"

"If I was a crop picker from Wyen, and my father was an urchet care giver, and if I knew no kaavl… Would you still want me? Would you still pursue me?"

"That is an unfair question. If you were none of those things, you would not be you. I am drawn to you because of who you are. I want us to be joined in union. Together we would be a force to be reckoned with."

"So it *is* about power," she whispered.

"We are the same, Methusal. We belong together. You feel it, just as I do. I will give you everything I have. You would want for nothing."

Except for love. He'd said nothing about love.

"So I'd be a possession to you. A tool to gain even more of the power you lust after?"

"We would be partners."

"But here's the problem. I don't want power."

"What do you want?"

"I want to be loved." Her voice caught.

He stood abruptly and turned away. He picked up a writing instrument, fiddled with it, and then faced her from across the desk. "I do not know if I can love anyone."

"You love Hendra."

"Yes. I care for her. I protect her. It is the same with you. And I feel a deep, consuming passion for you. But real love…I do not know if I am capable of it."

Her soul began to bleed. "Thank you for being honest."

"I can give you my loyalty and passion. You will want for nothing. I will make sure of it. You will have everything you desire."

"Except for you."

"You will have everything of me that I can give you."

Softly, she said, "Are you afraid to love?"

"No," he said harshly. "I think I am too selfish to love."

She stared at him.

"What you see of me, Methusal," he lifted his arms, "all of it I will give you. Is it enough?"

Will you accept me, as I am? His words from yesterday whispered through her heart. She wanted to love him, more than anything. She *did* love him. But if she was honest with herself, she knew she could not endure a cold marriage. Her heart would shrivel up and die if she had to live on meager scraps of his attention.

"I'm afraid," she whispered.

"Why?"

"Because I can't endure a cold union with you. It would kill me. It's not enough."

"I will make it be enough," he said harshly. "I will give you passion. I will make sure you never feel cold or alone."

Yes, she could well imagine the scorching passion at night. But during the day, and at all other times, he would treat her as a favored possession, at best. "It's not enough."

Red touched his cheekbones. "You would endure a passionless marriage with Behran? That would fulfill you?"

"This is not about Behran." Soon she would tell him the truth about the broken engagement, but first they needed to finish this conversation. "I do care about him..."

"As a *friend,*" he snarled. "His tepid attempts at love would quench the fire in your soul."

"Stop it." Tears burned her eyes. "This is hard, Mentàll. I'm sorry, but I can't be with you." He had no idea how sorry she was. Her soul felt like it was ripping in two right now.

Clearly, however, he did not love her. He only saw her as a possession who would help him gain more power. And since he couldn't give her what she needed—love—he'd keep hurting her, over and over again, without even meaning to do so. She wouldn't put herself in that position. What was more, it wasn't fair to him, either.

He stared at her in disbelief. "It is *not* over, Methusal."

"I'm sorry. It is. You can't say anything to change my mind."

"Then I will not use words," he said grimly.

A shiver slipped down her spine. He didn't like to lose. He would not give up, and worst of all, they still had one more performance to give the Presidente.

"You won't change my mind," she told him in a strong voice. "Accept it."

His choked laugh sounded like a snarl. "It is not over."

"Goodbye," she whispered, and swiftly escaped from the room.

Δ Δ Δ Δ Δ

Last week Goric had tried and failed to get a job as a houseboy. He would try again today, but Deccia wasn't prepared to wait any longer. She was desperate to get Timaeus out of prison before the Presidente returned. He was probably sailing back to Zindedi now. It was time to take matters into her own hands.

Unbeknownst to either Goric or Riln, she had decided to set out early this morning to line up with the other women at the palace wall. They were interviewing for maids today.

Deccia wore a demure white tunic and a tan skirt that she'd purchased from her current job, which wouldn't start for another hour. She should have plenty of time to make it through this line. She was only in seventh position.

She took slow breaths, trying to calm her racing heart. She had to get the job this time. She just had to.

Long minutes dragged by, and she slowly moved forward in line.

"Next." The olive-skinned, black-haired woman at the table looked familiar. With sharp hand movements, she impatiently waved Deccia forward.

Deccia smiled. "Good morning."

A frown creased deep between the woman's eyes. "Weren't you here before?" Before she could speak, the woman cut her off. "I can't hire you. Next!"

"But..."

"Next!"

Flabbergasted and angry, Deccia stumbled away.

She *couldn't* hire her? What was that supposed to mean? Obviously, the woman remembered her. Equally clear, she'd made up her mind to never hire her.

Disappointed and angry, she arrived early at work. Euphira was pleased to see her, at least. But Deccia wondered why the palace supervisor disliked her so much. What had she done?

It seemed like fate was conspiring to keep her out of the palace, and away from Timaeus. Tears filled her eyes at different points throughout the day as she ruminated on the morning's disappointing disaster.

She got home before the men did, and threw all of her frustrated energy into making dinner. Timaeus filled her mind. She remembered kissing him goodbye for the last time, and how strong and healthy he'd looked then.

Riln had heard nothing in weeks. Had he lost a lot of weight? Was he in pain? Had his gunshot wound and amputated finger been properly cared for?

Just the thought of Timaeus' finger made her burst into tears. The food on the counter blurred. She wanted to curl up on her bed and weep.

"Timaeus," she choked out. Blindly, she grabbed for a vegetable and chopped it in half. She could not fall apart. For Timaeus. For Timaeus. She *had* to think of a way to rescue him.

The door slammed, and she averted her body and wet face. She wiped her eyes on her sleeve and continued chopping.

"What's for dinner, lunatic?"

"Stew," she said shortly.

A thump came from the couch and Riln popped the top of a spirit bottle. Silence ensued, which was just fine with her.

With Riln there, she couldn't cry. Maybe that was a good thing. She concentrated on cutting up meat and vegetables into bite-sized pieces.

It was dark outside, and a delicious, savory smell simmered from the pot by the time Goric finally got home.

"You're late, rocher," Riln belched. "Spend time tickling your fancy?"

Goric flushed.

Riln laughed, and his black gaze slid to Deccia. "Of course not. If you weren't so pathetic..."

"Cut it!" Goric snapped. "I just came from the palace."

Deccia swallowed a soft gasp. "Did you get the job?"

"Yes." He offered her a thin smile. "I'm a houseboy, with full run of the third floor."

"That's wonderful!" she cried out. She flung her arms around him and hugged him tight. "Oh, thank goodness. Thank *goodness*." Tears rolled down her cheeks again.

Goric pulled free and retreated a full step. He eyed her with guarded concern. "What's wrong?"

"Nothing! I'm relieved. Now we can finally help Timaeus."

Riln snorted. "If the rocher's got the guts to tiptoe down to the prison."

"Riln, stop it!" Deccia said. "This is the break we've been waiting for."

"Yeah? What's your plan, apte boy? I heard that seven soldiers guard the main prison door. How're you going to get through?"

"I don't know. But I've been thinking about a rescue plan."

"You have? What is it?" Further relief grew in her. Finally, things were turning around.

Goric shoved his hands in his pockets and his gaze flickered from Deccia to Riln. "You may not like it."

"Tell us!"

"I heard a report today that Timaeus is still all right. He'll probably be safe until the Presidente returns."

Deccia felt even more relieved. "That's great. We'll get him out before he gets back."

Goric did not answer directly. "The ship from Koblan will probably arrive here about the same time as the Presidente's ship."

"So we have two weeks to rescue Timaeus."

Goric hunched his shoulders. "I'm thinking we should wait to rescue him."

"*Wait?*" Deccia cried in disbelief. "What are you talking about?"

Riln bellowed with laughter. "You're running true to form, apte! Running from a fight. Wanting to hide where it's safe, behind mama's skirts." An evil smile twisted his lips. "Deccia's skirts, I mean."

Goric's eyes blazed. He advanced on Riln. "You *scienth!* Shut it."

"Ooh." Riln waggled his massive hands. "I'm scared, rocher boy. Go scuttle under your rock."

"Stop it!" Deccia shouted. "What do you mean, *wait,* Goric? You can't be serious."

His hot glare turned from Riln. "Think about it. We don't know what kind of shape Timaeus is in. We hope he's healthy. Even if he's not being tortured, he could still have...complications."

Deccia felt suddenly sick. "His wounds could be infected," she whispered.

"Maybe. And think of another thing. When the soldiers find him gone, they'll mount a massive search for him. If he's injured, and we can't run far, then that'll be it for all of us."

Riln mumbled derisive comments under his breath.

"If he's sick, we need to get him a doctor!"

"If he's sick, we won't get far," Goric repeated in a quiet voice. "The soldiers are probably under orders to keep him alive for the Presidente. That means they're giving him the basic medical attention he needs. I think we should wait to rescue Timaeus until after the Koblani ship arrives."

"But the Presidente will probably be back by then, too."

"Koblan's ship might get here first."

"No Goric! That's crazy. I want Timaeus out *now. Right now.*"

Goric retreated a step to lean against the counter. He folded his arms. "That's what I think."

Silence ensued. Deccia could not believe that Goric had suggested such an outlandish plan. The whole idea made her feel sick. At least she could be sure that Riln would be on her side.

"I do not like it," she said quietly. "I do not like that plan at *all.*"

Arm resting on the back of the couch, Riln fingered his stubbly beard. He smiled. "I like it."

Aghast, Deccia stared. "Since when do you want to run from a fight?"

He smiled, showing his teeth. "But think of the prize, lunatic." He whipped out his knife. With a glazed look, he pressed the flat edge against his own throat. "A slice..." he moved the blade gently, "...and the Presidente's bloody reign will end."

She gasped.

"What about peace, Riln?" Goric challenged with a hard look. "He's signing a peace agreement."

Riln shrugged. "I don't trust him. The only good Zin is a dead one. Corpses don't start wars. And they don't torture innocent men, either."

Riln's crazy plot made Deccia's heart beat faster. An alarming rush of fierce, primal anger followed. The Presidente did deserve to die.

Riln fingered the sharp blade with his thumb. "I'm with you, Goric. We'll wait for the Presidente. When the ship gets here, I'll slip in and cut his throat. You two losers will rescue Timaeus. Problem solved. And we'll sail merrily home."

Goric's features looked tight, and potent dislike glowered. "We're here on a *peace* mission, Riln. Killing the Presidente could destroy all the work Mentàll has put into the peace agreement."

Riln shrugged. "I don't trust the rocher. He'll show his true hand quick enough, trust me. How about we give him one day to release Timaeus. But if he doesn't, I'm going in for the kill. Who's with me?"

"I am," Deccia said quickly. Her heart pounded in hard, heavy beats.

Riln grinned. "Well, lunatic. Glad to see you want to spill his blood, too. We'll work it out, with or without rocher boy."

Goric scowled, and his dirty blond hair spiked like an unhappy exclamation mark between his brows. "I'm with you."

"So we're all agreed." Riln said. "We give the Presidente one day to show his hand. Then we'll kill him, and everyone else who gets in our way." He grinned. "I'd like to flay into Fitrn, too. He's the one who took Timaeus' finger." He slid a glance at Deccia. "Or maybe you want me to save him for you?"

Deccia trembled. Part of her did want that. She wanted to make the General suffer, just as he had made Timaeus suffer. She closed her eyes, feeling strangely off balance. It wasn't right to feel this way. Was it? Her fingers curled into her hair. "Let's see what happens," she whispered at last.

"Yeah," Riln smiled in approval. "You're coming around, lunatic. I like you."

Goric sent her a murky, disbelieving look, and disappeared into the relief chamber.

Riln chuckled. "Apte boy probably needs to put his head between his knees. Just thinking about all that blood, and worse, that he'll have to fight. He might run, like the rocher he is. Doesn't matter, though, lunatic. Between the two of us, we'll get the full, bloody revenge the Presidente and his son deserve."

Deccia nodded weakly and sat down. She felt sick. Was this the right plan? If so, then why did she feel so lost inside? Didn't the Presidente and General deserve to die for what they had done to Timaeus? Not to mention the scores of people they had killed on Koblan.

But as she thought more about it, she realized something else. Their small team was Koblan's last defense against the Presidente. If the Presidente would not uphold the peace, then they would need to take action. They must prevent him from attacking their homeland and murdering more innocent Koblanis. Riln was right. Killing him would be the only way to stop him.

Help me, The One. Help me to follow the right path. And please protect Timaeus until the ship gets here.

△ △ △ △ △

The Presidente, his officials, and all of the Koblani chiefs were already sitting at the breakfast table when Methusal and Mentàll arrived. Mentàll had followed her to the dining hall. Without a word, he pulled out her chair.

After a soft, "Thank you," she greeted her parents. She also noted that the Presidente's bags were stacked near the front door. He meant to make a speedy escape this morning.

Calbn murmured to the Dehrien Chief, "You are late." A knowing smile curled his lips. "All went as you planned, I assume?"

"Not yet," he said shortly.

A servant placed a bowl of fruit before her. Methusal ate silently. In low voices, her parents discussed what time to leave for Rolban tomorrow. The earlier the better, as far as she was concerned.

Erl murmured. "We have much to prepare. Methusal's wedding and the Presidential elections are both in four weeks."

Hanuh glanced at Methusal. "You haven't told him yet?"

"Told me what?"

The Dehrien Chief stilled, obviously listening for her response.

"Let's talk about it later." She didn't want to lie about the engagement anymore, and yet she needed Mentàll to think it was over between them. Irrevocably. Perhaps that was dishonest—well, of course it was dishonest. But he would learn the truth soon enough. She just needed to get away from him first.

Concern sharpened Hanuh's gaze, but she said nothing.

Erl said, "Should we hold them both on the same day? A morning wedding and an afternoon election? The chiefs might enjoy a good party."

Methusal changed the subject. "Maybe you'll be elected as Presidente, Papa."

"That would be convenient, because Mentàll thinks the central government should be in Rolban."

Of course he did. What better way to get a deeper foothold into Rolban?

Erl continued, "It's the most protected community on the continent."

"You have my vote," Methusal said. In fact, alarm overcame her at the thought of Mentàll winning. Then he'd constantly be in Rolban, performing his Presidential duties. She briefly closed her eyes at that thought.

Breakfast passed swiftly, and she felt both relieved and surprised when Mentàll made no effort to speak to her. However, she noted the tension in his body. Worse, his expression could only be labeled as cold and determined.

"Presidente," he said, when the Zindedi leader had placed his napkin on the table. "When you are ready, the documents await our signatures in Calbn's office."

The Presidente's unpleasant dark eyes sought out Methusal. "Your fair bride will attend, as well."

Mentàll's mouth looked like a hard slash. "I would have it no other way."

The chiefs, Zindedi advisors, as well as Mentàll, Methusal, and the Presidente slowly filed into Calbn's office. One entire length of the table had been cleared, a chair flanked both ends, and a chair faced the long side of the table. Two documents lay on it.

The chiefs and advisors made a semicircle around the table. To Methusal's surprise, Mentàll urged her to Calbn's chair, which was at the end of the table. "You will want to sit in comfort," he murmured, and gently pushed her into the plushly padded seat.

"Presidente Solboshn. Please. You must sign first," the Presidente said, gesturing with a thick hand.

"I would be honored." Mentàll sat down, took up the finely sharpened writing stick, and signed his name to the top of each document with bold, decisive slashes. Then he rose and handed the writing instrument to the Presidente.

When the Presidente signed, a great cheer went up.

After the Presidente stood, Mentàll said smoothly, "Now the documents will need the signature of witnesses. Presidente, your men may sign first, if you'd like."

Red flushed the Presidente's face. Perhaps in Zindedi no witnesses were required. His name alone was law. But he handed the writing stick with a modicum of grace to Artn.

Mentàll retreated to Methusal's side as the other chiefs and advisors lined up to sign the documents. Calbn gestured to a comfortable chair where the Presidente could sit at the other end of the table.

Slowly, each man wrote his name. The Zindedis appeared a bit awestruck that their names were needed. The moment seemed to weigh more heavily upon the Rolbani chiefs, however. Each signed with slow, deliberate strokes, as if the weight of Koblan rested upon each of their shoulders.

"So you see, Methusal, we have done it," Mentàll murmured behind her. His fingers curled over her shoulders and began to knead, his large hands disarmingly gentle. "We can do anything together."

Methusal drew a quick breath. "You deserve most of the credit." She struggled to keep her voice level and to ignore the very pleasant sensations his hands wrought. "You put everything together."

"But you convinced the Presidente to come to Koblan."

His thumbs slowly stroked over her muscles and spine, again and again. Hypnotic, mesmerizing. Thrilling.

"Our success is a result of our true partnership." His fingers slid up, under the cover of her hair and teased the back of her neck and the base of her skull. He murmured, "Each of us is not complete without the other."

Her breathing accelerated, and she struggled to ignore the circles of pleasure his skillful hands created. So this is how he meant to torture her one last time. Luckily, no one was paying any attention to him, and her hair hid what he was doing, too.

"You...will do fine alone." She cleared her throat. "As will I." The tips of his fingers slid through her hair, increasing the pleasure and tension spiraling inside her. Her heart pounded as she absorbed his touch, and an empty ache began to grow, deep inside of her.

She didn't realize how sharply she longed for more of his touch until he suddenly withdrew, leaving her alone.

Mentàll's breath warmed her ear, making her inhale sharply. His light gaze met her agitated one. "I see how much you want to be alone," he whispered. "You cannot live without passion, Methusal."

"Stop it." Her face was very warm. Thankfully, no one was watching them at the moment except for the Presidente, who did so with a squalid, speculative sort of interest.

"I think you like my caresses. And if you were bold enough, you would ask me to do far more." His eyes gleamed suddenly. "Shall we return to our room?"

Methusal gasped. "In your dreams!"

He laughed. Threading his fingers through her hair again, he cupped the back of her head and kissed her. Against her will, her lips clung to his, and her heart beat loudly in her ears.

He broke the contact and smiled. His discerning, intent gaze ran over the blush warming her features.

"Mentàll," Calbn said.

Regret flashed, and he looked up. "Yes?"

"The documents are signed." Two scrolls lay on the table, each bound with a leather lace.

The Presidente and Mentàll moved toward each other and shook hands. Mentàll handed a scroll to the Zindedi leader. "Thank you for coming to Koblan. I look forward to many years of peace."

"Yes," said the Presidente. His thick, stocky body shuffled toward Methusal. He extended his hand to her. "I must apologize to your bride for my conduct in Zindedi."

Methusal glanced at Mentàll, whose eyes had narrowed. But she lifted her hand to the Presidente, who kissed it. His lips felt hot and moist, like a boiled slug. She managed to affix a smile upon her face. "Thank you, Presidente."

Zindedis and Koblanis milled around for a few minutes, shaking hands and saying goodbye, and then everyone filed out the door. Methusal followed close behind.

Hendra and Hanuh stood near the main door, and she quickly joined them.

After hearty farewells, the Zindedi horde left the mansion, accompanied by the chiefs, Mentàll, and the Koblani guards. And then they were gone.

Methusal expelled a shaky breath and sat down on a nearby chair.

"Are you all right?" her mother asked.

"It's over. It's finally over."

"Yes." Hanuh's eyes narrowed in concern. "Your father and I were talking. I think we'll head home first thing tomorrow morning. Will you come with us?"

A weight like a stone lodged in her heart. "Yes." Slowly, she stood up again. Mentàll was gone. Now was her opportunity to pack up and vacate his room before he returned. "I need to do something. I'll see you later."

Mentàll's suite seemed quiet and empty. Quickly, she packed. Last of all, her hand went to the marriage necklace at her throat. Should she leave it on his desk?

Much as she wanted to avoid him—and planned to avoid him for the rest of the day—that seemed cowardly. She'd give it to him personally.

She left the necklace around her neck, although she refused to ask herself why.

△ △ △ △ △

Methusal and Hanuh went out to lunch, and she told her mother about Mentàll's conversation with Calbn last night. And her decision to leave him.

"Are you sure?" her mother said softly. "It seems to me you're confused and hurt. Take some time to think about it."

But Methusal didn't want to think about it anymore. She was tired of thinking. Her mind was made up.

After lunch, Hanuh headed back to the mansion and Methusal walked on the beach by herself. She wanted to be alone.

The Presidente's ship set sail at the same time she started her walk, and its huge red and black sails billowed open to receive the southern breeze. It headed east, which surprised her. Zindedi was to the north.

Methusal passed children playing in the gentle surf, and their watchful mothers, who lay on towels. When her steps finally slowed down, Quasr was a lump of green in the distance, and the Presidente's ship had telescoped to a tiny black dot on the eastern horizon.

Cool water rushed over her skin, and sand sucked at her feet. A few prickly shells poked into her toes, and she dug down and discovered one perfectly shaped spiral shell. It was a translucent, pearly pink—the color of a perfect sunrise. She put it in her pocket and continued on.

The rush and crash of the waves filled her mind, and the sun warmed her face. She didn't have to think. She didn't want to think. Mentàll's marriage necklace still hung around her neck, hidden beneath her tunic. Its weight felt warm and silken, and as familiar as her own skin. Soon, she would take it off. When she got back to the mansion, she would give it to him.

The sun slowly dipped toward the horizon. Quasr was only a small smudge on the horizon now. She'd come too far. She'd have to hurry in order to make it back before dark.

She didn't want to go back.

The weight of her empty future hung like a dark stone around her heart.

She stood still for a while, allowing the waves to wash over her toes and lick around her ankles. Oh, to stay in this one perfect moment. Heartbreak lived in Quasr, and she didn't want to go back.

The afternoon light muted to a golden color. The sunlight reflected off of the rippling waves, and the silence felt drowsy and peaceful.

At last she turned west, into the setting sun. Her heart felt heavy, and she lifted her hands to Mentàll's marriage necklace. With fumbling fingers, she unclasped it. Emptiness and grief enveloped her spirit.

But this was the way it had to be. She had made her choice.

Her neck felt cold and naked now. With trembling fingers, she slipped it into her pocket, and with resolute steps walked faster for Quasr.

She wouldn't think about anything, beyond the fact that she had to find Mentàll and give him the necklace. It was time to end everything, once and for all.

△ △ △ △ △

Hendra put a hand to her smoothly brushed hair, took a trembling breath, and left her room. Nerves beat in her belly like frantic insect wings. She felt sick. Tonight was the night.

Surreptitiously, her fingers checked inside her purse for the small item she'd bought yesterday. She'd found it in a small shop far from the main road and the waterfront. Embarrassment had scalded her when she'd paid for it, although the tiny, dark-haired woman matter-of-factly took her money as if it was a common sale in her store.

Doc waited in the main hall with his back to her. A crisply pressed tan shirt outlined his straight, broad shoulders, and he wore dark breeches. Both were made of Zindedi cloth. He looked very handsome.

"Hi," she said softly.

He pivoted, and an appreciative grin creased into his ruthlessly trimmed beard. "You look beautiful."

She blushed. "Thank you." Tonight she wore a simple, sleeveless dress that she'd bought in Quasr. It was white, and beautifully embroidered with brown flowers and shimmering brown beads. Leather sandals completed her outfit.

He offered his arm, and they walked together through the dusky twilight to Poctlo, the seafood restaurant on the harbor.

"I'm glad the Presidente is gone," she murmured, as they were ushered to a polished table in the small restaurant. The waiter offered a parchment menu to each of them.

After drinks were served and their order taken, Hendra said, "Do you think the peace will last?"

"No."

A chill went through her. "You're sure? Already?"

"The Presidente is a manipulator. He'll only do what serves his own interests."

"But he's afraid of Mentàll. Why would he cross him?"

"The Presidente thinks he's much smarter than any Koblani." Doc smiled faintly, showing his teeth. "He's in for a big surprise."

"Do you think Mentàll suspects the same thing?"

"Yes. The Presidente is a fool to underestimate him." He lifted his water beaded glass and his smile widened, reminding her briefly of her cousin's feral one. "Here's to breaking the Presidente's power forever. And may the flames of hell soon welcome him home."

"Doc," she gasped.

"He's hurt too many people, Hendra. It's time for the killing to end. I believe Mentàll will defeat him. And if he needs my help, I'm more than happy to volunteer."

"I hope it doesn't come to that. I hope it's over."

"We'll find out soon. A man like the Presidente can't pretend humility for long. If it's a trick, he'll attack us soon, and viciously."

Appalled, she said, "You think he'll attack soon? How can you say that so calmly?"

"It may be for the best. I think Mentàll is waiting for an excuse to destroy the rest of Zindedi's military." Ice clicked as he drank tea. "I have to believe we'll win this war."

And she'd thought it was all over now. Her dismay must have shown, because Doc gently covered her hand. "For tonight, we have peace. I want to focus all my attention on you, Hendra."

"Nothing is ever easy, is it? One country wants peace. The other plans for war. And when they meet, will they destroy each another?" In an oblique way, it reminded her of her questionable plan for tonight. "Or will a better, more healing peace prevail?"

Doc's intent, smoky gaze watched her, as if trying to read the meaning behind her words. "Anything you'd care to share, Hendra?"

She forced a smile. "No." Nerves fluttered. She couldn't bring it up. Not yet.

The waiter's arrival was a welcome relief. She watched as he placed steaming plates of seafood and crisp vegetables before them, and then she smiled at Doc. "It smells delicious, doesn't it?"

His features relaxed into a smile, and when the waiter left, he lifted his glass. "To a beautiful evening." More softly, he said, "May it be everything you've ever dreamed about."

May it not be my worst nightmare.

Hendra swallowed. Her throat felt dry and chalky. "To us." Her voice squeaked. "To new beginnings."

△ △ △ △ △

Methusal made it back to the mansion just as dusk crept over the land. She was tired. Servants bustled about, readying to serve dinner. Few place settings had been laid at the tables tonight, so she guessed that many of the chiefs had already gone home.

Her parents, Behran, and Sozla headed for a table, and she waved to them, but kept going. Mentàll was nowhere to be seen. She had to find him. She needed to get this over with right now.

As she headed down a hall, Aali grabbed her arm. "Have you seen Dastn? Do you think he left with Wyen's chief?"

Methusal knew the Tarst runner was special to her cousin. It would hurt Aali very much if he'd gone without saying goodbye.

"No. I'm sure he's still here. I think he's traveling with us tomorrow." Of course, Aali, with her broken leg, could not leave Quasr for another few weeks.

"That's what I thought." Her careless shrug didn't erase the anxious expression from her eyes. Her cousin hurried on.

Methusal finished the distance to Mentàll's door. Heart pounding in sickening thuds, she rapped hard, twice.

No answer.

Maybe he was in Calbn's office? She relaxed into kaavl and fanned out her hearing, listening for his familiar low voice. Nothing.

He hadn't left with the other chiefs, had he?

Of course not. He was still recovering. Doc wanted him to stay in Quasr for at least another week.

She walked to the end of the hall. At the other end, a shorter one branched off into the garden.

He wasn't in the garden, either. She turned back into the larger hall, but before she'd gone two steps, the Dehrien Chief appeared from the direction of the main hall. His steps slowed down when he saw her.

His expression looked remote. That hurt, but not nearly as much as what she was about to do. She pulled the necklace from her pocket. It snagged around the perfect pink shell.

Mentàll silently watched as she disentangled it. After dropping the shell back into her pocket, she extended the necklace. Its long strands dripped through her fingers. "This is yours."

He opened his hand, and she let it stream into his wide palm. Without a word, he tucked it into his pocket. It was over.

She briefly closed her eyes. Nothing bound her to this man anymore. His acceptance of the necklace proved it.

"Goodbye," she said in a low voice.

"Methusal." The husky word made her glance up. Pain contorted his expression.

She'd hurt him. Her rejection had hurt him. It came as a shock. He seemed impenetrable to pain, as if everything rolled off of that hard, icy wall of his without ever touching his soul.

"I'm *sorry*," she whispered. And she was.

With a step, he came to her. Not certain what he intended, she backed up. Her heel hit the wall. Looming over her, Mentàll planted one hand on the wall, and the other cradled her jaw. Before she could do more than gasp, he kissed her, savagely.

She responded to him instinctively, and completely against her will. His kiss swiftly stoked a fire deep inside her. A fire she was helpless to resist.

With a tiny moan, she abandoned the fight and melted into him, giving him everything he wanted, and more. After long moments, his plundering lips gentled and stroked her own, pulling a response from deep inside of her.

Her eyes opened and unexpectedly met his. Vulnerability lived in them...and an almost childlike plea for something more—for affirmation. He needed her to affirm that he was worthy. That he was valuable, and worthy of affection.

"Mentàll," she whispered. Curling his fingers tightly into his shoulders, she pressed closer to him. He was worthy of love, and she wanted to make certain he knew that.

With tears in her eyes, she kissed him tenderly, trying to express to him all of the love in her heart. His hungry kisses drank in her response like it was food for his soul. A shiver rippled through him, and as she gave to him, she felt sucked closer and closer to his heart. Powerful emotions exploded, overcoming her mind and heart with sparks and light, and deep, unbearable love.

His lips slid from hers to press into her hair. Their chests heaved in tandem. Methusal felt deeply shaken.

When Mentàll pulled back, his eyes were clear, so that she could see into his soul. Just like that one night in Zindedi, when he'd nearly taken her for his own. The ice he wore to shield his heart from the world had melted, and the games, manipulations, and power plays had been stripped bare.

Seeing this side of him eased her fears.

He stared into her eyes, and then his closed again. With a soft, harshly muttered word, he pushed away. He pivoted on his heel and left her.

She pressed a hand to her mouth to stop a small, involuntary sound.

Was she doing the right thing, leaving him? Suddenly, she didn't know. Worse, she was rejecting him, just like his father had done. In fact, now she saw very clearly that she was just one in a long line of people to hurt him, over and over again.

△ △ △ △ △

A few minutes earlier, in the entrance hall

Aali wondered if Dastn had left Quasr yet. But he hadn't said goodbye. He always said goodbye.

She scanned the great hall. Hallways branched off each side of the hall. Paintings framed in gold covered the cream covered walls.

The Presidente was gone, and Aali was glad. He was a whip. She didn't like him or trust him, but he seemed to have a healthy respect for Mentàll. Who wouldn't? The Dehrien was scary in a dangerous, controlled sort of way. And the Presidente wanted the ore, so he'd probably honor the treaty.

The tall Dehrien Chief appeared from her right, his cool gaze scanning the room. It rested briefly on her, and then moved on.

She knew that neither Hanuh nor Deccia could get a full read on him. He was a remote, cool, and very self-controlled man. But the question was—was he still dangerous? Should he be the Presidente of Koblan?

Aali watched him turn left down a hallway, and then dismissed him from her thoughts. Where was Dastn?

She scanned the room again. Maybe he had left already. Maybe he was down one of the other halls.

Aali peered down the closest one. Nope. She peeked down the one into which Mentàll had disappeared moments earlier.

A good distance down the long hallway she saw Methusal and Mentàll. Her cousin put something into Mentàll's hand.

Aali hesitated. Okay, maybe she was being nosy. But this looked interesting. She knew their charade was over, since the Presidente had left. What more did they have left to say to one another?

Methusal hadn't been herself ever since she'd returned from Zindedi. Aali had thought it had something to do with the mission. But maybe not.

Movement down the hall drew her attention again.

Mentàll leaned in and put his hand on the wall over Methusal's head. He touched her cheek, and slowly ducked in and kissed her cousin.

And what was this—did Methusal kiss him back? Aali's mouth dropped open in shock. What in flying aptes...? The Presidente was gone. It was an act for no one.

Someone stopped beside her. It was Hanuh.

Methusal's mother watched the two embrace for a moment, but no surprise registered. Quietly, she walked away, just as Mentàll pushed back from Methusal. When he left, Methusal stared silently after him.

Aali finally blinked. Was Mentàll suddenly interested in Methusal, for real? Was it mutual? Her cousin hadn't exactly pushed him away.

Another thought entered her head. What about Behran? She saw him now, talking to Hendra across the hall.

"Spying again?" Dastn's voice came from behind her, and she spun. At least, she spun as fast as she could on crutches.

A tiny grin teased up the corner of his mouth. "Can't seem to help yourself, can you?"

She frowned. "I'm not spying. I was looking for you." Immediately, she knew she'd said the wrong thing. "I mean, I was wondering if you'd left yet. Finally."

"Can't stand it when I'm gone?" His grin edged up.

She gave a big eye roll. "It looks like *you* came looking for me, runner man."

His brown eyes gentled, and became intent. "Any message for me?"

Aali felt momentarily confused. Message for *him*? Then she saw the gleam in his eyes. He was ruffling her on purpose. But she decided to play along.

"For *you?*" she cooed. She touched a finger to her lips, and noticed his gaze followed the movement. With a small grin, she said, "Yes! I do have a message for you."

His dark gaze now looked wary. "What is it?"

"Tell my father I'll be home in four weeks. And I'll have a surprise for him, and for a few others in Rolban, too."

"Surprise? You and surprises don't mix. They're more likely to explode."

She waved away the incident from the war that Dastn had unfortunately witnessed. Loftily, she said, "I've matured. Can't you tell?"

"I can tell you're still a troublemaker."

She drew a dramatic hand to her chest. "You wound me."

His eyes narrowed. "Stop playing games."

"But I'm just a kid. Isn't that what you expect?"

He reached out and flicked his thumb and finger through the ends of her long hair. "We're leaving early tomorrow."

"I'll miss you," she said sweetly.

"Will you." His gaze looked knowing, and with a small smile, he left her.

Aali wanted to stomp her foot. Her good foot, of course. But that would be immature. And she wasn't! Not anymore. Really.

How had he won that conversation? The whip. The slug. The cute whip beast. She watched him walking away, and then she frowned, noting the hint of a swagger in his step. The whip!

△ △ △ △ △

After a delicious dinner, Hendra told Doc that she'd like to walk on the beach. He easily agreed. Nerves twisted inside of her. Step one accomplished. Now for step two.

A breeze had kicked up, and it was cool along the waterfront. Good. This fit into her carefully detailed plan.

"I'm a little chilly," she said, before they headed down the steps to the beach. "That vendor sells light blankets. I...I think I'll buy one." She fumbled in her purse for the money she'd brought for just that purpose.

Doc's hand stilled hers. "I'll buy it. They're not expensive."

"Oh... Well, thank you."

She watched Doc haggle with the sharp-nosed business vendor. He was completely oblivious to her devious plot. She felt bad, because she was tricking him. Uncomfortably, she wondered if her plan would upset him.

Doc put the soft, light-weight blue blanket around her shoulders. His arm lingered around her. "Is that better?" he murmured.

"Much, thank you." The happiness she felt walking close to him battled with the nerves making her feel sick to her stomach.

Holding their shoes in their hands, they walked down the beach. Warmth still lingered in the sand as her toes squished into the fine, powdery substance.

"It's a beautiful night." Doc's arm slipped around her shoulders, holding her close to him.

"Yes." Joy and despair thundered in her heart, mirroring the soft boom of the waves, and the gentle slide of the cold water as it curled around her toes.

Hendra glanced over her shoulder. The lights of Quasr were far away. They were alone on this deserted section of beach. Maybe they had come far enough.

...Or maybe they should walk a little further. She felt chilly now. Her hands felt icy, and her palms sweaty.

"You're cold," he murmured, and directed their path onto the warmer sand again.

After a little while he slowed to a halt and they faced the enormous black ocean. The waves thundered on the beach. Ryon's pale green beams sparkled off of the tiny wavelets.

"It's a perfect night," he said softly.

"Yes," Hendra whispered. She swallowed, working up the courage to speak.

Doc faced her. His eyes looked very dark in the moonlight, and his warm hands curled around her cold ones, holding them securely in his. "You know I'll be going home tomorrow."

She nodded.

"You'll stay here another week, with Mentàll?"

"Then I'll go to Rolban and visit until Methusal's wedding."

"Good. Rolban and Tarst aren't far apart."

She opened her mouth to speak, but he gripped her hands more tightly. "I don't want to leave you at all. You know that. But my patients need me."

"I know," she said softly. "Of course they do."

His thumbs stroked her hands, and he took a deep breath. "Hendra. You've grown to mean the world to me. I think you know that. You fill my whole heart and my soul. I love to be with you. I don't want to leave tomorrow. In fact, I don't ever want to be apart from you again."

"Doc." A quick, breathless panic surged.

"Listen to me," he said softly. "I love you. I want to spend every minute of the rest of my life with you."

"Doc." Her voice sounded strangled.

"Hendra, will you..."

"Doc! *No*. Wait." She pulled her hands free.

He stared at her. "What's wrong?" His voice sounded suddenly rough and unsure. "You don't feel the same way?"

"Yes. Of course I feel the same way."

His teeth gleamed white, and he reached for her hands again, but she backed away. "Yes, I love you with my whole heart. That's why I can't...I *won't*...make a promise I can't keep."

"What do you mean?"

"I have to know if I can be...everything you need me to be."

"I love you just the way you are. You don't need to prove anything to me."

"But I have problems," she whispered. "Have you forgotten?"

"I love you, and you love me. Trust our love to get us through any problems that might come." His voice lowered. "Marry me, Hendra."

"I can't," she whispered. "I can't marry you, knowing that I might fail you."

"You could never fail me."

Gathering up her courage, she blurted, "Make love to me. Right now. Here on the beach."

He stepped backward, his whole body visibly tensing with shock. "No!" he said, clearly appalled. "I will not compromise you. How could you ask such a thing?"

"I need to know if I can be a real wife to you." Desperately, she said, "You can't marry a woman who's afraid to be touched!"

"You are not afraid." His tone was calm now. "We hold hands. We kiss. You let me hold you."

"But that's not enough. Not for a real marriage. You deserve it all, Doc. And I refuse to marry you until I know I can...can be with you in that way."

Now he took her hands, and his grip was firm. "Trust me. It will be all right."

"It won't!" she exploded, ripping free. "I'm still afraid. I still feel that panic. It hasn't gone away. I won't be a failure to you. I won't! I don't want you to hate me!" She burst into tears.

"I could never hate you."

"I *need* to do this!" she whispered. "Don't you see? I need to know that I can. I planned it all." She fumbled in her purse and took out the small, embarrassing item. "I even bought this, and we have a blanket. ...No one is here. No one will ever know."

Doc stared at the tiny package in her palm. "No. I will not compromise you."

"Even if I want you to?"

"I won't do it," he said evenly. "Put that away. Now."

Tears streamed down her cheeks, but she did as he asked.

Gently, he said, "Now listen to me, Hendra. We can work this out..."

"Prove it, then." She swiped away the tears. Another idea sprang to mind. It, too, would prove once and for all if she was healed enough become Doc's wife. "Put your hands on my waist. Hard," she ordered. "Pull me close. Kiss me."

His gaze darkened and his weight shifted backward again. "I won't hold you like Jascr did."

"Do it." Cool resolve strengthened her. She had to know if she could marry him. Surely he could compromise this little bit to see if their marriage had a chance. "Prove we can work through my fear together."

A dark, forbidding frown said he wasn't happy to be forced into this situation.

"Please," she whispered. When he didn't move, she grabbed his hands and put them on her hips, exactly like Jascr had done so long ago. Holding her like that, Jascr had pinioned her to the wall and forced his attentions upon her, repeatedly. For years.

Doc's eyes closed. "Don't do this."

Even holding his hands in place made her flesh creep. "Hold me harder," she said. "Kiss me." She stepped closer, making it easier for him. When she let go, his hands still gripped her, hard.

His expression tense and tormented, he leaned forward.

Hendra wanted to scream with fear, but didn't. Her lips wobbled, and tears slipped down her face. She could endure this. She *would* endure this for Doc.

The pressure on her skin increased imperceptibly when he drew her the last little bit closer to kiss her. Something snapped inside of her. With a strangled cry, she wrenched free and stumbled backward.

Doc stared at her, breathing heavily, fists clenched at his sides. He was angry.

"No!" she whimpered, and ran.

"Hendra." His quick footsteps followed.

Gasping with fear, she ran faster. Panic seized her. He couldn't catch her. Jascr couldn't catch her!

Her foot hit a half-buried piece of driftwood and she fell and landed hard. Sand sprayed inside her mouth. When the footsteps stopped beside her, she wept into the sand.

He touched her shoulder.

She flinched.

"Hendra. Look at me. Please."

Trembling, she slowly sat up and brushed the sand from her clothes and spit it from her mouth. She felt ashamed. She'd run from him like a crazed woman.

"I'm sorry," she whispered.

He knelt beside her. "No. *I'm* sorry. I should never have let you... Hendra, I would *never* hold you like that." Anguish made his voice sound bleak. "I would never hurt you."

Feeling empty inside, she struggled to her feet. "I know. But you're not the problem. You are never the problem. *I* am. I'm still broken. This proves it. I can't be the woman you need me to be."

He gripped her shoulder. "You can."

Panic flared.

With a quick turn of his head, he muttered something and swiftly let go.

He took a deep breath. "This proves nothing. I would never hold you like that. I would never force you or hurt you. I want to cherish you. I want to *love* you."

Tears slipped down her face. Arms crossed, and trembling, she said, "Then love me now."

Aghast, he said, "I can't, and I *won't*. You're so upset you're shaking, and frankly, I'm not doing much better."

Dully, she said, "Later, then."

"No!" he said with force. "I will not compromise you. I will not violate you. I won't treat you like garbage, like Jascr did."

"Then it's over." Legs feeling wooden, she headed back toward the lights of Quasr.

"Hendra!"

"I'm done talking. Leave me alone. Please." She quickened her pace. Tears streamed down her face. Doc matched her strides, but remained silent beside her.

Once inside the compound, she ran from him. In the dark, quiet of her room, she wept in agony. She'd never be whole. Tonight had proven that she could never marry him.

Chapter Twenty-Four

Day 27

THE WIDE, open rolling sea gently rocked the Presidente's ship. He lounged in comfort in his opulent cabin, which took up half of the ship. A bump against the hull a few minutes earlier had indicated that his guest would soon arrive at his door. He inhaled deeply of his smoke stick. Sharp pain skewered his chest, and he gasped.

The door opened, exposing his coughing fit.

"Father." General Fitrn entered without invitation and nonchalantly toed the door shut.

The Presidente glared as he gasped and choked, trying to gain control of himself.

"Do you require a cloth?" his son asked solicitously. He pulled one from his breast pocket, but when he started to dab the Presidente's chin, the Zindedi leader lunged forward and slapped him.

A red mark flared on the General's cheek. Quickly, he stepped back. Hatred glittered. "I see I've wasted my time by coming here." He pivoted for the door. "Hostn!"

"Stop!" the Presidente bellowed, and coughed again. "Sit. We have plans to discuss."

His son did not comply. "Five minutes, Father. I'm coordinating a strike team as we speak. You are wasting my time."

The Presidente wanted to put his hands around the young pup's neck and squeeze, but his chest pained him terribly. He sat back, hands across his paunch, and tried to control his wheezes. He hated the contempt in his son's eyes. Did he look weak? Pitiable?

He stiffened his spine and spoke with as much force as he could muster. "I have ordered Kilum to bring Methusal to me on the northern coast. If it takes him longer than three days, he'll bring her to the Iignon coast. You will ensure her safe arrival in Zindedi."

"What else?" Fitrn glanced at the door, his averted posture already dismissing the Presidente's next directives.

The Zindedi leader's hands tightened into fists. "Report your progress!"

"Two teams are cutting a path around Eerpor. We have not been detected. All will go according to plan."

"It had better!" he wheezed.

"Rolban will be mine in a matter of days. You have nothing to fear, Father. Except, perhaps, your own health. If I were you, I'd rush back to Zindedi so your doctors can run to their panicked deaths, trying to extend your pitiful life. Do me a favor, and don't kill them all before I get home. Although it is unlikely, my men may require a good physician or two."

"Don't bother to come home unless your ships are loaded with ore," the Presidente growled.

"When I come home, the ore is not the only plunder I will take as my own."

He scowled. "Are you threatening me?"

"No, Father." The General's thin lips curled back, revealing straight, perfectly sharp teeth. "I am encouraging you to put your affairs in order. Spend your last days indulging in every sinful pleasure your corrupt body lusts after. When I come home, I will grant you one last choice. You may kill yourself, or I will do it for you."

The General spun on his heel and exited.

Rage engulfed the Presidente, and his heart thundered so hard it felt like it was about to explode. Panic seized him. Was he about to die? *No!* He tried to cry out, but it sounded like a woman's mewling cry.

A steward cautiously poked his head into the room. "Sir? Do you require assistance?"

The Presidente caught his breath. "Set your fastest sails! I want to go home."

The steward scuttled away.

After long minutes, the ship slowly began to move again. The Presidente laboriously breathed in and out. The view out of the porthole caught his attention, and his lips curled back. The General's ship slowly slid by. Only the barest breeze filled the black sails. His only satisfaction was that it would take his son at least a day to return to the Iignon coast with these uncooperative winds. Unfortunately, it would also take longer than normal for him to return home, too—after the brief delay to pick up his hostage, of course. His sailors had already received their explicit orders.

The Presidente closed his eyes and counted each successful breath. He thought about the future. Should he passively allow himself to be slaughtered like an apte when his son returned to Zindedi? Or should he kill the General, and neutralize the threat?

The last idea appealed. But he wanted his blood son to rule Zindedi. The line must go on, and his son knew this.

But he was not ready to die. Not yet. He had one last prisoner to execute, and he would draw that out for many, many pleasurable days. Methusal should prove interesting, as well.

He smiled, and the tension in his chest eased.

△ △ △ △ △

Methusal heard Hendra weeping, off and on, for most of the night. The other girl didn't want to talk. And it didn't keep Methusal awake, because she couldn't sleep, either. Her agonized heart also felt like it was torn in two.

Love for Mentàll urged her to accept him as he was, and to love him forever, no matter the cost—even if that same love would ultimately destroy her. Her head, on the other hand, said she should go home and put time and space between them. She knew her feelings were too confused right now to be able to think clearly about anything.

In the pale light of dawn, Methusal readied for the day. Hendra had finally fallen asleep. Tears traced pale, dried silver tracks down her cheeks, and her eyelids looked bruised.

As Methusal tied up her pack, the Dehrien girl sat up with a start. "Is it time?" she mumbled. "Are you leaving now?"

"After breakfast. You can rest for a while longer."

Hendra yawned, but didn't answer, besides putting her head in her hands.

"Are you all right?" Methusal asked softly.

"I'm fine," she whispered. After rubbing her face, she turned away to gather clothes for the day.

Clearly, she still didn't want to talk about it.

Methusal knew Doc would travel with them today, since he intended to head home to Tarst. Hendra had elected to stay for a while longer in Quasr, with Mentàll.

Methusal wondered what had happened between the two on their date last night. Clearly, it had ended in disaster. As she left the room, she said a silent prayer for Hendra and the red-headed doctor from Tarst, and wondered why love couldn't ever be easy.

Eggs and sweet rolls awaited the travelers at breakfast. Mentàll sat at the head of the table, and while she felt his gaze upon her, he made no attempt to speak to her. She told herself that she was glad.

Hendra emerged a little later, looking wan, and picked at her breakfast. At the end of the meal, Doc squatted beside her, but she shook her head in reply. Regret and despair scored lines into his face, but he quietly left her.

After breakfast the travelers, including Pan, all lined up outside and said goodbye to Mentàll, Calbn, and his wife. Sozla and her parents came out too, and Methusal and Behran both gave her a quick hug. After Behran released her, Sozla's cheeks looked pink.

"I will come to Rolban in a few weeks," she said. "My parents have said I may stay for two weeks."

"Good," Behran said. "That will give me plenty of time to show you the water systems."

"Yes," Sozla said quickly, smiling. "I am looking forward to that. And to attending your wedding, of course."

Behran glanced at Methusal. She opened her mouth, but he shook his head. "Later."

Methusal discovered that Mentàll now stood beside her.

He murmured, "Soon, I will send a ship to Zindedi for Deccia."

"Soon?" She searched his cool, pale eyes. "When?"

"After I discover if the Presidente can be trusted or not."

She wondered what that enigmatic statement might mean.

"We're ready," Pan said. Men waited with two urchets at the gate of the compound. They were loaded with tents and supplies. They must be Pan's, from Tarst.

So. It was time to go. She glanced at Mentàll again. Leaving him hurt, like a physical pain.

"Goodbye, Methusal." She could read no emotion in his eyes. They looked remote. Cool. It hurt badly. But wasn't this what she wanted? Wasn't this for the best?

His large, warm hand closed around hers, and then let go.

She felt bereft, and pain gouged deep into her heart. Was she making the right decision? "Goodbye, Mentàll," she said softly.

Sharp awareness flared in his gaze, and he watched her more closely.

Behran stepped up. "Goodbye. We'll see you in Rolban for the elections. Ready, Thusa?"

"Yes." She cast one more troubled glance at the Dehrien Chief, and then followed Behran to the gate. She felt Mentàll's gaze boring into her back.

"Hiy!" Pan cried, and the urchets lurched forward.

She cast another look over her shoulder. He still watched her. His hand lifted in farewell, and she lifted hers, as well.

Afterward, Methusal didn't look back. The emptiness inside of her grew deeper and hollower the further she walked from Calbn's compound.

Hanuh appeared by her side, and Methusal clutched her arm. "Am I doing the right thing, Mama?"

"You'll see him again, and soon. I guarantee it."

"But am I making a mistake, leaving him now?"

"No, I don't think so. A great deal has happened. I think it's best if you take time to sort it out. You must decide what *you* want. And what you're willing to live with, or live without."

Her mother was right. Hanuh's affirmation leant a bit of peace to her soul.

Methusal knew that she could not live without love. And Mentàll had said he did not love her. He would probably never love her, even if she returned and threw herself at him. She needed to be smart. She had to make a wise decision, no matter how much it might hurt.

Unfortunately, she didn't know if being separated from him would hurt worse than being *with* him—even if he could offer her a few small scraps of affection, as in the latter case.

She closed her mind to the endless, frustrating questions. If only he loved her, she would go with him to the end of the world, if he asked her. What he had done in the past wouldn't matter. And it wouldn't matter that he wanted to become Presidente and have kaavl sons that only she could give him. She loved him, and she desperately wanted to be with him. She would gladly give him kaavl sons, and anything else he desired, if only he loved her.

After a while, Behran moved over to walk beside her. "Are you all right?"

"I'm fine. But I think it's time to tell everyone the truth about our engagement. I can't keep lying about it. And my father needs to be told, too. I've felt bad that I haven't told him sooner."

"I understand." He remained silent for a moment. "But it's over with Mentàll?"

"I think so."

With a sharp frown, he looked at her.

She had to tell him the truth. Gently, she said, "I love him. That will never change. But can I be with him? No. I don't think so."

He nodded, and said nothing more, although his face looked grim. "I understand. Should we tell Erl now?"

"Yes." Impulsively, she grabbed his hand and whispered, "Thank you, Behran. For everything."

A wry smile twisted his lips, and he leaned close to kiss her cheek. "I feel the same way. I don't regret a single day we've had together."

She smiled. "I don't, either."

Together, they headed for Erl.

The long, hot day slowly passed by. The small group refilled their water skins in the river, and then trudged on to their first camp spot. It was the same tiny alcove where the Zindedis had attacked them on their way to Quasr last year. As they set up camp, Methusal found herself scanning the trees on the hills to the north, remembering how the black uniforms had popped up, and how guns had crackled death down on the camp.

To the east, sheer cliffs made of white rock rose to the sky. Ten months ago, Mentàll had been injured there, and she'd cared for him for several days in a cave. It had been a miracle they'd both survived without killing each other. How he had hated her then.

Dusk came swiftly, and she ate dried rations and fresh Quasrian bread by the campfire. Soon after, she crawled into her tent to sleep. Pan had thoughtfully brought several extra tents on his urchets.

Insects chirped into the night. Pan, Dastn, Doc, and Behran shared one tent, and Erl and Hanuh another. Methusal was alone. She was glad. Because being alone, she did not have to pretend to anyone. Being alone, she could face the weight in her soul and cry.

△ △ △ △ △

Aali warily eyed GG across the dinner table, and wondered when might be the best time to antagonize the old woman.

For a vital purpose, of course.

GG claimed that she was glad everyone had left the mansion. Now she could safely travel within her own halls again. She'd stayed in her rooms for most of the time the Zindedi delegation had been there. However, Aali didn't know if she'd done it of her own free will, or because Calbn had banished her there. He'd probably wanted his unpredictable grandmother safely removed from the peace negotiations.

In any event, GG had announced that she'd join them for supper tonight, and here she was. Actually, only Aali, Trori, and Rartn were in attendance. But the presence of the children didn't guarantee that GG wouldn't throw one of her legendary fits when Aali introduced the topic on her mind.

"What are you looking at, girl?" GG said irritably, stuffing bread into her mouth. "Afraid I'll snap your head off?"

"Nope. You've been cooped up in your room. I think you'll be on your best behavior. Unless, of course, you'd like to eat alone again."

GG scowled. "You are a most impertinent girl!"

Aali smiled. "Isn't that why you like me? Because I remind you of yourself?"

GG scowled harder, but a smile glimmered. "Pshaw," she grumbled.

Time to turn the subject to more interesting matters. "The elections will be held soon in Rolban."

"So?"

"My leg should be healed in time to get home. I can't wait to see Sims. And of course Methusal will be there, and Mentàll, too. What about Calbn? Is he going?"

"Probably." The old lady's eyes narrowed to unreadable slits.

"It'll be a dramatic day," she mused. "And Methusal will be marrying Behran on the same day the election is held. Can you imagine?"

GG made an incomprehensible noise.

"What do you think it will be like, GG, to have everyone all together?" Aali rested her chin in her palm. "Just think of the things they might talk about, or the ways the conversation might turn to the most unusual of subjects. Maybe old matters, long forgotten, will be brought up."

"I know what you're doing."

"Do you?" she said innocently.

"You think you know something."

"Do I?"

"You know nothing!" the old lady informed her. "And I'm not going to Rolban. I'm too old to travel."

"Of course you're too old to travel," she agreed. "But you can be sure, GG, that certain topics will be brought up. I'll make sure of it. So now is your opportunity to tell me all the details. I want to be sure to explain every piece of the puzzle."

Pink flushed the old woman's face. Warily, Aali watched GG's fingers tighten around her spoon.

Through pinched lips, the M'ntoyan matriarch said, "It's not your story to tell."

Aali smiled to herself. "True. But how much longer can we wait? You're not getting any younger."

GG glared. The gnarled hands curled tighter around the spoon. She shook it. "You don't want me to frighten the children, do you?"

Trori piped up. "It's okay. We know you have 'trocious manners. Daddy warns us all the time. He says if we act like you, he'll take a switch to us."

GG's jaw dropped, and she stared into her great-granddaughter's round, innocent eyes. She lowered the spoon. "Your friend Aalicaa is trying to pester me into going to Rolban."

"Would Daddy let you?" Trori wondered.

Aali stifled a giggle.

GG frowned, and sat up a little straighter. "Your father has no say over my comings and goings," she said crisply.

Although Aali remained silent as she watched the clear struggle taking place within the M'ntoyan matriarch, she couldn't quite smooth out the smile quivering on her mouth.

"Fine!" GG slapped both hands on the table. "I'll go. But things will unfold *my* way, you impertinent girl. Do you understand?"

"Of course."

GG muttered, "I'll have to think of the best way..." Her posture remained ramrod straight, and a calculating light gleamed in her eyes. Going to Rolban appealed to her, despite her cries of indifference.

Aali lifted her glass of urchet milk. "To family."

With surprising alacrity, GG raised her own small tumbler. "To justice. And power. And all wrongs righted."

Trori lifted her own glass. "I'm thirsty. Can I have more?"

GG chuckled. "Aali will get it for you. She's a busy schemer, like your grandmother. She needs plenty of work to keep her out of trouble."

∆ ∆ ∆ ∆ ∆

Methusal dreamed that she was in Zindedi.

Rough hands dragged her by the feet to the Presidente, who sat in his splendid office. She tried to cry out, but something filled her mouth. It almost choked her. Hard hands lifted her up, over a thick shoulder. Cold night air bit into her skin...

Methusal woke up, and felt completely disoriented.

She was hanging upside down, over a man's shoulder. A thick, stocky man, and he smelled like an unwashed wild beast.

Panic screamed through her mind.

Her hands were tied, and so were her feet. She was gagged.

Who was he? Why did he want her? What did he intend to do with her?

Methusal convulsed, and plunged her knees into the man's chest. Air *oomphed* from his lungs. Vile curses colored the night. To her shock, he threw her on the ground. Her head hit a stone. Tears pooled in her eyes, and stark terror seized her.

He knelt beside her and his pale, round face glowed in Ryon's green light. Kilum!

He was a Zindedi. She'd always suspected it. Now she knew for certain.

"Listen," he snarled. "I can make this easy or hard. You want to be knocked out?" He raised his gun. "Or do you wanna walk? What'll it be?"

Fear crawled through her gut. How could she speak with the filthy rag in her mouth?

"Walk?" he prodded.

She nodded, and he produced a long, wicked looking knife. It flashed in the moonlight, and it cut the bonds at her feet like a spoon through pudding. He gestured with the knife. "Get up."

It was hard to maneuver into a sitting position with her arms tied behind her back. He helped by grabbing her hair and jerking her up. Her scalp burned, but she didn't cry out. From there, prodded by his painful yanks, she scrambled to her knees, and then to her feet.

"Get moving." The knife poked into her back and she walked north, as he directed.

Long hours passed. Any time her steps lagged from exhaustion, or because of a sly attempt to get close enough to attack him, the knife poked deeper into her back. It stung. She was sure he'd drawn blood more than once. And how could she fight without the use of her arms? Especially when he had both a knife and a gun. She prayed for a wild beast attack. Then he'd have to shoot. Maybe someone would hear.

CHAPTER TWENTY-FIVE

DAY 28

UNFORTUNATELY, NO WILD BEASTS ATTACKED. When dawn lightened the horizon, Kilum prodded Methusal east, and ordered her to climb into the hills. The gritty soil was a light, whitish gray. The surroundings looked vaguely familiar, and she soon realized why. Once, when fleeing from the Zindedis, Mentàll had set up a temporary kaavl camp here. Now Kilum was directing her to the same place.

As daylight brightened the sky, Kilum shoved her into a cave entrance, sending her sprawling. He grabbed her by the feet and dragged her to the back of the large, shadowed cave. There, he tied her feet again, and left her lying there like a trussed animal.

"Don't go anywhere. If you're good, I'll give you food later."

She fell into a light, exhausted sleep.

A kick woke her again. "The invincible Methusal," he jeered. "Kaavl didn't help you much. I kidnapped you as easy as skinning an apte."

She'd been asleep. All the same, she knew this would never have happened to Mentàll.

Mentàll. She longed for him, and for his protective arms. But he could not help her now.

Kilum's balding head looked dirty, and so did his face. His dull black eyes radiated pure evil. They reminded her of the Presidente's eyes. Either man would kill for pleasure. Fear crept through her innards.

"You're more trouble than you're worth, if you ask me. But the Presidente wants you alive." He shrugged, as if there was no accounting for tastes. "I got food." He showed her a crust of bread. "Want it?"

Sullenly, she stared back. He grinned and popped it in his mouth. "Didn't think so." He left her again.

So, the Presidente had ordered her to be kidnapped. Clearly, he had no intention of upholding the peace agreement. The only good news was that Kilum wouldn't murder her. She closed her eyes again.

Sharp jabs into her ankles and wrists woke her a little later. The tight bonds loosened. And the gag was gone.

Unaccustomed to the sudden freedom, she swiftly sat up. Kilum now stood at the cave entrance, gun trained on her. "Get out there and take care of business."

Her skin crawled, but she took advantage of the opportunity, hiding herself as best she could behind a rock. Afterward, he waved her down to the stream, where a water skin waited, as well as a hunk of bread. "Drink up. This is our last stop for a long while."

She did, and while she fumbled with the water skin, filling it, she managed to fish the pink shell from her pocket. If anyone followed her, she wanted to leave a clue. Kilum ordered her to climb east. She managed to lurch close enough to the cave entrance to toss the small shell inside, and then she started climbing.

Would anyone find it? Was anyone looking for her?

Methusal would not allow herself to despair. As she scaled the familiar hills, she remembered climbing them with Mentàll. And she remembered fighting and winning over their Zindedi enemies. If only he was here now. So many times he'd saved her life, but now, alone, she'd failed to save herself. She missed him so much.

He would never even know she was missing.

If she couldn't find a way to escape from Kilum, soon she'd be on a ship to Zindedi. She'd never see Mentàll, her family, or Behran, ever again.

She didn't want to cry, but tears slipped down her face anyway. She scuffed her feet where she could, leaving a mark in the pale, gritty earth, and prayed for help to come.

△ △ △ △ △

Aali cleared her lunch dishes, and then stepped into the courtyard to gauge the angle of the sun. A few more minutes, and then she'd find Trori and Rartn. She'd promised them a trip to the pier this afternoon.

The gate at the far end of the courtyard flew open, and a familiar figure darted inside. Aali's heart leaped. "Dastn! Why are you here?"

He slowed down so she could walk beside him. His breath came in quick pants, and his dark brows were knotted. "Methusal's been kidnapped. I'm reporting it to Calbn."

"Kidnapped! By whom?"

"A Zindedi. Last night. The tracks looked like they were left by one man."

"Probably Kilum," Aali quickly deduced, remembering the disturbing encounter with him a few days ago. "I'll bet he's been an invader all along."

"Yes. And he was probably Verdnt's helper with the thefts a few years ago."

"Why would he want her?"

"I don't know. I have to report it and head back." He dashed inside the mansion.

Aali's heart pounded in hard, sickening thuds. She remembered Kilum's dead, evil eyes. He might kill her cousin.

Someone had to help her. Surely all of the people who loved Thusa—Behran, Erl, and Pan—were searching for her now.

But it wasn't enough, she suddenly knew. Methusal needed everyone—the very best tracking her. And she knew who that one person was. His injury would not stop him.

She darted back inside the compound and sprinted down hallways until she found the right door. Her heart pounded harder, but with a bit of nerves now. She'd never spoken to this intimidating man before.

She knocked.

After a moment, the door opened. Aali found herself staring at a broad, bleached-leather clad chest...and right in the center hung a silver disk. She couldn't stop staring. So here it was. Proof of her wild theory.

"Yes?" The Dehrien Chief's harsh voice jerked her back to reality. A quick glance upward encountered frowning, cool blue eyes. He dropped the disk inside his tunic.

Curiosity overrode her better sense. "Where did you get that?"

Mentàll gaze evaluated her, clearly deciding whether or not to answer her impertinent question. She offered a small, hopeful smile that hid her strong inclination to run away.

The cool eyes chilled further. "Why are you here, Aalicaa?"

Although he hadn't answered, she'd already guessed the answer. Facts clicked together in her head like a puzzle.

"Aalicaa."

She blinked. What was she thinking? "Methusal! She's been kidnapped. Dastn just told me. He's telling Calbn now."

Fear flared in the Dehrien's eyes, but was quickly masked by a brusque, urgent efficiency. "When? Where?"

"Last night. Dastn can tell you where."

The Dehrien Chief retreated into his room long enough to grab a pack, water skin, and a handful of other items. Then he shoved by her, out the door, heading fast for Calbn's office. He overtook Dastn halfway there, and spoke to him urgently. Both men disappeared into Calbn's office.

Aali clasped her hands in an urgent plea to The One. *Please let him find her before it's too late! Please.*

△ △ △ △ △

Methusal walked as slowly as she dared all day long. Her back burned from the stabs of Kilum's knife. They hiked east, and then gradually angled north, toward the sea.

In the late afternoon, Kilum allowed her to relieve herself again. She found a short, slim stick and hid it in the back waistband of her pants. It was too small to use as a weapon, but if he tied her up again, maybe she could use it to work the knots loose.

At dusk, she felt ready to keel over from exhaustion. She'd slept fewer than two hours in the last two days, and felt groggy and thick headed, and her stomach growled in sharp bursts. She'd eaten nothing since breakfast.

Kilum stopped in front of a cave, cast a calculating look at the sun, and then the horizon to the north. "Almost there," he grunted. "Sit. Eat." He threw another hunk of bread at her.

Her stomach growled again, painfully. She snatched it up and devoured it like a wild animal. All the while, she kept a wary eye on Kilum as he gathered brush and wood for a fire. With a firestick, he set it ablaze. The fire's warmth felt good in the chill dusk.

"Had enough?" he asked, when she'd gulped water.

"No."

He laughed. "Good. I'll let the Presidente feed you." A wicked smile showed chipped, misshapen teeth. "When he's good and ready, of course."

"Mentàll won't be pleased that you broke the peace."

"I don't care."

"They'll figure out you kidnapped me. They'll kill you."

He laughed. "Don't worry about me. You're my ticket home."

"The Presidente just signed a peace agreement with us!"

"What's that to me? I have a job to do. If you give me trouble, I'll kill you." He said it with ugly calmness. "Now shut it."

"You'll regret this. They'll find..."

"I *said*, shut it." He swung the gun and pain exploded. Everything went black.

△ △ △ △ △

When Methusal awoke, she lay with her cheek smashed into the dirt. Her head throbbed, and it was dark. Firelight flickered a short distance away.

After a few slow blinks to try to clear her mind, she took inventory of her situation. Her hands and feet were tied up again, and she was lying in the cave.

She didn't see Kilum, so she relaxed into kaavl to listen. Small pebbles rattled a short distance away. He was heading back toward the cavern.

Methusal rolled, so her back faced the wall of the cave. Her fingers felt numb from the tight rope around her wrists. Still, she managed to poke two fingers into her waistband and pull out the stick. Jamming it into the knotted rope that secured her hands was a tricky, painful matter. The sharp stick gouged her wrists several times before she found a rounded knot to stab.

Kilum crouched by the fire as she silently worked at her bonds. Her fingers and wrists soon ached. Worse, she couldn't tell if she'd made any headway. But she had all night. She needed to escape before dawn. Once she was trapped on the Presidente's ship, it would be too late.

Kilum shot her a glance, and she swiftly shut her eyes and lay very still. He didn't approach her. From then on, Methusal kept her eyes shut and remained in kaavl, listening to his few movements. Patiently, she worked at the knots, and only stopped for a few minutes when her fingers cramped.

Exhaustion pulled at her mind, but fear kept her awake, and so did the sharp ache in her head.

Kilum smoked outside, apparently enjoying his own, solitary company. Smoke blew in, filling her nostrils. Warmth from the fire blew in, too.

Long minutes crept by. The rope was as tight as ever around her wrists. She was so tired. The warmth and her exhaustion softened her grip on consciousness.

When she awoke again, Kilum lay snoring on the other side of the cave. Her mind felt a little clearer, although it still ached from the blow he'd given her. Methusal resumed picking at her bonds with the stick. A knot gave. Elation soared, and she wiggled the stick, loosening the knot still more. The rope fell slack, and she pulled her hands free.

She didn't dare make a noise, for fear of waking him before she was fully free. Still keeping her hands behind her, she bent her knees, bringing her tied ankles within reach of her hands. She worked at those knots, too, only pausing when an excruciating cramp seized her right leg. She lay perfectly still until the cramp eased. After another couple of tugs, her legs were free.

Kilum's knife and gun lay close to his side. Only small pebbles surrounded her. The slender, jagged, pointed stick was her only weapon. Methusal wished she had her knife. Cautiously, she sat up, praying that Kilum wouldn't wake up before she escaped.

So far, so good.

She rose to her knees, and then to her feet. Bent double in the low cave, she stepped forward. Small pebbles rolled, and Kilum twitched. Methusal stepped again, and gravel crunched. Kilum snorted, and she bolted outside.

"Hey!" he screamed. A metallic snap indicated he'd primed his gun. As she scrambled frantically up the steep hillside, her kidnapper barreled out of the cave. "Stop!" The gun exploded, and a rock shattered near her left ear. "Move again, and I'll kill you," he snarled.

Methusal kept going. Kilum swore, and climbed after her. She heard him reload the gun. Another shot scalded her arm.

She ran up the hill, and then darted down the other side. Ryon's light was her only help...and a curse. Kilum could clearly see her.

Kilum tackled her. She fell hard, and her shoulder and hip slammed into rocks. He was strong and heavy. He grabbed for her hands, but she twisted onto her back, trying to free herself. His gun arced for her head, but she blocked it with her forearm. She still gripped her meager stick, and with all of her strength stabbed it into his groin. He screamed.

Enraged, he cursed and grabbed for her throat. She kicked and struggled and stabbed at his chest with the now broken stick.

The One, help me!

His wicked, silver knife gleamed in her side vision. He was too strong. *She couldn't escape.* She was going to die.

With a swift, aggressive lift, he pulled his arm back, and suddenly froze. Mouth opened wide in a soundless cry, he arched backward. A high, animal moan wailed, and then he convulsed and toppled onto her.

Panting with fright, Methusal pushed frantically at his heavy weight. What had happened? Maybe a wild beast...? Sobbing, she pushed at him, until suddenly Kilum's dead weight lurched sideways, shoved by an unseen force.

Terror choking her, she brandished her broken twig. Then she gasped in shock.

"Where is your knife, Methusal?"

Chapter Twenty-Six

Was she dreaming? How could he possibly be here? But when Methusal blinked, she still saw the Dehrien Chief's large, powerful form standing over her.

"Mentàll!" She scrambled to her feet. "You're here," she said, and burst into tears. He drew her into his arms and held her tight.

Pain stung her arm, and she flinched.

Immediately, he loosened his grip. "You are hurt!" His voice sounded thick and strangled. His hands swiftly ran over her upper body—her bloodied arm, her shoulder, the sticky mess on her stomach...

Her cheeks heated, and she grabbed his strong wrist, stopping him. "I'm okay. A bullet creased my arm, but I'll be fine. The rest is Kilum's blood."

"You are sure?"

"Yes." She swallowed another sob. Needing to be near him, she cautiously leaned into him. Did he still want to hold her, after all that had happened between them? To her relief, his arms went around her and he pulled her hard against him again. She felt comforted and safe, being so near to him.

"Good," she heard his harsh murmur against her hair. "I am sorry I did not get here sooner." She felt the fleeting brush of his warm lips against her temple. For some reason that made her tears flow faster. "*Ce'cemone*," he whispered. "Please do not cry."

After her sobs slowed, Methusal sniffed, "How did you find me?"

He did not release her, and she felt content to stay where she was. "I can track a whip beast. And I can easily track a woman kaavl player scuffing her feet."

Methusal smiled for a second. "But your injury." She looked up at him. His face looked pale in the moonlight.

"I am healed."

"Not completely."

He dismissed this with a flick of his eyes. "Well enough."

"How did you know that Kilum captured me?"

"Dastn told Aali, and she told me."

"You must have left..." Methusal did quick mental calculations, "immediately?"

"Of course."

"Thank you."

"I would do nothing else. You know that."

"Yes," she whispered. He had proven, yet again, that he would move heaven and earth to get to her. To protect her, even at the cost of his own health. "You should rest." She looked at Kilum's body, which lay sprawled on the stones. "What should we do with him?"

"Leave him for the wild beasts."

"Mentàll. We can't leave him like that. We need to bury him."

"Morning will be soon enough. Come. Your arm needs tending, and we are both tired."

True. And Kilum wouldn't care one way or the other.

Methusal shivered when she left his arms. It was getting colder outside. At the cave entrance, Mentàll added more wood to the fire, making it blaze high into the night sky, and then he pulled supplies from his pack. Food, a small medical kit, and an extra shirt.

"Sit by the fire, and take off your tunic," he directed.

"I won't." A blush heated her cheeks. "And I can take care of the wound myself."

A bemused smile pulled at his lips. "How will you clean the wound? Through the small rip the bullet made?"

She saw his point. And she did have a bra on underneath. Her face felt hotter than the fire warming it. "Fine." She turned away from him and pulled the tunic over her head.

Breath hissed between his teeth.

"What?" she said.

"Sit."

When she did, she glanced behind her. Mentàll stared at her back. Anger seared red high into his cheekbones. "What did he do to you?" His voice was much too quiet.

"He stabbed me when I slowed down. It doesn't hurt much anymore."

In silence, he set to work swabbing her back with a cloth soaked in spirits. She flinched against the burning, stinging pain. "I am sorry," he murmured. Cool, soothing gel followed, applied with gentle fingers. Then sticky tacky leaves.

"Thank you."

"Do not thank me yet." He examined her arm. "It is not deep, but this will hurt."

"I know."

"I am sorry." The cool cloth bit into her flesh, and she choked off an involuntary cry. Teeth gritted, she endured the necessary torture, and felt intense relief when cooling coltac gel at last soothed the wound. He affixed tacky leaves, and bound a cloth around it all.

She shivered now. Her back was warm, but her front was freezing. She pulled on her tunic again, glad for the meager warmth, and to be covered again. She felt too vulnerable exposed to him like that.

Mentàll piled more wood on the fire, and then rummaged through Kilum's pack, which lay on the far side of the cave. He pulled out a leather cloak. "This will do."

He sat against the cave wall, a length away from the fire, and held out an arm to her. "Come to me." Perhaps he intended to hold her all night long.

It sounded unbelievably good. With alarming eagerness, she nestled up beside him. He put his arm around her, so her head rested on his shoulder. Then he arranged the cloak so it enveloped their upper bodies completely.

He was so warm. Methusal shivered, and brought her clasped hands to her lips and blew on them. His large hand covered hers, enveloping them in warmth. She smiled and breathed in the scent of him. Leather, light sweat, and the essence that was purely Mentàll.

She loved touching him, and being so close to him. Her eyes closed. Right here, right now, nothing else mattered. She could be with him, and neither the future nor the past mattered.

"Thank you," she mumbled again. As she relaxed into warm, secure slumber, his lips brushed her forehead.

"Sleep well, *saltisienna*."

CHAPTER TWENTY-SEVEN

DAY 29

METHUSAL AWOKE SLOWLY. She felt warm and comfortable. Daylight brightened the world beyond her eyelids. Mentàll. She was sleeping on his chest.

He'd come for her last night. He'd saved her life yet again. Did that make it eight times now?

She didn't want to move. His slow, powerful heart thudded beneath her ear. She'd never felt safer or happier in her entire life.

His lips pressed into her hair, and warm breath caressed her skin. He was awake. She should let him know that she was, too. With a hand on his chest, she levered herself into a straighter position. Her eyes met his, which were dilated dark in the shadowed cave. His gaze looked softer than normal, and his mouth very approachable.

"Good morning," she said shyly. She'd never slept so close to a man before. Zindedi didn't count, because half a length had always separated them. Except for that one, brief time. Her gaze dropped to his lips.

"Good morning." To her delight, his mouth came closer. His lips gently touched hers, and she closed her eyes at the warm, delicious pressure.

"Mentàll." She touched his jaw, holding him close so she could return his kiss. Prickly stubble scraped her palm.

Their shared, languorous kisses continued until pleasant warmth curled deep inside her. "Mentàll," she whispered.

His fingers curled into the hair at her nape, and he kissed her exquisitely, as if she was the most precious thing on earth to him. She felt like she was drowning.

When he gently urged her backward, to lie on the floor, she did not resist, and in fact curled her hands tightly into his shoulders and gave herself over to the ecstasy of his gentle, plundering mouth. Her breath caught when he positioned himself partly over her, and his thigh urged hers apart. Her heart thundered, and an unbearable yearning gripped her.

His body felt hot, and hard tension tightened his muscles. He wanted her. Her skin burned where he touched her, and every touch of his lips brought shimmering bursts of pleasure.

"Mentàll." She felt drugged, barely able to think. She didn't want to think. He felt so good. And he was so very good at this. Sanity surfaced for the barest moment. She mumbled, "You aren't trying to seduce me, are you?"

"What better way to make you mine?" His eyes gleamed, and he kissed her again.

More unwelcome sanity cooled her mind. If he took her, she would belong to him. Forever.

He kissed the edge of her jaw. Pleasure pooled like a heavy, silken weight in her blood. His kisses were perfection. He could take her so easily.

And yet if he did, he would ruthlessly and honorably insist that she marry him. And her father would agree.

With feeble hands, she pushed at his chest. His kisses stopped, so she could look into his eyes, which were clouded with passion.

"Really?" she whispered. "Would you really do it this way?"

"Do what?"

"Seduce me, so I'd have no choice but to marry you?"

He hesitated, and although his eyes cleared a little, they remained darkly dilated. "It is not beyond me. I am a wild beast, as you know." He bent to nuzzle slow, scorching kisses under her chin.

"Mentàll," she moaned, clenching her fists, trying to resist him. It was so hard.

"What?" His lips trailed a warm path down her neck. "Shall I stop?"

"Yes, you shall stop!" Her body felt on fire, and with her last shreds of sanity, she struggled and wiggled free, scooting backward to get away from his potent, drugging kisses. She quickly stood and crossed her arms, feeling a lot safer at this distance. Blood still rushed in uncomfortable pulses and swirls of pleasure throughout her body. Trembling, she looked down at him. "You are a wild beast. Aren't you?"

He slowly sat up. A faint flush rode his cheekbones, and his chest heaved deeply. Long moments passed. He did not answer.

She pressed a trembling hand to her forehead. "Of course you are. You're always determined to get your own way. You'd manipulate and seduce me so I'd *have* to marry you." Overcome with sudden rage, she shouted, "That's not the way it works!"

He regarded her rather calmly. It infuriated her still more.

"You won't even deny it."

"It was not my first intent, but it did cross my mind. I will not lie."

"Do you think that would be a good start for us? To trap me into marrying you? As if we don't have enough problems already."

"What other weapon do I have? You refuse to trust me. You refuse to give us a chance."

"And this is exactly *why!*" she cried out. "Mentàll, I hate you, and I love you...and...and I could just kick you. You infuriate me no end!"

The barest smile touched his lips. "You love me?"

"*Rrr!*" She clenched her fists and glared at the ceiling. "You drive me crazy. And this is why. Kisses are not supposed to be weapons!"

"How else can I make you see that we belong together?"

"Give me your heart. Tell me you love me more than all that power you lust after. Tell me you love *me.*"

"I cannot promise what I do not have to give."

"You *do* have love to give. Everyone does. Either you're too selfish to open up your heart and give it, or you're too scared."

"I would give you my life, Methusal. It is all I have. Is it not enough?"

She wavered. She read the truth in his eyes. "I don't know," she whispered. "I just don't know. Sometimes I see your heart, and others, it seems like ice surrounds you. And on top of all that, you keep manipulating and pushing to have your own way. How can I know I can trust you?"

"I want you," he said harshly. "I have never wanted anything more. Trust that."

He did. She did believe that. She eyed him with uncertainty.

Harshly, he said, "Call off your wedding to Behran, Methusal. Call it off."

It was time to tell him the truth. But first, she said, "Your behavior right now would not convince me to do anything."

"Forgive me, then. Please." He rose to his feet. "I am not a perfect man." Even more harshly, he grated, "But do not fault me for pursuing what I want. I will not run in fear."

Her mouth dropped open. "Are you saying I am?"

"If the moccasin fits." He bent, rapidly shoved his belongings in his pack, and straightened. "I will not beg for you. Marry Behran, if he is all the man you can handle."

He strode out of the cave.

Scowling, she stared after him, and then reluctantly followed. His words hurt, because they were true.

Mentàll now had a stick in hand, and scrawled a message in the dirt.

Thusa is fine. Go N. to coast. Then Quasr.

"Do you think they're close behind?"

"They will be here within the hour."

How could he know that, except... "You have hidden kaavl talents." At one time, she'd thought he had no special talents at all. But more than once his otherly sense had led them in the right direction. To safety. And last night, to her.

"Look deep. Perhaps you will find something more to admire about me, Methusal." He strode up the hill. The rigid set of his shoulders said he was angry.

Well, she didn't feel any happier. She felt confused and hurt and angry. Wasn't he at fault? Hadn't his unscrupulous behavior started this argument?

She followed him with a frown.

On the other side of the hill she remembered Kilum, and searched for his dark, crumpled form. But he was nowhere to be seen.

Mentàll slowly picked his way through the rocks, obviously looking for clues, and his finger traced a dark stain on a stone. A red stain. "The wild beasts took him."

"That's awful!"

"He deserved his fate."

He hiked north again, and Methusal silently followed.

An hour later, they crested the last hill, and the sea sparkled before them. A ship rode the waves fifty or more lengths from the beach.

"The Presidente's ship," he said grimly.

"He's waiting for Kilum. And me."

She saw no rowboat on the shore, and none bobbed alongside the ship, either.

"Now what?" she asked. "We can't go to the beach, or he'll see us. We can't let him know I'm free, or he'll know that *we* know the peace is broken. He'll suspect a strike from us before we can deliver it."

Approval warmed Mentàll's ice blue eyes. "We will stay hidden among the rocks until we round that point to the west." The point he indicated was a good half hour hike away. He pulled out a package of dried meat and bread and gave half to her. "We should reach Quasr by early afternoon."

Methusal nodded. They would make much better time once they reached the beach. She ate silently, and then gulped water. The sun was already growing warm. She glanced at him as he tucked the water skin back in his pack. His blue gaze snared hers, and his fingers slowed their ruthless knotting of his pack.

He said, "I hate it when we're angry with one another."

"I hate it, too," she admitted.

In a low voice, he said, "Will you forgive me? I did not plan to seduce you this morning. Trapping you into marriage was not my first intent. My blood burns for you, Methusal. I wanted you, and so I justified that perhaps I could have you. That perhaps I *should* have you, so I could make you mine forever." Harshly, he finished, "I am sorry."

"It's okay." She smiled, and he smiled back. Her spirits lifted. "I have something to confess."

He waited.

"My engagement to Behran is over."

Triumph flared in his eyes.

"It's been over for several weeks. Ever since I heard you and Hil talking on the ship."

Disbelief registered. "But why?" he said. "Why would you continue the lie?"

"Behran wanted to protect me, and I needed to protect myself from you. He called it a 'reconsideration' period."

"He didn't want things to end between you."

"That's true."

"It was a lie."

"Yes. And I'm sorry. My only excuse is that you confused me terribly. I needed a way to separate myself from you so I could think for a while. But I'm not sure if it helped much."

"Lies never do."

"Neither do half-truths."

He said nothing.

"If we'd both been honest with one another since the beginning of this trip, we'd be in a different place right now."

"You may be right."

"Where do we go from here?"

"We forgive one another."

"Yes."

"And we try to do better. I am not a perfect man, Methusal, as I said before. I have never pretended to be one."

"And I definitely am not perfect, either."

His teeth flashed in a small smile. "Then we both agree that we are human."

She smiled and impulsively hugged him. "I'm sorry," she whispered.

His arms closed tightly around her. "And I regret every word and action I have done that has hurt you."

Finally, she pulled away. "At last we have peace."

"We have more than peace, Methusal. I think you know that."

"Yes."

They did have peace. If only the other, remaining issues between them could be resolved as neatly. But it was a start. And at the moment she didn't want to think any further. She just wanted to enjoy her time with him. Right now, nothing else really mattered.

"Come. I want to make good time."

"Don't forget your injury."

"I am fine."

But several hours later, after walking on the beach, even after holding Kilum's cape and Mentàll's tunic overhead for protection against the sun, the heat had sapped even

Methusal's energy. Mentàll's face looked exhausted and drawn.

"Let's rest when we reach that next point," she suggested. "Maybe we're almost to Quasr."

But when they rounded the point, another point loomed a short distance away. And in the center, squatted by a smoking fire with his back to them, was a man with grizzled white hair. A tunic of patched fur covered one brown shoulder, and his vibrant, bass voice mixed with the boom of the waves. At intervals, his skinny brown arms flew skyward, as if sharing sparkles of joy with heaven.

The Prophet.

Their steps slowed down as they neared him, and Methusal listened to his strong, joyful melody.

Praise The One, O my soul,
and forget not all his benefits—
who forgives all your sins and heals all your diseases,
who redeems your life from the pit
and crowns you with love and compassion,
who satisfies your desires with good things
so that your youth is renewed like the eagle's.

Wait for The One and keep his way.
He will exalt you to inherit the land;
when the wicked are cut off, you will see it...
The righteous will inherit the land and dwell in it forever.

I know that my Redeemer lives,
and that in the end he will stand upon the earth.
And after my skin has been destroyed,
yet in my flesh I will see The One;
I myself will see him
with my own eyes—I, and not another.
How my heart yearns within me!

The Prophet's voice quieted, and he turned on his heels to face them. Dark brown eyes sparkled in his brown face. "Methusal and Mentàll. Come. Join me." He did not appear surprised to see them. In fact, she had the oddest feeling that he had been waiting for them.

They sat cross-legged around his fire. A cool breeze flowed through the area. It felt like gentle, soothing fingers of ice on Methusal's hot cheeks. The sun went behind a single, puffy cloud and shadowed the land.

The Prophet smiled at them. "Why have you come?"

"I was kidnapped. We're heading back to Quasr."

His smile widened, and he reached for his staff, which lay near his feet in the sand. "You do not know why you are here," he said softly. "You are as lost as ever."

Methusal didn't know how to respond to that. "We're heading home. We've been fighting for peace with Zindedi."

"And yet you are trapped by another enemy." The Prophet stared at them both with bright, expectant eyes.

She didn't know what he was talking about. Feeling a bit stupid, she glanced at Mentàll, who wore a reserved but tolerant expression.

The Prophet's brow wrinkled. "You cannot even guess?"

"I'm sorry," she said. "But I have no idea."

The Prophet frowned and mumbled to himself, and then wrote in the sand. At last, he looked up. "It is as it should be. You need help to find the right path."

Mentàll spoke. "What path, Prophet?"

Compassion softened the old man's gaze. "You, my son, are the one who is most lost."

Mentàll's muscles infinitesimally stiffened.

"Do not fear," the Prophet said softly, his eyes kind.

"I fear nothing," Mentàll said harshly.

"You fear punishment. You fear many things. Abandonment, for one. You think your father left you. You fear losing power and control over your life. You fear that The One hates you. You regret your many sins, but do not know how to put things right." He shook his head. "No wonder you are afraid to love. Listen well. You must find the courage to make things right with The One before you can make things right with anyone else."

His kindly gaze traveled to Methusal. "Fear not, child. When it is time, you will know the right decision to make."

The Dehrien Chief's shoulders moved restively. He wanted to go. He felt uncomfortable. But respect for the old man kept him where he was.

The Prophet smiled. "Your friends approach. I will leave you with one last word from The One who created you, and who loves you."

With a small hum, he sang,

There is no fear in love.
But perfect love drives out fear,
because fear has to do with punishment.
The one who fears is not made perfect in love.

He gave a throaty cackle. "Humble thyself in the sight of
The One, Mentàll. And he will lift you up."

△ △ △ △ △

The cool cloud slowly slid by the sun, and bright warmth
again spilled across the landscape. The Prophet chuckled and
stood, drawing his cape up and around him.

"Thusa!" Behran rounded the eastern point, and Dastn
was close on his heels.

Methusal hurried to meet them.

"Thusa!" Behran's arms closed tightly around her. "I was
so worried."

"Mentàll killed Kilum." Methusal looked over her
shoulder. "And we were just talking to the Proph..."

Although the fire still smoldered on the beach, the
Prophet was gone.

Behran's arms slowly loosened, and he released her. He
flicked a hard glance at Mentàll. "You found her."

"Of course," he said, in a coolly arrogant tone. "Did you
expect nothing less?"

"Thank you."

"Methusal has already thanked me quite thoroughly."

Warmth leapt to her cheeks, and she frowned. "Mentàll."

His smile looked like a wild beast's, complete with
gleaming fangs. "I speak only the truth. He deserves no less."
With ice in his tone, he added, "And Behran, let me offer my
sympathies on your broken engagement."

Behran glanced at her, and then back to the Dehrien
Chief. "I would do anything for Methusal. Don't ever forget
that."

"She does not require your services any longer."

"I will remain her friend for life. Treat her right, or I will
be there to pick up the pieces."

Methusal didn't like the tension between the two men.
She touched Behran's tense arm, and tried to catch Mentàll's

hard gaze, but failed. "Please stop. I don't want you two to fight with each other."

Behran broke gaze with the Dehrien Chief first. "I said all I needed to say. " He glanced at Mentàll again. "Don't forget it."

After a look at Methusal, Mentàll said nothing more, although temper flushed his cheekbones. He turned his back on the younger man and headed for Quasr. He was upset, but Methusal was grateful for his restraint.

"What happened with Kilum?" Behran asked.

"Mentàll killed Kilum just as he was about to murder me. I'm grateful he got there in time."

As they headed west again, Methusal told Behran and Dastn everything that had happened since Kilum had kidnapped her. Everything, of course, except for the private moments in the cave between herself and the Dehrien Chief this morning.

She slid a glance at Mentàll, who silently stalked beside her now. Although he didn't join the conversation, she sensed that he held himself under control by the finest of threads. He did not appear to appreciate that Behran was monopolizing her attention. His one glance at him spoke volumes.

Dastn said, "So that was the Presidente's ship. I wonder what he'll do when Kilum doesn't show up."

"Maybe send out a search party," Methusal said. "And when he's realized that Kilum failed, maybe he'll go home."

"Do you really believe it will be so simple?" Mentàll spoke at last.

She glanced at him. "You don't?"

"No. He is plotting much more. We need to discover what it is."

Unease slid through her. "Do you think he's planning another attack? You blew up half of his ships. And their powder supplies are low."

"He is weakened. But even a wild beast with few fangs is a dangerous threat." His gaze impaled Behran. "His move against Methusal was an act of war. I will send a ship to Zindedi to deliver retribution. In the meantime, we will plan offensive strategies."

"But all of the chiefs have gone home."

"They will meet again in Rolban for the election. I will deliver messages before then, so we can come prepared to make a plan of action."

"But what if the Presidente plans to do something before then? We only saw one ship. But who's to say he hasn't sent others? Maybe they're offshore right now, planning an attack."

Behran spoke up, "They don't have enough men or arms to attack our whole continent again."

"Maybe they'll attack only one place. One strategic place."

"Where would that be?" Dastn wondered.

Mentàll said, "He wants Rolban's ore."

Horror filled her. "The coastal community closest to Rolban is Eerpor."

"Yes," he agreed harshly. "Eerpor is isolated and defenseless. No patrols protect the Iignon coast, because it is impassable."

"The only way to Rolban from the east coast is through Eerpor."

"Sozla. And her family." Behran's steps faltered, and his face drained of color. "They're in danger. Mentàll, have they headed home yet?"

"They left yesterday morning. They should arrive home tomorrow." Mentàll's sharp gaze rested upon Behran. "You are worried about Sozla?"

"Of course. Her whole family is in danger. We have to warn them."

"I'll go," Dastn offered promptly.

Behran frowned. "But if we're right, they'll need extra men to defend themselves."

"If you would like to help, you could run over the mountains and warn Eerpor's chief," Mentàll suggested. "I would give Dastn a message to my first-in-command in Dehre. My men will readily help defend Eerpor. In the meantime, I will send messengers to the other chiefs, asking for help to defend both Eerpor and Rolban."

They had just rounded the northernmost tip of the Quasr Mountains. Up ahead the green trees of Quasr dotted the horizon, and to the south stretched the flat plains.

"I would like to go." Behran sent Methusal a worried look. "But..."

"Go!" she encouraged. "They might be in terrible danger. Do you have enough rations in your pack?"

"I have enough," Dastn spoke up. "And I can trap animals along the way. We'll be fine. Mentàll, if you write that missive, we can leave now."

Mentàll pulled out an old piece of parchment, which was already covered in writing on one side, and scrawled bold, dark words on the back. He rolled it up and gave it to the Tarst runner. "Be swift. Many lives may depend upon it."

"Yes, sir. Ready, Behran?"

Behran glanced with obvious regret at Methusal, and then pulled her close and hugged her. "I'm glad you're safe. Stay that way. I'll see you at home."

She became aware of Mentàll's tense silence. She gave Behran a quick hug in return, and released him. "Be careful. Please."

"I will. 'Bye." He strode after Dastn.

Mentàll's tension visibly eased as the two men jogged south.

"You don't need to be jealous, you know," she said softly. "I'm not in love with Behran."

"That may be true. But he holds a piece of your heart. If he could, he would take it all."

"No. I've made it clear that won't happen."

"But he thinks it's over between us, too, doesn't he?" Mentàll asked with unnerving perception.

"Yes," she admitted. "And it's true. We're not together."

"Not yet," he said with his usual arrogance. "However, until he realizes his wishes are dead, he will continue to hope."

"He's not a threat to you."

"Oh yes, he is. I see that quite clearly, Methusal, even if you do not."

His words unsettled her. In silence, they finished the final distance to Quasr. Mentàll's face grew drawn and pale the longer they hiked. Although he'd never admit it, his body clearly needed more healing time. He should never have come after her. And yet she was so glad that he had.

Her mind turned to other worries as they entered Quasr. Had the Presidente already sent war ships to the tiny town of Eerpor? If so, she knew who would lead the attack.

General Fitrn.

Fear, like black poison, bled into her heart. That insane, vicious man would leave no Eerporian man, woman, or child alive. Behran, if he was there when it happened, would die, too. And when they were all dead, General Fitrn would march for Rolban.

△ △ △ △ △

Hanuh greeted Methusal with tears of joy and relief, and her father with an unexpectedly teary, solid hug when they reached Quasr. Hendra, Aali, and even Doc also hugged her, but Methusal noticed that Hendra, although her gaze repeatedly rested upon Doc, stayed far away from the Tarst doctor.

Everyone, including Pan, Calbn, and Lylitha, sat at the long dining table while Methusal again told the story of her kidnapping, and how Mentàll's swift tracking had saved her life.

"Mentàll, we owe you more than we can possibly repay you," Erl said. "We are truly grateful."

"I was happy to do it," the Dehrien Chief murmured. The pallor that had lingered after the long trip had begun to fade. Methusal was relieved. "Your daughter means a great deal to me."

Methusal smiled, but felt the need to redirect the conversation. "How many times have you saved my life now, Mentàll? It's getting to be a habit," she told her parents.

"Eight times." His thumb stroked his cold, beading water glass. His light gaze held hers. "If old legends are to be believed, you would now be bound to me for eight lifetimes."

Methusal flushed, and glanced down at her cup.

Erl's brow raised, and he glanced from Methusal to Mentàll. For the first time, speculation gleamed in his eyes.

Methusal felt an even stronger urge to change the subject. "Mama, what happened when you found out I was missing?" Neither Behran nor Dastn had had time to tell her the whole story.

Tears welled in Hanuh's eyes. "It was awful. At first we thought you'd gone for a walk. But when you never came back..." tears slipped down her cheeks. "I was beside myself. Dastn, Behran, Pan, and Doc tracked you."

Doc took up the tale. "Your clear path led into the mountains. Behran and Dastn followed that. Pan and I followed lighter trails to the north and east, but they all ended up being dead ends."

Erl said, "Last night we came to Quasr. But when we heard those shots last night in the mountains..."

Hanuh pressed a hand to her heart. "I was so afraid, Methusal. You have no idea. Thank the *One* that horrible man is dead."

"Our troubles are not finished," Mentàll said harshly. He finished the saga.

Afterward, a tense silence fell. Then the other chiefs plied him with more questions. As the afternoon wore on, they formed a tentative plan. Runners would ask Aestoff and Wyen for reinforcements for Eerpor. Unfortunately, it would take days, perhaps even a week, to contact the other communities, and for the soldiers to travel all the way to Eerpor. If the General was already marching, their help could come too late.

Methusal left the men to their discussions. After collecting her pack, which her parents had carried back to Quasr, she took a bath and changed into clean clothes.

It felt good to wash all of the filth and grime from her body. She cleaned the wound on her arm easily enough, but the ones on her back were harder. She finally went to her mother for help.

"My goodness!" Hanuh sounded horrified when she saw Methusal's back.

"That's what Mentàll said. They don't hurt much."

"He patched you up?"

She nodded.

"He did a good job. They're starting to heal nicely." Her mother finished smoothing on the last tacky leaf. As she put away the medical supplies, she said, "Are your feelings for him becoming any clearer?"

"I know how I feel about him."

"You love him."

"Yes."

"That's a start. You must decide what to do next, Methusal. He will not wait quietly in a corner while you try to make up your mind. He'll try to make it for you. He's a very forceful man."

"Don't I know it."

"Methusal. I see the way he looks at you. And the fact he left Quasr, still injured, to find you—it's clear he won't let you go without a fight."

"I know. I told him that my engagement with Behran is over. But he still feels threatened by Behran. They almost picked a fight with one another on the way here today. But what Mentàll doesn't seem to realize is that this is not about Behran. It's about one thing, and one thing only. He doesn't love me, Mama. He's said so. All he wants is power and kaavl sons. He doesn't want *me*."

"Are you sure?"

"He told me that he's not capable of loving anyone."

"Do you believe it?"

"I don't know. The Prophet thinks Mentàll is afraid to love."

"What do you think?"

"I'm afraid to speculate. I'm afraid of fooling myself into seeing something that isn't there. All I know is that I will not marry a man who doesn't love me. It would kill me, slowly. Every day. I couldn't bear it, Mama. To love him with my whole heart, and to get nothing back, except a few scraps of attention...I *can't*."

"I think he'd give you more than a few scraps of attention."

Methusal blushed.

Her mother said quietly, "I've seen him kiss you. And they are not the kisses of a man trying to seal a deal or manipulate to get what he wants. He feels something for you, Methusal, whether he'll admit that to himself or not."

"He feels *passion* for me. Lust." Methusal's cheeks warmed still more. "He'll readily admit that. I'm afraid that's all he feels for me."

"Then you're at an impasse, aren't you? Unless he can tell you he loves you, it sounds like you won't marry either Mentàll or Behran."

"If only I loved Behran! Logically, he's the best man for me. He's good and honorable and full of integrity, and I respect and trust him. I care about him very much. He would never hurt me on purpose. He never *has* hurt me, period. On the other hand, Mentàll and I hurt each other all the time. We do it so well. It scares me."

"It's because you feel great passion for each other. That's the only reason why you can hurt each other so much. If you're honest, maybe that's why Behran has never deeply hurt you. He doesn't have the key to the deepest part of your heart. So he can't reach in there and grab your soul with his fist."

"The Prophet said when it was time, I would know what to do."

"Then be patient. I am sure you'll see Mentàll again in the next few weeks. See what happens."

But Methusal didn't see how anything would become any clearer in the next few weeks. In fact, it seemed that the more time she spent with the Dehrien Chief, the more confused she became.

△ △ △ △ △

Hendra couldn't stay in her room and avoid Doc forever. It had hurt, horribly, when he'd left the first time. She couldn't face seeing him again, and even worse, saying goodbye to him again.

All the same, she had to eat. She found a spot to sit between Hanuh Maahr and Methusal in the dining hall, and ate dinner quickly, listening to the conversation around her, which focused upon thwarting the Presidente's possible plans.

Doc sat across the table a short distance away. His gaze, which looked dark and brooding in the dim light, often flickered to her. When she dumped her dishes in the bin and then turned, planning to make a cowardly escape to her room, she found him standing at her elbow.

"Hendra." He placed his dishes in the bin, also.

Nerves fluttered. "Hello. Well... Goodnight." Before she could take a step, his hand closed around her wrist.

"Don't run from me again." An edge roughened his low tone. "You're not a coward."

"Aren't I? Isn't that the whole problem?"

"You are not a coward," he insisted gently. "Walk with me in the courtyard. Please."

"Nothing has changed. Please, let me go." She twisted at her wrist. He released it, but his hand slipped down to enfold hers, instead.

"Please, Hendra."

She looked into his eyes, and that was a mistake. Love for him welled up, making her heart ache. "All right," she whispered. "But only for a few minutes."

Outdoors, they silently meandered over the dim pathways of the lush, green courtyard. Light glowed from small lanterns, high overhead, and moisture beaded the warm air. Sporadic bird chirps peppered the silence, and she wondered if they were bidding each other goodnight.

Peace filled her heart as she walked silently beside Doc. His company was undemanding and accepting.

He was a wonderful man.

In fact, she realized with painful clarity that he was too good for her. He deserved only the very best, and that was not her. As much as it would kill her, she had to make him understand that fact tonight. Once and for all. For his own good.

Fragrant, flowering bushes crowded a nearby bench. When Hendra moved toward it, Doc sat beside her. He still held her hand, and, weak as she was, she didn't try to break the contact.

"I think it's best if we say goodbye now," she said quietly. "Don't you?"

"No." He did not sound perturbed. Just calm.

"We've established that I can't be a real wife to you—"

"We have not."

"Then what was that horrible mess on the beach about?" Unwanted tears swam in her eyes.

"It was a mistake. Every piece of it. I should have stopped it before it went so far."

"I became hysterical. You can't ignore that."

"I should never have touched you like that."

"You did the right thing. How else could we find out the truth? I'm afraid, Doc. I'm broken. I don't want to be, but I am."

Gently, he took her other hand. "I love you, Hendra."

"It's not enough."

"It is, if you'll let it be."

"I won't disappoint you. I won't hurt you like that."

"Don't you think I should decide what I want? Do you love me?"

"Of course I do. But..."

"Shh." He gently kissed her. And then, to her utter shock, he slipped down and knelt on the ground.

"No," she whispered.

"I love you. I accept you as you are. Even if we can never be intimate, I accept that. I can't live without you. I need you more than my next breath. Please agree to be my wife."

"I can't." Tears spilled down her cheeks. "It wouldn't be fair to you."

"*Please.*" Stark need underscored his low tone. He meant it. He loved her so much that he was willing to sacrifice everything for her. It shouldn't be this way.

"I love you so much. I want to say yes, more than anything, but..."

"Then do it," he said with fierce urgency.

She wiped away her tears. "I can't. You'll grow to resent me. I couldn't stand that."

"Hendra." Anguish constricted the word.

"No. I love you with my whole heart, but the answer is no."

His hands tightened around hers. "Take a chance on us. I know we can make it."

Tears relentlessly rolled down her cheeks.

He kissed the back of each of her hands. Huskily, he said, "I won't give up on us. I won't give up on you. I will wait for you."

"Don't," she choked out. "It'll just hurt more."

"How can it possibly hurt more than it does right now?" Tears gleamed in his eyes, and that made her burst into jagged sobs.

"Shh." He sat beside her again, and drew her into his arms. He kissed her hair. "It'll all work out. I promise."

She clung helplessly to him and sobbed into his chest. She hated herself for being so weak. She needed to be strong and let him go now. Otherwise, the hurt would continue to fester, and he'd never make a clean break and find someone new...someone better. Someone who could love him the way he deserved to be loved.

Gasping on a breath, she jerked free and leaped to her feet. "It's over. Goodbye. Please...please don't talk to me ever again." She fled for the mansion.

She had done the right thing. She *had.*

She curled up tight on her bed, shuddering violently with misery.

Oh, she hated being afraid! A low scream escaped. She hated Jascr! She *hated* him!

She dug her fingernails deep into her pillow, wishing it was his face. Wishing that she could rip him apart, just as he had ripped her entire life apart.

Chapter Twenty-Eight

METHUSAL AND THE OTHERS STOOD at the gates to the compound, much as they had done three days earlier. The urchets pulled restively at their bridles. She waited near one smelly beast, with her pack at her feet. Erl, Calbn, and Pan were deep in discussion, but she hadn't seen more than a glimpse of Mentàll this morning.

She'd heard that Doc had briefly examined both Mentàll's wound and Aali's leg last night, and prescribed that they both stay in Quasr for a minimum of one more week. She could well imagine how that restriction chaffed at Mentàll's fiercely independent spirit. Especially with the election coming up in a few short weeks.

Hendra had bid them a quick goodbye inside the mansion, promising to come to Rolban soon with Aali. Afterward, she had quickly turned away, but Doc had stopped her. With a hunted look, she'd stared at him. Methusal hadn't eavesdropped on his low words, but it had been hard to ignore Hendra's emphatic head shake. Then she'd dashed away.

Now Doc looked grim. He stood by himself a short distance away. Something terrible must have happened, and Methusal felt bad for them both. They loved each other. That was clear. But she knew all too well that love didn't necessarily mean that everything would work out in a happily ever after ending.

"Methusal."

The low, harsh grate made her jump. She spun. Jsan and Tumel stood beside Mentàll.

"I am sorry for startling you." A faint smile glimmered. "Jsan and Tumel will go to Rolban with you. They will protect you."

Methusal glanced at the two burly bodyguards. "Is that really necessary? Kilum is dead."

"Do not argue, please. They are your bodyguards, and will remain so until I see you again."

She offered them each a smile. "Thank you."

Mentàll said in a low, intense voice, "I want to protect you myself. Perhaps I should."

His fierce desire to protect her unexpectedly made her feel cherished. "Thank you. But you need to take care of yourself. You need to finish healing."

"Stay here with me, then," he said harshly. "Until we are sure Rolban is secure."

"I can't," she said softly. "You know that, and you'd feel the same in my position. If Rolban is in danger, they'll need me. You've taught me a lot, and sometimes I feel so close to the Primary level it's unbelievable. Maybe one day I'll make it. In the meantime, I promise I won't get captured again."

"Stay focused."

Her one, repeated failing. "I will. I'll do my very best."

"You know, Methusal, that is the only reason why you have not fully advanced to the Primary level." His matter-of-fact tone and level gaze told her that it was the desire of his heart that she advance. He wanted the very best for her.

She smiled. "Thank you. Everything will be fine. You'll see."

She didn't want him to worry. And, for once, it was time for her to stand on her own two feet. If it was necessary, she would face and fight General Fitrn alone. And win. She hoped.

His frown lingered, but eased when Pan approached. The Tarst leader offered a hand to Mentàll. "We're leaving. I'll see you in four weeks."

Mentàll shook it firmly. "I will send you every piece of information I receive about the Zindedis."

"And I'll send my men into the Tarst Mountains. If Zindedis try to get by Eerpor, we'll spot them."

"Good."

Pan moved away, and a moment later, a "Hiy!" and clopping urchet steps indicated the caravan was rumbling forward. Jsan and Tumel followed. Methusal lingered near Mentàll, although when she realized it, she moved away.

"Methusal."

She glanced back.

"I do not like this." It was clear by his tormented expression that he did not like being weak, and unable to travel, either. "Reconsider. Stay here with me."

She touched his hand, and her fingers closed around his. "I'll be fine. And by the time I get to Rolban, your men will already be hiking to Eerpor. General Fitrn, if he's even coming, probably won't make it to Rolban."

He relaxed a bit.

Methusal realized that she was still holding his hand. "I have to go," she murmured, and attempted to release it.

But his long fingers tightened around hers. "Be safe." His unexpected kiss came as a shock. She felt it clear through to her toes, and trembled when his lips lingered.

He murmured, "Remember this, Methusal. You belong with me. I will make sure you realize that when I see you next."

The maddening man. From gentle to arrogant in a heartbeat. "The last time I checked, I don't belong to anyone."

His pale gaze burned with determined fire. "I will see you next week in Rolban."

"Is that a threat or a promise?"

His mouth stretched into a humorless smile. "A promise." The blue gaze slowly, deliberately, dropped to her mouth again. She flushed. "Until then, fair Methusal." He turned on his heel.

The man burrowed under her skin so easily. He infuriated her, and yet she loved him.

She hoped a nasty surprise did not await them in Rolban. While she'd managed to sound confident to Mentàll, she did not feel that way at all.

Last night, General Fitrn had invaded her dreams. She'd relived the torture of when she'd hung, cold and dripping wet, from the rings in his basement. She remembered the pitch black, and her fear, as bitter as blood on her tongue.

Was he in Koblan? The thought scared her more than she wanted to admit.

While General Fitrn lusted for power and ore, experience had taught her that he lusted for blood still more. If he came to Rolban—if he took over their community—his first order of business would be to torture her to death. Methusal knew this as certainly as she knew the sun would rise. She'd escaped from him once before. But if he gained power over Rolban... Suddenly, she was glad for Jsan and Tumel's protection.

The One, please protect us all.

△ △ △ △ △

Hendra sat huddled on a bench in the garden. The sun shone and the sky was a cloudless blue, but she was alone. So alone. Again, tears overcame her. Already, she missed Doc so much.

She wrapped her arms around her knees and buried her face in them. She sobbed out the aching emptiness in her heart.

"Hendra?" Her cousin's voice startled her. Quickly, she wiped her eyes. With a frown, he sat down beside her. "What is wrong?"

"Oh, Mentàll." Without thinking, she leaned into him, and he just as easily pulled her close. It was the first time she had ever turned to him for comfort. She cried quietly into his shoulder.

"What is it, little cousin?" he asked gently.

"I told Doc goodbye," she wept. "Forever."

"Why?"

She cried harder. She couldn't tell her cousin her deepest shame. How she was unfit as a woman, and unworthy of Doc's love.

"Tell me, Hendra. Perhaps I can help."

"You can't. No one can!" She burst out, "I'm worthless, Mentàll. I'm not worthy of his love."

"Did he tell you that?" Anger darkened his tone.

"No! Of course not." She bit her lip.

"Then why did you say that?"

"Because it's true!" Her face hurt from the tension of crying so hard, but she couldn't seem to stop.

Mentàll waited, saying nothing. The silence became overwhelming, begging to be filled with the truth.

Should she tell her cousin her darkest secret? He already knew about Jascr's attack on her years ago. Could this revelation possibly be any worse? Suddenly, she had to tell him. She had to tell someone.

"I cannot love him...as a woman loves a man," she whispered in shame.

He said nothing for a long moment, evidently trying to piece together missing information. "Because of Jascr?"

"Yes. But not just because of him. Because of all of the beatings from my father, too. I'm afraid to trust men, Mentàll. I've tried, but I can't."

"You trust me."

"But that's different. You're..." she looked up into his dear, familiar face, and stopped.

He smiled. "Some would say that I am a dangerous man. And yet you trust me."

She hugged him. "You're a good man, Mentàll! You saved me from Jascr. And you've protected me all of these years. I know you'd never hurt me."

"And do you think Doc will?"

"No! Of course not." With a frown, she pulled free. "The problem isn't him. It's me."

"You do trust him, then?"

"Of course. Doc would never hurt me."

"I agree. So what is stopping you? Fear?"

"Yes. He asked me to marry him, but I said no. I'm afraid I'll never be able to be a real wife to him."

"Does he know your fears?"

"Yes."

"Then he knows the risks. He is willing to face them in order to win you."

Hendra looked down. "I'm afraid he'll stop loving me if...if I can't..."

"You must make a choice. Either choose to fight, or choose to live alone. But be sure that you can live with your decision."

"How do I make the right choice?"

"Fight for what you want. Let nothing stand in your way."

Hendra glanced over at his suddenly ruthless tone. "As you will fight for Methusal?"

His pale eyes narrowed. "As I will fight for Methusal."

He left her then, and Hendra mulled over his words. She did want to marry Doc. No question about that. But she wouldn't accept his compromise. She couldn't stand the possibility of becoming a disappointment and a burden to him. Or that he might grow to resent and hate her.

She crossed her arms tightly across her midriff.

Still, she had come a long way. Back in Dakarra, she had refused to let Riln intimidate her. She wasn't afraid when Doc held and kissed her anymore. Could their love defeat the remaining fear? She remembered the words of the old Prophet. "Perfect love casts out fear." Of course, he meant The One's love.

The One. Why hadn't she asked him for help? He had helped her before.

Hendra bent her head and asked for deliverance from the curse of her past. And she prayed for her cousin, too. It didn't show on the outside, but Mentàll was just as broken inside as she was.

Hendra wanted to hope. Could love ever heal her? Could it ever heal either of the Solboshn cousins?

Chapter Twenty-Nine

THE ROLBAN MOUNTAINS loomed up ahead. Clouds enshrouded their peaks. It felt cool outside for this time of the year, and it smelled like rain. Methusal hoped the storm would hold off until they made it inside Rolban's gates.

The trip south had been incident free, and thankfully boring. They had seen no Zindedis.

Now they neared the large, cliff-faced mountain that housed Rolban's community. It jutted east into the Dehrien plain, and a flat plateau topped it. No one was working on the upper crop plateau right now. It seemed quiet...almost too quiet. Of course, it was almost time for the evening meal.

Hanuh's nose flared as they approached the western end of Rolban.

"What is it?" Methusal said.

Her mother hesitated. "Nothing."

Methusal slipped into kaavl and listened for unusual sounds...for cries or struggles inside Rolban's gates. But all was silent, except for quiet murmurs. A visual carry revealed that Rolban's gates were wide open, and a familiar guard watched the entrance. A child scuttled up the Grand Staircase, crying for his mother.

"Everything's all right," she said. "The Zindedis aren't here."

"I know." But Hanuh's gaze went to the mountains towering over Rolban. She said nothing more.

CHAPTER THIRTY

DAY 34

AFTER THE JOY OF RETURNING home and sleeping in her own bed again, Methusal found it difficult to fall back into her old routine.

An inexplicable feeling of edginess woke her up multiple times during the night. Without thinking, she automatically concentrated into kaavl each time. In fact, she dreamed of a conversation in the whaal room, and then later wondered if it had been a dream at all. Her unease made little sense, especially since today a Dehrien runner had reported that no ships had been sighted near Eerpor. In addition, all was quiet on the Iignon coast, as far as men could safely hike to see.

Were they all paranoid about nothing?

All the same, Eerpor's chief had asked that Behran stay for a few extra days. The Dehrien soldiers, who had recently arrived in Eerpor, would also remain until they received new orders from Mentàll.

On the other hand, the men from Aestoff and Wyen had not yet shown up in Rolban or Eerpor.

The unsettled feeling grew stronger in Methusal as the day waned toward twilight. At dinner, a lingering frown scored a line between her mother's brows. It reminded Methusal of the time that Dehre had been about to invade Rolban. Hanuh had known something bad would happen. But she hadn't known when.

That night Methusal had a difficult time falling asleep, and dreamed of wild beasts stalking the mountains. Worse,

General Fitrn, with a wicked blade clenched between his teeth, ruled them all.

A sharp exclamation woke her in the pitch dark before dawn.

"He's dead! No. Two...three people!" In her parents' room, Hanuh gasped aloud and began to cry.

Methusal sat straight up. Fear coiled like a whip through her gut.

CHAPTER THIRTY-ONE

DAY 35

AALI PLAYED CATCH with Trori in the courtyard. Almost three weeks had passed since the twins were born. That vile Presidente had left nine days ago. In three days Hendra, Mentàll, and she would all head for Rolban. Her time in Quasr had gone fast. Aali and a woman from the village took care of Trori and Rartn now. Lylitha was regaining her strength, but slowly.

"Good catch, Trori."

The little girl giggled, and then squealed and dropped the ball. "Dastn!" She ran and was swept up into the runner's strong arms.

Aali's heart flipped when she saw him.

He kissed the top of the little girl's head and put her down. "You've grown an inch since last time, Trori."

As Aali watched the two of them, a warm smile blossomed in her heart. She couldn't help it. Even though Dastn had been maddening the last time she'd seen him, she couldn't help how she felt about him.

Trori turned to Aali. "Look, Dastn! Aali's all better."

As he came closer, his brown gaze held hers. It looked warm this time. Not teasing or amused. "No more crutches."

She smiled, and her heart thumped harder. "Nope. Looks like I'll be able to make it home in plenty of time for the election."

"No surprises planned?"

She smiled impishly. "Maybe I do have a few surprises planned for election day."

That wicked brow tilted up. "Guess I can't miss it then, can I?"

"I hope not. How long will you be here this time?"

"Just tonight. Mentàll will probably want me to deliver a few more messages."

"Trori!" The woman from the village called from the mansion's doorway. "Time for dinner. Come wash up."

"Play whaal with me later, Dastn," Trori begged. "You too, Aali."

"Whaal?" Dastn teased. "Isn't that game too old for you?"

"I'm smart." The child proudly lifted her chin. "Aali taught me. Rartn's too little, though."

"We'll play later," he promised.

Trori ran off, and Aali's gaze returned to Dastn. He looked tired, but wonderful. "Isn't that pack heavy? Here, I'll take it." She attempted to tug the shoulder straps off his broad shoulders.

His fingers closed over hers. "It's too heavy."

"Please," she scoffed. "I'm stronger than I look."

He lifted his hand and allowed her to tug the pack completely off of his shoulders. It fell heavily into her arms, and she staggered forward a bit. Then she caught her balance and with a strain, pulled it up onto her own shoulder.

"What do you have in here? Rocks?" She tried not to topple over.

He laughed. "I'm carrying trade items between Pan and Calbn. Dried wild beast meat this time, and oil, too. Pan wants a few straw goods for Aenill when I go back."

"That should be lighter, at least," she huffed. The weight cut painfully into her shoulder.

"Give me that." He lifted it free, and the relief made her sigh. He grinned.

"I'm hungry." With an impertinent smile, she said, "Will you take me out to dinner again?"

"You'd like that, wouldn't you?"

"Yes. And I can even pay for it. Calbn's giving me money for taking care of Trori and Rartn now."

"I'll pay."

"But it's my idea. My treat to you, since you toiled all the way here. Come on, Dastn, say yes."

"I'll clean up and give Calbn his messages. Meet you back here in thirty minutes."

"I'll be here," she grinned.

She rushed to her room and brushed her hair until it shone like silk. Then she put on a new scoop necked, soft blue shirt that Lylitha had given her. The tired mother had claimed that it was too small for her now. And she'd said it matched Aali's eyes.

Aali hoped Dastn would like it, too. She didn't forget the money, either.

She returned to the courtyard extra early and waited on the bench. She tapped her foot impatiently. Then she jumped up and inspected flowers. It felt so good to be able to walk again without those hampering crutches!

She sniffed a particularly beautiful, dark yellow flower. The petals felt so soft, like a baby's new skin.

"Ready?" Dastn's warm hand curled lightly over her shoulder.

Aali's heart pounded at his casual touch, but she flashed him a smile. "Isn't this a beautiful flower?"

He plucked the flower by the stem and tucked it behind her ear. His eyes slowly scanned each feature of her face. "Yes."

Warmth flushed her cheeks. She didn't know how to respond, and as a result, felt like a doltish slug. Finally she found her tongue. "Thank you. Are you hungry?"

"Yes," he said again, and then his fingers closed around hers. "Where are you taking me?"

Her heart raced. Feeling breathless with joy, she curled her fingers around his strong, warm ones. Had he truly taken her hand? She felt like she was floating on air. "The same place, if that's okay? I loved it."

"Fine by me."

Dastn glanced down at their hands, and a sharp breath whistled through his teeth. Abruptly, he released hers. "Sorry," he said gruffly.

Her joy dove down to the soles of her feet. "Don't be."

"Aali." No mistaking the warning in his low tone.

She told herself not to feel upset. He'd taken her hand and held it for a second. Maybe not on purpose, but he'd done it. It must mean something positive.

Her mind took all kinds of happy flights of fancy on the way to the dock. She chattered with him about everything she saw—the houses, the trees, and the goods for sale.

At the same time, she was very aware of his arm that occasionally brushed hers as they walked side by side down the road. As if they were almost, but not quite, on a date. Like a real boyfriend and girlfriend.

Maybe she was imagining too much, but she felt giddy. A few times she stumbled over pebbles in the street.

His smile curled up at one corner. "Are you watching where you're going?"

She giggled. "Not really."

They reached the dock, and claimed the same table they'd had before. Dastn refused her money, and retrieved delicious food for them from the hut.

Sunshine filled her soul, and she chattered and smiled at Dastn during the meal. She knew she could be wildly misinterpreting his fleeting, casual hand holding. But the fantasy and the hope were too good to let go.

Finally, they finished. The sun hung low on the western horizon.

"Time to head back," he said.

"Already?"

"I need to make an early start tomorrow."

As they headed for the main road, she spied a booth that was still open. It had cute little straw dolls. She grabbed his hand. "Look! Don't you think Trori would like one of those?" Each wore pretty little patterned dresses and had cheerful, painted faces.

Gently, Dastn disengaged his hand. "She probably would."

She tried to ignore that he'd deliberately dropped her hand, and also tried to pretend that everything was normal.

She picked up a little stiff doll in a patterned blue and white dress. It had yellow hair and painted blue eyes. "Maybe this would remind Trori of me." She looked at the price tag. It would take a good chunk of the money she'd earned. "I'll come back and get it as a goodbye gift for her. I'll need to find something for Rartn, too."

"They won't forget you. And I think your time with them has been enough of a gift."

Gently, she replaced the doll. "Thank you." She flashed him a smile, and glimpsed an affectionate smile and a tender look in his eyes.

He turned away. "C'mon," he said gruffly.

But he couldn't fool her. Not only had he held her hand for one second tonight, but that smile hadn't been his usual teasing, cocky grin, either.

Spirits lifting, she chattered to him all the way back home. At the compound, everything was quiet. The guard let them in and closed the gate behind them.

Dastn stopped in a shadowed turn of the path, and she turned to face him.

"Aali." His tone sounded warning.

Her spirits plummeted a bit. He'd guessed what she had been thinking and hoping. It mustn't have been hard. She'd been chattering and acting like a giddy teenager all evening.

She knew what he was about to say, and couldn't bear it. "No." She put a finger to his lips. "Don't say it."

His lips felt firm and warm against her fingers. They moved, just the slightest bit. Did he just kiss her?

His hand closed around her wrist, lowering her hand. "I think..."

"No!" she said fiercely. "Don't think."

"Why not?"

"Because then you'll say something stupid. You'll ruin the whole evening." She felt frustrated, and tears prickled in her eyes.

His hands closed around her upper arms. "Aali."

Mutinously, she stared up at him.

"Stop looking like you want to bite me."

"I don't want to bite you! I want..." She flung her arms around his neck, and quickly pressed her lips to his.

Dastn did not respond. He stood rigid, as if ordering himself under control. Tears filled her eyes, and she buried her face in the hollow of his throat. It hurt that he hadn't kissed her back. Maybe he *wasn't* as interested in her as she wanted him to be.

"Aali," he murmured against her hair. "Aali, look at me."

Finally, reluctantly, she looked up. His thumbs brushed the tears from her cheeks. "You're a special girl. I enjoyed every minute of tonight."

She sniffed. "You did?"

"Yes! And I want," he took a breath. "I want more of them, The One help me."

Her spirits soared again. She gave him a watery smile. "Really? That's wonderful. So do I."

"Aali," the warning tone was back, and she didn't like it. He hesitated, as if searching for the right words. "We can be friends. That's it. Nothing more."

"But that's ridiculous. If..."

"I *will* do the right thing by you." He expelled a harsh breath. "You're only sixteen. In two years you'll be eighteen. We can reevaluate our relationship then."

"Age is just a number. I am not a child, for the billionth time. I have the feelings of woman."

"I'm sure you do. But I have the feelings of a man, and I will not compromise you in that way. It's friends or nothing. Do you have any idea how fast things could go out of control if we crossed that line now?"

Her heart pounded at the idea. "I think I want that."

"No. You don't. Either we work together on this, or I'm going to have to stay away from you." He meant it. But his dark eyes looked conflicted, and that gave her heart hope.

"So what do you propose we do?"

He gently put her from him. "Talk. Maybe have dinner together. But never spend time alone together again."

"Like now?" she smiled at him.

"Yes," he said roughly. "Exactly like now."

She continued to smile, but did not agree to his neat little plan. He had feelings for her. Just as she had strong feelings for him. They would not stay in the box that Dastn was constructing.

Maybe one of the surprises in Rolban would be for him.

"I'll see you in a few weeks?" she said softly.

"Yes. I'll see you then." He gave her shoulders a gentle squeeze, and strode toward the house.

Aali watched him go, hugging her arms around herself. Her heart burgeoned with her feelings for that one, single Tarst runner. He was wonderful, decent, kind, and gentle—not to mention strong and handsome and thrilling. Did he feel anywhere near as much for her as she did for him?

If so, that nasty box he'd just constructed would come tumbling down in Rolban. Time to start working on one last plan.

△ △ △ △ △

Heeding Hanuh's distressed cry early that morning, Erl had sent men to scour both the nearby plains and the mountains looming over Rolban. They had returned at twilight, reporting seeing no one at all.

At dinner, Hanuh sat hunched at the table. Fear contorted her features.

"What do you sense, Mama?"

"They're coming," her mother whispered. "As silent as shadows and as invisible as ghosts."

Methusal shivered. Her father had sent extra guards to the plateau, and additional men patrolled the locked entrance gate downstairs in the Grand Hall. She had remained focused into kaavl for most of the day, but now she concentrated into it again.

As she finished her soup and bread, she listened carefully, projecting her hearing up onto the plateau. Nothing except for a few soft footsteps. Maybe seven or eight men—in keeping with the number of guards her father had stationed up there.

The plateau would be hard to approach undetected. It faced a sheer mountain wall, and the Rolban River bisected the plateau from that wall. Steep bluffs protected Rolban's plateau on the other side. They weren't impossible to climb, but they were difficult. Invaders would be spotted before they'd climbed far.

And outside the entrance gates...she fanned out her hearing, trying to filter out the murmur of the guards inside the gates, and the aptes scuttling across the rocks to the east.

Nothing. She returned to the plateau, and then down to the gates again, listening... More tiny scuttles. The aptes were busy tonight.

A rock rolled, fifteen lengths from the entrance. She leaped to her feet, overcome with horror.

Now she heard the footsteps. Now she knew why the aptes had been running.

"Papa!" she screamed. "They're here! The gate!"

Rolbani men ran for their weapons. Knives, bows and arrows, and swords were kept in a storage room down the hall, next to the Chief's office. For once, Methusal actually wore her bone-handled knife tied to her shin. She yanked it free.

Men shouted down to the guards at the gate, warning them.

A long moment of silence elapsed, and then guns thundered. Men shouted. A few screamed.

Hanuh stared with stark terror, her hair straggling in wisps down around her face, punctuating her confusion. Erl grabbed her arm. "Both of you. Go into the compartment behind the kitchen." Even now, women and children ran for the one place where a heavy stone door would protect them until rescue—or until the Zindedis defeated every single Rolbani and found them and killed them.

Hanuh ran, but when she realized Methusal wasn't following, she turned back. Her face twisted into a soundless cry. "Thusa! Come on!"

"No. This is my fight, Mama. This is was why I was born." Methusal felt this truth, deep down to her toes. It was no accident that she'd been blessed with her ancestor's greatest kaavl gifts. He'd lived in a time of war, and he'd helped his community. And now she lived for the same purpose.

Matron Olgith, Petr's aunt, grabbed Hanuh's arm and they both disappeared into the room behind the kitchen.

The guns continued to report. And between the blasts, an ominous sound reached her ears. The squeak of the opening gate. "They've opened the gate, Papa!" she cried.

White-haired Petr Storst brandished a wicked looking knife. Fear reflected in his red, resolute, bearded face, but he moved for the Grand Staircase with the other men. Jsan and Tumel flanked him. Already, archers had taken up positions on the staircase and fired down into the Great Hall.

Methusal paused in the upper hall. Her task, she knew instinctively, was to find and kill the head of the beast. General Fitrn.

She briefly contemplated her diabolical, cold resolution to kill. It wasn't like her to want to kill anyone. In the past, she'd helped to save lives. She was a healer. And the men she'd killed during the Quasr War still haunted her dreams.

But General Fitrn was the snake which would kill them all. With him dead, only one threat remained: the Presidente.

Tightly gripping her knife, she carried with both hearing and vision. It was as effortless as if she was a flying beast swooping around corners, rising and dipping to see and hear the bloody carnage.

The Primary level. At last.

Downstairs, the black clad soldiers had stopped firing their guns and now hacked swords into Rolbanis. Bloody corpses, both Zindedi and Rolbani, lay scattered on the floor. The carnage made her feel sick. But she could not think about how many men lay dead. She had to find the General.

He would not be downstairs. Instinctively, she knew he would sneak in a different way. A safer way.

The plateau.

She bolted from the dining hall. A Zindedi soldier had gained the top of the Grand Staircase and she shoved him, sending him tumbling backwards, into his comrades. Men shouted, and swords clashed.

She dashed down the supply room passageway. Old Sims stood in the doorway with wide eyes. He clenched a knife in his fist.

She paused. "Hide!" she urged him. "Lock the door."

"No," he said. "An old man's life isn't worth much. I'll kill Zindedis until my dying breath. ...Wait! Methusal. Another blade, just in case." He shoved an old sword into her hand. "Some say the blade's been blessed. The One go with you, my girl."

She tucked her small knife into her waistband and grabbed the sword. "Thank you, Sims. Pray for us all."

"I will. That I will," he mumbled.

Methusal crept closer to the stone steps that led to the plateau. Multiple feet scuffled overhead. Zindedis! How had they reached the plateau unseen? She sent a prayer heavenward. It was time to join the battle.

Overhead, nails scraped against the trap door. Drawing a quick breath, she pressed her back against the passageway wall.

The trapdoor flew open. Black Zindedi pant legs descended. She gripped the sword tighter, her hands slick with sweat. When the man's belly was at eye level, she thrust. He screamed and tumbled to the ground. Overhead, Zindedis cursed. The man she'd killed was young—he looked like one of the green recruits she'd seen on the docks in Carachki.

"Two of you go at once," said General Fitrn's sharp voice.

Horrified, she backed up, and discovered that Sims was standing stolidly beside her. Two more young Zindedis dropped down, bypassing the stairs. Sim's blade flashed, and so did hers. The men fell, but pain seared her arm.

Sims and Methusal valiantly battled in the narrow passage, but as more Zindedi pairs descended, they found themselves forced backward, down the hall. Their blades whipped with frenzied precision.

She wondered how much longer they could prevail. A minute? Seconds? At the back of the pack, she glimpsed General Fitrn's black cap, perched at the perfect angle on his blond hair.

Sims cried out. A sword had slashed a line from one of his armpits to the other shoulder.

Fueled by fear and desperation, Methusal redoubled her efforts, but too many Zindedi knives swept toward them now.

Sims cried out again, and staggered. She shoved him sideways, into the supply room, but without his defensive sword, the Zindedis voraciously fell upon her. She stumbled to her knees. One man kicked her hand, sending the sword skittering down the hall.

"Halt," came the General's cool voice. "This one is mine."

The Zindedis parted like a stream of black water. With slow, deliberate steps, the General approached. He looked down at her, and his sword tipped up her chin.

"Methusal Maahr." His smile curled into a debased leer. "You are a delicacy I will enjoy at length. Once the battle is won, of course."

He kicked her. "Get into the room. With the old man."

When she tried to stagger to her feet, he grabbed her hair and shoved her hard, so she landed on her hands and knees.

Coldly, the General said, "Find your prey, men."

The black hordes rushed down the hall. In the distance, a man roared. Methusal's heart leaped. It sounded like Barak.

Swords clashed.

The General smiled. "This could be bloody." To Methusal's surprise, he slipped into the supply room and shut the door behind him. One lone lamp flickered near the door.

She scooted back, away from him. Sims lay nearby, bleeding heavily.

Why had the General come in here? To escape from the battle because he was a coward? Or for a more diabolical purpose?

Warily, Methusal watched him, afraid to move. She wanted to help Sims, but didn't dare. If the General suspected that she cared for the old man, he might torture him, just out of spite.

The lamp illuminated General Fitrn's sharp features, and glowed off of his fine, light brown hair. He didn't look quite real—as if he was a doll, or a statue. And yet the heart of the foulest wild beast lived inside him.

Screams peppered the hall. The General smiled again. "Give me your knife."

"I have no knife," she lied.

He grabbed Sims by the hair and forced his head back, exposing his neck. "Give it. Or the old man dies now."

Sims' eyes flickered open. A feeble glare shone. Instinctively, she knew he didn't want her to give up the knife. Even if it meant his death.

The good thing about the supply room was that all sorts of odds and ends were tucked about the room. And, since Methusal had been Sims' apprentice for the last three years, she knew exactly where they were.

Slowly, she withdrew her knife and tossed it to her left.

"Very good." Fitrn released Sims, who sagged like a deflated ball. Anger still sparkled in Sims' eyes, however, giving Methusal hope that he wasn't finished yet.

As General Fitrn advanced toward her, she scooted backward, pretending to be terrified. Instead, her hands scrabbled for lengths of twine coiled behind a stone pot.

An evil smile curled his lips. "What shall I do to you first?"

She offered no expression. Instead, she watched his every step as carefully as a whip stalking an apte. At the same time, her ears catalogued every scream, every sword clash in the hall. Barak shouted orders to Jsan.

It wasn't over yet.

General Fitrn smiled. "You are not frightened enough. Don't you know that Rolban will soon be mine? Five shiploads of my men are swarming her now. You have no hope. All of your loved ones are being cut down like rutting rotarhudges right now."

Five shiploads.

He smiled. "Yes. Now you see. Where is your lover?"

She didn't answer.

"Your death, and that of Mentàll Solboshn have been ordered by the Presidente. Too bad you cannot share your last, bloody breaths in a passionate embrace."

"You're sick." Hatred tensed her body. Methusal wanted to punch off the General's perfectly placed beret. He looked so neat and clean and perfectly pressed. He made her skin crawl.

"After we have defeated Rolban, we will obliterate each and every community on Koblan. It will be a pleasure."

Keeping her expression neutral was difficult.

"On your feet. Go on, get up."

She slowly rose to her feet. The string remained balled up in her fist.

Fitrn smiled. "I will not kill you yet, of course. After I have won the battle, I will make rings and string you up. Then you will watch as I slowly torture each of your family members." His gaze swung to Old Sims. "Perhaps I should start with him first. Right now. I like that idea."

"You're a coward."

His gaze swung back, and narrowed to slits. "I'm *what?*"

"It's easy to torture a woman and an old man. Why aren't you out fighting with your men?"

A snarl contorted his features. "You insolent..." His blade flashed, but her kaavl string whipped out still faster. It spun around the blade and ripped it from his hand. Unfortunately, another gleaming blade instantly replaced it.

The General lunged for her, slamming her back against the wall. His cold, sharp blade pressed beneath her jaw. "Don't move, or you will die."

His jaw twitched, and so did his left eye. Angry men were more dangerous than calculating ones, and more prone to make fatal errors.

Provoke him? Or not? Making a quick decision, she taunted, "You would kill me so quickly? What little patience you have."

The knife twisted under her jaw. When it pierced her skin, she sucked in a breath.

He hissed, "I shall take great delight in killing you *slowly.* I like to make people scream."

Much as she tried to ignore it, fear pounded in her head. The man was sick. Twisted. One easy slice, and she would be dead. He wasn't as controlled as she had first believed. Even in the dim light, red flushed his skin. His eyes gleamed like a madman's. He wanted to kill her now. In fact, she suddenly believed he would.

For one infinitesimal moment, her thoughts slowed down to perfect clarity. Maybe she was meant to die. Maybe she had no future at all—with Mentàll or without him.

But the man who filled her heart and her mind would never give up. *Never.*

And neither would she. In the back of her mind, she heard his snarl, "Concentrate, Methusal. Defeat the *scienth*! You can do it."

"What shall it be?" The General's knife pressed harder. "Death now? Or will you obey my every instruction?"

"I will obey," she said woodenly.

Manic delight sparkled in his eyes. The knife pressed harder. "Move away from the wall. Slowly."

Methusal obeyed. She took one small step, and then another...and then swifter than thought, she jammed her knee into his groin. He grunted, and his knife sliced down her neck.

The calculated risk had paid off. She wasn't dead. Methusal felt no pain as she grabbed his knife wielding hand and twisted it backward. He snarled as she smashed on his instep and kicked his knee.

He unexpectedly leaped upon her with an inhuman scream. She crashed backward, onto the floor. They rolled, struggling with the knife. She grabbed his wrist with both hands, trying to force it backward. The horrible man was strong. Too strong.

Relax. Concentrate.

Although it made no sense, she trusted the words of Mahre...of Mentàll. Her brain relaxed utterly into kaavl, and clarity sharpened her mind.

Methusal rolled on top of him again. Shoving her legs sideways, and maneuvering her body at an angle to his, she used her feet for traction and surged forward. The knife blade wavered a mere inch from her nose. Fitrn bucked, trying to roll her again, but the angle of her body prevented it.

Another crawling surge forward, and she managed to shove her elbow into his windpipe. A strangled sound escaped from his throat.

He fought maniacally, but she scrabbled her feet against the floor, preventing him from rolling. The knife poked near her ear, but she grimly pressed on his throat until the knife fell from his fingers.

The General's face was purple. An unintelligible gurgle escaped from his throat. It sounded like a bizarre battle cry. With an insane surge of strength, he bucked free.

Methusal sprang to her feet. As quickly as Fitrn rolled for the knife, she jumped for it, meaning to land first and kick it free. But he rolled faster than she'd expected, and her feet landed hard on his neck. An audible "crack" rent the air.

Horrified, she stumbled to the floor, but retained the presence of mind to kick the blade free. General Fitrn lay sprawled on his stomach, his face toward her. His brown eyes were open, and appeared to be watching her. But no expression lived in them.

The thin, pale man lay absolutely still. A wrinkle creased his uniform. His black beret had rolled away.

The door slammed open, and Barak surged inside. "You freed yourself," he panted, his great chest heaving. Then his gaze fell on the Zindedi General. "Is he dead?" Jsan was close behind, and immediately knelt beside Sims.

"I don't know. I jumped on his neck. He...he's *staring* at me."

Barak grinned at the motionless man and kicked him. Something flickered in the Zindedi's eye. "He's alive." He looked at Methusal. "Would you like to kill him, or shall I?"

It was awful, staring at the Zindedi General, who stared right back. The man lay there like an insect. Trapped in a shell of a body that would no longer work for him. She swallowed. "Barak..."

"'Nuff said." He raised his sword high above the Zindedi General. "Time to put you out of our misery, rocher." With one vicious thrust, he ran the General through.

The brown eyes dulled to lifeless orbs.

Methusal felt sick. The snapping of his neck would haunt her forever. "I can't believe he's dead."

"Why not?" Barak swiped his blade clean on Fitrn's spotless black jacket.

"He's the General. The Presidente's son."

Barak's thick lips curled back, showing his teeth. "I'll share the good news with the others." His gaze centered on her neck. "You're bleeding."

"I am?" She lifted her fingers to the point just under her jaw. They came away slick with blood.

"I'll get you a doctor." Barak lumbered for the door with surprising speed for such a huge man.

"And for Sims," she called after him.

Methusal felt light-headed. She was probably in shock, she decided, and sat down near Sims, who was breathing shallowly. Jsan pressed cloths onto Sims' injuries to stop the bleeding.

Her gaze returned, as if drawn by some sick fascination, to General Fitrn.

The man was insane. And evil. Just like his father. She crossed her arms, trying not to think about the ways he might have tortured her if she hadn't freed herself.

Right now, everything felt like a nightmare. After the escape from Zindedi, and Kilum kidnapping her...what more could happen?

Finally, she'd saved her own life. And at long last, she believed she'd finally reached the Primary level, although only the Dehrien Chief or Pan could promote her. She'd achieved it through battle. Through killing men. The realization produced little joy.

The elderly doctor, D'Wit, appeared and carefully cleaned up Sims' wound. Pouring spirits over it made Sims moan. D'Wit frowned over the injuries. One was in Sims' shoulder, one on his chest. "Flesh wounds," he muttered. "Need lots of stitches."

"They can wait," Sims said faintly. "Methusal's bleeding from the neck. See to her."

The doctor frowned over her wound, too. Methusal couldn't see it, and decided that was a good thing.

"Nasty looking," was his only comment, and poured spirits over a fresh piece of lynnte weed. She flinched when he cleaned it.

"What's happening out there?"

"Aestoff's men just arrived, led by a Captain Swartzi. I believe the battle will turn in our favor soon."

Captain Swartzi! She remembered the tough, swarthy man and his men who patrolled Koblan's west coast.

"You're lucky," D'Wit told her, applying tacky leaves. "You only have one small puncture wound, and a thin cut down your neck. Neither require stitches."

"Good."

The sounds of battle in the hall retreated.

"Now for Sims' stitches." The doctor pulled out more spirits, along with a needle and thread. Methusal gripped Sims' hand throughout the entire ordeal. It took a long time, and Sims was pale and barely conscious when the doctor finished.

D'Wit gathered up his bag. "I need to tend the wounded. I could use help, Methusal."

After making sure Sims was comfortable with a pillow and blanket, Methusal collected medical supplies and followed the doctor. Many Zindedis and Rolbanis lay dead in the hall. Barak stalked among them. If a Zindedi twitched, he stabbed them. If a Rolbani moved, the doctor and Methusal ministered as best they could. Many would die, but she helped make them feel as comfortable as possible, and fed them strong doses of pain powder.

The devastation made her feel sick.

Downstairs in the Great Hall, the sounds of battle hadn't abated. But it appeared as if the last battle was centered there now. Kaavl told her that the surrounding hallways were quiet.

After making sure the passageways were safe, Barak charged back into battle.

It was after midnight when the sword clashes ceased.

Barak lumbered back upstairs, sweating and dripping blood. A giant slash scored one arm. "It's over."

"Let me tend that."

He scowled. "It's nothing." But he sat docilely enough when she insisted. He wouldn't sit still for the doctor's stitches, though. "We need to take care of the dead."

The night passed by in a daze for Methusal. Twenty-seven Rolbanis died—all of whom she had known her entire life. As well as Tumel. And scores of Zindedis. The men from Aestoff helped carry the dead to caverns. They would be buried in the morning.

Finally, bleary eyed, she found her mother and father, both safe, along with Petr, in the dining hall.

Her father rubbed his face. "It's over. Thank The One that Mentàll sent for Aestoff's men. And thank goodness they decided to stop here before hiking over the mountains. Most of all, thank The One for Captain Swartzi. His swordsmen are the most skilled I've ever seen."

"Did the Zindedis attack Eerpor?" Methusal was still worried sick about Behran, Sozla, and her family.

"I don't know. We'll find out more in the next day or two."

"I hope more Zindedis aren't coming."

"I doubt it. In my opinion, with Fitrn dead, it's over."

But was it? Exhausted, Methusal said goodnight and curled up into a tight ball in her compartment. How could it possibly be over? The Presidente was still alive. And even when he died, who would take his place?

Despair rode her exhausted mind, pressing it into the black oblivion of sleep. How could they ever win over such a relentless, vicious enemy?

CHAPTER THIRTY-TWO

DAY 38

INFORMATION ABOUT THE ZINDEDI ATTACK trickled into Rolban over the next few days. It appeared that the Zindedis had scaled the sheer, Iignon cliffs with ropes and metal climbing gear. Then they'd snuck along the high, treacherous ridge at night, bypassing Eerpor. However, Tarst men had surprised them on the Tarst ridge the morning before the attack on Rolban. The Zindedis had killed three of them, just as Hanuh had sensed.

Eerpor remained safe, and so did Behran, which relieved Methusal.

It turned out that scores of Zindedis had retreated from Rolban the night of the attack. By the time Captain Aestoff's men and the Rolbanis pursued them over the dangerous Iignon region, the Zindedi ships were dots on the horizon.

The dead were buried. Rolban was quiet and in mourning. Never would things be the same again. Methusal felt closer to her family than ever before in her life. Sims lay in bed, but chaffed at it. Methusal divided her time between running the supply room and helping the doctor with the many wounded.

And in the quiet moments, she felt lonely. She missed Mentàll terribly. It seemed strange that he was not with her, sharing the crisis with her. And for the first time, she realized that every time something horrible had happened to her in the last year, he had been there. In fact, only now did she see how deeply he had comforted her, and given her the strength to go on. She longed to see him. Her heart ached for him.

Mentàll had promised that he would come soon. She couldn't wait to see him.

Chapter Thirty-Three

Day 40

THE PRESIDENTE HAD ARRIVED back in Zindedi last night. Deccia wondered if he had signed Mentàll's peace agreement. She felt sick with worry. According to Goric's friend in the palace prison, no orders had been given yet to kill Timaeus. But how quickly that could change.

She did not know if the Koblani ship had arrived yet.

Tensions were running higher than ever at home. Riln was ready to attack the Presidente at the slightest provocation, but Goric insisted the Koblani ship must be in Zindedi before they made their move.

Deccia couldn't bear the thought of going to work today and standing helplessly in the shop across the street from the palace. She had to do something to try to help Timaeus.

So, just after dawn, she struck off toward the harbor and followed the coastline west. Maybe the ship had arrived. If so, a note from Mentàll should be on the ship, indicating if the Presidente had signed the peace agreement or not.

She pushed through the dense undergrowth and rounded the last curve to the secluded bay. A ship gently pulled at its anchor chain. *Sea Mistress*!

Deccia couldn't believe it, and almost burst into tears of relief. After all the setbacks and all the problems, home was finally within reach.

She jogged down the hill, waving her arms and yelling to catch the attention of someone on deck. Several men looked her way. They were too distant to identify, but one skinny man looked like Skyl.

"Hello!" she shouted.

Men levered the rowboat into the water and the thin blond man rowed toward her. A gun lay across his knees. The boat ground ashore.

"Skyl!" she cried out, but he pointed the gun straight at her heart, so she stopped short. No recognition registered on his blank face, and then she realized why. She plucked off her glasses. "It's me. Deccia! How is everyone? Did Mentàll make it back home alive?"

With a sheepish grin, Skyl lowered the gun. "Everyone's fine. In fact, Mentàll sent two notes. He said Riln would know what to do with them."

One was a folded parchment, and the other was a sealed envelope with Riln's name written across the front. Deccia unfolded the parchment and quickly read the bold, dark print.

The Presidente signed the peace agreement. But afterward he ordered Methusal kidnapped. Methusal is safe, but the Presidente cannot be trusted. Riln, you know what to do. Act immediately. The ship will take you home when your mission is complete. — Mentàll

"Oh, no!" Deccia whispered. Timaeus was in grave danger. They had to rescue him immediately. Oh, how she wished they'd tried to rescue him sooner!

Skyl said, "If you need us, we'll be here. Get those notes to Riln now."

△ △ △ △ △

The day passed by with excruciating slowness for Deccia, although after she'd received the notes from Skyl, she'd gone into work late, because she had no way to contact Goric or Riln until that evening. Her explanation about a family emergency seemed to placate Euphira regarding her tardiness.

Deccia had a difficult time focusing on her job, however. Fear and impatience churned within her. She wondered what was happening to Timaeus. And what they were going to do about the Presidente.

Most frustrating of all, she couldn't give the notes to Riln until he'd finished work for the day—providing he didn't go directly to a spirit house first, and squander half of his pay.

Anxiously, she stared out the window. Euphira watched her with a slight frown. In the late afternoon, she said, "Maybe you'd like to leave work early today."

"Could I?" Deccia felt relieved, but still agitated. Riln would not get off for another hour.

"Will you be in tomorrow?"

Deccia tore her gaze away from a black cart leaving the palace. "Um. I'm not sure. I might have to travel home for a few days."

"Of course, Hanuh. Take all the time you need. But if you're gone longer than a week, I'll have to look for a replacement."

"I understand. Thank you, Euphira, for everything."

The woman gave Deccia her dascals for the day, and then watched her go with a sad, almost severe look. She seemed to sense that Deccia wouldn't be back.

For the next hour Deccia waited in the park, keeping a close eye on the side palace gate. She'd nab Riln before he could escape into one of his night time haunts.

Eons seemed to pass by before she spotted his tall, muscular frame.

"Riln!" Quickly, she crossed the street.

Surprise lifted his heavy brows. "Lunatic. What're you doing here?"

"The ship is here. Mentàll sent you two notes."

He read the parchment quickly, and to her surprise, he smiled. "Just the news I've been waiting for." He stuffed the envelope into his pocket.

Goric joined them. "What's going on?"

Deccia repeated the news, and Riln reluctantly relinquished the parchment.

After a swift read, Goric's eyes narrowed. "What mission?"

"None of your business, rocher." Riln refused to say more. At home, he stuffed an extra shirt, food, and a water skin in his backpack, and headed for the door.

"Where are you going?" Deccia demanded. "We need to rescue Timaeus. The Presidente could execute him any minute!"

"Sorry, lunatic. If all goes well, I'll be back tomorrow night."

"Tomorrow night?" she cried out. "But Timaeus!"

Riln slammed the door behind him.

Goric pulled on his backpack. "I'm going with him."

Deccia couldn't believe it. Both men were abandoning her, just when Timaeus needed help the most. "No!"

He sent her a sideways look. "Timaeus is still all right. But I don't trust Riln."

"He's acting under Mentàll's orders."

"Yes. But Riln's a hothead. Do you really want to leave Koblan's fate in his hands?"

Deccia saw his point. "Fine. But be careful. And please hurry back!"

He settled the backpack more comfortably across his shoulders. "I'll be back. Lock the door."

CHAPTER THIRTY-FOUR

DAY 41

BEHRAN AND SOZLA had arrived last night, and today he was showing Sozla all of Rolban's water systems. Both seemed to be enjoying themselves immensely, and Methusal didn't want to intrude upon their happiness. She was glad Behran was home, but she'd missed talking to him while he was gone. He'd asked her to eat dinner with him tonight, and she was looking forward to it.

She brushed the lunch crumbs off her lap and stood. Her long hair fell forward, over her shoulder, as she'd worn it lately in an attempt to hide the red wound on her neck. Although it had healed over, the redness would last for a while. She was tired of people staring at it. Commenting on it. Congratulating her on how she'd contributed to the death of General Fitrn. It all felt so awful. So wrong.

The memory of snapping his neck underfoot still haunted her. And so did the guilt and horror she felt about killing the young Zindedis. She'd for asked forgiveness from The One. Of course, the killings had been done in self-defense. But she'd killed eleven men last week, and three more during the Quasr War. It made her soul weep.

Methusal forced her mind away from the ugly memories. The Great Hall was busy today. The entrance gates were flung wide open. Sunshine streamed inside. Maybe later, after helping the doctor, she would go outside and practice kaavl. It soothed her soul like nothing else could these days.

A flicker of white caught her eye.

Bleached leather. A tall, powerfully built man with white-blond hair. Her heart stuttered, and then thundered. Mentàll. He was *here*.

Joy surged. She'd missed him terribly—so much so that right now she could barely breathe. She didn't move from her spot at the back of the cave. She couldn't seem to take her eyes off him.

The Dehrien Chief's gaze flicked over the occupants of the hall, and a jolt went through her when it found her. A faint smile curved his lips, and he headed straight for her.

"Methusal." He looked well. No paleness lived under his tan. Just healthy color. Vitality emanated from him.

"Mentàll." Her heart fluttered crazily. She blurted the first words that came to mind. "You're here to campaign for yourself, I assume?"

"Do I have a chance in Rolban, with your father running?"

"Opposition is strong."

"Headed by whom?" His pale eyes gleamed down at her.

She couldn't help but grin. "No one. My father is Chief. Whom else would we vote for?"

"Who will *you* vote for?" he murmured.

"Does it matter?" she said with a teasing smile. "After we gather up all of Rolban's votes, my father will cast Rolban's Presidential vote for the winning candidate. He will win the most votes here. So my vote won't matter, one way or the other."

"It will matter to me." His arm slid across her shoulders, and he urged her to walk beside him. "Perhaps I need to woo my fiercest opposition."

She liked his warm weight around her shoulders. Against her better instincts, she leaned into his hard, warm body and drew him still closer.

"You are docile now?" he murmured into her hair. "Will a kiss persuade you to vote for me?" When she didn't answer, he pressed a warm caress into her hair. "Do you like that?" he said softly. "Perhaps a dozen more will persuade you to ask others to vote for me, too."

"No," she said, and tried to pull free.

He didn't allow it, and in fact turned her to face him, a spare handbreadth from his chest. She frowned at him for manhandling her in such a way. "You are a wild beast," she told him. "You'll be lucky to get one vote."

"Perhaps you need more persuasion," he murmured.

Her cheeks flamed at his not so subtle insinuation. "Kindly take your hands off me."

"If I were kind, perhaps I would." His light eyes narrowed with amusement. "But you know better, Methusal."

"Let go."

"After I secure a promise from you."

"What promise?" she said warily.

"Dine with me tonight."

"Sorry," she said sweetly. "I have obligations. And I promised to eat dinner with Behran."

"Behran is one of your obligations?"

"No!" He was riling her on purpose. He looked too pleased for it to be anything else. "I want to dine with Behran."

He didn't like that. His quick frown made that clear. "You delay the inevitable."

"Now what do you mean?"

"We will finish this conversation. Be sure of it."

She stepped free of him. "We have nothing left to discuss." With an arch brow, she added, "Except, perhaps, your concession speech. I'm sure humble words aren't in your vocabulary. I'll make you a list, since you like to be prepared for every occasion."

A rusty chuckle erupted from his throat. "You are a woman in a continent. Two, in fact. That is why this conversation does not end."

Exasperated, she left him.

How could she have felt glad to see him? And she'd thought she'd missed him? She was crazy. She'd missed nothing about that maddening man. Nothing.

△ △ △ △ △

The Presidente strode for his office with short, purposeful steps. A sense of anticipation heightened his surprisingly vigorous health today. By contrast, the last few days of the sea voyage home had been hellish. It was the sole reason he'd been unable to visit his office yesterday. At least that is what he'd told his advisors.

Today he felt in the prime of health, and ready to set in motion his many plans of torture—large and small—with which he'd amused himself all the way home from that barren, fetid land mass called Koblan.

He flung open his outer office door and strode inside Yalin's secretarial sanctuary.

"Presidente!" Yalin rushed forward and dropped to his knees. His hands quivered. "I welcome you home. How may I serve you?"

It was an appropriate and well-fitting welcome after his long voyage. The Zindedi leader eyed Yalin with benevolent pity. It truly was a shame. For a boy, Yalin had done a remarkable job as his secretary. However, when Fitrn took over the role of Presidente, it was a simple fact that he would shred Yalin limb from limb—as he would every advisor who'd obediently worked in close trust under the Presidente.

His own plans would be much, much kinder to Yalin.

"Rise," he commanded. "Come into my office immediately."

"Yes, sir!" Yalin hastened to open the office door for the Zindedi leader.

The Presidente strode forward and then stopped, because the delightful aroma of ortangia blossoms filled the room. Their tender, velvety blossoms bloomed from every corner and crevice of the office. It overpowered his senses like an aphrodisiac of the highest order. He inhaled deeply, closing his eyes with pleasure. Then he breathed again. With wonder, he said, "Who ordered these in?"

Yalin bowed deeply. "I did, my Presidente, most honorable and without peer."

The Presidente's mouth worked. An unfamiliar sensation filled his eyes. His hand went up to investigate. Tears? He looked down at Yalin's bent blond head and still trembling hands, and felt remorse. If only this young man...

He drew a deep, shuddering breath. There was no help for it. General Fitrn was his son. Gently, he said, "You have done well, Yalin. But..."

Yalin seemed to shrink. "Yes, my leader?" he whispered.

"When my son returns, my rule as Presidente will end. Do you understand what that means for you?"

"Yes, sir." Yalin swallowed audibly.

"If you wish, I will keep you on as my secretary until that day. Or..." he could not believe he was about to say this, "you may leave now. Escape in safety to your family." He did mean it. For these few seconds, Yalin could take him up on his offer without fear of retribution.

Yalin hesitated for a long moment. Anger bit into the Presidente's goodwill, embittering it. If the young fool did not speak soon...

Yalin bowed again. "No," he whispered. "I will stay with you, my Presidente."

Powerful emotion burst in the Presidente's chest, and he gasped from the wonder of it. Someone had chosen *him* over his own life. Without coercion. With no hope of a future, except for with the Presidente.

Emotion choked his voice, making it scratchy. "I will see that you are richly rewarded this day, Yalin. Richly rewarded."

His secretary murmured, "Thank you, my Presidente."

The Presidente swallowed. "Resume your duties at once."

With a bent head, Yalin slipped back into his office.

The Presidente took deep breaths, trying to understand the emotions surging inside him. How could he feel so moved by the subservient fealty of a single, unimportant man?

And yet he would write out his rewards this minute. Yalin could choose any of them he wished. Overcome with a feeling of largesse, the Presidente settled into his comfortable desk chair and took out a parchment and writing stick. With bold slashes, he prescribed three rewards for Yalin.

He chuckled, and stroked the words of the last offering fondly. If Yalin was as wise as he'd begun to think, he'd quickly agree that the last choice would serve him best of all. But whatever pleasure Yalin desired, he would order it fulfilled beyond Yalin's wildest imaginations. He chuckled again, imagining the incomprehensible delights that lay ahead this night for the young man. He wished he was young, so that he could fully enjoy such delights again, also. But with his troubled heart, he had to choose his pleasures few and wisely.

"Yalin!" he barked.

The secretary entered at once, as if waiting for his command. As of course he had been, the young fool, the Presidente thought with acute fondness. He handed over the folded slip of paper. "You may choose your reward. I will order the arrangements myself."

Yalin opened the paper and read the three options. His eyes lingered on the last one, and the Presidente smiled. "Any?" he whispered.

"Of course."

He pointed to the third option. "If...if you are sure..."

The Presidente smiled widely. "I will order my three best women prepared for you."

Yalin's eyes widened, and he stuttered, "Yes....yes, sir."

"Now," the Presidente said, "bring my mail."

"Yes, sir. *Thank you,* sir." Yalin scuttled out.

To the Presidente's surprise, a knock came a moment later. "Enter!" he growled.

Wearing a fearful expression, Yalin slipped back inside. "I apologize, Presidente. But this message just arrived." Swiftly, he delivered it to the desk. As he headed again for the door, a muffled *boom* exploded outdoors.

The President swiveled to stare out the northeast window. Smoke plumed skyward, and a sudden earthquake shook the palace. Yalin stumbled to his knees. The open door walloped his temple.

"*What was that?*" the Presidente roared. Military artifacts jumped off the shelves. Vases of ortangia blooms exploded in a crash of water and glass on the floor. "*Who did that?*" he screamed.

Yalin grabbed the door to stop its pounding assault. "I...I will find out right away, sir!" he gasped.

The Zindedi leader reared up in rage. "It's those Koblanis! Those foul Koblanis have done this!"

He cleared his desk with one vicious arm sweep. More flowers and vases crashed to the floor. The bruised nectar singed his enraged nostrils.

"Clean this up!" he screamed. "Clean this up at once!" How dare the Koblanis defile his heavenly, fragrant sanctuary? And the eastern powder mine... His rage knew no bounds.

Yalin was already at the desk, mopping up the mess with a towel.

"This is unconscionable. *Unconscionable!*" the Presidente screamed, muscles bunching tight in his neck. His heart pounded alarmingly hard. "They will pay!" He swore filthy, obscene words while Yalin silently mopped. At one point, Yalin placed a sopping wet parchment on the desk.

The Presidente recognized the note that Yalin had delivered before the explosion. He ripped it open, splitting it in half. Bold dark slashes, indicating the writer had written it in a temper, blazed into his eyeballs.

Kilum is dead. Methusal is alive and well. The peace agreement is void. Zindedi will receive no ore. Today you will receive payment for your treachery.

Further treachery will be severely punished. The choice is yours. Choose peace, and we will allow you to live in peace. But choose war, and Zindedi will suffer, and I will order your death. Choose wisely.

Mentàll Solboshn, Presidente of Koblan.

The Presidente gasped with rage. His gaze flew to the official Koblani seal at the bottom of the page. Beside it were the signatures of every chief on Koblan. He'd suspected that the unification of Koblan was a bluff. But here was proof that Koblan was unified under one man.

That Dehrien bastard! The Presidente shredded the soggy paper into bits, and ground them beneath his heel.

Yalin quickly looked up, and then down again, swiftly and efficiently performing his duties. The Presidente wanted to hurt someone. He wanted to *punish* someone for the destruction of the eastern powder mine. Obviously, Koblanis were still in his land. Where was his son? Why hadn't he stopped it?

Everyone. *Everyone* had failed him. And when Fitrn came home, he would kill the Presidente.

Everyone was against him—everyone except for Yalin. He sat down heavily in his chair and took comfort from the close proximity of his secretary. He watched the young man's bony shoulder blades moving industriously. He could not harm the poor, cowering pup.

Then whom could he punish?

Of course! A short laugh barked from his throat. Who else but his Koblani captive? His brother's murderer! Oh, he would suffer, and he would suffer dearly. The Presidente rubbed his hot hands together.

Tomorrow, at dawn, the tortures would begin, and he would witness every flinch, and every scream. All day, if possible.

"Rise, Yalin," he commanded. "Take down an order."

At once, his secretary miraculously produced a writing stick and dry parchment. The Presidente dictated each specific torture the vile Koblani was to suffer. Yalin turned paler with each edict, and his hands quivered by the end.

"Yalin," the Presidente said kindly, and the black, terrified eyes of his secretary stared blankly at him. "I would never inflict such tortures upon you. Not ever. You are my loyal, obedient servant. As long as you completely and promptly obey me, I will continue to richly reward you."

"Yes, Presidente."

"Yes, *my* Presidente. I like it when you say that."

"Yes, my Presidente," he whispered.

"Now give that to the guards, but come back quickly. You have much work to finish in here."

"Yes, sir." Yalin quickly left.

The Presidente's sense of satisfaction faded as soon as his secretary disappeared. Anger rose in blistering waves from his soul.

Who would have thought that the Dehrien Chief he'd tried to manipulate into conquering Rolban three years ago would become *Presidente of Koblan*?

It did not matter. He was a rocher to be squashed.

His son would soon execute judgment for him. Much as the Zindedi leader resented the General for his youth and good health, his son would not let him down.

With a shaking hand, the Presidente gulped wine. Yes. He would plunder Rolban, and by using the ore and the powder still remaining in his largest quarry, he would continue his plan to take over Koblan. Even better, he would order the General to stay in Koblan until that Dehrien was dead.

The war had just begun. Tomorrow he would kill his brother's murderer and send his body back to Rolban. It should arrive by the time that small village had been well trampled under his finest son's boot. It would demoralize them all.

Yes. The perfect beginning of his triumphant reign.

△ △ △ △ △

When the earth shook under Deccia's feet and she spotted black smoke billowing up in the northeast, her heart sank like a stone. The Presidente would be enraged beyond all reason now. And on whom would he exact his bloody vengeance? Timaeus.

She crumpled onto the couch and burst into tears. How could she rescue Timaeus now? Goric and Riln were the only ones with access to the palace.

"The One help me!" she cried out, fists clenched against her temples. "Tell me what to do!" She had to do something now to help Timaeus!

And yet how could she possibly get into the palace? Maybe Euphira or Tineia knew a way inside. Or she could round up the men from the *Sea Mistress*. Maybe they could all overpower the soldiers guarding the maze.

Perhaps that was the best idea. They could do it tonight. Hopefully, Timaeus would still be alive then.

If Methusal was here, what would she do? Or Mentàll? Surely it wouldn't be so difficult for them. After all, they knew Mrn. M, who had connections to the Presidente...

Mrn. M! Deccia sat up straight. And Ceri! Surely, if Ceri was here... *Oh, please The One, let her be!* Even if she wasn't, maybe for Methusal's sake, Mrn. M would help her. All she needed was a toehold into the palace. Once inside, she'd find a way to rescue Timaeus.

She ran to the bathroom and splashed cold water on her face. What should she tell Ceri or Mrn. M? The truth? Or a close version? If necessary, she'd beg and plead, if that's what it took.

She hurried back out, but stopped short. Goric stood in the doorway. His pale face looked drawn and his shoulders slumped.

"Goric! What is it?"

He said nothing for a long moment, and then shrugged his pack onto the floor. In a dull voice, he said, "Riln's dead."

"*What?*" she said in utter disbelief.

"Riln's dead."

"He died in the explosion?" Then Deccia realized that wasn't possible. The explosion had happened just minutes ago. Goric could not have made it back here with the news that quickly.

"No. He set a timer for it to blow later. He went in that mine at midnight, but never came out."

"He had a timer?" Deccia repeated. "How do you know he's dead? Maybe he's captured. Did you try to rescue him?"

Goric turned away, his shoulders hunched. "I'm sorry, Deccia. I couldn't help him."

"Are you sure he's dead?" she persisted.

"They threw his body outside. I'm sorry," he said again. "I had to leave him. I had to tell you what happened."

Deccia could barely wrap her mind around this horrible new fact. Crass, overbearing Riln was dead? It didn't seem possible. He'd seemed larger than life. As if nothing could ever defeat him. Even though she hadn't liked him, tears stung her eyes.

"We have to rescue Timaeus now, Goric."

"I know. Maybe..."

"No maybes. Come on. I know who will help us."

"Who?"

"A friend." She hoped Ceri would be there. *Please, The One.*

Deccia and Goric walked swiftly through the Carachki streets. When they turned onto Feldon Street, Goric's steps lagged behind hers. "Why are we here?"

"My friend lives here."

Goric looked strangely uneasy. "Listen, Deccia, I..."

"Come on!" she snapped, not understanding his odd reluctance. She grabbed his hand and pulled him inside Mrn. M's gate. "These people are nice. They won't turn us in. It'll be all right. You'll see." She rapped sharply on the door.

Goric shifted from foot to foot behind her.

"Coming!" said a voice from within the house. It sounded young, and Deccia's hopes soared.

The door opened, and she cried with relief, "Ceri!"

Ceri blinked, and then stared at Deccia harder. "Deccia? You've cut your hair!" Her delighted smile flickered to Goric and froze. Her smile twisted into a snarl. "What are *you* doing here?"

△ △ △ △ △

Methusal headed for Behran's compartment. It was time for the evening meal. Aali and Hendra had arrived shortly after Mentàll, and she'd enjoyed spending the rest of the day with them. In fact, she'd just left them in the Great Hall.

She knocked on Behran's door.

"Come in," he called. When she stepped inside, she was surprised to see Sozla sitting on the floor with him. Sketches lay between them.

"Oh!" Sozla jumped up. "I must go. Thank you, Behran." The Eerporian girl hurried out.

Methusal stared after her. "Why did she run out like that?"

"I don't know." He frowned.

"Is she okay?"

"I'm not sure." His frown lingered. "She's been acting a little strange lately."

"Is she homesick for Eerpor?"

"I don't think so." Behran gathered up the sketches and dropped them on the small table next to the wall. Not for the first time, Methusal admired Behran's compartment. The warm glow of the lamps made the dyed leather cushions on the chairs and couch glow with color.

His mother, Poli, worked with Methusal's mother in the garment room. Poli had a knack for sewing colorful bits together to create beautiful pillows and wall hangings. Behran's new compartment showcased many of her efforts. It was a warm, comfortable room, and Methusal had often looked forward to sharing it with him after they were married. Sadness crept into her heart.

As they walked toward the dining room, she asked, "Did you draw those sketches? What are they for?"

"They're improvements I want to make to our water systems."

"I didn't know you were interested in making changes. That's wonderful."

Behran shrugged. "Motr has to approve them first."

"I'm sure he will."

Behran grinned, and his fingers caught hers. "Thank you, Thusa. For believing in me."

She stopped and looked into his deep blue eyes. Her hand tightened around his. "Of course I do, Behran. You're the best." She looked down at their linked hands, and sadness slid through her once more. She wondered, yet again, if he was still hoping for more between them. It hurt that she might have been encouraging his false hopes.

She should never have continued the engagement. "Behran." Taking a breath, she tried to find the right words.

"Methusal," he said softly. He knew. She saw it, deep in his eyes, and he released her hand. "It's not over with Mentàll, is it?"

She shook her head.

Others brushed by them in the hall, but they paid no attention.

"I'm sorry, Behran. I never should have…"

"Stop. I've known the truth for a long time." His gaze gentled, and he pulled her into his arms and held her tight. Her eyes filled with tears. He held her close for a long moment. Then his lips brushed her hair and he let her go.

"I'm sorry," she whispered again, and wiped her eyes on her sleeve.

Behran hugged an arm around her shoulders. "Come on," he said quietly. "Let's eat dinner."

When they headed back down the hall again, she saw Mentàll. He stood stationary, half out of a doorway down the hall, watching them. Obviously, he'd stopped in midstride. His usual arrogance had been replaced by bleakness and a harsh set to his lips. Silently, he turned and strode for the dining hall.

Methusal's heart felt even heavier now. Everything was such a mess! She'd hoped for a quiet dinner with Behran so they could talk and catch up, and now Mentàll had the wrong idea about the two of them.

After they'd heaped their plates with food, Behran said, "Look. Sozla's alone. Would you mind eating with her?"

"Of course not." The Eerporian girl looked lonely. "Good idea."

Sozla looked up as they joined her. "Oh." She blinked, as if taken aback. "You must not dine with me. You must dine together. See, I am finished." Hurriedly, she lay her fork down on her half full plate.

Behran's hand gently touched the Eerporian girl's wrist. "Stop. We want to eat with you."

She sent Methusal a troubled look. "But why? You must want to be alone." She made a move to stand.

"Sozla," Methusal interjected. "You're our friend. Don't you want to sit with us?"

Her hand fluttered, as if she felt flustered. "Well, yes, of course. I only wish not to intrude."

"You're not," Behran said. "Now eat your food. You can't afford to lose any more weight."

Methusal eyed the other girl. Sozla had always been thin, but Behran was right. Her face looked peaked, and her skin looked stretched tight over her cheekbones. She frowned. "Are you sick, Sozla? What's wrong?"

"I am not sick." She waved a dismissive hand, and forked up a bite of meat.

"Then why have you lost weight?"

Sozla looked from one to the other of them, and tears sparkled in her dark eyes. She swallowed the meat. "It is of no importance. Please forget me."

Methusal sent Behran a worried frown.

"Talk to me," he told Sozla quietly. "Please."

She blinked quickly, and pressed her hand on Behran's for a fleeting second. "Thank you, Behran, for your care. But I am fine. I must go now. Goodnight." She gathered up her plate and utensils, and quickly left them.

"What was that about?"

Behran continued to frown. "I'm not sure. But I'll find out."

Realization slowly dawned upon Methusal. "Did you and Sozla become good friends on the trip?"

"Yes. I suppose. We worked together on the bombs."

"I see." And they'd spent a great deal of time together in Eerpor, too. Methusal watched Sozla hurry from the dining room.

"Behran, have you told her that our wedding is off?"

"No. I didn't think of it. Why?"

"Maybe you should. And soon."

The Eerporian girl had fallen in love with Behran—of this, she felt certain. And Behran obviously cared about her, too. Perhaps more was blossoming between the two of them than Behran realized yet. The thought gave her joy. More than anything, she wanted for him to be happy.

Her gaze found Mentàll. He sat across the room with Erl and Petr. Their conversation seemed intense, judging by Petr's flushed face and his finger jabs to the east. They were probably discussing General Fitrn's invasion.

Her gaze lingered on the Dehrien Chief's broad back. The man confounded and ruffled her. Logically, any future with him would be full of bumps and challenges. But foolishly and illogically, she realized she wanted that future. She loved him. All of a sudden she knew that if he could tell her he loved her—even a little bit—she'd willingly go headfirst into a deeper relationship with him. She would entrust her entire heart, her life, and her future into his hands.

△ △ △ △ △

Deccia felt shocked that Ceri knew Goric, but rushed on with her plea for help, ignoring the strange coincidence. "Ceri. Timaeus is a prisoner in the palace. The Presidente is going to execute him."

Ceri gasped aloud. "I'm so sorry!"

"Your mother knows the Presidente. Could she get me inside the palace? Or convince the Presidente to pardon him?"

Distress darkened the Zindedi girl's eyes. "I'm so sorry, Deccia. I wish I could help! But my mother can't go to the palace unless she's invited. And she holds no influence over the Presidente. To him, she's just a pretty toy." Her gaze turned to Goric, and her lips curled back. "Unfortunately, *he's* the only one who can help you."

"What do you mean?"

To Goric, Ceri said, "What game are you playing? When I saw you in Dakarra I had no idea you were with Deccia and the others." She looked at Deccia. "You don't know who he is, do you?"

"You saw him in Dakarra?" She felt more confused than ever.

"When I was running away from General Fitrn I came across him in the woods. I slapped him. Which you deserved, didn't you, Goric?"

His face turned a dull red. Deccia remembered when he'd "run into" a tree and ended up with a red mark on his face. "What do you mean? How could Goric possibly help me rescue Timaeus? He hasn't been able to help so far."

"Why not, Goric? Why haven't you helped your *friend,* Deccia?"

"It's complicated."

"Complicated. Like how you left me behind without a goodbye? I mourned you for two years! Finally, I realized you're just another one of your father's puppets. You have no spine of your own. You could have told me why you left. But you didn't. Because you're a slug."

"I'm sorry. I cared about you, Ceri, but I was stupid. And yes, I was weak and ruled by my father."

All of the pieces slid together in Deccia's head, but she couldn't believe the picture they made.

"And now?" Ceri said, with a bite to her voice. "Are you your own man? Or do you still play for the Presidente?"

"I am my own man," he said softly.

"Then why haven't you told Deccia who you are? Why haven't you helped her?"

"I have..."

"*No.*" The one word cracked through Deccia's lips. Everything was now horrifyingly, blindingly clear. Tabor wasn't the spy. *Goric* was. Even worse, he was the Presidente's youngest son. A devil spawn of that demonic family. He was the one who had broken Ceri's heart years ago. And he'd been a master spy in Koblan for the last seven years. Worst of all, he'd given the Presidente Timaeus' description. Goric was the reason why Timaeus was in prison in the first place.

She stared at him, feeling utterly betrayed. But she couldn't attack him here, in front of Ceri. Ceri still didn't know she was a Koblani. Now, more than ever, Deccia had to stay undetected—if that was even possible, thanks to Goric's duplicity.

She turned to her friend. "Thank you, Ceri. But I have to go."

"I'm sorry. If I could help you, I would. Maybe if Goric decides to grow a spine, he'll help you. 'Bye." Slowly, the door closed.

But Goric, the Presidente's youngest son, would not help her. *Why would he?* He hadn't yet. She walked fast, blindly heading south. Goric's footsteps matched hers.

She hissed, "Are you going to take me to prison now?"

He said nothing.

"*Speak* to me!" she snarled.

"I'll talk when we get home."

Home. Deccia wanted to laugh and cry at the same time. But most of all, she wanted to scream at him. She remembered the nightmare when she'd woken and discovered that she'd bloodied his nose and split his lip. She wished she could do it again. He deserved *so* much more!

Maybe she should feel scared to be alone with him in their rented house. Would he hurt or kill her? More likely, he'd turn her over to the military.

Just to be on the safe side, she wouldn't go inside the house. She'd accost him in the back yard. Then she could run away if she needed to.

Tears pressed hard on her eyes, but she wouldn't let them fall. She was too angry. The ten long blocks were accomplished in silence, and when Deccia reached their back yard, she whirled on him.

Now, for the first time she saw the similarities between Goric and his insane brother, General Fitrn. The same dirty blond hair. The same sharp features and slight body. Only Fitrn's face was square, whereas Goric's was narrower. And the General's light brown eyes were dead, while Goric's gray ones looked wary.

She said through her teeth, "You killed Riln."

He didn't answer.

"*Didn't* you?"

"No. Riln was a hothead. He killed himself. I had nothing to do with it."

"You are *unbelievable*." She clutched her head, fighting to keep the tears in. "It's *your* fault Timaeus was captured. Why he's been *tortured!*"

He flinched. "I didn't intend for Timaeus to get caught."

"That's no excuse! You described him. You named Riln in the false papers, and then you framed Tabor as the spy. Both were innocent men."

"I'm a Zindedi, Deccia. I have a mission. I can't let Koblan destroy my country."

She laughed bitterly. "Zindedi is the aggressor. *You* attacked *us!*"

He said nothing, but looked uncomfortable.

Her chest felt tight. She still couldn't fathom the depths of his betrayal. "You could have helped me, and Timaeus, all this time, but you *didn't*." Her voice broke. "You ordered those washer women not to hire me, didn't you? You delayed Timaeus' rescue."

"Yes."

"*Why?*"

"To protect you."

"To protect *me?*" Deccia broke into heaving sobs. She could barely think. She could make no sense of any of this. Only one thing was clear. "You can help me save Timaeus."

He did not answer.

"Help me save him now."

Goric remained silent.

"Please!" Deccia dropped to her knees.

"Stop it." He sounded angry. "Get up."

Deccia charged back to her feet, fueled by fearful hope. "Please, Goric. I'll do anything."

His gaze flickered to her mouth, and then away. Her heart beat faster. At last, she acknowledged her suspicions. Goric harbored feelings for her—deep and hidden, as was everything about him. Before she could stop herself, she blurted, "*Anything.*"

Those murky gray eyes met hers at last. He knew what she meant and what she offered.

"No."

She had to change his mind. "Help me. Please," she begged.

His posture stiffened, and he visibly retreated into that remote place inside himself.

Deccia grabbed his shoulders and pressed her lips to his.

He trembled.

She whispered, "Anything, Goric," and slid her lips against his. His body remained stiff for so long that she was about to give up in despair, when a sigh shuddered through him. He kissed her back.

Deccia felt a sick, scared sort of triumph. She was winning. She could do this for Timaeus. She would do anything to save his life. Tightening her grip on his shoulders, she put all of her concentration into kissing Goric. For a second, his mouth moved with hers, but then he unexpectedly jerked back with a harsh gasp.

She moved closer and insistently pressed her mouth to his again, urging a response from him. Only a moment passed this time before he kissed her back. This one lasted longer than the first. He pulled back with another tiny, harsh gasp.

"Goric," she whispered, and found his mouth again. His arms went around her now, convulsively tight. At last, he responded with hunger.

Deccia felt triumph...and despair. This was so wrong. But for Timaeus she could do it. To save his life, she would do anything. She opened her mouth, inviting him to take more. Her heart pounded and she cringed, waiting for his response.

He froze. Feeling sick with herself for knowing exactly how to manipulate him, she persuasively ran her tongue across the seam of his lips. He shuddered hard and whispered, "The One. *Deccia.*" Abruptly, he released her and staggered backward, creating distance between them.

Her heart pounded and she looked away from him. Would he expect still more? Could she do it? She struggled to gather up her courage again.

Softly, he said, "Deccia, stop. I will not take advantage of you."

She quickly looked back. "But..."

"I'll help you rescue Timaeus."

"But why?"

"Because you're one of the few people who has ever been my friend."

Deccia smoothed her trembling hands down her tunic and struggled to find words.

"Thank you for not..." She couldn't finish.

His gaze looked sad. "Your heart doesn't belong to me. I won't continue my family's crimes against you."

"Thank you," she whispered.

"I'm sorry about Timaeus," he said abruptly. "I went to the palace that first day, to stop the torture."

"You did?"

"I bribed the guard with that hundred dascals. He was an old acquaintance. I knew he'd do anything for money. He didn't have time to talk then. The next day I found out it was too late. Timaeus' finger...I'm sorry."

Deccia tried to take it all in. "If you could get into the prison—if you could help him get out... Why didn't you?"

"My brother would have hunted him down. I told you that. He would have found you, too. I couldn't let that happen. Timaeus was safe in prison as long as I kept sending a steady stream of dascals to the guards."

So that explained why Goric never seemed to have any money.

"Why?" she said simply. "You're a Zindedi. You could have turned Riln and me in to the military. You didn't have to help Timaeus. Why did you?"

He shrugged and looked away. "Because of you."

A silent moment beat by. He cared about her, just as she had suspected. And she'd just tried to exploit that for her own purposes. She changed the subject. "So you'll help me rescue Timaeus. Tonight."

"I'll go alone."

"No."

A slight smile tipped his lips. "I knew you'd say that. We'll leave at midnight."

"How will we get in?"

"I know every secret passage into that palace." Now his smile looked twisted. "Thanks to my father, sometimes I'd stay lost for days at a time."

Tonight they would rescue Timaeus. Tonight she'd go into the palace of the man who'd ordered Koblan's destruction, and who had ordered Timaeus' torture. Hatred shivered through her.

Behind her, Goric let himself into their house. Apparently there was no love lost between him and his father. But two could keep secrets. She wouldn't tell him the other reason why she intended to accompany him to the palace tonight. Riln was gone, so now she was the only Koblani left who could prevent the Presidente from slaughtering more innocent Koblanis. After they rescued Timaeus, she would need to execute one final mission for Koblan.

But without Riln, could she do what needed to be done?

△ △ △ △ △

In the dead of night, Goric led Deccia deep into the Presidente's gardens. Only the thin crescent of Ryon lit their path. The green light made Goric's pale hair shimmer. Deccia had to trust him not to turn her over to the military, or his father.

Over the last few hours she'd wondered how many ways Goric had betrayed both the kaavl team and Koblan. It made her sick to think about it. She didn't want to know.

Quietly trickling water reached her ears.

Goric skirted a pool of water and climbed a few steps above a miniature waterfall. He held out a hand to help her up. After a hesitation, she took it. She had to pretend to trust him, even though she felt as if she didn't know him at all anymore.

"Back here," he whispered, and disappeared into the thick forest. But the forest only appeared to be thick. It ended in a dark wall. Goric paid no attention to this, however, and instead ran his fingers over a huge tree trunk. "Here it is."

Metal squeaked, and Goric grunted. "Hasn't been used in a while," he muttered. "That's good." When he stepped back, a black hole yawned open in the tree. "I'll go first. Be careful. There's a steep ladder going down. Sixteen rungs."

Feeling cautiously for each foothold, Deccia followed him into the pitch black trunk of the tree. A light flared below, revealing that Goric held a taper cupped in his palm. "We'll have to move fast if we want to get there before this burns out."

Deccia followed close on his heels as he swiftly navigated the serpentine twists of the narrow dirt passage. "You said there are a lot of secret passages in the palace. Why?"

"My grandfather was paranoid. He ordered servants to spy on guests and listen for plans of mutiny. All suspects were quickly executed. He built these outside passages so he could escape from the palace. This one was his favorite. He ordered it built with twenty-five twists and turns. He figured an enemy couldn't get a straight shot and kill him."

"So your family has been in power for how long?"

"Two generations. ...Here we are."

"Where?"

"The prison."

Deccia's heart jerked hard with wild, fearful anticipation. "And Timaeus?" she whispered. "Is he near?"

"We'll need to go down one level."

"What about the guards? What should we do?" Her fingers curled around the knife she'd tied to her leg, just inside her boot. She'd placed a thinner blade through the back strap of her bra. Goric didn't know she carried either one.

"Follow me." He slid aside a panel that revealed more pitch black nothingness on the other side. "It's a storage room," he explained, climbing through the small opening. "Prisoner's personal items are kept here."

"Are they ever returned?" Deccia said acerbically.

He didn't answer, but cracked open a door. A sliver of light streamed in when he peeked out. "Rotations," he muttered. "We'll need to wait."

"How long?"

"Until my friend comes on duty. It should be soon."

Deccia's heart beat harder with nerves while they waited. Could she do what needed to be done? *How* would she do it? First, of course, Timaeus must be rescued.

"Stay here." Before she could protest, Goric slipped out.

He returned a moment later. "It's set. I'll get Timaeus. You stay here."

"No! I'm coming with you."

He hesitated, his face a pale shadow in the dim room. "Don't you trust me?"

Deccia didn't answer. "I want to come," she insisted. "I'll be safe with you, right?" And she'd get a good look at the prison, too.

He hesitated, clearly reluctant to agree to her plan of action. "All right. But walk close beside me. They can't suspect you're a Koblani."

"Fine."

To her surprise, Goric took her hand when they entered the hall. A massive guard, dressed all in black, waited for them. His thick, furry brows scrunched hard together when he saw her. "Who's this?" he rumbled.

"My girlfriend. She wanted a thrill. She's never been in the palace before."

He growled. "My neck's on the line. Get the guy and get out." He cast a glance over his thick shoulder. "Zindh will be back in five minutes. If he sees either of you..."

Goric swiftly pulled Deccia over to a large wooden door and pushed it open. Torches lit a round, circular stone stairway. It smelled damp, and of urine.

Deccia didn't care. She'd crawl through filth to find Timaeus. And to think he was just at the bottom of this stairway!

Just in time, she remembered her plan. "Is there another passage out of here, in case something goes wrong?"

"One. But it leads inside the palace."

"Where is it—just in case?"

Goric stopped at the bottom of the stairs, which forced her to stop, too. His sharp gaze searched hers. "Why?"

Deccia lied smoothly, "I feel vulnerable. And scared. Anything could happen. Will you trust *me*, and tell me the other escape route?"

He continued to watch her. Something flickered in his eyes, and then vanished. "I trust you, Deccia. Even though you don't trust me."

"I'm here with you. Doesn't that prove that I trust you?"

"Wouldn't you make a deal with the devil to rescue Timaeus?"

"Where's the passage?" she repeated.

"Out this door and to the left. It's at the end of the hall. The seventh stone up. Push it, and a trap door opens. Be prepared to fall."

Heart thumping, she nodded.

His gaze still didn't leave hers. "Are you ready?"

"Yes."

"Don't do anything foolish."

Uncomfortable with his intense, discerning stare, she said, "Let's get Timaeus."

The hall was deserted. Goric plucked a ring of keys off the wall and sprinted to the fourth door on the left. Deccia crowded close behind him as he worked the lock. Finally he pushed the door open. It swung into the black, dank interior.

"Timaeus?" she whispered. She elbowed by Goric and ran into the room. "Timaeus, are you here?"

"Deccia." It was a weak whisper.

Where was he? The dim spill of light from the hall didn't illumine much.

She moved further inside, and then Timaeus appeared out of the gloom. He moved slowly, with a shuffling limp. A dark beard obscured half of his face, and his once muscular frame looked thin.

"Timaeus," she gasped, and flung her arms around him. He smelled, and his hair felt greasy. But he was Timaeus.

He hugged her tightly for a long moment, his heart beating noticeably hard in his chest. "I can't believe you're here," he whispered. "And Goric. Thank you."

Deccia pulled back and examined his face. "Are you all right?"

He gave a short, mirthless laugh. "I'll live. Maybe we should get out of here."

"Yes." Finally, she looked down and reached for his hand. He jerked it behind his back, but not before she'd seen the red, seeping stump of his finger.

Tears filled her eyes, and she wanted to burst into hysterical sobs, but he watched her warily, clearly afraid of her reaction. "Oh Timaeus," she whispered, and tightly hugged him again with shaking arms. "I love you so much. Everything is going to be all right."

He drew a harsh, almost sobbing breath. That steeled her determination into a fierce resolve. The Presidente would never hurt anyone again. Never. "Come on. Goric knows the way out."

Goric checked both ways down the hall. "We need to be fast. Zindh will be back any second."

Goric went first, and then Timaeus. Deccia exited from the room last. But instead of turning right to follow the others, she turned left, and sprinted down the hall.

"Deccia!" Timaeus' shocked whisper cut like a knife through her soul.

As her palm hit the seventh stone, she looked over her shoulder. Timaeus' mouth was open, and Goric looked furious, but not surprised. And then the floor opened up beneath her and she fell.

△ △ △ △ △

Deccia's feet hit the floor and she tumbled sideways. Above her, the stone opening slid shut. Her hip and elbow hurt, but they still worked. It was pitch dark, but she had to get going.

She quickly discovered that the passage was too low for her to stand, so she bent double and walked fast, with her hands acting as feelers in front of her.

She believed that Goric would do the prudent thing and get Timaeus home safely. Timaeus, whose leg obviously pained him, who'd been malnourished...whose *finger*... Tears blurred her eyes, but it didn't matter. She couldn't see anything, anyway.

The Presidente would pay for what he had done to Timaeus. So would the General, when she next saw him.

Her plan was ridiculously simple. She'd make every attempt to find the Presidente on her own. Logically, she wouldn't be successful. She would, however, definitely succeed in getting captured and thrown into prison. Afterward, she felt fairly certain the Presidente would call to see her. Especially if he thought she was Methusal.

She knew her plan was bold and reckless, but she didn't care. At one point or another, she would be alone with the Presidente. That's all she wanted. Once chance. Soon, his reign of terror would end.

The passage ended. She slid aside the panel she discovered and peered out. Feet shuffled by, and then all was silent. Deccia wished she could carry with vision, like her sister could. Since that wasn't possible, she listened carefully, and then slid out.

Stairs rose to the left, and she sprinted up them. Methusal had told her that a room on the second floor hid a secret passage that led straight to the Presidente's office. She only needed to find it, and then all would be well.

"Hey!" Hard fingers grabbed Deccia's arm and spun her backward, hard into the wall. She gasped as the air left her lungs

The black-haired guard growled, "Who are you?"

"Methusal Maahr. Tell the Presidente I've come to speak to him."

Chapter Thirty-Five

IN THE BLACK SILENCE before dawn, the Presidente meticulously shaved his jowly face. He wiped the finished perfection with a fluffy towel. "Etin!" he shouted.

His manservant had left minutes before to answer the door. Dawn was fast approaching, and the Zindedi leader wanted to get dressed. Soon the opening ceremonies for the day of torture for his brother's murderer would begin. He did not want to miss a single moment.

"Etin!" he bellowed again. He dropped his robe and pushed his thick arms into his crisp red shirt. If the fool didn't get here in one second...

"I am here, sir." The white-haired, stooped man appeared in the doorway. He appeared reluctant to enter. That fact made the Zindedi leader suspicious. Etin had served him since he was a boy in the palace. The old man knew him too well.

"What is it?" he said. "I am waiting to be dressed." To illustrate his point, he pulled on his trousers with violent, sharp jerks.

Etin slowly entered the Presidente's dressing room. "I...I bring bad news." The little white updo of hair on the top of his head shivered.

"What?" the Presidente scowled, reaching for his belt.

"The prisoner escaped. With help. Early this morning."

"What?" The Presidente stared at Etin, unable to fully comprehend the meaning of the manservant's words for a long moment. Then rage billowed. "How is that *possible?*" he screamed.

"I...I do not know, sir." Raising his hands, Etin backed away. "I do not know, but..."

The Zindedi leader attacked him with the belt. The old man cried out and turned away, but the Presidente viciously walloped the frail old back again and again, with as much strength as he could muster. Etin fell to his knees. He scrambled forward, and somehow surged to his feet and ran out the door.

Sharp pains pierced the Presidente's chest, making each breath a painful, laborious effort. He doubled over, resting his hands on his knees, pretending to feel exhausted. Pretending that he had allowed Etin to escape, rather than letting the sly old servant outmaneuver him.

"Send for Yalin at once!" he commanded, his voice little more than a wheeze.

Etin speedily exited from the outer bedchamber.

The Presidente grabbed the arm of the chair and slowly sank down into it. His heart raced. It did not slow down, and the painful pressure building inside his chest felt like a blown up child's toy of animal intestines, ready to explode.

Fear gripped him, and he closed his eyes, trying to breathe shallowly. He could not die. Not now. Too much still needed to be accomplished.

A shuffling movement alerted him. Two Yalins stood before him. He blinked hard. Now there was only one skinny, frightened looking secretary. "What happened to the prisoner?" he said in a hoarse voice.

"Guards saw a man and a woman enter the prison. The man and the prisoner escaped."

So. The prisoner had escaped with help.

"How could this be, Yalin? How could this *be?*" He tried to keep his voice calm, but it was impossible. Rage and the desire for vengeance ate through his blood like a hot fire. "*What did you do?* How did you let this happen?"

Terror struck the young man's expression. "I...I didn't, Presidente. I gave the orders to the guards yesterday, just as you ordered. I...I do not know how the outsiders got past the guards, or into the prison."

"The Koblanis learned that their comrade was to be executed this morning, Yalin," the Presidente said through his teeth. "That is why they came. How did they learn that detail? *How?*"

"I do not *know!*" he cried out, visibly trembling. "I told no one. I swear my loyalty to you, Presidente."

With a twisted snarl, he reminded, "*My* Presidente."

"My Presidente. I swear. I told no one. I would *never...*"

"Even when my women plied you with pleasures?" he said sarcastically. "You did not bleat your most secret confidences while in the throes of passion?"

Yalin reddened. "I...It did not happen last night."

"You did not go to the women, as I commanded you?" the Presidente mocked, his voice rising in contemptuous disbelief.

"I...I went, but they said...they said they had received no orders." His voice lowered to a hushed, ashamed whisper. "They threw me out, and laughed at me."

The Presidente roared, "You are an incompetent imbecile. *Incompetent!* You deserve their contempt if you cannot take what is yours."

Yalin rocked back on his heels, his eyes still trained at the floor. "I have further news. The female Koblani has been captured, and she is in prison. She says she is Methusal Maahr, and wishes to speak to you."

He snorted. "Truly? That is impossible. General Fitrn has not returned yet." The Presidente continued to scowl at his cowering secretary. The pup needed a spine, and he knew just how to give it to him. It had worked well on each of his sons. He doubled the belt in his hands.

Yalin froze, terror in his eyes.

"You are as dear to me as a son, Yalin," the Presidente said, licking his lips in anticipation. "As a father disciplines his sons to become men, so I will discipline you now."

"But what did I do?"

But the Presidente did not answer. He used every ounce of his strength to flay into the young man's flesh. Rage for Mentàll Solboshn, Methusal Maahr, his brother's murderer...the flagrant escape last night...all coalesced into a hot ball of fury, and he took out every stroke of anger on his helpless secretary. Sweat streamed down his face. When Yalin finally collapsed to his knees, the Presidente felt much better.

Breathing heavily, he threaded the belt through the loops, looking down at the shuddering young man. Blood seeped through his clothing. He felt a small stab of remorse. Perhaps he had been a little harsh.

He found a parchment and ink and wrote a short command. He thrust it into Yalin's limp hand. "Go to the women now. They will tend to you."

Yalin took it. Without looking at the Presidente, he staggered to his feet and exited.

It seemed very silent after he had gone. Unease slithered through the Presidente. His hands stung from the thrashing he had administered. The young pup would survive, and be stronger for it, just as his sons had been, he assured himself.

He returned to his chair, and sat there, alone. Something would need to be done about the Koblani woman. But right now, he could not muster up the desire to do it.

△ △ △ △ △

Deccia was hungry and cold. The soldier had stripped off her jacket and boots, and her knife, as well. When he'd found it, he'd backhanded her. Then he'd thrown her in the jail cell and left her. Luckily, she still had the knife hidden in her bra.

Would he tell the Presidente that she'd come to see him?

She tried to think about Timaeus, and to take comfort from the fact that he was surely safe. Goric would have brought him home. Wouldn't he? Yes. She trusted that he would have done that for her.

Although she was freezing cold and it was uncomfortable sitting on the cold, damp floor, she felt calm. More than that, she felt resolved.

"'*Vengeance is Mine, I will repay,' says The One.*" Unbidden, the Prophet's words slid through her mind.

"I've waited long enough. I have to do *something*," she whispered. "The Presidente will keep making war on Koblan. He'll keep killing our people and *torturing* them." Tears welled, but she swallowed them back. "I have to stop him."

The war would end today.

"*Timaeus.*" Her throat ached. She wanted to be with him, but he was the reason why she was here. The President and the General had committed enough atrocities. It was time to stop them for good.

Could she do what needed to be done?

When would the Presidente call for her?

△ △ △ △ △

Methusal hadn't seen Mentàll all day, and wondered if he was avoiding her.

She also hadn't seen Behran or Sozla, which she took to be a good sign. Motr, Behran's supervisor, had sent Behran into the mountains to check the water levels in the high lake. Sozla had gone with him.

It was almost dark, so they should be back soon. She hoped Behran had told Sozla about their ended engagement, and that progress had been made in their own relationship today.

She ran a quick brush through her hair, readying for dinner, and wondered if she would see Mentàll tonight. After their "discussion" yesterday, and her misleading embrace with Behran last night, she wasn't sure what he was thinking.

She needed to speak to him.

With a sigh, she let herself into the lamp lit hall and stopped short. Mentàll's large body lounged against the opposite wall. He was clearly waiting for her.

She closed the door. "Hello," Her heart leaped with joy. "It's nice to see you. But why are you here?"

"It is my turn to enjoy your company at dinner tonight."

She couldn't help but smile. "Did *asking* me cross your mind?"

A return smile glimmered. "I did not want to give you the opportunity to say 'no.'" To her surprise, uncertainty flickered across his features.

Her heart softened still more. "I would be glad to have dinner with you. Thank you."

His smiled widened. "Good. When I become Presidente, I will be here often. I hope to enjoy many meals together then."

She rolled her eyes. "*When* you become Presidente. You won't stop, will you?"

"I want only the best, Methusal."

"Complete power, you mean? Complete control over every circumstance, so you can achieve your every goal?"

The faint gleam in his eyes said he enjoyed her impertinent remarks.

Encouraged, and squashing a smile of her own, she said, "Tell me, Mentàll. What is your ultimate goal? Power over the entire world?"

His lazy smile resembled a predatory wild beast's. "No. My goal is simple. To make you mine."

Methusal's heart beat accelerated. It seemed suddenly too quiet in the hall. He'd laid down the gauntlet. No more games. No more hidden agendas.

She lifted her chin and shoved aside the irritating hair that had been tickling her neck all week.

The Dehrien's gaze focused on the point beneath her jaw. He frowned, and his teasing smile vanished. "What is that?"

Her hand flew to her neck. She'd forgotten it, and now felt vulnerable with it exposed to him. "The mark of the General. I'm sure my father told you all about the attack."

His pale gaze cooled to deadly ice. "Of course."

"He was going to kill me. But first, he intended to torture me." A shudder slipped through her.

"You killed him."

"Almost. Barak finished him."

His attention returned to the mark on her neck. "Does it hurt?" he asked quietly.

"No. Only the memory."

He leaned toward her, and before she could guess his intent, he dipped his head and she felt his warm lips on her skin. Right on the closed up puncture wound.

She gasped at his intimate touch and closed her eyes, instinctively arching to give him full access to the sensitive area. Pleasure spiraled through her. And healing soothed her soul.

She felt his hands settle, lightly but possessively around her waist. His lips remained still, pulsing electricity through her flesh. Then they moved, trailing a row of kisses down her throat, following the line of the injury.

Her fingers dug into his powerful shoulders. "Mentàll," she breathed.

He looked up, his gaze uncharacteristically gentle. "More? I want to do it."

She stared at him, her breaths coming rapidly. "No." She released her grip on him. "No. Thank you." More kisses, and she'd lose her grip on reason.

He released her and she felt a sense of loss. He straightened. "Still you claim you do not want my touch?"

"It's not..."

"You want *me,* not Behran."

"I..."

"*I* want you."

Her breath caught in her throat. "Do you?" She searched his eyes. "Once and for all, I need to know. Because honestly, I want to be with you, too."

His gaze intensified at her blunt admission.

She drew an unsteady breath and plunged forward. If she wanted to have a future with him, she needed to be brave enough to resolve the major issues that stood in their way. She hadn't meant for this to happen here, in the hallway, but no one was around. This was as good a time as any other.

She said, "Maybe I'm being presumptuous, but in Quasr, I overheard and got the impression that you may want a future with me."

"Yes." His voice was a gravel rasp.

"We could go about this the traditional way, and you could court me. But it would make no difference. We know each other very well. If I'm honest, I would gladly step forward into a future with you, if you can answer just one question for me."

"Ask it," he said roughly.

"Do your feelings for me go beyond your desire for power? For kaavl sons? I need to know how much you want *me*. And I don't mean physically."

He was silent for a moment. "I care for you, Methusal. I have told you that."

"How much? Like a pet apte?"

"No!"

"Then what do you feel for me?"

"I do not know. I will provide for you..."

"No. I'm asking what you *feel* for me. Do you love me, even a little? Or am I just a prize to you?"

His eyes narrowed. "A prize?"

"I want to know if this is about love, or power. I already know you want power. And kaavl means the world to you. But at heart, do you want *me*? Or do you only want what I can provide for you?"

He frowned. "And what can you provide?"

"Calbn said it best. You want a close alliance with Rolban. You always have. So it would benefit you to marry me, the Chief's daughter. And if you marry me, you will be able to mix your bloodline with the great Mahre's. Isn't that what you've always wanted? Power and immortality. And you can get both through me."

He stared at her without speaking for a very long moment. Then he uttered a harsh Dehrien word. Red etched his cheekbones. "Face the truth, Methusal!" The words sounded like a gunshot.

"*What* truth? Tell me. Please!" Gathering up her courage, she whispered, "I'll tell *you* the truth, Mentàll. I love you. With my whole heart."

"You love me?" Uncertainty flickered, but red still burned on his cheekbones. "And that is why you continue to lead on Behran?"

"I am not!"

Harshly, he said, "I saw you hug him last night. If you truly love me, then why are you feeding him lies?" He paused. "Or maybe I am the one being played for a fool."

"No!"

"Do you require two men? Is that it? Does that feed your vanity?"

"Mentàll! No..."

"Speak the truth at last, Methusal. Who do you want? Him or me?"

Frustrated, her temper surged. She'd just told him she *loved* him! And he still wouldn't answer her one, simple question. "*You* tell me the truth," she snapped. "You manipulate, you play every underhanded trick in the book to get your own way, and *my* motives are suspicious? One minute ago you were gentle, and now you're arrogant and demanding. Who are you? And what do you really want?"

"You know who I am, Methusal."

"Yes! I know you are all those things."

Harshly, he said, "Can you accept me as I am?"

"Yes. I could. But..."

"Then choose. Behran, or me?"

Infuriated, she glared. "Behran knows it's over between us. This is not about him. It is about *you*. Tell me the truth. Why do you want me? Is it for the alliance? For kaavl immortality? Or is it *me*, and me alone that you want?"

"The truth, Methusal?" Fury still scored his cheekbones. "I do want you for those reasons. Why would I not?"

Devastated, she stared at him. "So, that's all it is?"

For a long moment, torment clearly wrestled in his blue gaze, as if he longed to say something deeper, from his heart. But then it cooled to distant ice again. "I have proven over and over again that I care for you." He uttered a soft curse.

"And my blood *burns* for you. It is a fire that keeps me awake every night—is that not enough? Do you want me to say I need you? That I cannot live without you? That I love you? I cannot. I will give no one that much power over me. Not ever. Accept that."

She swallowed a soft, disbelieving gasp. "Then you're a coward! I hope your arrogance and pride comfort you at night. Because you'll never have me! *Never.*" Tears filled her eyes. "Go! I never want to see you again."

He stared at her in complete disbelief. The red in his cheekbones drained to white. Without a word, he stalked away.

Methusal escaped into her compartment. Sobs shook her entire body. *He didn't love her.* He never had, and he'd just sworn he never would. *Never.*

She sank to the floor and wept.

△ △ △ △ △

Rolbanis lined up at the buffet line, piling their plates with food. Hendra's stomach rumbled, and she glanced around, looking for a friend with whom to eat dinner. Behran was there, with Sozla.

But Mentàll had been on her heart all afternoon. Normally, he was one of the first in line, but she didn't see him. Another scan noted that Methusal was missing, too. Were they together?

Or was something wrong?

Instead of joining the buffet line, she left the dining hall. Her steps slowed down near the Grand Staircase.

Down below, the Grand Hall was quiet and shadowed. A few torches flared on the walls.

She slipped down the stairs. Only a solitary guard stood near the entrance gate, looking out into the night. The rest of the hall was deserted.

When she turned to head back up the stairs, a pale flash in a far, dark corner caught her eye.

Mentàll. He stood with his head bowed, and his fist and forearm were pressed against the rock wall. Quickly, she hurried over. White edged his clenched jaw.

"Mentàll. What is it?" she said softly. "Are you all right?"

He did not respond. He looked frozen.

Deeply worried, she said, "What's wrong? Can I do something?"

"No." His head turned on his forearm and faced the wall. "You can do nothing."

"It's Methusal."

His fist tightened, and he drew a strangled breath.

"What did she do?"

Mentàll laughed once, a bleak, choking sound. "She hates me. She never wants to see me again."

"Why not?"

"She thinks I want her for a permanent alliance with Rolban. And to mix my blood with hers to produce Mahre's kaavl descendants."

"Is that true?"

"Partly."

"Tell her the full truth, Mentàll."

"I cannot love her," he said harshly. "That's what she wants. What is worse, Behran can give her love and everything else she desires, too."

"She loves *you*. Not Behran."

He laughed without humor. "She will not have me unless I love her in return. If I cannot love her, Behran will be waiting."

"I've never known you to give up."

He faced her then, and she gasped at the misery etched into his face. Never before had she seen her cousin display such intense emotion. He said, "You love Doc. Fight for him, then."

Hendra drew a sharp breath. She'd missed Doc horribly over the last two weeks. In fact, the pain grew worse every day. "That's different. And he's not here."

"He would be if you sent for him."

Tears blurred her eyes. "You're changing the subject. I can't love Doc. I've told you that! I could never be good enough for him." She still feared this was the truth.

Mentàll swore. "So how are we so different, Hendra? We are both broken, and unable to love. We are both unworthy!" His fist smashed into the wall and blood ran from his knuckles.

"Mentàll."

"We are both bastards! And we are both cursed by our hellish family!"

"That's not true. You've escaped. You're Chief, and people want you to be Presidente."

"That is not enough!"

"Then what is enough?"

For a long moment she didn't think he would respond.

"Love. Love is enough, Hendra. Go after your Doc."

"I can't!"

"Then I will send him to you."

"Mentàll, no."

He cursed. "You are giving up. You are letting that *scienth* win!"

"No." And yet she was. That knowledge made her feel sick.

"Doc loves you, and he will accept you. What more do you need?"

Hendra twisted the subject back to him again. "What do you need, Mentàll? Go after Methusal. It's not too late."

"Methusal will not accept me. I cannot love her."

"Of course you can. I know you can."

Mentàll picked up the pack at his feet. Hendra hadn't noticed it before. "I am leaving," he said harshly.

"Fear is a lonely companion."

"Now you think *fear* is my problem?" he snarled.

"And pride. You're afraid to love her. You won't admit that you need her. You think you don't need anyone, but you're wrong. Haven't you been miserable for long enough?" Hendra felt anguished for her stubborn cousin. He could so easily make battle plans and political alliances, but he could not forge an alliance to heal his own heart.

"And you. Haven't you been miserable for long enough?" The words hung between them for a long moment, and then he said, "I will be back for the election!" With quick strides, he disappeared through the gates and into the black night. Wild beasts howled in the distance.

Her cousin's words circled through her brain.

Hadn't she been miserable for long enough?

How long would she allow Jascr's abuse to paralyze her? How long would she endure misery because she was afraid to embrace the possibility of hope and love? Hadn't she lived in the dark for long enough?

Hendra wiped the welling tears from her eyes. She loved Doc so much, but she and Mentàll were truly two of a kind. Both broken—but in different ways—and both unable to forge a deep, loving relationship with another human being.

Despair wrapped around her heart. She was so sick of being afraid. So sick of being alone. She was still afraid—terribly afraid—of failing Doc and being an utter failure to him as a wife.

But did she want to let Jascr win?

Of course not.

Maybe it was selfish and greedy, but she needed Doc's love. She loved him so much.

Two weeks had passed. Did he still want her? By all rights, he shouldn't. She'd foolishly given up when he'd refused her dumb, compromising proposal. As well he should have, she knew with shame. She'd put him in an impossible situation. And yet he'd pledged to endure a celibate marriage, just because he truly loved her. Surely he would never give up on her.

For the first time in weeks, hope blossomed.

If both Mentàll and Doc believed in her and loved her, maybe it was time that she believed in herself, too. After all, if she could face down a bully like Riln, surely she could find the courage to put her body in the hands of the man she trusted and loved more than her own life.

If she did all that—if she took that chance—maybe the love she yearned for would finally heal the last broken places in her heart. Maybe she would be whole again. Maybe she could love Doc completely, the way he so deserved to be loved.

For the first time in two long weeks, hope lifted her spirits. She knew what to do. But first, she would do one thing for Mentàll. Hendra headed back upstairs.

△ △ △ △ △

Methusal still sat crumpled on the floor, blocking the entrance to the compartment.

The door latch clicked, and the door pressed into her back. She couldn't summon the energy to move. A knock rapped. "Methusal?" her mother said. "Is that you?"

Her throat ached from crying so hard. How many tears lived in her? Apparently more, and more...and ever more.

She scooted sideways and the door flew open.

"Thusa?" Her mother immediately sank down and wrapped her arms tightly around her. "What's wrong, sweetie?"

"Oh, Mama!" Gulping on more tears, she burrowed her face into her mother's shoulder. "Everything's such a mess!"

"You love Mentàll." Hanuh stroked her hair. "I know. And maybe this doesn't help, I saw this moment coming a long time ago."

Methusal choked back a miserable laugh. "You did?"

"Remember when the Quasr War started? I said your life would never be the same."

"I remember."

"I hoped things would not change. Behran is such a nice boy. And Mentàll..."

"Is not." Methusal hiccupped.

"Two months ago, when Mentàll came here with plans to make peace with Zindedi, I saw then that he'd made up his mind about you."

New tears overflowed. "He doesn't love me, Mama. He said so. All he cares about is power."

"Are you sure?"

"He *said* he doesn't love me. He swore he never would. He said he'd never let anyone have that much power over him."

Hanuh remained silent for a while. "Interesting."

"Why is that interesting? It's cold-blooded. I hate him!"

"You love him."

"I don't *want* to love him," she sniffled. "How can I love him?"

"You love him because you see something deep and valuable in him. He's a complex man, Methusal, and he has all sorts of walls. It doesn't take an empath to see that. But I think during your time in Zindedi you saw into his true heart. Is that fair to say?"

Methusal pulled back. "He can be so gentle, Mama," she whispered. "And sometimes I *feel* like he really does love me."

"Maybe he does. Perhaps he's just afraid to admit it— maybe he's afraid to love anyone. Look at his past. His mother died when he was very young. He never knew his father, who abandoned him. His uncle, as far as I've heard from Poli, abused him terribly.

"Methusal, no wonder he's afraid to love. He pulled himself up by his own bootstraps to become Chief of Dehre— at age twenty-four. He's learned that the only way to protect himself is to grab power and manipulate others to get what he wants. He might think that if he keeps his heart shut, he'll never be hurt again."

Methusal wiped away the last of her tears. Quiet hope unfurled inside of her. "Maybe. That makes sense. I'd never thought about it that way before."

Hanuh stroked the hair away from Methusal's forehead. "I don't pretend to know everything about Mentàll. He's a closed man, and very difficult to read. But I do see how he treats you, and combined with what you've told me about him, I think that maybe it's time we *all* give him another chance."

"Yes." Maybe there was hope... Possibly.

A knock sounded at the door. Methusal stood aside as her mother opened it. "Hendra."

When the blond-haired Dehrien girl saw Methusal's face, she said, "I'm so sorry. I didn't mean to disturb you."

"It's all right," Methusal assured her. "What's wrong?"

"I thought you'd want to know... He's gone."

"Who?"

"Mentàll."

She went very still. "Where did he go?"

"Dehre."

"Now?" Fear and disbelief knotted within her. "But the wild beasts!"

Hendra offered a small smile. "Dehriens aren't afraid of wild beasts. Not like Rolbanis are. We've fought them away from our village all of our lives."

It didn't ease the worry in Methusal's heart, or the guilt she felt. He'd left right now because of her. "When will he be back?"

"For the election."

She bit her lip. "We had a horrible fight."

"It's not too late," Hendra said gently. "You can go after him tomorrow and tell him how you feel. You love him, don't you?"

"Yes. So much."

Her face lit up in a big smile. "Good. Because he needs you. Desperately. But he'll never admit it. He reminds me of the orphans I care for in Dehre. They hunger for love. They need to be told, over and over again, how much they're loved. Mentàll is the same way. He's never opened up to anyone like he has to you. He's pursued no woman like he's pursued you. I think he does love you, but he's afraid to admit it."

Hanuh smiled. "Your perspective confirms what we were just discussing."

"Methusal, do you truly love him?"

"Yes!"

Hendra smiled. "Then help him. Heal him. *Love* him."

CHAPTER THIRTY-SIX

DAY 43

AFTER THE DETERMINATION AND HOPE she'd felt last night, doubts assailed Hendra when she piled items into her pack that morning.

She wondered if Doc's feelings for her remained the same. If he had doubts, that would be understandable.

Hendra tied her pack shut. Her hands trembled a little as she contemplated what she was about to do. This trip could change her entire life. First, she would tell him how much she loved him, and apologize for forcing him into that uncomfortable position in Quasr. And then... She wasn't sure what she'd say next.

Yes. Surely it wasn't too late. She strapped on her pack and went looking for Dastn.

He waited for her at the entrance gates, and grinned when he saw her. "You're ready. We should get to Tarst by early afternoon."

The sooner the better, as far as she was concerned. Her nerves already felt drawn as taut as a bow. "Thank you for taking me with you."

"I have a message for Pan. It works out well." He eyed her bulging pack. "Planning to stay awhile? Do you have a place lined up?"

Hendra flushed. "Not really. I...I hadn't thought that far ahead."

"Doc's mother will be glad to meet you. She has a spare room."

She nodded, feeling a bit taken aback by the thought of not only pledging her life to Doc, but meeting his mother, too. "His father died, didn't he?" He had never said much about his family.

"Twenty years ago. A fall from an urchet broke his neck. Doc is an only child. Lucky for him, he had my sister and me for cousins." With a faint grin, Dastn added, "Although, to be honest, we were the lucky ones. He was like a brother to us."

Dastn told Hendra more about their family as they rounded the eastern end of Rolban and headed north, across the plain.

△ △ △ △ △

Methusal set off for Dehre in the cool of the morning. Hendra had told her last night that she'd decided to travel to Tarst today with Dastn. She hoped everything went well for Hendra and the Tarst doctor. They both deserved so much happiness.

And today she was hiking for Dehre with the same hope for herself and Hendra's cousin.

At midday, as she neared Dehre, her heart hammered with the anticipation of seeing him. The sun toasted her skin, and although she'd brought water, she looked forward to ducking into the shade of Mentàll's tent.

The outer shacks of Dehre still looked dilapidated, and a number had a sad, neglected air about them, as if the people who owned them were too poor and tired to care about appearances. At least the drought had ended this year. And to the north, she'd spotted green crops. The wall around the small town was almost finished. Only the eastern wall needed to be built. Another improvement for the small community.

She crossed the outer perimeter, which was interspersed with blackened smoke pits. The fires still kept the wild beasts at bay during the night.

Children in ragged clothes watched her, and one scraggly apte followed her. Maybe a pet.

The interior of Dehre looked better, as if recent attention had been paid to it. The houses stood upright. Flowers were planted out in front of a few of them. The central business street boasted a few vendors. One cart advertised that it was from Quasr, and displayed intricately woven baskets. Dehrien women haggled over them.

She cut northwest. Soon the Dehrien Chief's white tents came into view. The chief's compound covered a large circular area. The tents were made of fine leather. Five smaller ones encircled a large one, which she knew was the dining hall. And the medium-sized tent to the east was Mentàll's. Heart thrumming faster, she headed for it.

She felt sticky with perspiration, and guessed that her hair looked straggly by now too, but what could she do? Mentàll had seen her look far worse. All the same, she wished she'd had the foresight to bring a brush. She rapped twice on the wooden knocker beside his tent flap's entrance.

Silence.

She knocked again.

A short woman carrying an armload of laundry swerved in her direction. "Are you looking for Mentàll?"

"Yes. Is he here?"

"You're Methusal?"

"Yes." She wondered how the woman knew.

The woman nodded. "Come with me."

Methusal followed her into one of the side tents. It took a second for her eyes to adjust to the dim interior. But instead of seeing Mentàll, as she'd expected, a man who looked remarkably like Tabor sat behind a desk.

"Methusal is here," the woman told him, as if this should be significant to him. With a nod to Methusal she left, clutching her laundry tightly in her arms.

The mud-colored brown eyes of the man were sharp and discerning. He offered a calloused hand to shake. "I'm Toriln, Mentàll's first-in-command." His voice was very deep.

"You're Tabor's brother."

"He was my twin."

Twins. "I'm so sorry."

"Thank you." He pulled a package from a sack. "You've saved me a trip. Mentàll asked me to give this to you."

Methusal accepted the leather wrapped package. It was flat and square, like a shallow box. The uneasy feeling within her grew. "Where is Mentàll?"

"He left this morning."

"For where?"

"He didn't say."

"He didn't say? When will he be back?"

Toriln shrugged. "I don't know." His sharp eyes appeared to be sizing her up.

"You mean he's disappeared? That's not like him."

"No. It is not. Then again, he was nothing like himself when he returned last night."

"What do you mean?"

"I'm not one to read a man's thoughts. But my guess is that he wanted to be alone."

"Oh." And it was because their fight last night. Toriln appeared to be a perceptive man. He'd probably guessed that she was the reason for the Dehrien Chief's abrupt departure. "Could I leave a message, then? Will you give it to him when he returns?"

"Sure. If he comes back before the election."

The election wasn't for two weeks. Did Toriln really think Mentàll would be gone for that long?

Toriln handed her a bit of parchment and a writing stick. Methusal simply wrote,

Mentàll, please come to Rolban. Or I'll come to Dehre. Whatever you want. I have something important I need to tell you. I love you. Methusal.

Toriln said, "I imagine you'll head back to Rolban now?" His brusque demeanor indicated that he recommended it.

"After I refill my water skin."

His curt nod was a clear dismissal.

"Thank you," she said, and left. What a taciturn man. Obviously, he felt as if she'd done Mentàll wrong. Perhaps she had, by dismissing him when she'd felt so hurt. But now she wanted to make things right. She prayed it would be possible, and that it was not too late.

The laundry woman saw her when she exited, and directed her to the well. Then she insisted that Methusal eat lunch in Dehre, too. "The sun is hot," she fussed, and insisted that Methusal eat in Mentàll's tent, at his table. Unlike Toriln, she seemed to harbor no ill feelings toward Methusal. In fact, the soft light in her eyes indicated that she might be a romantic at heart.

The tent was quiet. It smelled so much like Mentàll that it made her ache with longing for him.

Before eating lunch, she slowly unwrapped the package he'd arranged to give her.

After unfolding only one side of the wrapper, she softly gasped. It was the *Second Book of Kaavl*. The book he'd stolen from her hands near the end of the Quasr War.

A folded note inside was addressed to her in Mentàll's bold, decisive scrawl.

Methusal, I am sorry for the many ways I have hurt you. I am a greedy and desperate man to think I can have it all. This book belongs to you. I finally understand that I can never make you happy. If Behran can, ce'cemone, then marry him. You have my blessing.

Forever yours,
Mentàll

He had given up.

Methusal couldn't believe it. She read the note again. "No," she told the absent, frustrating man. "It's not over. It will *never* be over."

△ △ △ △ △

When Dastn and Hendra had traveled for only two hours, the runner frowned and peered into the distance. "Who is that?"

To Hendra's alarm, he pulled the bow off of his shoulder.

"Just to be safe," he said grimly, stringing one sharp arrow in place. "Zindedis might have left spies behind."

The thought had never crossed her mind. Dastn urged her to hide behind a large, prickly tagma bush. He waited beside her, bow flexed, and at the ready.

Hendra peered through the thick, prickly branches at the lone man who was approaching. He walked with quick, purposeful strides, as if eager to reach his destination.

"Fool," Dastn snorted, and unexpectedly lowered his bow. "Almost got himself shot," he muttered, and strode out to meet the man.

When Hendra rounded the bush, she finally saw the sun glinting off of dark red hair. *Doc.* He was *here*. He was coming to Rolban.

She felt faint with joy and shock.

When Doc spotted them, his steps slowed down for a second, and then doubled.

Minutes later, Dastn raised his arm and slapped hands with him. "We were coming to meet you, cuz."

Doc smiled, but his gaze, as it had for the last several minutes, remained upon Hendra. "I was heading to Rolban."

"Funny," Dastn said. "I think Hendra was heading there, too."

She flushed. "Actually, I was going to Tarst, to see you."

Doc grinned. "To see me?"

"I need to deliver a message," Dastn interjected. "Is Hendra safe in your hands?"

"Always. Thank you, Dastn."

"No prob." The Tarst runner loped for the Tarst mountains.

Hendra was suddenly not sure what to say. "Why are you coming to Rolban?"

"To see you. I was hoping to change your mind." Hope softened his eyes. "But maybe you've already changed it?"

She drew a deep breath, and blinked back tears of happiness. "You have no idea how much I've missed you."

With a smile, he said, "I think I might have a small idea."

"I'm sorry for what I did to you in Quasr. For asking you to... You know..." Her voice lowered, "Behave inappropriately."

A faint smile answered her apologetic confession. "It tempted me, but for only a second. I could never— I love you too much, Hendra, to ever dirty you like that. You deserve a beautiful wedding, and flowers—everything I can give you, and still that wouldn't be enough to show you how much I love you. Or how much I want to cherish you for the rest of our lives. Hendra, you have no idea..." His voice broke, and Doc, the direct, unflappable Tarst doctor, blinked back moisture.

Hendra folded her hands around his. Softly, she said, "I love you so much. I'm sorry I ran from you and told you I never wanted to see you again. That was a horrible, horrible lie. I've missed you so much." Now it was her turn to blink. "I love you. And if you'll still have me, I would be so happy to say 'yes.'"

His grin looked a little unsteady. "To be perfectly clear... you will marry me?"

"Yes!"

Doc folded her tightly in his arms and his lips touched hers. Elation, fire, and joy seared through her. She found herself clutching his shoulders to steady herself.

Doc kissed her again, and then they stared at each other. To her surprise, he looked just as dazed as she felt. Not much fazed him, and she'd seen him calm and steady in every situation under the sun—in Zindedi, under attack, and in battle.

"Hendra," he murmured, and drew her closer. He pressed his cheek against her hair. "Hendra." It sounded like a quiet ache from his soul.

In his arms, the last of her old fear began to melt away.

Could it happen, so quickly, so easily? And yet she felt it *all* melting away. She could barely believe it.

Hendra wrapped her arms around him, and quiet tears slid down her face. She whispered, "When you hold me, I'm not afraid anymore."

He laughed a little. It sounded choked. "Then let me hold you forever."

△ △ △ △ △

Deccia had slept little last night. Nightmares swooped in like black beasts of prey. Even though she'd chosen this prison sentence, she couldn't forget her weeks in Quasr's dungeon, and the fear, helplessness, and humiliation she'd suffered. She would not be sucked into that mindless pit of terror again.

She would not.

When would the Presidente call for her? Or would he, ever?

Was this part of his strategy? To break her down? To wait for fear to strangle her soul? Did he hope to make her beg for mercy?

Not this time. Never again.

Hours passed. Footsteps clumped in the hall. Each time her hopes lifted, but no one stopped at her door.

What time was it now? Afternoon? The evening of the second day? The only thing the guard had left behind that first night was a small pail of water. It was half gone, although she drank from it sparingly.

Would they leave her in here forever? Would they forget all about her?

Fear slid like insidious poison into her spirit as the endless black day surely edged into night again. The fear made her feel angry. The Presidente would not win.

He would not.

Her stomach growled. She hadn't eaten in two days.

Deccia closed her eyes and slept.

The General hissed, "How foolish, to sacrifice yourself for the others. They won't appreciate it. But I will. Come with me."

"No."

"Come."

She refused.

"Guards," he said in a bored tone.

Rough hands dug into her armpits.

"No! No." Wildly, she struggled. "Never again!"

The door opened, and the light in the hall felt hot, like a furnace. "Where are you taking me?" she cried out.

"You've crossed over to my side, love. Be prepared to enjoy the fruit of your labors."

A burning fireball exploded and hurtled down the hallway. It engulfed the General, leaving only black eyebrows and maniacal, flaming eyes.

The guards screamed, but the fire consumed their hair and clothes, and then they exploded into nothingness.

"Come, my pet," the General's voice hissed and popped. "Take the final step."

"No!"

Cold water hit Deccia's face. She gasped and reared back against the wall, her eyes wide, terrified.

Rough hands hauled her to her feet. "The Presidente has called for you. Get a move on."

Chapter Thirty-Seven

Unfamiliar guards—neither was Goric's friend—flanked her, each with a tight grip on her arm. They hustled Deccia up countless stairs, and then pushed her into a large room.

Polished wood paneled the room, and a large red and black woven rug lay on the polished floor. Red curtained windows framed the black night. A narrow-faced young man, wearing a cramped, frightened look, worked behind a small wooden desk.

The guard on Deccia's left growled, "Tell him we're here, Yalin."

The young man slowly slid upright, wincing in apparent pain. With a baleful look at the guard, he rapped lightly on a massive door.

"What?" demanded the Presidente's muffled voice.

"The girl is here."

Silence.

The young man faced them. "You will need to wait." He gingerly resumed his position at the desk.

The guards did not seem surprised. They marched her right up to the Presidente's massive door. Her nose was only two fingerbreadths shy of the polished wood. And they waited.

It seemed like hours, but surely it was only twenty minutes before the Presidente shouted, "Enter!"

The guards shoved her inside.

A quick glance assessed the room. It was decorated in a similar fashion to the outer office. Polished wood and red were the predominant themes. Military swords, knives, and guns lined the walls and served as artistic additions to the book shelves. Her gaze immediately zeroed in on the stocky figure seated behind the large desk. Black hair. Amber eyes.

Her heart almost stopped beating, and then surged into overdrive. It couldn't be! And yet he looked just like...

She felt dizzy, and was glad for the painful, unyielding support of the two guards gripping her. The man behind the desk looked just like General Greisn. The man who had repeatedly raped her in Quasr. The dead man who still stalked her dreams.

"*No,*" she gasped.

The high ranking military man leaned forward. A frown of interest scored into his wide brow. "What do you see?"

"You...you're not General Greisn," she gasped, clinging tightly to reality.

Speculation glittered in his eyes. Now she saw they were a darker brown than the General's. And his body was a little thicker—perhaps a result of sitting at a desk for too long. And his face was squarer, and his gaze focused. He laughed. "No. I am not my brother. And you, my dear, are not Methusal Maahr."

Deccia felt as if she was losing her advantage much too quickly. "I'm Methusal's twin sister."

"Of course. But what use are you to me?" His voice sounded like General Greisn's, too. It was uncanny. Fear licked into her soul.

"Reconsider the peace agreement," she told him. "Give us a sign of good faith, or all of your powder mines will be destroyed."

Anger hardened his features. "Do not threaten me. You are lucky I have agreed to see you at all. Surely you must realize what an easy, delightful matter it would be to put a young woman like you in her place." His insolent eyes on her body made his intent clear.

Hatred and rage coalesced into a tight, hot knot inside of her. The Presidente was just like the General. No. He was worse. Because of him, General Greisn had come to Koblan and raped her. Because of *him* Timaeus had been tortured and mutilated.

If the Presidente had his way, he'd rape Koblan's ore and murder every Koblani, too. Even that would not be enough for him, because her empathic abilities sensed the darkest truth. Nothing would satisfy this man's lust for two things:

power, and inflicting unspeakable atrocities upon others. In the Presidente's blackest heart, world dominion would never be enough. He'd only be satisfied when every single person was whipped and cowering before him. And then he'd want to torture them still further. He was sick and twisted, and evil to his core. He had to be stopped.

Through her teeth, she said, "Do you choose peace? Or war?"

"*You* chose war when your people attacked my land again. There will be no peace." He glanced down at the parchments on his desk and flipped one over. Without looking up, he said, "Take her away. Do whatever you like with her."

The guards pulled her backward, but Deccia fought them. Inspiration struck. "We've identified your deepest spy."

The Presidente's head lifted. His raised hand halted the guard's efforts to wrestle her out the door. "Explain yourself."

"Goric is your son. If you don't release me, my friends will kill him." Deccia had never been a very good liar, but the Presidente scowled.

He snapped, "Kill him, then."

She couldn't help but gasp. "He's your son!"

"So? He's weak and lazy. I had high hopes for him, but he's a mama's boy. He's worse than useless for my purposes. Now he's blown his cover. He deserves what's coming to him."

"Even after he delivered Timaeus right into your hands?"

"After weeks of silence!" the Presidente roared. "His reports from Koblan were sketchy, even during the Quasr War. He is useless!" Spittle flew. "If your people don't kill him, I will." Returning his attention to the papers, he wiggled his fingers at the guards.

The man was insane. Deccia could do no more than gape at him. He must be. And cruel beyond measure. He'd gladly kill Goric, just as he'd kill all of his other enemies. As the guards yanked her backward, she whispered, "He deserves better than you."

The Presidente froze for a second, and then slowly looked up. "What did you say?"

"Goric is a hundred times the man you will never be."

He stared at her as if she were curious species of animal he'd never seen before. "And yet you would kill him."

"It's not my decision."

"You speak so highly of my son, even though he has betrayed Koblan's trust for years?" He paused. "He has betrayed *your* trust."

Deccia tried not to flinch. "At least he still has a soul."

The Presidente laughed. "And mine is lost?" His brown eyes hardened to black. "You threaten my son's life one moment, and defend him the next. Curious. Tell me the truth. You would not kill him at all, would you?"

"It is not my..."

"You wouldn't kill him," the Presidente repeated. "You would never kill him." The words hammered, like nails into a coffin. It bizarrely felt as if the Presidente wanted to subject her to his will. It reminded her of when General Greisn had tried to make her into a nonentity; like a disposable piece of human flesh.

Deccia wished her arms were free. She wanted to tear out her knife and prove that he was not all powerful. That *he* should fear *her*. She *wanted* him to fear her. She hungered for it more than anything she'd ever craved before.

The guards' hands bit more painfully into her arms, and she realized she was pulling forward, trying to break free. A snarl curled back her lips.

The Presidente opened his mouth, but a rap at the door made him scowl. "What?" he bellowed.

"A note from General Fitrn's fleet." Yalin's voice trembled. "It...It's urgent, sir. It says an officer will be here soon to speak to you."

"Get her out!"

"What should we do with her?" a guard dared to ask.

"Drown her. And if you see my son, drown him, too. I should have put him out of my misery years ago."

Deccia struggled like a wild beast, but the guards kept a firm grip on her. They marched her downstairs, literally carrying her when she dragged her feet. She wanted to cry and scream and beg for her life, but would not.

She had utterly failed. She'd been unable to attack the Presidente. This was all for nothing. He would win again.

In her head, she silently screamed.

"This way," said the guard on her left.

"Oh, come on," whined the other one. "Let's have some fun with her, first."

"Got a weak stomach?"

"No, but look at her. It's a shame to let all that go to waste."

"I'll do it myself, then. Get back to the prison."

Her last hope—the guard who wanted to rape, rather than murder her—left her alone with the burly guard, who now grabbed both of her arms, preventing her from grabbing for her hidden knife.

He hustled her toward the back of the house. Deccia wondered what he planned to drown her in. A pool? A pond? Surely, he'd loosen his grip for a moment. Maybe she could pull him into the water with her. Maybe in the water, she could wiggle free long enough to grab her knife. Then she might have a fighting chance.

The guard shoved her into a room lined with books.

"She's all yours." The guard thrust her forward. Across the room, a man stood with his back to her. He wore the crisp black of the Zindedi military, with a beret perched perfectly, at a slight angle, on his blond hair. He turned around, and she gasped in surprise.

Goric. He looked hauntingly—disturbingly—like his brother.

"Thank you," he said quietly. The guard left.

"What are you doing here?" she said, bewildered. Goric wearing Zindedi black looked ominous. "Does your father know?" She answered her own question. "Of course not. He just ordered to have you drowned, just like me."

Goric stood very still.

"Why are you here?" she asked.

"To right wrongs."

What did he mean? "If your father catches you..."

"I'm not afraid of my father. Not any longer."

His stillness seemed unnatural and a little scary. Cautiously, she said, "What do you mean?"

"First, I'll help you escape." At last, he moved. With a touch to the base of a wall torch, a whole section of books moved. Surprise, surprise. A dark secret passage lay behind the bookcase.

After she followed him inside, the door rolled shut again behind them. Goric lit a taper, which revealed that the passage forked left and right. In addition, straight ahead stairs led upward. Three paths to choose from.

"Where do those stairs go?"

"You don't need to know." He headed left, and in a few minutes he descended down a long flight of stairs.

Even though Goric was offering her freedom and the opportunity to see Timaeus again, her footsteps lagged. She didn't want to leave the palace. The Presidente had to be stopped. A plan formed as she obediently followed Goric.

After a long while, the path sloped upward. Goric stopped and pressed a lever, and overhead a panel moved. Cool night air caressed Deccia's cheeks.

"Go on." Goric's push at her shoulder felt rough. "Timaeus is at the house."

"Tell me what you plan to do, Goric."

The taper made his face look sallow, and the detached look in his eyes scared her. "Goodbye, Deccia."

Slowly, she climbed the ladder. Goric followed. She knew he was watching to make sure that she left. With a final glance backward, she whispered, "Goodbye," and slipped into the tangle of tall flowers and clipped bushes of the Presidente's garden. After ten paces, she stopped and listened. Nothing. Goric had not followed her.

She waited for a few minutes, and then retraced her steps. The panel was closed. It looked like a flat stone from this side. She knelt on the grass and searched for the opening lever. It was easy to find, because it was hidden beneath one corner. Soundlessly, the stone slid aside. She listened intently for footsteps, or for breathing down in the passageway. But all was silent. Goric was gone. Deccia climbed down the ladder and slipped back toward the palace.

△ △ △ △ △

A rap came at the Presidente's door. The Zindedi leader had been staring at the wall, thinking about little. It was late, and he was tired. Ordering the Koblani girl's death had inspired no pleasure. His orders to kill her had been half-hearted, at best. What was wrong with him?

The ennui had lingered since yesterday. Ever since the powder mine exploded everything had aligned against him. Not only had the mine exploded, but the prisoner had escaped. He'd been *right* to discipline Yalin yesterday. He had.

The delicate scent of ortangia blossoms still permeated the room, but he'd grown so used to it that he could barely smell it anymore.

The rap came again at the door.

"Enter, Yalin," he commanded, straightening his spine, and folding his hands on his desk.

The young man entered partway and slid a glance his way. "The officer has arrived, Presidente. He says he carries an urgent message for you."

"Send him... Wait. Come here, Yalin."

Yalin's brows knit into a nervous line, but he obeyed.

The Presidente cleared his throat. "I think I treated you too harshly yesterday."

Yalin's gaze flickered up, and then away.

Why was he apologizing to a lowly servant? Frustrated rage rose in him, but he pushed it back down.

The truth was, he'd missed the fawning devotion Yalin had lavished upon him when he'd arrived back home. The flowers had been extravagant, and his obedience quick and heartfelt. No one had treated him with such devotion before, except for an old pet. He closed his mind to the unfortunate end to that beast.

The fact was, his sons did not like him, and women tolerated him, but Yalin had seemed to worship him. The Presidente missed the adulation from his secretary. What was more, he deserved it, and he wanted it again. He could afford a few scraps of condolences in order to return matters to the way they should be.

"I was angry," he finished. "But not at you. You must put it behind you."

"Yes, Presidente." Yalin still hung his head, refusing to meet his gaze.

"That is the end of the matter," the Zindedi leader stated with finality.

"Yes, Pr... Yes, my Presidente."

Relief flooded the Zindedi leader. "Good. Now usher in my visitor." As soon as he leaves, you may retire early to your rooms." Uncommon largesse struck his heart. "Visit my women. They will make sure that you mend as good as new. Would you like that?"

Interested alertness lifted Yalin's chin. "Yes, my Presidente. Thank you."

"Good." Overcome with a sense of wellbeing, he scribbled on a parchment, and gave the note to the boy. "Finish your duties, and be quick about them."

The secretary ushered in a thick figured Commander, and then discreetly closed the door behind him.

He sat up a little straighter in his chair. "Why are you here? I ordered all ships to stay in Koblan until their holds are full of ore. Has this been accomplished already?" Something told him it had not, because an aura of gravity pulled the Commander's jowls into bleak lines.

"No, Presidente. I sailed on the fastest ship home so I could warn you, and impart my sympathies."

"Sympathies?" Pain darted through the Zindedi leader's chest. He did not like the sound of this. He thundered, "What sympathies?"

The Commander did not flinch. If anything, his sea weathered eyes appeared even graver. "I regret to inform you that your son, General Fitrn, is dead."

The Presidente gasped. It felt as if an urchet had kicked him in the chest. "What? That is not possible!"

"General Fitrn bravely led the troops to Rolban and attacked. In the midst of the fighting, Methusal Maahr killed your son."

The Presidente gasped again. *Methusal Maahr?* "But Kilum..."

"Kilum is dead," the Commander said without emotion. "Rolbani forces slaughtered half of our men in Rolban. Eerporians caught our rear flank. It was an utter defeat, and the other ships are heading home."

"*No!*" the Presidente screamed. Pain skewered through his chest. "No," he choked out. "It cannot be."

The Commander clicked his heels together. "What are your orders, Presidente? I will carry them out immediately."

His mind jumped from one jolting death blow to another. Almost all of Zindedi's powder had blown up. Two-thirds of his ships and men were decimated. His brother's murderer had escaped. Kilum was dead. His *son* was dead.

The Koblanis had won. Mentàll Solboshn had succeeded in destroying every one of the Presidente's most prized weapons and men. Now nothing was left. He did not have enough men, arms, or ships to attack Koblan again. And without his son, who would lead them into battle?

"No!" he roared. His eyes bugged out, and his lips contorted, mirroring the hellish pain blazing inside of him. "*No!*"

He surged to his feet. "Get out! Get *out*, you bastard! Tomorrow you die. Prepare for your torture and death!" Spittle flew. He threw vases, books, and guns after the fleeing Commander. And still he continued to scream. He couldn't seem to stop.

The pain in his chest felt like a heavy, throbbing weight. Like a bomb, ready to explode. His office lay in ruins, and he could barely move because of the pain. Panting, he staggered back to his chair. An outraged sob mewled from his chest.

His son was dead. *Fitrn was dead.* As was everyone who had failed him. His heart pounded in thick, heavy thumps. The movement felt unnatural and wrong. It pounded once hard, and then twitched to the side.

"Yalin." Even though it was little more than a whisper, his secretary entered, carrying a spirit bottle and a small glass filled with amber liquid.

Tears stung the Presidente's eyes. "You think of everything, Yalin. You are a good boy."

With a shaking hand, he grabbed the glass and gulped down the tawny contents. It went down smooth and sweet, and burned a pleasant path to his stomach. "Pour me another."

Yalin obeyed. The Presidente drank half of this one, and closed his eyes. His head swirled. He did not feel right. He opened his eyes again to speak to Yalin, but his secretary was gone.

He was alone.

The Presidente closed his eyes, feeling a sick, black emptiness inside.

It was wrong. It was all *wrong*. Nothing should have happened this way. How could he accept this defeat? It was unthinkable.

He was all powerful. *He* was the one everyone had feared for years—whom everyone must continue to fear. And yet he sat here alone. Worse, he had the sickening feeling that the The One he refused to acknowledge was laughing at him.

He remembered a scripture his mother used to say about his own father, before his father had ordered her executed.

Her soft voice whispered through the Presidente's mind. "He laughs at the day of the wicked, for he knows their day is coming."

"It is *your* doing!" Spittle flew, and he shook his fist skyward.

He shook his fist again, but he felt impotent. A bitter taste coated his tongue, but before he could reach for the spirit glass again, another pain blazed through his chest. He gasped for breath.

A blurry vision passed before his eyes.

"Brother?" he whispered.

The image disappeared, replaced by another vision. A door, with steps leading downward. The heat of the flames sucked at his soul. Far in the distance he saw his brother, who looked like a skeleton. His mouth was wide open in a tortured, screaming grimace.

Panic filled him. And fear. He did not want to go to that place.

But the flames licked higher, warming him from the inside out. His chest felt hot. His stomach felt like it was on fire. A burst of white hot needles shot from his midsection and poked into every part of his body. Pain screamed through his mind.

Flickering, translucent orange flames surrounded him, and beyond them... He gasped. Was that Goric, his son? In his office?

"My son!" he gasped, and extended beseeching hands. "Come to me. It is so hot. Rescue me from the flames."

Goric came closer. The Zindedi leader could not see Goric's eyes very well, but his face looked cold. His son pushed a spirit glass into his hand. "Maybe a sip is what you need."

"Yes." With a grateful, shaking hand, the Presidente brought the glass to his lips. Goric and Yalin were both so solicitous and concerned about his wellbeing.

He sipped the smooth, sweet spirits, trying to wash the bitter taste from his mouth.

But he could choke down no more than a mouthful.

With a shaking hand, he lowered the glass. It collided with the desk, and wetness slid onto his skin. *He felt so hot.* He was amazed that the wine didn't sizzle on his skin. He pulled at his neck cloth. "Help me, Goric."

But his son had disappeared.

The Presidente was alone again, encircled by translucent, dancing flames that flickered higher than his head.

Pain clawed at his gut. It felt as if a giant fist had closed around his heart. It squeezed harder and harder.

Pain radiated down his arms, his spine. Every piece of him burned, and felt as if it might explode. To his left, the staircase appeared again and descended into darkness. He smelled a noxious fragrance. Cries wailed upward, and he shrank backward. He didn't want to look.

"Please," he whispered. "I don't want to go there. I *won't* go there."

Hadn't he fought this battle before? He would fight it again, and he would win. He would shake his fist at the all-powerful The One, and he would win this fight. He was the Presidente of Zindedi, after all. *He* chose his destiny.

The opening to the stairway widened, and he saw molten orange liquid lapping at the steps. Horrible, shrieking wails spiraled upward. Those awful screams, combined with the fiery pain consuming his innards almost made him lose bodily function.

Those screams...they sounded like those of the first man he had ever tortured.

The opening grew wider, inches now from his boots. Panic consumed him. This was *wrong*. He did not belong in that place.

"*I will not go!*" he screamed, and spat vile curses at The One.

The giant, inexorable fist tightened around his heart.

Everything suddenly seemed to go perfectly still—the excruciating pain, the helpless feeling, as if he was a rocher, about to be ground to dust under a giant, cosmic boot. The awful realization that no more choices remained to him filled him with helpless terror.

And then, one by one, the faces of every person he had ever ordered tortured or killed passed through his vision.

Some faces were contorted in excruciating pain, but then relaxed into joy. Other bodies crumpled into sizzling piles of ash.

His sons passed by. Goric, angry and defiant, running far from him. Fitrn, exploding into a fine ash of nothingness. And last of all, Yalin, his back streaming blood, his face cast downward, to the floor. When he finally lifted his eyes to the Presidente, hatred blazed.

The fist closed tighter and tighter, so he could hardly breathe. Was this hell? Was this the endless pain before the blessed relief of death?

Or would the pain continue, even beyond the grave?

"Please," he whispered to The One.

The One did not answer.

This was hell. But he was still alive...wasn't he? His solitary agony went on and on... And on.

△ △ △ △ △

Deccia swiftly retraced the steps she had walked with Goric. After climbing the stairs, she immediately turned left and climbed the next set of stairs—the ones whose destination Goric had refused to tell her. She had a good guess where they ended.

It was unnerving to walk in the pitch dark, but she traveled as fast as she could, using her hands as feelers. The path ended in a smooth wooden door. It was easy to find the small lever. Holding her breath, she carefully depressed it and the door slid sideways.

She'd entered some sort of a coat closet. Light seeped under the far door. Carefully, she edged it open and peered out. It was the Presidente's office, just like she had hoped.

It was quiet, and she wondered how much time had passed since she'd been there last. It seemed like an eon, but was probably only an hour or so. All the same, it must be late evening. Perhaps the Presidente had retired for the night.

She pulled out her secret knife and cautiously widened the door opening. Large chairs formed a circular conversation area in the far corner of the room. She hadn't noticed it before. The room appeared to be empty.

Her gaze slid to the massive desk and her heart spiked. The Presidente!

Instinctively, she shrank back, and then peered out again. The Presidente lay slumped forward on the desk, his head in his arms. Was he asleep?

Incredulously, she stared. Could it be any easier? The room was empty. No guards were present. And the Presidente was sleeping!

Moving on tiptoe, she exited from the closet. She held the thin, pliable blade tightly in her fist.

What if he suddenly woke up? Would he attack her?

But his thick shoulders and black head didn't move. From this angle, his resemblance to the General was uncanny.

Fierce elation hit her. It would be so simple. So swift.

Deccia now stood right behind the Presidente. His exposed neck was the perfect target. She gripped the blade tighter. Her palm felt sweaty

Do it, she told herself.

Just lift the blade and plunge it into his neck.

But where? Where would be the best place to stab him? Examining his neck from the clinical perspective of trying to find the perfect kill point made Deccia's own throat close in revulsion.

"Do it!" she whispered out loud. "What are you waiting for? This man is *evil.*"

And yet, looking at him resting there, so helpless and exposed, he looked like any other man. Vulnerable. A life The One had created.

"He's *evil,*" she reminded herself desperately. He was sick and depraved, just like General Greisn. The Presidente would never rest until every Koblani was dead. He'd ordered Timaeus' torture. She could never forgive him for that, or for what the General had done to her. They were evil. *Evil.* Someone had to stop them.

She looked at the blade in her hand and gripped it harder. Tears formed in her eyes. If she didn't do it, then who would stop this madman?

Her hand felt cold, and it trembled. With a shaking arm, she raised the knife, clenching it so tightly it bit into her flesh.

She couldn't believe that he was resting there so placidly, completely unaware that he was about to be murdered.

Murdered. Tears spilled down her cheeks. Her hand wavered.

She couldn't do it.

The tears came harder. No matter what he had done, she could not kill him. She would not become like him.

She suddenly sensed a warm presence behind her. Strong fingers pried the knife from her grasp. "No, Deccia."

She spun.

Goric.

Her heart fluttered in panic. He'd seen her poised to kill his father. Would he kill her now?

"You're too late," he told her.

"What do you mean?"

"He's dead."

"Dead?" She stared at the Presidente, and then at his son. Suspicion arose. "Did you...?"

Goric's lips twitched, but his eyes looked like unreadable stones.

"Tell me you *didn't*, Goric!"

"You came here with murder in your heart."

"But I couldn't. I didn't."

"And neither did I."

She drew a shaky breath of relief. "Then what happened?"

"His heart has bothered him for years. It probably exploded."

Deccia looked at the dead Presidente. "I can't believe it."

Goric lifted a parchment from the desk. "I think this note killed him. My brother is dead. Methusal killed him when he attacked Rolban."

Her jaw dropped. "Your father and your brother? *Both* dead?"

"Yes." The paper fluttered back onto the desk.

"Now what? Your whole family— Who will take power in Zindedi?"

"I will," he said quietly.

"*You?* But will they listen to you?"

"Yes," he said simply.

Goric seemed like a remote, coldly resolved stranger. And she suddenly believed that he could do anything.

She whispered, "What does that mean for Koblan?"

"You and I have formed a bond of peace, Deccia. That bond will last forever."

"You mean you'll stop the war? You'd do that for *me*?"

He smiled faintly. "For you. But also for peace. I'm sick of war. For years, I was weak and quick to judge. But now I know Koblanis are people, just like me. And flawed, just like me. I want peace, if Koblan will extend peace to us."

Deccia nodded. "We will. You can trust me."

He smiled. "I do trust you. And that is the foundation of our peace alliance. I ask only one condition. For all future negotiations, I ask that you always be present."

It was a request. She saw that in his eyes. And it was also a plea for something more—for the fragile bond they'd formed to continue. He wanted her to remain a small part of his life.

Discomfort and another, unknown emotion slid through her. On some level, this wasn't right. Goric knew it, but he waited. For Koblan. For peace...

"I would be honored," she said simply.

He offered his arm. "I'll walk you out. It's best if you leave through the secret passage again."

He lit a torch and she followed him down the same passage as before, and then out into the cool garden. This time, he walked with her to the edge of the Presidente's garden.

A guard stood in the shadows, and he nodded when he saw Goric.

Goric walked a few steps further, onto a path bordered by high ortangia bushes. There he stopped. In the dark, he looked sinister again with the black Zindedi uniform and beret. He looked so much like his brother.

As if sensing it, he took off the cap. With his blond hair gleaming in the feeble light of Ryon, he seemed more like the old Goric again.

"Goodbye, Deccia."

"Goodbye. Thank you for everything."

He laughed quietly. "Not for everything."

"For rescuing Timaeus, and for rescuing me, too."

He smiled slightly and leaned forward. His lips brushed her cheek and lingered. "Go in peace, Deccia."

She found his fingers in the dark and squeezed them. "Always," she whispered.

He smiled. "If you ever want to return to Zindedi, you will always have a place here."

She laughed. "I don't think Timaeus would like that."

"Of course not. But one day, if..." Roughly, he said, "It would be a shame for both of us to be alone forever."

"You'll find someone who loves you, Goric."

"Maybe." But she clearly sensed that he did not believe her. The Presidente's son once again retreated into that quiet, lonely place inside himself. "Go with The One, Deccia."

"You, too." With one final look, memorizing his pale face in the moonlight, Deccia turned quickly and left him behind. The guard silently accompanied her, evidently commanded to keep her safe.

Sadness pulled at her heart. How could this be? She thought she'd grown to hate all Zindedis, and yet she didn't want to say goodbye to the one Zindedi who had been the biggest threat to them all along.

The One, please take care of Goric. Keep him on the right path, and please provide someone for him. He needs so desperately to be loved.

△ △ △ △ △

Deccia hurried home, eager to see Timaeus. At the house, she thanked the guard nicely, and then burst inside. Her husband sat on the couch.

"Timaeus!" she cried out.

He grinned and rose fast. With a quick, limping stride, he met her halfway across the room. She slammed into his arms and held him tight. How long she'd dreamed and prayed for this day!

He'd shaved and smelled clean, and wore Riln's clothes, which hung loosely on his spare frame. He felt stronger than he had in the jail cell yesterday.

"Timaeus," she whispered.

"Deccia," he murmured into her neck.

Suddenly she was sobbing, and he held her tight. When the storm eased, he kissed her forehead, her cheeks, and then her mouth. "I love you, Deccia. Goric got you out?"

"Yes. I've missed you. I love you so *much!* You have no idea how much I've worried and prayed for you."

"I felt your prayers. Knowing you were waiting for me kept me going. I wanted so much to see you again. And when you came, it was like a mirac..." His words choked off. "*Why* did you run away? I couldn't *believe* it, and then Goric said you were captured. Good thing he had that job in the palace."

Clearly, Timaeus still didn't know who Goric really was.

She whispered, "I wanted to stop the Presidente from ever hurting anyone again. And I wanted to make him pay for what he did to you. And for what he and the Generals have done to all of us."

"You planned to kill him?" Timaeus sounded shocked. He pulled back and urged her to sit down beside him on the couch. "That doesn't sound like you at all."

"I know. I felt a cold, dead kind of rage. I was willing to do anything to stop him." She whispered, "Even murder. I don't know how I got to that place."

"I do," he said grimly. "General Greisn did it to you. And your nightmares didn't help."

"But when the General took *you*—that's when it got so much worse. And when I learned how you'd been tortured..." Her voice broke, and she gently touched his hand. "And mutilated... That was my snapping point. I was terrified for you, and furious with the Zindedis. When Riln talked about killing the Presidente, it sounded like a good idea to me. That night we rescued you, I carried two knives. They found one. But tonight, after Goric rescued me, I slipped back to The Presidente's office with the other one."

Timaeus blanched. "You went back?"

Deccia looked down at her hands, so tightly clasped that they looked white. "He was sleeping at his desk. Or that's what I thought. I stood over him with the knife. I tried to figure out where I should stab him, and I...I just couldn't. It was wrong. It was evil." She dissolved into tears.

Timaeus pulled her into his arms. "Shh," he said. "It's all right."

"I almost committed m...murder, Timaeus! What's wrong with me? What sort of a terrible person have I become?"

"You're not horrible. I would have killed him. I'm glad I killed General Greisn."

"But you killed him in battle. Not in cold blood. Not while he was...sleeping."

"Maybe. But you didn't do it."

"No. It turned out he was dead already."

"He's *dead?* How?"

"Goric was there. He thinks it was a heart attack." She shivered and went deeper into Timaeus' arms. "I almost became just like them. A cold-blooded killer. The Prophet's words kept going through my mind. That vengeance is The One's to repay. I didn't want to listen. I *refused* to listen. I wanted my own revenge." She shuddered. "But even though he was an evil man, murdering him would have been wrong."

Timaeus held her tighter, and kissed her hair. "Yes," he said softly. "I'm glad you didn't do it, for your sake. That family has taken enough from both of us. I'm glad they didn't take your soul, too. Killing him would have destroyed you, because you have a kind, tender heart. You wouldn't have been able to live with yourself."

More tears fell.

A long time passed, and Timaeus helped her mop up. He said, "We'll go home tomorrow. You'll never have to see Zindedi, or any of the Presidente's sick, crazy family again."

"It isn't over."

He frowned. "What do you mean?"

"Even though the Presidente's dead, and so is General Fitrn..." She paused, searching for the right words.

Joy lit his features, and he pulled her into a quick hug. "Then it *is* over! How did you learn about Fitrn?"

"Goric told me."

"We owe Goric a lot. I never would have guessed it. Where is he, anyway?"

Deccia drew a deep breath. "He's preparing to assume power of Zindedi."

Timaeus' face went blank. "He's *what*?"

Deccia told him everything, from beginning to end. Including her attempt to seduce Goric so he'd agree to rescue Timaeus, and how unnecessary that had been. And she finished with how Goric had laid down his peace terms with Koblan.

Timaeus said nothing for a very long time. His fists clenched and unclenched. At last, he said, "I don't know whether to be grateful, or to kill the bastard."

"I think Goric was conflicted the whole time he was with us. Especially in Dakarra. The Presidente said he was a horrible spy and a disappointment to him."

"He betrayed us," Timaeus said tightly. "My papers were missing several paragraphs and the Presidente's seal. That's why they picked me up. He gave you incomplete papers to copy. And the description he gave the Presidente matched mine."

"I know. But he named Riln, instead of you. He told me he didn't want you to be imprisoned, and he hated Riln. Looking back, I think in Dakarra he was trying to separate the pressure he felt from his father and his loyalty to his country from the strange kind of loyalty he felt to us. He never turned any of us in, although he easily could have."

"So he's a saint," he said sarcastically.

"No. But when I was in prison I thought a lot about something he said to Ceri. He's tried for years to figure out who he is, and how to be his own man. I believe that either in Dakarra or here in Carachki—or on the ship, when he volunteered to come with me to Carachki—he finally made the decision to break away from his father. That's when he started to follow his own path. That must have been a conflict for him, too. He'd chosen to turn his back on Zindedi and help a Koblani, instead. Last of all, he gave the guards money so they'd stop torturing you."

"He did it to help you."

"Maybe."

"No. From the beginning of the trip, you had a connection with him. I saw it."

Deccia shook her head. "I just tried to be a friend to him. I sensed he needed one. It's ironic, really. The whole time I was haunted by nightmares and starting to hate the Zindedis more and more, I was becoming friends with the biggest Zindedi threat of all."

Timaeus said again, "He did it all to help *you*."

"Partly, maybe. But not completely."

His grip on her hand tightened. "He's in love with you. Isn't he?"

"I don't know." She felt uncomfortable, but Timaeus' dark gaze demanded answers. "Maybe. ...A little. Eventually, that will fade. What matters is that he's pledged peace with Koblan. And I believe him. I trust him."

Timaeus searched her eyes. "Then I will, too."

"So it *is* over." She sighed with relief.

"Except for the ongoing peace negotiations."

Deccia kissed him. "We can handle that, can't we?"

"As long as I'm there with you, Goric can negotiate until he's blue in the face."

Deccia giggled. "You don't need to be jealous, Timaeus."

"I do. But I'm prepared to remind you why you love me best." He unexpectedly stood and swung her up into his arms. She shrieked.

"Timaeus, you're still recovering!"

"I'll be fine," he growled. "I need you now. And if it takes all night to erase Goric's kisses from your mind, then that is what I'll do."

She clung tightly to his neck, but when he lay her gently on the bed, she didn't let go.

"My heart belongs to you, Timaeus. *All* of my heart. Always and forever."

"And mine belongs to you."

Her husband invested the entire night in proving that fact to her. And Deccia loved him so completely that by morning, no doubts remained in Timaeus' mind, either.

Chapter Thirty-Eight

Day 49

AALI ITCHED FOR THE ELECTIONS TO ARRIVE. For one, she didn't get to see Dastn as much as she liked. Messages were flying fast and furious between all of the communities. Last time he'd only been in Rolban for an hour. After giving her a quick, affectionate squeeze around the shoulders and muttering a few teasing words in her ear, he'd run off.

Worse, he'd seemed excited to leave. He was charged with energy, and delivering messages as fast as he could take them. Yesterday he'd taken off for Aestoff. His mission was to find Mentàll. No one had seen the Dehrien leader in a week. Very mysterious. However, she had little doubt that he'd show up for the election.

GG had better come to the election, too. All of Aali's surprises would be ruined if she didn't. But at least she could count on one thing—the old lady loved creating a good drama. That, if nothing else, would pry her out of Calbn's mansion. She was counting on it.

Chapter Thirty-Nine

Day 53

Mentàll was officially missing, and Methusal was worried sick. Quickly, she descended from the plains plateau where she'd been practicing kaavl, and ran back to Rolban's entrance. Dastn had just arrived, and she wanted to hear his report.

Last week a runner had informed Erl that Mentàll had been seen in Aestoff more than a week ago, but the Dehrien had abruptly left after his meeting with Chief Aarabst.

No one had seen him since. And with the runners flying between all of the communities, it was easy to verify that he had traveled to no other village to garner support for his campaign. That wasn't like him. Not at all. It was as if he'd disappeared off of Koblan.

Surely he was all right. Surely the wild beasts hadn't eaten him. That thought made her feel sick with worry. Then she told herself for the millionth time that he could take care of himself. He always had.

Then where was he?

Methusal slowed down as she entered Rolban's entrance cavern. Hendra stood listening to Dastn with a frown. When she spotted Methusal, she said, "Someone saw Mentàll with the Prophet five days ago."

"Where?" she asked Dastn.

His shrug looked apologetic. "I don't know. I heard the rumor in Aestoff. I didn't talk to the person who saw him."

Five days ago he was safe. But why was he with the Prophet? In Zindedi, Mentàll had freely admitted that he and

The One weren't on speaking terms. What was more, he didn't care to be. So why would he want to spend time with the Prophet?

Aali trotted up to Dastn's side. Immediately, the Tarst runner's muscled arm curled around her shoulders, squeezed briefly, and let go.

Hero-worship shone on her cousin's flushed face. "How long will you be here today?"

"Only an hour. I have to talk to Erl."

"I'll come with you."

He grinned. "Afterward, let's have lunch."

"Dastn, wait," Hendra said before he headed for the staircase. "Please, if you see Mentàll, would you tell him about my wedding? I want him to be here in plenty of time. I'd like for him to give me away."

"If I see him, I'll tell him."

"Thank you." Hendra's worried gaze followed Dastn for a second before turning to Methusal. "I hope I haven't made a mistake."

"Of course you haven't. Deciding to hold your wedding on election day makes sense. Mentàll will be here. Wild beasts couldn't keep him away." Methusal hoped. The knot of worry in her heart hadn't loosened much with Dastn's news. Mentàll was still missing. Where was he? Why had he disappeared? Was he hurt?

"He's fine, Thusa." Hendra touched her arm. "I think I'd sense it if he wasn't. You probably would, too."

"I'm sure you're right." Methusal forced her thoughts back to Hendra's concerns. "I'm glad there'll be a wedding on election day, after all. And my father is thrilled to have a party to go along with the election. All of the chiefs will like it, too. And they'll especially love all the food Aenill will make." Aenill, Pan's wife, was the best cook Methusal had ever met. "And all of Doc's family will be here. It will be fine."

"I hope so." Worry still shadowed her eyes. "Mentàll is the only family I have. The only one who counts," she added in a soft, sad tone. "If he's not here, I...I don't want to get married."

"Don't worry. He will be." Optimistic advice she should believe, too. The warm aroma of meat and simmering vegetables wafted to her nose. Matron Olgith must have removed the lids from the stew pots. "I smell lunch. Want to head up?"

"Thusa, wait." Hendra twisted her hands together. "Doc and I were talking. We each want someone to stand with us at the altar. Doc will ask Dastn, and I...well, I'd like to ask you."

"*Me?*" she said, surprised and deeply touched. "I would be honored! Thank you."

Hendra smiled. "Good." More softly, she said, "You're the best friend I have. And...well, I just wanted to let you know how much your friendship means to me."

Tears swam in Methusal's eyes, and she hugged Hendra. "You mean the world to me, too."

With a smile, Hendra pulled back, and they headed upstairs together. Her mind returned to Hendra's cousin, however. The man they both loved. Where *was* he?

CHAPTER FORTY

CHIEFS HAD BEEN ARRIVING all day, but Mentàll was still conspicuously absent. Toriln, his first-in-command, had arrived in the mid-afternoon. When Methusal had questioned him, he'd reported that Mentàll had not been to Dehre in two weeks. And so Methusal's message had not been delivered to him, either.

Aenill had arrived yesterday, and today she was helping to prepare delicious food for lunch, but Methusal could barely eat it. She felt sick. Surely Mentàll would arrive tonight. All of the chiefs were scheduled to arrive today.

Tomorrow would be the big day. In the morning Rolbanis would vote for Presidente. The votes would be counted during Hendra's wedding, and after the reception lunch all of the chiefs would cast their official votes for the Presidente of Koblan.

Methusal paced in the upper hall. The deepening shadows in the Great Hall indicated that the late afternoon sunlight had faded to twilight. Only Mentàll and Chief Calbn had yet to arrive. Nervous flutters beat in her stomach. Surely Mentàll would arrive soon.

A commotion downstairs made her sprint down the Grand Staircase. Urchets pawed the ground outside the main gates. Her spirits plummeted when Calbn entered the hall. No Mentàll. Two men hovered by a fidgeting urchet, and then carefully bore a small, black-robed figure to the ground. The bent, elderly woman nodded to each of them, and shuffled forward on her own power. GG.

Aali darted for the old woman. Methusal wondered why, and unthinkingly slipped into kaavl to listen. These days kaavl was becoming second nature to her. It felt like slipping on a well-worn leather jacket. Comfortable—perhaps too comfortable sometimes. Just like now, eavesdropping without consciously deciding to do so.

"He's not here," Aali hissed. "Have you seen him?"

"No." The old woman's eyes snapped. "But he will be. Don't worry."

"If you say so."

"Don't fret."

Methusal's father had just finished shaking hands with Calbn, and now bowed deeply to GG. "We are honored that you made the long trip here, Matron M'ntoyan."

GG's eyes sparkled, lapping up the attention with delight. In a regal, if slightly condescending tone, she said, "I am pleased to be here, young man." She shuffled forward again, her gaze searching the hall.

"Has he come yet?" Sims appeared by Methusal's side. His wounds had mostly healed, but he still walked stiffly, and also with a noticeable stoop now. Sims had always had strong, square posture. The stoop scared her, because it made him look unbearably old and frail.

"No," she said. "And it's almost dark. Even though Hendra said he's not afraid of wild beasts, he probably won't come tonight."

"Not if he has half a brain," Sims snapped. Years ago, his son had died in a wild beast attack.

Personally, she agreed with Sims. Wild beasts were far too dangerous. Traveling at night tempted fate. Only the foolish—or supremely confident—man would dare to take that risk.

"Straighten up, old man!" Methusal hadn't noticed GG's black garbed figure until she poked Sims' chest. Her pale eyes glared. "You look a hundred years old."

Sims jerked upright. Shock evolved into recognition. A bark of laughter escaped. "M'tilde! Well, my girl. I see your tongue is as sharp as ever."

"Is that all you can say, old man?" GG's lips pursed, as if she'd eaten something sour.

Sims laughed again, and it suddenly sounded decades younger. He kissed GG's hand. "You're as lovely as the day I first met you."

"Oh, pshum!" But GG's tiny smile said she was pleased. "I trust you've prepared prime accommodations for me?"

Methusal wasn't sure if she was talking to her, or to Sims. "We've given you one of our best guest compartments."

"*One* of the best. Hmph!" With a sniff, GG offered Sims her arm. "Take me up, old man. We have much to discuss."

Sims obliged. His wide smile said that GG's drama amused him. "What brings you here, M'tilde?"

"You, of course. I figured I'd better come before you keel over. You're two years older than me, you know."

"How could I have forgotten?"

As Methusal watched them slowly climb the stairs, she noticed Aali, a short distance away, watching them as well. A suspiciously satisfied smile curved her cousin's lips.

The clang of the gates drew Methusal's attention back to the dark landscape. Guards secured the locks against the night.

Mentàll wasn't coming.

Oh, The One, please protect him. Please bring him here safely! And soon.

CHAPTER FORTY-ONE

DAY 57

"TWO HOURS UNTIL THE WEDDING," Methusal said to Hendra. At the moment, she stood in the long line straggling from the dining hall, waiting for her turn to vote. Hendra had already voted, but she'd taken pity on her and stopped to talk for a minute while Methusal waited. "Will you go through with it?"

Mentàll still hadn't arrived, and it was past mid-morning.

Worry pinched Hendra's features. "Yes. I want to marry Doc, and I won't let him down. Your mother and Poli and Aenill have done so much, too. And all of Doc's family is here." She glanced toward the Grand Staircase. Her voice lowered. "This isn't like him. Where could he be? If he's not here by the afternoon, he won't be able to vote for himself."

"Toriln could."

"But would any of the other Chiefs vote for him? Even if their communities already voted to elect Mentàll and instructed their Chiefs to cast their vote for him, would they follow through? People are wondering where he is."

"I know." It didn't help the sick feeling in Methusal's stomach to know that Erl and so many others were deeply concerned about the Dehrien Chief's absence, too. Surely he wasn't hurt. Or dead.

"I'm going to go outside and see if I can spot him," Hendra said. "Then I'd better get ready for the wedding."

"Tell me if you see him."

She nodded, and hurried for the Grand Staircase.

The line moved forward a few paces, so now Methusal had a good view of the dining hall. GG and Sims sat near the tea counter. Their gray heads were bent together, and they were deep in an excited discussion, if GG's wild hand motions were any indication. They had been inseparable ever since last night, and again, Methusal wondered what was going on, and how they knew each other. However, she had no doubt that Aali would reveal GG's and her scheming plots at the appropriate moment.

Sozla and her parents sat at a different table. Last night Methusal had learned that Sozla had asked her father to release her from the marriage contract to which she'd been bound. Because of Behran, no doubt.

Behran dropped his folded vote into a large wooden box and headed for Sozla.

A pang of sadness twisted through her. It surprised her, because she wanted him to be very happy. Maybe she was mourning the future with him that would never be.

Methusal moved forward again. Out of her peripheral vision, GG rose. It surprised her when the M'ntoyan matriarch headed straight for her. A well-manicured, claw-like hand curled around her arm. "I need to tell you something. But later. To both you and Mentàll."

"If he gets here."

GG patted her arm. "Don't give up hope." A giggle caught her attention, and Methusal followed her gaze. Aali clutched Dastn's arm, laughing. The two headed down the hall, following a man carrying decorations.

"Young love," GG said, with a nostalgic smile.

The wedding would take place up on the plateau. A beautiful spot, with a stunning view. Already men had wrestled benches upstairs for the chiefs and a few others to sit upon. The other attendees would have to stand.

"Remember," GG said. "Later. Be ready."

Frankly, the old lady's words seemed optimistic. Mentàll wasn't even here. Maybe he'd never arrive at all. Maybe he was dead.

Tears gathered in her eyes. She couldn't think that way. He'd be here. He had to be.

When it was her turn to vote, she smoothed the rough parchment flat and carefully wrote, "Mentàll Solboshn for Presidente." With a heavy heart, she folded it and dropped it into the voting box.

The wedding would start in an hour. Methusal headed for her room to change. She didn't feel like socializing. She just wanted to be alone.

△ △ △ △ △

Methusal finished buttoning her long dress. It was one she'd bought in Quasr, and was made of a soft, beautiful green cloth. It reminded her of the gown she'd worn to the ball in the Presidente's palace.

Where Mentàll had been shot.

The despair of that moment washed over her afresh, echoing the misery she felt now. Why had she sent him away in a fit of anger? Why hadn't she seen what her mother and Hendra had—that he was afraid to love? She had rejected and hurt him, just as so many others had hurt him before. She loved him, and she missed him. And she wished desperately for another chance to make things right.

She glanced into the small mirror on the wall that she'd brought from Quasr. Her eyes looked shadowed and her cheekbones prominent. She'd lost weight.

It didn't matter. Hendra and Doc deserved every happiness in the world, and she was glad that someone would feel joyful today.

She attempted a small smile, but the mirror told her it didn't look very convincing.

The smallest cool displacement of air touched her skin, and movement caught her eye.

She quickly turned, but her leaping heart told her who had entered her compartment before she saw him.

"Mentàll!" she gasped. Hand to her mouth, she stood still in shock. "You're here," she whispered. Her heart thumped like crazy, and her thirsty eyes drank in every line, angle and shadow of the man before her.

He looked tired, and his face gaunt. Faint lines that she'd never seen before etched the sides of his mouth, but his eyes...his pale eyes burned with fierce, determined fire.

"When did you get here?" she whispered.

He closed the distance between them. Unable to move, she stared up at him.

His harsh voice came, fierce and low, "Don't marry him."

Behran? "I already told you, I'm not..."

"I know the wedding is back on." His hands gripped hers. "I heard that it will take place today. Don't marry him!" His voice cracked.

She opened her mouth. "I..."

To her everlasting shock, the Chief of Dehre, and her mortal enemy for over three years, went down on his knees before her.

"Don't marry him, Methusal! Please."

Too stunned to speak, she gaped down at him.

"Marry *me!*"

"Mentàll." She breathed his name. And then an involuntary one left her lips. "Why?"

Immediately, she wanted to take it back. Did it matter why? He was here, and she loved him! She'd been hoping and praying for this moment.

"Why? ...*Why?*" His hands closed painfully around hers, and the ice in his eyes cracked again so she could see into his soul. "Because *I love you!*"

"You love me? But I thought..."

"I told myself I could walk away from you. That I could let Behran have you." Through his teeth, he said, "*It was a lie.* I *cannot* live without you. Leave Behran. Accept me. Please."

"You love me," she whispered.

"Yes. I love you. And if you will have me, I will spend the rest of my life proving it to you."

Tears slipped down her cheeks. "So my bloodline doesn't matter to you? Rolban doesn't matter to you?"

"No," he said harshly. "I want you, Methusal. *You!*"

"I love you, too. And I'm not marrying Behran. I told you that before. I love *you.*"

Hope flared in his eyes, but doubt chased it.

Methusal remembered how Hendra had likened Mentàll to an orphaned child. He needed love, and yet he couldn't quite believe that someone would actually love him. This strong, confident—even arrogant man—thirsted for love. It was why ice shielded his heart. It was why he was afraid to open up his heart and love anyone.

With a smile, she said again, "I love you so much, Mentàll. *Please* get up." When he finally rose, she flung her arms around him. Into his chest, she murmured fervently, "I love you. I *love you.*" She choked on a sob. "I love you so much." She held him tighter. "Please don't ever leave me again."

A shudder went through him. "Then you will marry me."

She choked on a laugh. How like him to say that. To try to secure his place, so no one could intrude on his territory. She kissed his chest. "I'm not marrying Behran."

"But the wedding preparations." Confusion roughened his voice. "Gifts are piled up in the dining hall."

She smiled up at him, unable to get enough of his wonderful face. "Hendra is marrying Doc. And she's been frantic with worry about you. We have to let her know you're here. She wants you to give her away."

"I am not ready."

For the first time, Methusal smelled the dirt and sweat on him, as if he'd been traveling for days. "Where have you been? I've been worried sick about you."

"It does not matter." His large hand cupped her jaw, and he suddenly kissed her with fierce possessiveness. "Nothing matters now. Except for you," he murmured, claiming full possession of her mouth. Her world spun away, and all she tasted and felt was Mentàll. And never had she been so gloriously happy.

She loved him. She loved him so much.

A knock intruded into her hazy, passion drugged mind.

Mentàll was the one with the strength to suspend their kisses. "Who is it?" His harsh tone warned the person to go away. He nuzzled her neck, exploring the line of her throat. She trembled.

"Mentàll is here!" Hendra burst in the door, and then hastily averted her fiercely blushing face. She covered her eyes. "I'm so sorry!"

Mentàll released Methusal, and immediately held out an arm to Hendra. Her long white dress swirled around her ankles as she went to him. He kissed her hair. "I am sorry I worried you, little cousin."

Hendra's uncertain glance went from Methusal to her cousin. Methusal hoped her own blush had subsided. "Where have you been? We've been so worried."

"I traveled the continent. It was time for me to face a few hard truths." His gaze went to Methusal. "The Prophet helped in my quest."

So the rumors were true. It was also clear that he still had much to tell her.

"I'm marrying Doc in a few minutes. Would you give me away?"

"I would be pleased and honored, Hendra. But first I need to clean up."

"Hurry, then." Tears brimmed in her eyes, and she hugged him again. "I'm so glad you're here."

"And I am glad to be home." But his gaze rested on Methusal. "You will wait here?" he said. "When I am changed, we will go to Hendra's wedding together."

"Yes." Happiness spilled out of her smile, and she watched Mentàll and Hendra exit—he with a last glance at her, as if reluctant to leave.

Mentàll was back. Joy burst like rainbows of sunshine inside her soul. And he loved her. He *loved* her.

△ △ △ △ △

Hendra waited on the plateau a short distance from the benches filled with people. Seven lengths away, Doc waited beside the minister, and she couldn't take her eyes off of him. His dark tunic fell in crisp lines from his straight shoulders, and his dark breeches hugged his trim hips. His gaze held hers, and pride and fierce joy burned in it. He thought she was beautiful, and he loved her.

People crowded behind the benches, too. A few murmured admiring comments about her dress. It *was* beautiful, and Hendra felt so grateful to Hanuh for making it.

Hanuh had bought the beautiful, silky material in Quasr, meaning to make a dress for Methusal's wedding, but had insisted on making the gown for Hendra, instead. It was long and white with soft, flowing lines. Intricate beadwork decorated the "V" neck, and also down the sleeves, which puffed out a tiny bit in the upper arms and then narrowed to a point on her wrists. Hendra could scarcely believe that Hanuh had wanted to do so much work to make something so beautiful, just for her.

The ceremony was only waiting for Mentàll and Methusal to arrive. She smiled, thinking about the scene she'd unwittingly interrupted. They loved each other. Her dearest hope was that Methusal's love would heal her cousin, just like Doc's had already healed her.

Friends sat on the benches, smiling at her. Aali grinned from her spot next to Dastn. GG sat with Sims, with her gnarled hand curled around his arm. Her bright eyes scanned the plateau behind Hendra. A sudden, approving smile crinkled, and she patted Sims' arm. "Blood will tell," she murmured, quite audibly. "Blood will tell."

Hendra turned. Her cousin, tall and broad shouldered and impossibly handsome in white leather and trim white breeches, held Methusal's hand. His smile looked peaceful and content. Never had she seen him smile like that before.

Joy spilled over in her heart, and as Methusal moved forward to take her place opposite Dastn at the altar, Hendra sent Doc a radiant smile, and then looked up at Mentàll beside her. He offered his arm, and she curled her hand around it. His warm hand covered hers.

Musicians, sitting to the left side of the altar, piped a beautiful melody, and Hendra moved down the aisle as if in a dream. She could not look away from Doc's face, and barely noticed when Mentàll kissed her cheek and went to go sit down.

At the altar, Doc's warm, steady hands took hers, and her nervous jitters stilled when she looked into his steady gaze, full of love for her.

The ritual of the ceremony proceeded, and Hendra vowed her love and her entire life to the man she cherished. As if made by physical, unbreakable bands, she felt each pledge knit her soul more securely to him. And each of his low-voiced promises secured her hope and trust in him and their future deeper into her heart. At the end, the minister asked if they had special words to speak to one another.

Hendra discovered that she was almost incoherent. "I love you so much," she whispered. "Thank you for believing in me, and for being persistent. Thank you for never giving up on me. When I met you, my heart was frozen. I couldn't feel very much. But as I grew to know you better, the ice finally started to melt. Thanks to your love, I'm whole again."

He smiled, and a faint gleam shone in his eyes. Tears? He cleared his throat. "I fell in love with you the first time I saw you. Remember? It was during that invader attack on our way to Quasr. Men were dying all around me, and I was doing my best to save them. And then, out nowhere, someone appeared to help me. I looked up and saw you. I thought you were an angel." He gave a short, shaky laugh. "I still do."

Hendra smiled at him through eyes brimming with tears. "I love you so much."

"And I love you." He kissed her. Applause exploded.

The minister chuckled. "I pronounce you man and wife."

As their kiss went on, teenage boys hooted, which pulled Hendra from her happy haze. With a blush, she pulled back.

Doc smiled. Tenderness and love warmed his smoky blue eyes. She loved him and trusted him completely. She knew he'd hold her heart securely forever.

For the first time, she felt a tug of anticipation for their wedding night. At last, she could be as close to him as she wanted to be. She blushed again.

As they stepped down from the altar, he murmured in her ear, "My sweet Hendra, what puts that guilty sparkle in your eyes?"

She blushed again. "You'll have to wait and see."

He chuckled and gathered her into his arms. Right in front of everyone, he gave her another deep, lingering kiss. The boys hooted again, but after finishing the kiss at his leisure, Doc sent them a lazy, tolerant smile. "You're just jealous. Go find your own angel."

And then the time for talk was over, because Rolbanis threw grain into the air. It showered down on Hendra and Doc. Squealing, she ran with him to the end of the rows. Laughing, and safe at the end, their shared, radiant smiles promised each other a lifetime of rich and enduring love.

△ △ △ △ △

What a perfect wedding. A bit dreamy-eyed, Methusal watched Doc help Hendra down through the trapdoor. The wedding reception now awaited them, and if the delicious aromas wafting outdoors were any indication, Aenill had prepared an unparalleled feast.

Mentàll waited for Methusal, and as soon as she stepped away from the altar, his large hand immediately enveloped hers, claiming her as his own. GG, wearing a dark blue dress made of severe lines, speedily hobbled up to them both. The old woman's fingers clutched Mentàll's arm.

"I want to speak to you after lunch, young man." Her bright, anticipatory gaze traveled to Methusal. "You, too. And young Aali and your families. We'll meet in the whaal room."

"Why?" Methusal dared to ask.

GG frowned. "Impertinent girl. Haven't you learned that you mustn't question your elders?"

"Methusal would challenge the devil himself."

Methusal sent him an exasperated look.

"We will be there," Mentàll assured the older woman. "You have my word."

"Good." GG grinned. She patted his arm. "Despite all of the strikes against you, you have promise. As it should be," she muttered, and shuffled away.

"What do you think that's all about?"

Mentàll shrugged one shoulder, but his gaze looked speculative. "We will see."

△ △ △ △ △

Methusal and Mentàll joined Hendra, Doc, Dastn, Aali, and Doc's family at the main table in the dining hall. Aenill had prepared a feast of roasted rotarhudge and tubers, salads of logne leaves and tagma berries, and warm, hot bread with butter. Tarts were for dessert. Mentàll grabbed three. He devoured them with a minimum of bites, and then cast repeated looks at the buffet, probably wondering if he could respectably go and get more.

Methusal took pity on him. When she returned to the buffet for her dessert, she piled five on her plate. Mentàll eyed them like a ravenous wild beast when she returned. She grinned. "What will you give me if I share?" she teased.

"My firstborn child. And perhaps another three or four more, as well."

"Awfully presumptuous."

His teeth gleamed white, like a wild beast's fangs. "Before this day is out, you will be pledged to be mine."

"Tell me again why I love an arrogant man like you?" Methusal handed him a tart, and his strong teeth neatly bit it in half.

"I prefer the word 'confident.'"

"Of course you would," she murmured. She toyed with another tart. "Why does such a strong, *un*sweet man like sweet tarts?"

He grinned. "That quality is lacking in my soul. Perhaps that is why I need more, more, and ever more. Perhaps it is why I want you."

"I'm hardly sweet," Methusal scoffed. "But thank you for your *sweet* words." She offered him another tart.

He did not take it. "I am quite sure that you are sweet," he told her. "And I can prove it."

"How?" Humor and suspicion mixed together.

"Feed me the tart. Then I will see."

It seemed like a dangerous idea. Also a little too intimate for such a large gathering like this. Methusal glanced at the others to her left. Doc's mother was telling a story about him as a child, and everyone, especially Hendra, listened with rapt interest. The Tarst doctor looked a bit red in the face. No one was paying attention to either Mentàll or her.

"All right."

With a wicked smile, he leaned forward so she could reach him more easily. The first bite was a clean snap of his teeth, which he swallowed extraordinarily fast "More," he commanded in a low voice. Methusal poked the last bit in his mouth, and to her surprise and shock, his lips closed around her fingers. His tongue swirled around the ends. She felt faint. Hot and cold blushes ravaged her cheeks as she mindlessly absorbed the sensual, pleasurable pulls at her fingertips. With a gasp, she snatched her hand back.

Her heart beat uncomfortably fast, and she felt very warm. He smiled. The light gaze took in every nuance of her expression. "As I thought," he murmured. "You are sweeter."

Methusal's cheeks felt scalding hot.

A sudden shout from the Great Hall came as a welcome relief. Men ran into the hall, and then fell back. Warm, hearty greetings peppered the air.

Someone had arrived, but who?

A tall girl with bobbed dark hair appeared, and a thin, dark-haired man stood beside her. It took only a moment to recognize them both.

"Deccia!" Methusal screamed, and flew across the room.

She hugged her twin tight, and suddenly they were laughing and crying, all at once. Methusal drew Timaeus into the hug too, and moments later Petr, Aali, Erl, Hanuh, and all the others gathered around, asking excited questions.

When everyone had quieted down a bit, Petr ordered that all of the tables be moved closer together so that everyone, including all of Koblan's chiefs, could gather around and hear Deccia and Timaeus' news.

Deccia sat down with obvious relief. "We've been walking all day," she explained.

"Tell us everything," Petr said. "When did you arrive in Koblan?"

"This morning," Timaeus said. "We sailed to Eerpor so we'd have a shorter distance to walk."

"I wanted to get here in time for Thusa's wedding." Deccia glanced at Behran, who was sitting next to Sozla, and then to Methusal with Mentàll, and her smile softened. "I see a lot has changed. "

"Hendra and Doc got married this morning."

"Congratulations!" Her smile widened.

"Tell us everything," Methusal urged. "How did you get Timaeus out of prison?"

Deccia and Timaeus took turns telling the story of Timaeus' imprisonment, Riln's death, Goric's duplicity, and the Presidente's death.

A shocked murmur greeted this last bit of news.

Mentàll had been leaning forward, paying close attention to each bit of news. "So the Presidente and General Fitrn are both dead. Who is ruling Zindedi now?"

Deccia and Timaeus looked at each other. "Goric."

"Oh, no," Methusal said. "Do you think..."

"No," Deccia said quickly. "I don't believe he'll continue the Presidente's war against us."

"How can you be sure?"

"I know," she said quietly.

"She and Goric formed their own peace agreement," Timaeus said.

"What do you mean?"

"He'd never do anything to hurt her." Timaeus and Deccia exchanged a look.

"That's right." A peculiar sadness tinged Deccia's small smile.

Timaeus watched Deccia, his brown eyes sober and considering, and then explained to everyone else the terms of the peace agreement. After a moment, Deccia seemed to become of aware of Timaeus' concerned gaze. Her smile widened and deep love softened her eyes. "I love you, Timaeus. With all of my heart."

He relaxed. "I love you, too, Deccia." They kissed.

Aali made a gagging sound.

Methusal guessed that much more had gone on in Zindedi than Deccia had said. She'd find out later.

Behran spoke. "So, Goric was the spy all along. It sounds like you both trust him now. I'm having a hard time with that idea. He's the reason you were in jail, Timaeus. Maybe he played a part in Riln's death, too. And we don't know how many other ways he sabotaged the mission, either."

"It all makes sense now," Sozla spoke up. "Remember? Goric and I were to blow up the big powder mine. I found it odd that he had such a bad sense of direction. And he claimed that he set the bomb inside, but it didn't blow up."

"He probably disabled it," Behran agreed. "We may never know how many other ways he betrayed us. Just think of the Quasr War. Did he warn the Zindedis about Kitran's attack on the munitions building?"

"Kitran only told his Tarst friends," Methusal said. "He didn't even tell me."

"Let's not forget Efron's death. And the attack on kaavl camp."

Hendra said, "Wortn was tortured. Didn't the attack come after that?"

"Yes." Methusal remembered the odd dream she'd had. Secrets had been tortured from Wortn and afterward, his dead body had been dumped on the plains. Goric had not given up kaavl camp.

"The Presidente said that Goric was useless," Deccia said. "Goric hated his father. In fact, when I was standing over the Presidente with a knife in my hand, and Goric was there...I wondered if he had killed him."

"Did he?" This was from Mentàll, and his hard, probing tone encouraged Deccia to pause. If Methusal knew her at all, she was using her empathic abilities to look deep into her memories.

"I...I don't think so. He said he didn't. But the Presidente was dead when I got there. And when I've thought back on it over the last few weeks, I keep sensing something else in the room. Something bad. Hatred. Hurt...revenge. Murder."

"Someone killed him," Mentàll concluded.

"But who?"

"Does it matter?" Behran asked. "He's dead. The threat is over."

"We hope," Mentàll said. "Unless the killer strikes Goric, too."

Deccia's face paled, and her fingers twisted into her napkin. "Surely not. Why would he?"

"It depends on the killer's identity and his purpose," Mentàll said. "It could have been one of Fitrn's men. Or an eastern Zindedi. Regardless, our new Koblani Presidente will need to send a peace delegation to Zindedi. We will learn then if they can be trusted."

"I don't want to go back," Deccia whispered. "Not yet."

Mentàll regarded her. "Then we will send a new peace agreement by ship. New details will be negotiated. But eventually, we will all meet together. And if Goric's one stipulation for peace is for you to be present, then you must be present, Deccia."

"Fine. Maybe...maybe in a few months."

Hanuh touched Deccia's shoulder. "You're exhausted. You need to rest."

"At least Goric's military is crippled," Behran put in. "At this point, it doesn't matter if we can fully trust him or not. I don't trust him, for the record."

Sozla spoke up. "Perhaps you are right, Behran. But I also think we are lucky to have this opportunity to have peace with Zindedi. It's just my opinion, Deccia, but I think your kindness to Goric made all the difference."

"*And* all the pudding she made for him," interjected Doc.

Everyone laughed.

Methusal said, "The Prophet told us at the beginning of the trip to love our enemies. He also said, 'When a man's ways are pleasing to the The One, he makes even his enemies live at peace with him.'"

Deccia's discerning gaze traveled from Methusal to Mentàll. "So, has that proven true in your own life?"

Methusal smiled. "We're still negotiating our peace agreement."

"Tonight it will be finalized," Mentàll asserted.

Calbn's fist rapped the table. "This is fascinating, but it's time for the Presidential vote."

It was the moment Mentàll had been plotting and planning for months. Methusal smiled to herself, and curled her fingers around his. "I voted for you. I hope you win."

A wide smile broke across his features, and he kissed the back of her hand. His lips lingered. "Your support means everything to me."

The Dehrien Chief followed the other chiefs down the hall to Erl's office. Each vote would be cast in secret, and then the chiefs who weren't running to be Presidente would tabulate the results.

The results would then be reported to the candidates, and to Rolban at large.

Methusal already knew that Erl had won the Rolbani vote a little earlier, so he would cast a vote for himself. Her vote had not mattered at all, except for to herself and to Mentàll. She fervently hoped he would win the election. He'd worked so hard for it, and he deserved to win.

△ △ △ △ △

The votes were still being tallied. GG hobbled up to Methusal and seized her hand in an extraordinarily strong grip. "Send Mentàll and your father to the whaal room when they've finished voting."

"All right."

With Aali's help, the old lady gathered up the remainder of her victims, and then disappeared down the hall. Again, Methusal wondered what Aali and GG were plotting. Ten minutes later Erl exited, and she relayed GG's wishes.

Fidgeting, she waited for Mentàll. At last his tall, broad shouldered body emerged from Erl's office. She hurried over to him. "Well? Did you get a sense of how the others voted?"

"None. Calbn will report the results in a few minutes."

She slipped her hand into his, feeling joy that she could freely do so now. "That should leave us just enough time for GG's mysterious meeting."

When they entered the circular whaal room, all the chairs were taken, and a few people stood against the walls.

Sims and GG sat side by side, and Aali stood behind them with an excited, mischievous grin.

"Come here, young man," GG commanded the Dehrien Chief.

Mentàll approached the hunched older lady, and then went on one bended knee, so he could look her in the eyes. She smiled approvingly and took his hand.

Slowly, the sharp old eyes scanned his face, and then she cackled to herself. "Yes, yes. The very image. He would be proud. Are you, Sims?"

Sims grinned. "That I am."

GG patted Mentàll's cheek. "You are a smart young man. Blood will tell. I always say blood will tell. And it has."

Mentàll watched her, as if waiting for something specific.

Regally, GG inclined her head. "You may kiss my cheek, my son...my grandson."

Methusal gasped in shock. Hendra clapped a hand to her mouth, and Aali grinned wider.

Mentàll, however, did not appear to be surprised. He gently kissed each of the old lady's cheeks. "Grandmother."

With a smile, GG clapped her hands. "Let us celebrate! A son was lost, but a grandson found." She peered at Sims. "And a father beholds his grandson. At last."

For the first time, shock registered on Mentàll's face. With a gruff word, Sims hugged GG, and then extended his hand to Mentàll. A smile wavered on his wrinkled face. "I hope you will accept me as well, my son."

"Yes!" Mentàll said. He stood and clasped the old man's hand. Child-like wonder glowed on his features. "You are the father of my father?"

"Yes, my grandson. M'tilde just told me yesterday. I had no idea. Tell me, Mentàll. What do you know of your father...my son?"

The old hurt tightened Mentàll's features, but he did not try to extricate his hand from the old man's grasp. "Very little. He abandoned my mother before I was born."

Sims nodded. Tears sparkled in his old eyes. "As I thought. Although I always knew I had a son, I didn't know Karish until much later, when he was a man."

"It's my fault," GG interjected. "I bowed to my father's wishes and married another. My father banished Sims from Quasr."

Sims took up the tale, "Karish sought me out, but we did not have enough time together. Not at all. He was a wanderer, as I was for many years. I'm sorry that I knew nothing about you or your mother, Mentàll. Karish died over thirty years ago in a wild beast attack."

"He...died?" Surprise flickered, and Mentàll stepped back, pulling his hand free from Sims'.

GG interjected, "He wears the medallion, Sims, did you know? Aali, my smart girl, spotted it. It confirmed all my suspicions."

Aali's grin widened.

"Let me see," Sims said, and Mentàll withdrew the round disk with the two peaks etched into it. The old man fingered it, and a gentle smile touched his lips. "He gave this to your mother, Mentàll?"

"Yes."

Sims nodded, and he looked at GG. "Are you thinking what I am thinking, M'tilde?"

GG gave a sharp nod. "It was a promise."

"A promise?" Mentàll repeated. It was unusual to see him looking lost, and trying to put together pieces he'd never known existed.

"His promise to your mother," Sims explained. "He would never have given her the necklace unless he'd planned to marry her."

Mentàll looked down at the medallion. He slowly fingered it. "He planned to marry her." His posture slowly relaxed, as he finally absorbed the real truth about his parents. He'd hated his father for his entire life because he'd abandoned his mother—an abandonment which had led to her death, and Mentàll's own horrible childhood. "He loved her. He meant to marry her."

"And I'm sure he would have loved you, too," GG said. Her pale blue eyes—even paler than Mentàll's—sparkled suspiciously. Methusal suspected tears did not come easily to the crusty M'ntoyan matriarch.

"He loved her." Mentàll still stared at the medallion, and emotion faintly flushed his face.

"You are one of us," GG proclaimed. "A M'ntoyan, through and through." A shudder went through Mentàll. "Come to me, my son." Mentàll bent and allowed GG to kiss both of his cheeks again.

Her gnarled old fingers reached for and gently cradled the medallion. "I was certain I would never see this again. Wear it proudly, my grandson. You will forever be one of us, and you will always have a place in Quasr."

"Thank you, Grandmother." As if finally coming to his senses, Mentàll kissed each of his grandmother's cheeks, and then shook Sims' hand again. Their eyes met, accepting and forging the bond between them.

A throat cleared in the doorway. Calbn. He wore a rare smile. "Ready for more good news, cousin? You have just been elected Presidente of Koblan. Nine votes to two."

The blood drained from Mentàll's face, as if he couldn't quite take in all of this good news at once. Methusal ran and flung her arms around him.

"Congratulations!" she murmured. "You deserve it. You deserve it so much." When she would have released him so others could congratulate him too, his arms closed more tightly around her.

"I am Presidente?" His voice was faintly disbelieving. Methusal grinned and held him tighter. For this one moment, his vulnerability was clear to all. In this moment, others could finally see the man she loved.

When Mentàll's arms loosened, she let him go and watched him give Calbn a brief, manly hug, and then everyone wanted to shake his hand.

Methusal watched with pride. Hanuh touched her arm and drew her into a hug, too. "You've found a fine man," she whispered. "Don't ever let him go."

"I won't, Mama. Not ever."

She could hardly believe that Mentàll was a M'ntoyan, and a member of the ancient, distinguished ruling family from Quasr. He'd risen from poverty in Dehre to become Chief, and now he was the Presidente of all of Koblan. Was GG right? It seemed so. Blood had foretold this day.

Mentàll, Sims, GG, and all of the M'ntoyans were family now. Her adopted grandfather was Mentàll's real grandfather. This revelation had been an obvious surprise to Mentàll. But it seemed as if he had already guessed he might be a M'ntoyan. Was that why he'd spent so much time in Quasr? Perhaps he had wanted to get to know his family. And he'd become good friends with his cousin, Calbn.

Mentàll reappeared by her side and put his arm around her. His eyes glowed with triumph. "We will celebrate!" he proclaimed to all. "And we will honor Erl and the chief of Wyen. They are worthy men, and fine opponents. Perhaps one day, one of them will take my place."

"Here, here," roared Wyen's chief, from the doorway.

Methusal hugged an arm around Mentàll's waist and smiled up at him. "I'm so proud of you. I don't know how this day could get any better."

"I do," he murmured. "After the celebrations this afternoon, meet me on the rocky portion of the crop plateau. The northern slope. I want to speak to you in private."

She smiled. "I'll be there."

"Good." He kissed her, and then the celebration party streamed into the dining hall.

Δ Δ Δ Δ Δ

Dastn spoke behind Aali. They were the last ones still in the whaal room. "Mission accomplished?" She heard the smile in his voice.

"And more," she said, quite pleased with herself.

"Congratulations." He moved to stand beside her, and his arm almost touched hers. Her heart gave a tiny flip.

"Thank you."

"No more Aali meddling is necessary."

She rolled her eyes. "I solved two mysteries. See how happy everyone is?"

His lips curled up at one corner. "You did a lot of good."

"For once, you mean. Don't say it."

He laughed. "I didn't."

"And it was a whole *lot* of good. Give me full credit!"

"We've watched a lot of happy endings today."

"All except for one." With her hands on her hips, she turned to look at him.

Dastn's smile vanished, and then reappeared again. His brown eyes looked darker. "I don't know what to do with you."

"Don't you? Well, I know what to do with you," she promised. She put her hands on his shoulders, stood on tiptoe and, heart pounding with fearful determination, touched her lips to his.

He stiffened and tried to pull back, but she buried her fingers in his thick, dark hair, and wouldn't let him go. Not yet. She continued her soft, shy kiss. It felt so wonderful to finally touch him in this slow, lingering way, and to be this close to him. Emotions surged in her, swamping her, until she felt dizzy.

He stopped trying to extricate himself.

"Aali," he murmured. His tone was soft and warning against her mouth.

She ignored him, and moved her lips in ways she'd seen her sister and Timaeus do.

"Aali..." Her name sounded choked now.

She stopped and looked up into his tormented eyes. "Kiss me, Dastn. Please?" she begged softly.

He heaved a deep breath, and then lowered his head. His warm lips met hers. For the first time, he kissed her. Aali trembled at the same time a shudder went through him.

He kissed her deeply, with intense hunger. She clung to him, buffeted by wild, sweet emotions. She loved this man with all of her heart. Who cared if she was only sixteen? She knew her own mind.

Dastn pulled back and buried his face in her neck, in the soft silk of her hair. "Aali..." It was a groan, an ache from his soul. He was as affected as she was, and the realization thrilled her.

She whispered, "I love you."

At first, she didn't know if he'd heard, but then his arms tightened, fiercely and protectively, around her. He pulled her close, head tucked under his chin, and close to his heart.

His gentle breaths warmed her hair, and she held him tightly, afraid to let go. Suddenly, she was afraid she'd lose him forever.

"Aali. You're only sixteen."

"Don't *say* that!" She pressed her face into his chest, unable to halt the sudden rush of tears.

He said softly, into her hair, "Grow up, Aali. I'm waiting."

She held him tighter. His warm, strong hand stroked her back.

Finally, she pulled away, unable to bear it any longer. She wiped her eyes. "You promise?"

His tender gaze held hers. "You're a girl in a universe. I could never let you go. You drive me crazy. You exasperate me. You make me whole."

Her lips trembled a little. "Do you love me?"

His mouth tilted into that special half smile, which was only for her. "Yes. But we'll take it one slow step at a time."

"That you will!" Petr's voice boomed, startling them.

Quickly, they both faced her father. Dastn said, "Yes, sir. I will never compromise Aali."

Petr's glare softened. "I know you won't, son. But hands off my daughter. She's not eighteen yet."

With reluctance, their linked hands parted. But Aali knew, looking into Dastn's eyes, that her future belonged with him. Always. And his smile promised her forever.

△ △ △ △ △

Methusal sat on the boulder strewn slope of Rolban's northern plateau. To her left, the sun flirted with the horizon, and straight ahead the stark peaks of the Tarst range soared skyward. The last, warm rays of sunlight glowed off the nearby boulders and soaked into her comfortable leather clothing.

Memories trickled into her mind. It had been a day of endings and beginnings. A day of hope, born out of the ashes of the past.

Over three years ago, she had met Mentàll on a plateau just like this one while she'd been practicing kaavl. Her first impression of him had warned her that the powerful Dehrien would be a danger to her. How right she had been! He had always been a danger—but most of all, to her heart.

Chasing the first memory was a second—actually, it was a nightmare. Mentàll had chased her through the pouring rain while men battled and died all around them. The dream had warned her that if she ran from The One's words, she'd die in the prison where Mentàll would bind her.

But now Mentàll had caught her at last. However, he no longer wanted to destroy her. He wanted to love her. And their happy ending was all thanks to the Prophet. Because she'd listened to him, and had tried to treat Mentàll with kindness, so many things had changed. Instead of hating and wanting to destroy her, he had been healed. Instead of the prison she'd fought to escape in the dream, she was bound to him with chains of love.

More events from their first years played with swift clarity through her mind. Their distrust of each other. The ways they'd hurt one another. How could The One create something good out of something so bad?

How grateful she was to the Prophet for telling her to love her enemy. And she was glad that she'd tried her best to obey, no matter how hard it had been at the time. The reward far exceeded the price.

Footsteps whispered up the steps behind her, breaking into the memories. Kaavl heard that he'd stepped out of the trapdoor and onto the plateau. His footsteps came closer, but she didn't turn around when he sat on the boulder behind her.

The familiar, harsh voice spoke, and its low tone resonated, filling her sensitive ears. "It's a beautiful sunset."

She still didn't turn around. "Yes, it is."

Another long moment elapsed. Methusal's eyes remained fixed on the horizon, watching the sun dip closer and closer to the line of the desert. A slight movement indicated that he'd edged closer. Still she didn't turn around, although her heart was beating very fast, and her breath seemed to have caught somewhere in her throat. This was it. Finally, it was time to face her future.

A little of the old concern mixed with her elation. Mentàll still wasn't fully tame, but her heart didn't care anymore.

Hard, lean fingers touched her temple, and then slid back through the soft, slippery strands of her hair. The light pressure was firm. Lingering. Sure. Like the man himself. He knew what he wanted. He always had. And he always would.

Her eyelids fluttered closed.

Each of his fingers ran through her hair this time, and then trailed down to her neck. Her breath exhaled in a soft gasp.

She felt his large hands curl around her shoulders, kneading them. Tingles rushed to every one of her nerve endings. Was she crazy—or a little bit foolish—to want to join her life with this man?

But she felt more at peace right now than she ever had before in her life.

Lifting her head, she opened her eyes and gazed at the horizon again. The sun set now in a blaze of glory, burning the sky with fiery orange, pink, and red colors.

She had made her choice.

The future lay before her. Rocky. Uncertain. But brighter and more glorious than she could ever have imagined.

As he moved to sit down beside her, the long, lean cut of his bent leg slid into her vision.

At last, she looked up. Facing her future.

How she'd fallen in love with this dangerous man, she'd never know. But she couldn't turn away from her fate now, even if she had wanted to.

His wide palm cupped her cheek with the gentleness she'd grown to see in him. He was still dangerous. A predator, some might say. Half tame, and half not... His eyes met hers, and for a long moment they both stared, not saying a word. Then she closed her eyes and his lips touched hers.

The bristle of his chin sensitized her skin. His silken kiss drew powerful, explosive emotions from her. She'd found her soulmate. The only man who'd ever be able to match her, and challenge her, wit for wit. Physically, he was stronger than she was. But in the future, their union would hone the sharp edges off of both of their personalities. Gentling them. Harmonizing them into a perfect unity.

Mentàll pulled back, and his gaze ran over her features, reading her expression. Methusal's heart already felt branded by this man. She belonged to him, now and forever. The thought was a little frightening, and yet wonderfully exhilarating, too.

His thumb brushed her lips, as soft as a feather. "You got under my skin from the beginning, Methusal. I never thought I'd get under yours, too."

She reached up and laced her fingers behind his neck. Feeling slightly breathless with her boldness, she pulled his head down for another, even more satisfying kiss. With a groan, he pulled her hard against him. His kiss was savage, and hungry. And it thrilled her.

When the kiss ended, he still held her tight. Cradling her. Caressing her.

She murmured, "I was remembering our past. It's a miracle, isn't it, that we're here together now?"

Silence elapsed. "I will never hurt you again, Methusal," the husky words growled from deep in his throat. "I swear it."

She believed him. She'd never thought it was possible, but she'd grown to trust this man. Just as she had fallen in love with him. Despite all of the obstacles, and all of the reasons why she should not. She'd seen a glimpse into his soul over the last few months. And she liked what she'd seen. His rough edges would only make life more exciting.

She smiled then, meeting Mentàll's icy blue gaze. "I know." With a sigh, she leaned closer to him. She felt a sense of wholeness and peace being with him like this.

Her mind returned to the worry she'd felt over the last two weeks.

"Where were you? I was so worried. I was afraid a wild beast might have eaten you."

He gave a low chuckle. "Perhaps it takes a wild beast to understand the ways of true wild beasts, but I am not foolish. I have a healthy respect for them. At the same time, I understand them. I sense them. I know where they are and how to evade them. I also know when they will not chase me."

"Your kaavl is extraordinary." She smiled. "But you still haven't answered my question. Where were you?"

More silence stretched. Finally, he said, "When I left here, I was furious with you, and also with myself, and consumed by a blinding, hellish pain. I felt like a wild beast who had lost his sight. I did not understand why you would not have me. Every goal I work for, I achieve. Everything I want, I manipulate and coerce until I eventually possess it. But not you. And I did not understand why it hurt like the fires of hell.

"I sent you the note and the *Second Book of Kaavl,* telling myself it was the best way to absolve myself of guilt and purge you from my life. I told myself I would forget you. It was over. So I went to Aestoff to continue my campaign for Presidente. But when I arrived there, I found I could not concentrate. I could not think about anything but you.

"When I left Aestoff, I was confused and scared. That hellish pain wouldn't leave me. It just grew worse, especially when I learned that a wedding—your wedding, I thought— was going to take place after all. I couldn't stand it. I wanted to go to Rolban and rip Behran's heart out, like the wild beast I am. Instead I cut south, trying to outrun my bloody thoughts. I did not want to be that man anymore, but I didn't know how to be a better one.

"The Prophet met me after I'd been wandering in the desert for five days. It was hot, and I'd run out of water. I wasn't thinking right, and I didn't know exactly where I was. He offered me water."

Mentàll's voice grew quieter, and more reflective. "Never had I drunk such cool, refreshing water. I asked if he'd found a stream nearby. The water was so cool, I knew he couldn't have carried it far. He said that the one who creates streams of living water gave it to him. I knew he was talking about The One, but I didn't say anything. The One and I have never been on the best of terms.

"The Prophet said, 'Son, are you ready to stop running? Are you ready to make peace with The One?'

"I was at the lowest point of my life. It was easy to see that I hadn't done very well by following my own path. I'd lost you. I'd perpetuated that dishonorable takeover of Rolban. And I'd hurt you more times than I could bear to remember. In that moment, I finally saw myself as I am. A power hungry, needy, greedy man. A selfish man, callously willing to hurt others to get what I want."

Methusal felt the need to interject. "You're not."

"Yes, I am, Methusal. At that moment, I felt as if I'd come to the end of a long, desert road. I was empty, thirsty, and hungry. I could not go back. I could not change any of the terrible things I had done. I could not have you. I did not want to go forward, either. I didn't want a life without you. It would be meaningless.

"I told the Prophet everything I just told you, and he smiled. Then he asked if I was ready to repent and ask for forgiveness from The One. He said that in order to be healed, I would also need to give away all of my fears and the hurt of my childhood to The One, too. Then The One would make my path straight again. After that, the Prophet disappeared." Mentàll fell silent.

"Did you repent?"

"Yes, I did, on my knees in the desert. I wept until the sun went down and darkness cooled the land. I fell asleep. In the morning, my soul felt as clean as the new dawn.

"For the first time since I was a child, I was filled with a feeling of hope and peace. I tracked down a stream and refilled my water skin, and then headed to the coast to think. Several things finally became clear to me. One is that I love you. I had been blind. I couldn't see it before—or maybe I'd been afraid to see it. Until that time in the desert, I never knew how much fear lived in my heart."

Methusal hugged him. "Is it any wonder, after the way you were treated as a child? All of your hope must have died then."

"You are too kind, Methusal. I chose the wrong path. And you were right. At the beginning of the trip to Carachki, I did think I could manipulate you into my arms, and then permanently into my life. But the opposite happened. The more time I spent with you, the more power you wielded over me." He gave a short, mirthless chuckle. "Will you forgive me?"

"I've already forgiven you. I told you that."

"Good." Tension eased out of his body. "I have peace with The One, Methusal. I have repented of my self-serving ways."

"You're an angel now?"

A harsh chuckle erupted. "I will never be an angel. You know that. But I will not deliberately turn my back on The One and follow the wrong path again."

She believed him. And security wrapped around her, as warm as the quilts and his body heat had done the night he'd rescued her from General Fitrn.

He had admitted to making mistakes. Doubtless he'd make more, and so would she. Neither of them was perfect. But at least from now on they would both make every effort to follow The One's precepts. She knew, without any doubt, that she could trust him, because he was a man of integrity. He would never lie, and he would never break his word.

She put her arms around him and buried her face in his chest. All of the powerful feelings she'd harbored for him—feelings she'd never understood, but which had cut to her soul from the first—had deepened and sweetened into a love so powerful that it made her feel giddy with wonder.

Lacing it all together was a fierce protectiveness. She never wanted him to be hurt again. *She* never wanted to hurt him again. Instead, she wanted to love him with every fiber of her being, all the way to her dying breath.

She pulled back. Voice trembling with fierce emotion, she said, "I love you so much, Mentàll. With my whole heart."

The ice of his blue eyes melted, and hope remained, almost childlike in its vulnerability. "You do?" Rough wonder sounded in the harsh undertone.

She wrapped her arms more tightly around him, and insisted from her full, overflowing heart, "Yes. I *love* you. With my whole heart and soul."

His fingers slid down her cheek. The finest tremor shook them. "Truly?"

"Yes. Truly."

"I love you, too." He captured her lips in an urgent, searing kiss. Within moments she felt boneless, and deep shivers trembled through her. Her soul had begun to fuse with this man, whom she loved so deeply.

After timeless moments, Mentàll pulled back. His quickened breaths matched hers. "Only one matter remains unresolved."

"What?"

"You will marry me." A faint smile accompanied the arrogant statement.

She smiled. "When?"

"Soon. I am not sure how much longer I can keep my hands off of you."

"Have you been trying?"

With a short laugh, he kissed her again, quite thoroughly. By the end, she could barely think. With infinite attention to detail, he then caressed her ear. "So," he murmured, "you agree, then. You will marry me?"

"Are you using ruthless tactics on me again?"

"Yes." His gentle, persuasive kisses seared below her jaw, and then lower, down her throat. "Please. Will you marry me?"

"Yes." Her voice was breathless, bordering on incoherent.

"And soon," he softly persisted, sliding to the hollow of her throat and raining slow, fiery kisses lower.

"Yes, soon," she gasped. "Very, very soon!"

"Good." After another lingering kiss, he looked up. Triumph glittered. "At last you will be mine, body and soul, forever."

She smiled at his typically arrogant statement. "You are an incorrigible wild beast, and I love you," she whispered, and kissed him again.

A long, slow shudder went through him. His kiss hungrily drank in her affection, and after a moment he returned stirring, soft ones of his own, until she wasn't sure who was giving to whom. "I love you," she whispered again.

He vowed in a low, harsh voice, "And I love you, *ce'cemone.*"

"What does that mean?" At last she would know.

"Dearest of my heart. You are the fire of my heart, *saltisienna.*"

"*Mentàll.*" How could joy this big fit inside her heart? It felt ready to burst. And the same emotion, mixed with wonder, burned in Mentàll's blue gaze.

He kissed her again, and joy flamed like the brightest comet in her spirit.

Their love was a miracle. A gift neither had seen coming, nor expected. A blessing. Her heart soared heavenward on wings of gratitude and joy.

Thank You.

The End

Author's Note

I SINCERELY HOPE you enjoyed *Kaavl Conqueror,* and the entire Kaavl Chronicles series. I wrote *Kaavl Conspiracy—* the first book of the series—to be a stand-alone novel a number of years ago. However, a character came on the scene then (Mentàll Solboshn) whom I never anticipated. More than any other character I have written, I felt compelled to write his story, as well as his and Methusal's happily ever after. It was not an easy journey for them, which made it all the more fun to write. After I wrote the first draft of *Kaavl Conspiracy,* scenes for the remaining books in the series germinated in my mind in the years that followed, and I wrote them down in a very large file. Finally, about fifteen years after *Kaavl Conspiracy* was written, I was able to find the time to write the remaining books in the series and complete their story. It has been a journey of love. I love the characters and their stories so much, and I hope you have loved them, too.

One final note. As a small press author, getting my books before readers is a real challenge. You can help! If you liked this book, please consider writing a short review on Amazon, B & N, or the retailer's website where you purchased the book. Each review encourages Amazon and other online retailers to promote the book to more readers. Each and every review counts, and means so much!

I love to hear from my readers. Please drop me a note at jennettegreen@jennettegreen.com.

Best wishes always,
Jennette